PETER MENDELSUND

SAME SAME

Peter Mendelsund is a writer and designer.
He lives in Manhattan with his wife and two daughters.

ALSO BY PETER MENDELSUND

What We See When We Read

Cover

The Look of the Book
(with David J. Alworth)

SAME SAME

SAME SAME

PETER MENDELSUND

Vintage Books
A Division of Penguin Random House LLC
New York

A VINTAGE BOOKS ORIGINAL, FEBRUARY 2019

Copyright © 2019 by Peter Mendelsund

All rights reserved. Published in the United States by Vintage Books,
a division of Penguin Random House LLC, New York, and distributed in
Canada by Random House of Canada, a division of Penguin Random
House Canada Limited, Toronto.

Vintage and colophon are registered trademarks of
Penguin Random House LLC.

Library of Congress Cataloging-in-Publication Data
Names: Mendelsund, Peter, author.
Title: Same same : a novel / Peter Mendelsund.
Description: A Vintage Books original edition. |
New York : Vintage Books, February 2019.
Identifiers: LCCN 2018009753 | ISBN 9780525435884 (pbk. : alk. paper)
Classification: LCC PS3613.E48223 S26 2018 | DDC 813/.6—dc23
LC record available at https://lccn.loc.gov/2018009753

**Vintage Books Trade Paperback ISBN: 978-0-525-43588-4
eBook ISBN: 978-0-525-43589-1**

www.vintagebooks.com

Printed in the United States of America
10 9 8 7 6 5 4 3 2

For K, R, V

PART I

THE SPOT

1

I was unaware, at first, that I had entered the Institute.

Sure, the dome appeared, briefly, far off in the desert. A bright semicircle, a second sun, perched upon the wavy horizon. I thought it was a business park or the reflective apron of one of the Freehold's honeycombed luxury developments. A stadium? One of those steroidal mega-mosques one reads about in the literature, perhaps. Something. It drifted along for a spell, during that endless drive out, along the rightmost edge of my vision, no matter how many times the car merged onto new roads. I could see it even through the double tint of my sunglasses and the vehicle's windows. The dome, known only as a flare. Other than that, there were the dunes of course—dune by dune—stuccoed to the sky behind. And these gray superhighways, colonized by sand along their shoulders, giving them lightly ragged edges like monumental pencil marks.

But nothing else, really.

Besides that distant dome. Which was there. Until it wasn't.

It vanished. Could it have been a mirage—a trick of the light? Idk.

But: no. No, I can see it again.

Oh, I see the dome, all right. Only I see it, now, from the inside; from underneath, I mean. I didn't notice a security checkpoint, so it will have been unmanned. There were no barriers to raise or lower; no fanfare, no ceremony. I was in the desert, outside of the Institute, and now I am within it. And the Institute is all about me. This uncanny oasis in the middle of a scorch-plain. And atop it all, the great upturned bowl of its metastructure.

The desert—and with it, my old life—now gone.

Poof.

And so the car hums along, through this entirely new, artificial ecosystem, past the tall palms which line both sides of the straight, clean avenue, casting their tarantula shadows. Off to the sides, parklands, lawns, copses, nature trails, etc. (How many gardeners must be employed here? No sign of them, though; nor of any of the Institute fellows.) The stubble of a few communications spars; small electrical substations; glints from far-off solar panels amid the greenery; what looks like a desalination unit; and now an enormous, brightly blue, artificial lake. Farther off, the buildings themselves. The campus.

The car scrunches onto an access road, and I can see that I am approaching an immense set of concrete-and-glass slabs—one of the first Western-style constructions in the Freehold, and the work of an influential architectural collective. The car slows, then stops in the building's shadow, and I debark. Mine is the only vehicle in the lot, and I have that persistent, unsettling feeling of being marooned in a city of one. The quiet air of a town after a massacre. I wonder where all the other Institute fellows are, but remember the time of day, and recall that at this hour they all must be hard at work on their projects, at their workstations, and in their studios, their laboratories, so on. Exhilarating to imagine—to imagine that I might belong to their number. Also exhilarating to discover that it is wonderfully cool out, under the dome. The work of the metastructure's air circulators. I stretch limbs, breathe in deeply, which reaps the strangest, almost autumnally crisp air. Air with a unique but unlocatable aftertaste—something citric, and rubbing alcohol. A chemical terroir.

Exhale.

Craning, I still can't see a soul.

I reach for my device again, whisper it awake, and it produces a sigh, and begins to faintly pulse. Pull up a map, pinch outward, fix Miss Fairfax's position inside. And so I follow an animated arrow guiding me toward the building's main doors, which obligingly swish open, and then I enter, meander through a maze of empty hallways, branching like bronchioles in a lung, past the empty lounge areas, the empty galleries, until I arrive in a bright atrium—a hangar, really—easily hundreds of meters across and just as high, housing the Landau-Schmidt glacier.

Maybe it's just a replica. The website claims it's the real

McCoy. Though the language is ambiguous, as in, "from the original." Either way, a large thing of any kind is always an event of sorts. I knew there would be such sites out here: enclosed ski slopes, so on. But still. Wow. Just look at it.

I snap a pic: caption, post.

Needless to say, as with everywhere else in the Institute, no one other than me is here to see the glacier—to climb, ski, or otherwise experience it. So there's more of the suthering silences of large, empty spaces.

A viewing platform. The escalator takes me up; the high platform descends into view, arrives beneath my feet. Modular tables and sleek, rounded chairs, a bar. Lots of white leather and orange plastic. It's all—the decor, the signage, the softly chirping music even—retro-futurism. This is what once passed as modern, bleeding edge, and now, curated thus, it is pure kitsch. Or maybe it's nostalgia. Nostalgia for another future.

I'm enjoying it. After all: What is nostalgia without kitsch?

Just plain old memory.

My new admin, Miss Fairfax, sits at a small table, looking just like the online versions of her. Same face (round), same hair (dark), same glasses (thick). I now realize that she reminds me, in a pleasant way, of other women I've known. A type of woman who wears glasses. I want to say that she is a specimen of this particular type. Even Irl, with its fuller, richer aspect. In any case I find her conformity to type oddly comforting. Next to her is a man I don't know. His type:

louche, and jaded. Very pale. Hair shaved along the sides, but flopping down in front along his forehead. His eyes are deep-set, feline, feminine, almost kohled. He wears a smart-looking tunic. Miss Fairfax wears one as well, albeit a different color. Odd, this—yet they both look so chic—especially in this setting, with the piped upholstery and softly lambent overheads.

My jacket is shiny at the lapels and elbows, and creased just about everywhere and obviously quite the wrong color for the climate. The sole of my left oxford is detaching itself in just one more emblem of my general dishevelment. I am wearing this rumpled clothing in direct contravention of my normal manner of dressing, which is kempt and orderly. I always say that "we are how we dress," or "the clothes make the man," or use some other kind of formulation in which a person is equated directly with his clothing, and so I feel that I am being misrepresented ("the rumpled type"; worn, déclassé). And as I stand here thinking these uneasy thoughts, suddenly, like a spooked herd, Miss Fairfax and her companion look up, simultaneously—the admin doing so over her glasses, slipping as they are along the bridge of her nose. She waves and smiles. The pale man does not. He seems unimpressed.

I approach. She rises. The pale man remains seated. I put out a hand, which everyone ignores. Miss Fairfax steps back to take me in and assess my extent, sliding those glasses up her nose with a practiced forefinger.

"Hello, Percy. Welcome to—"

The pale man interjects. "Welcome to nowhere."

————

His name is Dennis Royal. A moneyman, pursuing his work at the Institute's Business Center. "Derivatives. Derivatives of derivatives, actually. Topological models of markets. Mining data sets. Dull stuff, honestly. The gist is making money. Heaps of it."

He bends over a cigarette, half-mast between his lips, in order to light it. Miss Fairfax taps him, and shakes her head, and he shrugs, lets it fall theatrically from his mouth into a hand, and slips it back into his tunic pocket. "What's your bag, Mr. Frobisher?"

"I prefer not to discuss it, at least not while the work is in progress."

"Everyone talks about their projects here. It is, in some sense, the raison d'etre of the entire endeavor."

"Ah, well, I prefer to travel under the radar. And my project will only take a few weeks to finish. I'll be gone before anyone knows I'm here."

Mr. Royal chuckles.

"You're skeptical?"

"Weeks? They are nothing out here. Months are like days." He pulls the cigarette out again, remembers, and returns it, clicking his tongue in self-admonishment.

"No, no," I maintain, "in and out."

"Seasons like weeks, years like months . . ."

"Best to think hopeful thoughts, surely, Mr. Royal?"

"Think whatever you like, I'm merely giving you the lay of the land. The Institute has a way of encouraging one to . . . linger."

"Some of us haven't the luxury of so much time."

"But, of course you have," he insists, glint in his eye.

Miss Fairfax finally steps in: "You will see, Percy. It all seems strange at first, but, when the coin drops, it can feel like an awakening. Anyway, Dennis, don't be so gloomy. We must all play our part in helping Mr. Frobisher acclimatize."

"My part, my dear, in case you hadn't noticed, is to be the rotten apple," he counters, "and your part, Miss Fairfax, is to keep me in line. Though you, Percy. You are—"

"The ingénue. The new hopeful?" I suggest.

"Another credulous mind for the Institute to mold," Dennis offers instead.

"The Institute does nothing of the sort, Mr. Royal," says Miss Fairfax.

"So, have you been given one of these?" says Mr. Royal, turning back to me again, and pinching the fabric at his chest, "a fucking getup?"

Miss Fairfax now reaches down into her bag and pulls out a slim, plastic-wrapped package and slides it part of the way across the table.

Inside the parcel, carefully folded, some kind of outfit.

"A *uniform*," I protest.

"Well, of course," she replies.

True, many of the locals I've seen since arriving out here are uniformed in one way or another. At the airport even, and the hotel. Jumpsuits mostly. They must delineate class in some way. Color-coded or some such. Keep the tiers sorted. Make the castes intelligible to one another.

"Unfortunately, it's not optional," she adds.

All right, all right. My clothes were wrecked from the trip anyway.

"We have limited quantities. You only get the one." She nudges the package another inch.

Mr. Royal is smirking again.

I slide the package into my lap.

"Good," Miss Fairfax exhales. "Good."

Dennis shrugs.

"So," I say, addressing them both, "any other surprises?"

And so, more dialogue, here (though no more surprises). Instead, all of that expatriate talk about what everyone misses, and what, of the new experiences, are worth having; and more importantly, whose experiences have been the deepest; who has been most subsumed into sheer foreignness. In other words, who has remade themselves to the fullest extent. Both my new colleagues have a thing or two to say about fellowships in general, how this collective differs from others, in what ways it is the same. They tell me of a local oligarch (or sheikh or some such) who has paid for all this. How he wishes to furnish the desert with creatives. As Dennis puts it: "irrigating the place with culture. We are pumped in and diffused; the Freehold is hoping something will take root out here." We speak of the other fellows, the various disciplines they represent, though the gossip is what Mr. Royal clearly relishes. His distaste for those aspects of the Institute which are (I want to say: *institutional*) is unmistakable. Miss Fairfax seems visibly animated when discussing the Institute, the projects and their taxonomies. She is thorough on schedules and procedures, and I am sure I am retaining none of it. I pull my old fountain pen from my front pocket and spin it through my fingers. Twirl it mindlessly over my thumb. I can feel the vibrations from Mr. Royal's skinny leg, the one adjacent to mine, which is oscillating up and down like a sewing machine needle. I imagine him fashioning something under the table—a flag, emblazoned with money signs. Miss Fairfax's hands are resting in her lap. I can just make them out under the table. Her hands are facing upward, their fingers curling toward her palm, occasionally twitching or pulsing inward, like upended crabs. More importantly, I notice myself noticing these details, making such analogies, and realize that my mind is beginning to pull up anchor. Everything, now, seems put on. I cease to belong to myself. I notice the scurf on the pale man's right cheek, his obsolete earring-hole. I notice the petro-lime smell of the room's industrial cleanser. I hear cicadas buzzing inside the room, this room—from the speakers—Alpine Meadows; Coastal Tranquility? Nature, denatured.

"Denatured" is good. I remind myself to whisper that down to my device, later.

Now he says something, and she says something.

(Him again; then her. Her; him . . . or maybe they don't alternate, and it is the same voice all along. Idk.)

Another gap.

"Percy?" Miss Fairfax says, and again, a bit louder.

"Sorry."

"We'll see you tonight," she says.

PETER MENDELSUND

"Don't be late," Mr. Royal drawls, waggling a finger. Miss Fairfax swats at him with an Institute brochure, before sliding it neatly into the breast pocket of my jacket.

Miss Fairfax concludes with a quick smile, and a friendly embrace. Mr. Royal holds out a limp hand for me as if to kiss. I shake it.

Mission accomplished. I'm back in the car alone, a driver only implied.

Out on the Institute thoroughfare, I finally see the denizens of the place, leaking from the widely spaced, large concrete buildings—one is an outsized column punctuated by irregularly spaced windows; another a distorted triangle; a third is an enormous piece of Brutalist shrapnel. A scheduled period must have just ended. Fellows are swarming like ants from a hill; everyone dressed in uniforms, admins dressed in blue. Here and there, work crews, in pink coveralls and caps.

By the side of the road, a woman is sitting on a bench by the artificial lake. She is drawn, ascetic, virginal. Reading on her device. She doesn't look up as the car passes. She's wearing a similar getup to that worn by the other fellows. Her aspect and posture. So bony and severe. Her (I want to say: *foreign*) eyes. They are alert and bright, clear, newly minted. Her eyes. Her eyes as she reads.

I've passed her, and I whisper to my purring device as the car continues back down the palm-lined avenue toward the Residential Enclave. "Dramatis Personae," I say, and then I list everyone—Pale Man: Mr. Dennis Royal; Admin: Miss

Fairfax, adding in "the Mysterious Woman" as an after-thought, and tagging her "Tbd."

The car continues north, toward the Institute's interior—its nucleus—and away from the dome and its subtle boundary. I twist around in my seat to look out the car's rear window, and can see behind me, receding through the dome, the world of sand, stones, and senseless things; the lifeless world of heat and torpor. Farther out even, far off, I can still make out (barely) a dark gulf, scored like an old piece of slate. Beyond that is the white, illegible city.

Such epic spaces.

I think of my home, and its clutter—but here is empty and endless and I find these unbroken spans truly hard to fathom, or stomach.

Pivoting round again, I see the main campus approaching slowly through the front windscreen. I slink down farther in my seat, and find the tops of two Institute buildings to focus on. My mind relaxes and expands. These buildings move in relation to one another as my car continues along the road. Two buildings on two independent strata, as if painted on two distinct theater scrims: one in front of the other. (Three scrims actually, as the sky presses in from behind the buildings.) As the car moves, the buildings begin to shift positions; gradually. Eventually the structures drift together—line up into a single building. I feel something shift. A deep sense of being new to the planet emerges inside me, as a feeling remembered. I knew something once—what I knew was that I live on a large, planar surface. And that I was an object upon that plane, and shared this plane with other objects; people, structures, so on. And that I was like all of these other objects and elements present upon this planar surface. And life is made up of events such as these—events such as: *two buildings and the sky behind them and me the observer all forming a sequence*. We three objects are arranged: *just like so*. The two buildings, there; and me, moving among them, here.

It is a strange feeling. And the feeling is very old.

And eerily familiar.

I'd like to remember these buildings, take stock. There's an important lesson here, I think; a rare and valuable intuition.

But suddenly now, my device chimes out a shrill little *ping!* and I'm startled from my reverie.

Pity.

The device, adamant, pings again.

"I'm coming," I say, as I dig it out.

A message from elsewhere. From someone I don't know, or don't wish to remember. I didn't give out a forwarding number or address for just this reason.

It's an emoji. Of a smiling face.

A face, but . . . denatured.

(Delete.)

THE INSTITUTE WELCOMES YOU

. . . Core values representing . . . innovative models of . . . society of makers . . . Nurturing . . . Guided, encouraged,

assisted . . . inspired . . . free   play . . . outstanding . . . creatives . . . the future.

A man at the center of an installation of some sort. Another man, holding up some kind of molecular model, the structure of which appears to be made from bright and hard candies, light gleaming off of its lacquered surfaces. A woman crouches over a diorama. Four people in front of a whiteboard, greasy with hieroglyphics. An admin, proctoring.

. . . facilities set upon . . . one hundred hectares . . . land-art intervention . . . bleeding-edge . . . state-of-the-art . . .

The Campus—overhead shot. The Enclave from the outside. The swimming pools. Slender palms. The Landau-Schmidt glacier in its hangar. Hulking concrete pavilions, bright planes, geometric shadows.

. . . rejuvenation . . . world-renowned spa . . . sports facilities . . . the wellness center . . . dynamic results with caring empowerment . . .

Baths, saunas, pools, lounge chairs, massage rooms, gym equipment, medical gear, fellows beached on lounge chairs, half turned to one another, glowing with good digestion, scoured pores, and smiling conspiratorially. Towels, shower caps, paper gowns, slippers, etc.

... Supporting and operating programs in the designated mission areas ... excellence ... innovation ... key thought-leadership ... provocation ... collaboration ... success!

A glowing stage. A bright screen. The Institute's logo. An illustrious fellow: Jawbone miced, spotlit. A Discourse™ in progress, that is. I can hear the applause; the introductory music and: this, *this* is the dream right here. The dream. A Discourse.™ *My* Discourse.™ Mine.

... Staffed by ... to differing needs ... & which require diverse levels of ... specialized ... wide range of ... fully licensed & accredited ...

An enormously obese, bald man in a uniquely bright tunic, a long medallion around his neck. The profound dignity of his office. Next to him on either side, dwarfed, his admins. Everyone massed below an unseen photographer, who must be up on a ladder, or shooting down from a balcony, everyone looking up, and smiling, eyes shining, the composite form of all these Institute professionals forming a rough, dense circle, or something else. What, exactly, is unclear.

New possibilities ... far-flung ... adventure ... exotic ... novelties for ... fostering ambitious ... creatives ... building ... measurably better ... imagining the coming world ...

The Freehold itself. Ruins, malls, mines, camel rides, men and their retainers—in thobes, dishdashas, their heads banded by black agals—hunting with peregrines, Range Rovers out in the sand. (You get the picture.)

"Become the best you."

Sheesh.

I try to close the pamphlet, managing only to crumple it badly.

2

A solitary suitcase is trundled into my flat at the Residential Enclave. My identity papers go into the safe in the closet; my toothbrush peals into a glass by the sink. The enormous novel I intend to read during my stay here thumps onto a bedside table. My ratty coat is slung upon a hanger. I barely have a chance to look around before I am off to the Institute's Cavity Yard for a gathering of the fellows, this creative aristocracy: enfants terribles, singularities, radical highfliers from leading universities, captains of industry, prodigies of nature, mavens, the Institute's own gilt-edge investments. Everyone top of their class and field.

"I was just dazzled when I first arrived," Miss Fairfax says, handing me a fizzing glass. She's been here a year already. Learned a bit of the local language, and even picked up the shadow of a tan. "Some of those pesky rays get through. God knows how."

She's already made Senior Admin. *Admin5*, her name tag reads.

"For me—and I assume this is true for you now, as well," she says, "it's really like having arrived. To have the acknowledgment, the prestige, the—"

Rubbing my fingers, "The money?"

"An astronomical amount has been spent throughout the Freehold. The colonization of this desert cost, in currency sure, though also in labor."

We cannot contemplate the conditions under which this oasis was coaxed to blossom, can we, as we all tacitly agreed, by accepting this invitation, not to dwell on prices paid. We fellows would like to maintain a frictionless sojourn upon these inhospitable shores.

Meanwhile, these same fellows are everywhere in evidence—appropriately diverse—though all wearing the uniform. I've put on mine. And it fits. It fits very well actually, Imho. A marked improvement over my rumpled civvies. Looks and feels: good. But it smells odd; synthetic, sterile. And I didn't sign up for a cult, after all. W/e. Frankly, it is comforting to look, at last, like (I want to say: *no one?* Certainly like no one in particular).

"Looking spiffy," Miss Fairfax says, admiring my duds. "One of us."

Us, everyone, all the sundry creatives, promenading under the strings of the little lanterns. Hors d'oeuvres, smiles and simpers, chatter. Moving across the manicured grounds, avoiding the sprinklers, canapés in hand, gossiping, networking, making small provocations, navigating the stylized landscape with its barbered tufts of sage grass, its silvered pools, its sculpted totems. I hold tightly to Miss Fairfax's arm.

"Amazing, isn't it," she says, indicating the sky, the mediated sky; and that mediation itself, the metastructure.

Under the old dispensation, the zoning commissions and world bodies claiming some degree of oversight in these matters permitted the construction of large, air-conditioned open-air sites—but these (buildings, parks, stadia . . .) Swiss-cheesed the atmosphere to such an extent that we will never see their like again. So, the new outdoors is indoors.

"Out is in; in is out," she says.

Depending on the time of day, the metastructure reveals or hides itself, but now, the sunset is made prismatic by the dome's proprietary materials—its silicates and embedded filaments. The sky glitches, causing subtle artifacts, chrominance noise, wow and flutter. I must admit the effect, this aurora, is beautiful. We watch the sky slowly ooze and warp like antique glass. The lightest of breezes carries a slight but comfortable chill. Miss Fairfax shivers happily, and—as if the result of a molecular chain reaction bridging the gap between us—my body mirrors hers, and shivers in unison.

I take out my device, and, stepping back a couple of paces, point it at Miss Fairfax.

"Percy, for heaven's sake."

"Smile!"

Click. (Got her.)

Walking toward us is Dennis Royal now, in conversation

with another man. Dennis sees us and in greeting, mini-mally adjusts the height of an eyebrow (he looks—as I'm guessing he must always look—terribly bored). The man at his side seems much more animated. He is smaller, darker, with a trim, stiff little beard. Kind eyes. He's from here, I'm guessing—given his accent, and the kaffiyeh fastidi-ously wrapped about his neck. (In my typology, I think of him as "the Local.") The scarf contrasts with his donnish habitus—but the overall effect is academic-radical chic.

"Mr. Ousman Al'Hatif," Miss Fairfax tells me.

The dark man shakes my hand warmly. "Mr. Percy, I was told that you'd be coming and I've been eager to meet you." His voice is soft, and he vaguely trills his *r*'s.

Mr. Royal, sipping through a red cocktail straw, comes to the end of the liquid in his glass with a long sucking sound.

"Mr. Al'Hatif is the Archeologist," Miss Fairfax tells me, over this rudeness, "as well as a long-term resident here. Ousman knows all the ins-and-outs."

"I've been at the Institute as long as anyone here," he agrees, "so please let me know if I can advise you in any way, or help you to adapt to your new life here. We will all, of course, be seeing a lot more of one another."

"There's no avoiding it," sneers Mr. Royal.

"Yes, well," Miss Fairfax puts in, still perhaps rankled by his comments earlier, "that is rather the point, Dennis, isn't it. Cross pollinating with the other fellows. Speaking of which, we mustn't monopolize our newest member."

She tugs on my arm, and off we go to greet a succession of name tags: *the Cryptographer, the Sculptor, the Philosopher, the Actor, the Translator, the Set Theorist, the Miniaturist, the Critic, the Sociologist, the Composer, the Developer, the Astronomer, the Hedonic Psychometrician, the Philologist, the Financial Modeler, the Developer of Social Platforms, the Computational Linguist, the Urban Planner, the Percussionist,* so on.

"When did you . . . ?" "The trip out . . . ?" "Jet lag . . . ?" "Culture shock . . . ?" "*Frobisher*, was it?"

My name tag reads, merely, *Percy F.*, yet despite this withholding (or perhaps because of it) I'm expelling my facts in a slow but seemingly unstanchable leak. I can't manage to guard against it. The group feel, the institutional vibe overall, is one of inquisitiveness, curiosity, fierce intelligence, cattiness. So many questions. Sidelong looks. It goes on for a while, this bit, and I'm having trouble modulating my energies, but now, just as I am replying to yet another inquiry about the nature of my work, happily, someone begins clinking a glass, and everyone turns away from me and toward the sound.

Ding, ding, ding.

We draw closer together on the gently tiered lawns, murmuring, echolocating as a group, toward the toast-giver, and I can see, through the throng, that colossal man from the brochure, who must be the Director (paradigmatic case of "fat man"; heaving body, shiny pate). He is raising his glass up like a lantern, and I find myself on the outside rim of the large circle which surrounds him, and so can see only bits of the proceeding. Mostly, I see it all fractured onto the screens of the fellows' devices in front of me, each scene in miniature. Everyone assembled upon the darkening terrace is trying to capture the moment—the fat Director, and the occasion he embodies—and the scene comes to me like a broken monitor, an uneven scattering of pixels; the individual screens contributing to the general impression while also capturing it as well as themselves, these recursions, these mises en abymes, as if there were an infinity of parties like this one, going on and on; scores of identical Directors, identical guests . . .

He clinks his glass one last time for good measure, looks around him until the silence is total, and begins speaking.

The Director's toast to be indicated by asterisks

```
********* * * * **** * * * * * **** ******   ***
* * ** * ******* * * * * * * *** * * * * *  * ** ** * ** *
** ** ** ** ** **   *****   ** ******** ****** ** * **
* * * *   * ** * * * ** * * * *     ***   **** * * * * * **
* *       * ** ******** ***********   ******   ********
***       ******* ***** **** ****** * * ********** ****
* ****** ********* * * * * * * *       ****************
************ *********** *** *****************     ****
**** ******* ****   **** ****** ***   ***** *    ****
*   ***   *** * * *   ** * *            *
```

As I listen to the Director's speech from the periphery of the gathering, I notice that the audience encircling our master of ceremonies has been made (I want to say: *biddable?*). It is the theater of the thing. They cease to be an aggregation of individuals and instead have become a single organism: a creature that responds quickly and obediently to the prompts provided it; clapping, grumbling, cheering, etc. We are enjoying ourselves, I think. Or, they are. All of them. Committed, fervent. Feelings I simply can't manage.

I cannot merge. Never could. Recognizing this fact, I feel a pang.

My admin, Miss Fairfax, finely tuned to sense ebbing spirits, slides between several fellows to stand beside me, slipping her arm back again into mine. She looks up at me kindly.

"You're here," she says, smiling, stating the obvious, though I know what she means. She means that it is real.

The Director wraps up his address, and we, gently, applaud.

Alone again, back in my rooms, just before sleep, I examine my pics from the day. Time-stamped, most recent first. Airport. Road. Desert. Campus. Dennis Royal and Ousman Al'Hatif. Here's the one of Miss Fairfax; her look of embarrassment, but also of warmth. I enlarge it, shrink it, adjust the tints and levels, apply and then remove a series of filters. I put my nose to the device and inhale deeply, and am surprised to receive a sharp little electrical charge. I put the device down and reach for a glass sitting primly on a doily by the bed. Bring it to the bathroom, take the pleated skirt off the top, and run the tap. The world outside the dome is hot, but everything inside of it, including the water, is nice and cold.

Looking up, I notice something in the mirror. It seems to be on my chest. I reach up, and my uniform is damp to the touch.

Looking away from my reflection and down, there is a splotch—a moist spot, small, but spreading. A dark blue stain on the breast pocket of my uniform.

My pen.

Gingerly, with a tissue, I extract the pen, sticky with ink, wrap it in more tissue, and place the damaged article, like an amputated digit, on the edge of the sink.

I wash my hands, dab my fingers into the glass, and then rub them on the uniform, worrying the stain between my wet fingers.

But I'm only making things worse: it's only growing. ("You only get *the one*," Miss Fairfax said.)

Just the one. Fml.

Give up. Brush my teeth.

Time passes.

I suddenly feel the minty foam blooming its way down my throat and gag.

Spit. Ugh.

3

I am still wearing my robe—barely, it's dilating open—
there are sheet marks on my chest and face; the hair's an
apocalypse. The rug is softly burled under my swollen toes.
I'm fighting a fierce jet lag, tinged with the faint peripheral throb of a day-old hangover and/or withdrawal from
said hangover's root cause. Further state of the union: the
throat is scratchy; the mouth is dry; the eyes are itchy;
cheeks rough.

There's the low hum of the interior space mediating the
exterior. Pleasantly dim. Far above and out, penetrating the
AC, one can hear the metal-on-metal scree of some predatory bird. Silence. Then, fainter, one more bird cry. Gentle
water drops. Wind.

I reach over, turn off *Sounds of the Deciduous Forest*, sit up.
Plant my feet.

Good morning.

Let's kick the sheets off and grope out across the room,
vampiric, one arm folded across the eyes, the other a feeler
out in front, slither forward—slide the sheet of curtains

across the wall on their singing ball bearings and reveal, through a seamless pane of multi-ply plate glass, that remorseless sky, hung with its shocking sun. *Hiss.*

I smell my own breath, repelling, sourly warm off the glass. Squint, adjust, and here's what there appears to be: the top, hairy fronds of a date palm; its testicular pendules hanging below. A swimming pool, wormy with impossible teal. The long, gated rows of the Residential Enclave, arranged along an artificial river, a canal of some sort, ramifying outward. Culverts. Parklands. One or two geometric sculptures. A large, and mostly empty, car park. A series of tiny, darkly rainbowed and fluorescing oil spots. And past the metastructure: the desert.

Out there.

I crank open the window and the nicely cooled breezes blow in, jellyfishing the curtains. The perfect temperature, a faint tattoo of a spiky palm leaf, now spread out on the floor. I can smell lavender, and the pool is making rippled patterns on the wall and the desk, like floaters in a vitreous humor. A fair, languorous morning, full of promise. Though I also feel a strange, persistent tug at my conscience this morning, as if I'd been caught out in a lie. A vague sense of wrongdoing.

I turn and walk toward the bathroom.

The once-white soap in the dish is now covered in a light blue froth.

Bloody hell.

The ink.

I hold the soap under the tap, watching the semi-hardened blue scum soften and run off down the drain. The uniform, now bearing its moist spot, hangs over a chair. No time for regrets though. No time. I must get myself in order, as today is for touring the Institute campus, and for finding a space in which to compose my project.

(The project!)

The gracious Mr. Al'Hatif has volunteered (been volunteered, perhaps) to help orient me today. I am to rendezvous with him up at the Arts Pavilion. So, I make my way there, through the echoing concrete canyons, past the swimming pools, and gardens with their busy morning sprinklers, past the scuttling workers in their crayon-colored suits, down paths, under arbors, across atria.

"Hmm," Mr. Al'Hatif mutters, after we greet one another and I point out to him the dark, unsightly blemish on my uniform.

"What can I do? It looks indelible."

"They take these things rather seriously here, Mr. Percy."

"So I've been told."

"Have you tried the Enclave's concierge?"

"Not yet."

"Do. And if that doesn't work, well, you could take it to the Same Same."

"The—"

"A fix-it place. In town." He probes the spot one more time with his finger. "But, I doubt it will come to that."

We climb the long, open-air white marble stairway of the Arts Pavilion. Arriving at its first mezzanine, we get onto a lift, and take it to the topmost floor and stand out on a wide balcony, where we look over the property unfurling below us, the whole extent of which is visible from this height. There are the various structures, with their strange geometries, arranged haphazardly like upturned toys in a sandbox, or the aftermath of an explosion. An arbitrary torus, a distended cloudlet, some conjoined volumes, a grid-sleeve, an irrupted bird's nest . . . From this height, the site feels like a blueprint of itself. I already recognize some of these buildings: off to our right is the Residential Enclave, and that over there is the refectory, and the library, the Pleasure Center, the Mountain House, where I first met Dennis and Miss Fairfax . . . I ask Mr. Al'Hatif about a large and elaborately vented building just below us.

"That is the Presence Center, Percy. Site of the Main Stage."

"Is that where—"

"Yes."

I let it wash over me for a moment. I will—if all goes according to plan—be delivering my talk here, my Discourse™. The day will come soon, before I know it. I will be up on that very stage, in front of that famous, pellucid white backdrop, up there, telling the world of my work—my ideas, beliefs, findings and everything I say and each choreographed gesture I make will be simulcast and recorded, sent out via redundant fat-pipe systems over multiple platforms and viewed; repackaged and sold the world over. It's beyond belief.

Looking down now, I watch my new colleagues below. Them too, I think. They will also stride out to that heroic-mode, introductory synth-blast, and straight into the global consciousness. "Thought leaders," the pamphlet bragged. Yet, I feel now as though I could reach down and knock them off their paths, pluck them up and set them down elsewhere, spin them all, change their orientation and rotation. They are dwarfed by the Institute itself, these international superstars. Dwarfed by it, by me, at this vertiginous elevation. And once again, I marvel at the scope of the thing as a whole. The audacity, the hubris of it, the force of will necessary to construct this large-scale terrarium in the middle of what is surely one of the most unforgiving and uninhabitable regions on the planet.

"The campus is, as you can see, quite large—and there are any number of spaces which could be made available to you," Al'Hatif says, leading me back toward the stairway.

But we don't find anything which meets my standards in the Arts Pavilion. So we walk through the Science Center, past hermetically sealed white rooms, bursting with paraphernalia. Some of the gear is incredibly technologically advanced, but in other rooms, *wunderkammers* of various sorts, there are crucibles and alembics, as well as rows of strange bottles containing odd ingredients—materials which look grown or scavenged. As the doors open and close, hissing as they unseal and reseal, smells leak out—formaldehyde, turmeric, urine, something burnt and acidic.

Outside, we sit, and a mildly troubled Mr. Al'Hatif looks over my manifest. "Are you sure that you need all of . . . *this*, in order to finish your work?"

"Oh yes. Yes, I do."

"But for projects like yours—"

"What do you mean?"

"I don't intend to pry."

"My needs are complex," I say, wishing to leave it at that.

"And yet," he continues undaunted, "all you would truly need, I'd think, is a device, and if you had an old-fashioned bent, perhaps some paper—"

"Paper?" I grimace.

"Yes, paper; no? Some pencils, a pen. A device? Running the appropriate applications? No? Of course, you know best."

"I am not sure yet what my requirements are," I say, and, trying to remove some of the sharpness from my tone, add: "How could anyone be sure at such an early stage? But better to be over-outfitted than under, don't you agree?"

Which prompts the ever-refined Mr. Al'Hatif to snake a pocket square out from his suit pocket and wipe first his mouth and then his brow. "I suppose so, Mr. Percy." He is tiring. I am as well.

We soldier on.

"So the statue wasn't, in fact, indigenous to this region," he explains. "It was built by the religious nomads who were moving along the trading roads—such, at least, was the rationale for its demolition. That the builders were foreign."

Mr. Al'Hatif's project at the Institute is the reconstruction of an ancient statue; a statue recently destroyed by fundamentalist insurgents. I'm guessing that Mr. Al'Hatif is the only one of our small number to be working on a project germane to this locale.

"Look."

An image, a projection of the desert plain, which emanates from his device.

"It had been standing serenely in this spot for ages and had survived every manner of affront at the hands of man, beast, and nature; but still it stood."

Across red sand, here are remains, the broken stumps of stone or marble legs. Lots of rubble. Smoke still rising. Crews roping off the devastation. Forensic teams setting up lights. An unbroken ring of waste surrounding the scene.

"And all that's left now is this. What a calamity."

The crime scene: graticulated and labeled like a map. A grid, made of string or wire or light; whether forensic, or archeological, I can't be sure. Fragments of rock are marked with small yellow tags.

"The insurgents maintain that the attack was an assertion of faith—in opposition to older, illegitimate, tribal beliefs."

There's more to it than that though, I think. A crime like this one is . . . it is a repudiation of modernity, or some such.

"Of course, the funding is just pouring in for the rebuilding."

We enter the cavernous library. The corridors connecting the research and reading rooms are lined with read-only devices of every make and year. I reach out to examine one, but it is either dead or I don't have the proper signature to whisper it awake. Farther down, on the bottom tier of the building, there are rows of old periodicals on white acrylic stands, in neat colorful stacks. Several fellows are working down here as well, including Dennis Royal, who sees us from across the reading room and wryly doffs an invisible cap to us.

"Now look at these two, will you?" Mr. Al'Hatif juts his chin out toward the other end of the huge room, where two men seem to be engaged in a heated debate. "Always at it."

We stand there watching the disputants—red in the face, gesticulating—but their rancorous voices are smeared, and faint.

"Professional squabble," he adds.

"Seems personal."

"Debate is encouraged at the Institute. It is the very hallmark of an open society such as ours. You'll see."

We leave the library, and follow a footpath along the course of the artificial waterway. Everywhere, work crews in coveralls, bent over tasks. A project period has let out, just as it had on the afternoon of my arrival, and the fellows are streaming from their studios. Despite it being a Recess, some of the fellows have taken their work out of doors, and are huddled in small groups, studying and debating under the strange shadows of the brutal buildings. Some wander, and from the fuzzy looks in their eyes one can tell that they are going hard at some problem or another. Looking around, I realize that I am unconscious of the distance Mr. Al'Hatif and I have traveled, and it dawns on me slowly, but with eventual force, that the Institute belongs to a different world; a no-place; a kind of Cockaigne. How did I end up here, I ask myself.

At world's end. At world's fucking end.

"Well, here we are," says Mr. Al'Hatif. It is a new, clean, little set of rooms, and I know before entering that everything is just right. I inspect the ceiling, which is reasonably high. The few windows on the south and west sides of the building are clear, and louvered, sight lines good, so the lighting should not be a problem. Solid electric—lots of it—plenty of signal, etc., etc. The space is accessible to large deliveries, and yet it is also sufficiently secluded. It's too good to be true. Though the walls are flaking, I notice now, initials carved into them, of people who worked here previously, presumably. Someone has preceded me it seems.

Mr. Al'Hatif is smiling at me strangely.

I don't mind though. Np. I think I'll keep them, these marks. They seem important.

"I'll take it," I say, as if he were a Realtor. "Tell Miss Fairfax: it's . . . perfect."

"But, Mr. Percy—"

And I'm already imagining where I'll put my things. The equipment I require. Some technical specifications will have to be examined: the wiring will have to be double-checked.

But in the middle of the room is a desk. That will prove useful indeed.

I walk over to it, tug on the drawer handles, but the drawers don't budge. Seems as though the moldings and pulls are just for show.

"Mr. Percy?"

And there's nothing on the desk. The blotter's surface powdered and empty—though not for long. No sir.

Not for long.

"Mr. Percy?"

All this, Tk, that is, hopefully: soon. (After I get the ink-stained uniform taken care of.)

Now that I'm in the space, my work space, I can't wait to begin.

It's like I already have.

"Mr. Percy, but this is your room, already. Your room? We've walked you in a circle."

4

Nighttime.

Something is happening.

I sit up in bed and listen. I hear it once, and then again. Like the collective grunts of several men, followed now by the solitary, high, and reedy cry of one man. Contrabasses v. Oboe. A register of fear. The many against the one.

Difficult to understand.

Now: nothing.

I creep to the door, crack it, peer down the darkened hallway. Wait. No, nothing.

Time passes.

(More time passes.)

A very faint noise: croak or moan.

I ease the door closed until it clicks shut.

Back to bed. There for some time.

Still awake. I take a tablet. Have the bottle at the ready. Hopefully: kaput, right out. What *was* that hubbub though? Did somebody . . . cackle?

Tbd, Tbd.

Shhhh.

5

(TABLE TALK)

To work.

But first, a brief jaunt out to the dome's perimeter; to one of the Institute's "Observation Points." As long as I have come all this way to the desert, I decide that I might as well take a good picture of it. I head out from the flat, walk past the pool, down the winding, palm-lined paths, around the huge blue kidney of the lake (at one point I can hear, and then see: a pink jumpsuit in a golf cart following behind me at a discreet distance, the driver speaking periodically into his walkie-talkie, most likely making sure that I don't wander too far or otherwise come to ill; before he peels away eventually in a diminishing hum) out past the fountains, and huts and depots, and all the way to the perimeter and turbines. It takes a while, but I get here. I have made it right up to the edge where the green biome meets the desolate, arid one.

Here it is, an unending, billowing, landscape of rust.

Center it in the viewfinder. Take the shot.

Distance. Space. Sky. Rock. Sand. Unirrigated and austere. Same as on my screen.

Smells of nothing.

There's a single bench. Which seems to be here for just this purpose. "Desert Viewing," the small plaque reads. A scenic view.

Perching here, I can see the ten meters in front of me in impressive detail, the grains of sand. Then the plain behind, upon which are those quicksilver lakes of mirage, floating pools, hovering just a smidge above the ground, snakes of heat spiraling upward. But then the honeyed dunes behind that, the first wind-ruffled rank waving like eels, and each successive grade fading into vagueness in discrete degrees of blur.

Twenty meters, blurry.

Thirty meters, blurrier.

Etc., etc.

Detachment doesn't so much descend as it does remind me of always having been there. I am the only solitary presence out here. Everything else—sand, dunes, stones, the ragged clouds, even the sun, nestled in its own halo—are multiples.

And as my optical focus moves outward, my mind wanders inward, running over my memories of the last few days, playing back for me my insertion into Institute life. And I can feel an effort being made, just beneath this layer of consciousness, which constitutes the active formulation of a story. Something coalescing. I don't have much of it yet, but I know a few things. For instance, that nothing about me, here, at the Institute, is particularly startling, or

particularly novel. That this personal narrative of mine—
"Uncanny Tales of Percy Frobisher"; a story of genius, brave
endeavor; of adventure and personal growth; the concep-
tion and realization of a thrilling new project—all of it is
nothing but a tired trope out here. It's everyone's story. All
the fellows have seen, unpacked, drilled down into some
fascinating topic and traveled great lengths to pursue further inquiries. We are all brave explorers; and thus, none of
us are. I'm another in a number; another item on the shelf.
But then, but then: I didn't come here to stand out. I didn't
sign up for this psychotic geste—didn't utterly deracinate
and reformulate myself—in order to achieve celebrity, or
notoriety.

No. Just.

There came a juncture in my life when I found myself in
need of reinvention.

When I began to suspect that there was no bottom to
the dull satiety; when not another aimless and indistinguishable day could pass without my suffering a boredom
akin to pain; when all of the minutes of all of my dissolute
days were martialed in ranks against me, and there was no
longer anything for it but to desert my post. I up and left my
life—such as it was. I knew it would happen. Of course I did.
And it came to pass. The submission, the awarding of the
fellowship . . . It all arrived just in the nick of time, and I
accepted it without question. A change of state, a change of
charge and velocity. Regeneration; reinvention. *Finn-e-gan,
begin a-gain.* It had been time to go.

Past time.

But now things have become odd. Strange, and rather quick-like, under the metastructure. The disorienting exoticism. Directors and admins. Ideators and projects: all impressively idiosyncratic; all indicative of the bleeding-edge moment. The VR Modeler. The Historian of Prosthesis, the Creator of Cryptocurrencies—whose blockchain ledgers help further the abstraction of commodities already abstracted beyond understanding—the Man-Who-Assiduously-Tracks-His-Own-Life-Data, the Woman-Whose-Face-and-Hands-Are-Covered-in-Yarn (the Performance Artist?). In the line for breakfast this morning, a reedy and disheveled man beside me told me he was finishing up extensive work on a cylinder.

"The cylinder will be completed in a matter of days."

"Congratulations," I said. "What does it do?"

"Why should it do anything?"

"Ah, *art* then—"

"Hardly."

Such late times these are, to produce projects such as these.

A new life. "A new you." A new me.

No one said it wouldn't be strange.

God it's hot.

I rise from the bench, and give a last squint out into the actual. The Irl.

Smooth my uniform, hands ruffling over it, then I turn away from the meatspace, and turn back toward the mindspace and begin the walk back. A couple of steps toward the campus, outermost shoots of grass, mushy underfoot—and I'm already cool as could be.

A little farther on, and, hello: I see my Mysterious Woman once again. She's heading across the quadrangle, frictionless, reading her device as she walks.

And just as she is about to disappear around a wall, she suddenly lifts her eyes and smiles, nervous and timid as a rodent.

Blammo—contact.

Then she's gone.

A work period in which no work is done and none of this is worth dwelling on except to chalk it all up as a total loss. Distracted, I play with my device. My device, which continues to glitch. It's been acting strangely. Finicky. Intermittently unresponsive, then (worst of all) pinging uncontrollably. It's been doing this since somewhere over the last ocean. It never asked to come along with me—press-ganged through every manner of atmospheric change, new air pressures, radical heat fluctuations, not to mention shifts in time zone. It's having a tantrum. *Ping! Ping! Ping!*

"Hush," I say to it, stroking its hard membrane, "hush," feeling as though I am, periodically, glitching myself. I look down at the stain on my uniform.

Ping!

"I know," I say. "Ditto."

Brb.

―――――

So now my room screen. News; weather (outside the dome: scorching); and the football's on. I count twenty-one games in seven languages. I gather that here is where old players come to die. These athletes, they get a villa, sip drinks, get glad-handed about, visit the souks, camel races, fortresses, maybe train falcons. They have no competition; no yard-stick; no audience. It must eat them away inside. Money's good—but for what? Idk.

The Institute, on the other hand, provides nothing if not competition; a yardstick; an audience. I run my mind over recent events, and feel a sweat begin to rise again. The stain—leave it to me to ruin my uniform so publicly, so soon. I am, it would seem, unavoidably *me*. I feel the loss of control vertiginously, first as fear, but then as diminishment and as a dissipation of energy. Something has been drained away, as I was afraid it might be. Some critical authority. An authority rendered slightly less potent. Possibilities limited. I have been caught up, already, in a cycle of regression. No longer a cipher, a mystery, a rallying point for a set of new proclivities. I wish, now, that I could hoard my informa-tion; save it, or parcel it out according to a thoughtful and prearranged program. I need all the energy I can get. For me. For the project. For the Discourse™. Energy must not be squandered. I must not succumb to the heedless volun-tarism of closed social networks.

I walk over by the freshly made bed to the table, grab and open the small bottle lying there, and arc a pill into my mouth—open palm hitting my mouth making a faint *whop*.

It takes a moment, and then I am slowly disappearing, dispersing. My mind unmoors from my body and the world becomes a place without quality. I disassociate. There is no more feeling-of-what-it-is-like to be here. Here is hardly a "place," at all. But it is a place of sorts. I pull up a pornographic thought, a scenario, tailor-made, and sync it to the image of Miss Fairfax, which I now have on my device.

As always, I must affix my generalized sexual impulses to the Irl.

Could be anyone. "Might as well be her," I say to myself, through the gathering mists, as I envision Miss Fairfax disrobing.

And then I wait for the chemicals, and everything else, to really-and-truly kick in.

"Can you pass that? Thanks."

A row of brown tunics sitting at either side of the long refectory table. Sweating carafes of cool water, porcelain plates, big nickel-plated chafing dishes, tasteful amber lighting from licking candle flames—warm and guttering LEDs; which look pretty bloody real, Imho.

I'm sitting next to Dennis Royal. Seated with us are the two fellows who were arguing so heatedly in the library, during yesterday's tour. The first of these men is dignified, if a little shabby. He resembles that actor whose name eludes me. The other man a kind of classic "scholarly man" (though Nm; never mind all that, as I instantly think of these two men as "Disputant 1" and "Disputant 2," respectively). Next to the two men is Mr. Al'Hatif, and on their other side is the Architect (鼎福, or *Ting-Fu*). 鼎福 the Architect helps himself to the decanter, while Disputant 1 holds forth.

Disputant 1 is speaking on "maps and territories." Disputant 2 is on the left, and is eating noisily, stagily almost, as if to draw attention from Disputant 1. But Disputant 1, unperturbed, fails to notice.

"My scholarship pertains to the delineation and description of 'boundaries,' across various fields of inquiry. Their definitions, and the manners in which these boundaries are policed," declares Disputant 1.

"Hmph," says Disputant 2. Everyone ignores this.

"The Freehold must be of particular interest to you then," I posit.

鼎福 the Architect adds, "Out here on the frontier as we are? On the fringes?"

"Oh certainly," Disputant 1 concurs. "One does have the feeling of being *on the edges* of something, here. On several edges in fact. One hardly knows where one zone ends and another begins. It is all gray area, it seems. Which, of course, makes it all (you are correct, sir) quite pertinent indeed to my research."

Disputant 2 continues ingurgitating for our benefit, raising the volume of his chomping and lip-smacking slightly, tuning it all subtly, ever higher and louder. "Nobody cares. Nobody cares, Lou," he says.

"Shut it, Leo," Disputant 1 rejoins, before collecting himself.

Disputant 2 smiles triumphantly at having successfully provoked his adversary, having proven something discernible only to the two of them, locked as they are in perpetual conflict. A small morsel of something clings to Disputant 2's lip.

Disputant 1, gamely, attempts to continue: "The first boundary we learn is of course the 'inside/outside' distinction, gleaned when we are taught, as infants, to understand that selfhood and thought take place in an *inside* space, that the world, separate from us, transpires outside of this space, and that our bodies mediate the two realms. I am interested in the relative shapes, volumes, and extensions of the putative inner realm. For if it could be said to be a space, in direct contrast to the outer, and unlimited, space, then what kind of a space is it? Is it equally boundless? Does it have limits, walls, ceilings, capacities? Does it have shape or extension? Is this space experienced, or only inferred?"

A cup falls to the floor and clangs loudly. Someone bends down under the table to retrieve it. I only half listen to Disputant 1, occasionally stealing glances at the other fellows relishing the sumptuous courses provided by the Institute chefs. A *Daube a la Provencal*. Tagines. Apricots and almonds. Fancy, etc. There is a fellow here, a famous chef, and so all the menus are "curated" (as the brochure has it). Everything, delicious. We eat with abandon. Someone is yelling now. It is Disputant 2, though I can't locate him. Disputant 1 has had enough. He gets up from the table and excuses himself.

Someone in another conversation then says the phrase "rupturing the conventional discourse."

Dennis is holding two almost-contradictory expressions on his face: distaste and glee.

I see an administrator lingering over by the door. (Admin14? I mix them up, but one's always around. And I wonder where Miss Fairfax is.)

Time passing in this way.

Anyway, I think, these meals are strange, certainly, but exciting, and aren't I just soaking it all in? Inspiration. Convivial warmth. Prompts and challenges. All of it. I've been told I've been sat at "the good table," so there's that. We are each other's family, for the time being.

Mr. Al'Hatif is talking about his statue now, as is his wont. The Poet (a paradigm case of "thin man") is stuck on a line in his poem, and canvasses the group for opinions. He recites the problematic portion a couple of times. It's beautiful, but incomplete. He gives us several variants. In the poem, rather self-referentially, a poet is wrestling with creative confusion.

The Architect, helpfully, provides the poet with a series of prompts, in order to get his colleague unstuck:

"The Poet founders, but in foundering, reveals something about the nature of poetry itself?" he tries.

The Poet considers this.

"The Poet finds a solution to his problem, but is completely out of paper? The Poet never began his poem in the first place, which is to say that the poem is a delusion in the mind of the poet? The Poet is, himself, a species of poem?"

Prompts.

Prompts?

"One of the core techniques," Mr. Al'H. explains to me in sidebar. "A kind of nudging, or priming. The prompt is an essential tactic used here at the Institute. Anyone can provide a prompt to anyone. We are all supposed to remain receptive to the prompts of others," he says, spearing a *batata harra* out of its steaming, silvery coffin.

Someone new comes, and sits themselves down on my left in the spot that Disputant 2, it appears, has vacated. It's the Puppeteer, or some such. The chair where Disputant 1 once sat is now taken by Miss ☺, the Brand Analyst. (She also resembles a film actress, though a diminished version of one.)

Leaning forward over the table, the Brand Analyst extends a cheerfully manicured hand. She is vivacious, carbonated, and all her bodily tics are flirty and flip. She's the youngest of the fellows I've met thus far, and seems it, bless her. "So nice to meet you?" she blurts on an upward lilt, smiling flirtily, and I immediately have the impression that there must not be too many eligible male fellows about, and think it sad that she would expend such energy on me of all people (it is hopeless, really). I don't doubt that she would lack for suitors, would there be any proper men present.

The Architect, Mr. 鼎福, leaves off prompting the Poet, and begins chatting with her. She is new here, while he is a fellowship connoisseur; a lifer, trekking from one colony to the next, never setting down roots. The Architect is one of that gypsy band of itinerant thinkers who live permanently upon the charity and mercies of such places.

"What kinds of structures do you build?" she asks him.

"Full-surround. VR environments. Actually."

"Ah," she replies, batting more lashes than she probably has. My own eyes are pulled up in stock-wonder, this quickly becoming my favored, most economical response.

I put in: "Nothing real?"

"What do you mean," the Architect replies.

"I mean, do you actually make anything?"

"Yes, of course, as I've said."

"But, in real li—"

Dennis the moneyman accidently elbows me, and I knock over my fork. As I bend over to retrieve it, I see that Disputant 2 is down under the table, where he's been since he dropped his own cup earlier—hiding like a child. He looks at me guiltily. I smile reassuringly back at him, and rise again. Dennis Royal is now engaged with the Brand Analyst. He is explaining to her something involving *model inputs* and *stochastic processes*. His eyelids are now half-closed, not with drowsiness, but in a subtle species of erotic languor. There's some sort of ruckus in the kitchen behind us but no one seems perturbed by it.

I turn back to Mr. Al'Hatif, who has more to say on prompts.

"A prompt is provided *by* a fellow, *to* a fellow. It can be anything: visual, verbal, choreographic. The idea is to spur creativity."

"Does it work?"

"It does; often, yes."

"So I can just proffer a prompt to anyone, and they to me?" I ask.

"Yes," Miss ☺ the Brand Analyst says. The Architect nods, lazily.

The bedlam is building behind us. Still, no one seems to care. *Clank, clank, clank.* Yell. Wtf.

"For example," the Architect weighing in, "if you were stuck on your project, Percy, I could give you a sentence, a phrase, an idea, or a picture or a movement, so on, to catalyze forward momentum."

"Oh, that seems handy."

"It is; it is. In fact, I have just given you a prompt."

Someone is clipping their nails at the table. I can hear the muted snips.

"You did?" I ask, recovering. "What was it?"

"What do you mean?" asks the Architect, growing mildly impatient with my questions.

A couple of admins rush by, and disappear into a hallway.

"I mean, how will I know if I am being offered a prompt?"

Both the Architect and the Brand Analyst open their mouths to respond, but the Brand Analyst gets there first.

"It's all prompts, silly," she says as she lurches, now, coltish, out of her chair. The Architect stands up as well.

Dennis, next to me, has pulled out a vaping pen, draws upon it.

"All?" I ask.

"Sure, while you're here."

"Even this, now?"

"Yes," the Brand Analyst says over her shoulder, walking toward the door, "and *this* as well. And this . . ."

It is so real, the way she says it. By which I mean that she seems to mean it.

Dennis exhales noisily, releasing his mentholated steam.

Everything is motivation. Here. Everything for the projects.

And I think: Good. *Just* what the doctor ordered.

Clank, clank!

On my way back to my room, I run into the Enclave's cleaning lady, who emerges from a shadow behind the Enclave's convenience desk just as I'm walking by. So I point out the stain on my uniform. She casts an expert eye on the garment, muttering over it like a cleric.

"But what can be done," I ask, to which she simply shrugs. Nothing, that is. Nothing can be done. (But what was it Mr. Al'Hatif had said? About a shop in town.)

I wish good night to the concierge and head up the stairs and back to my solitude.

Though there is good news: tonight, in the Enclave, it is just as quiet as could be. And after only a few minutes attempting to read my book—the mammoth masterpiece I've promised myself I will eventually finish—my lids become scrims, and I fall right asleep just like

6

To work? I'm not sure. Is what I'm doing work? I lie in the middle of my floor, hands crossed behind my head, staring at the ceiling, wondering where creative momentum will come from. It's work, of a sort (Imo).

Begin with broad strokes, I tell myself. Begin with an outline. Begin with method.

I roll over and grab my device lying on the dusty floor beside me, and then pivot onto my back again. From this position, I whisper up my main schematics, *The Fundaments*, which contain the entire groundwork for my project, and I see now that, whereas the design of the project is strong, so much depends on how it is realized: the fine-grained particulars of the thing, all of which have yet to be considered.

No time like the present.

It is, unfortunately, just at this moment that my gaze lands upon the chair beside the bed, over which my uniform has collapsed—dark stain front and center.

Shit. Shit.

So I pop to my feet before the worry truly sets in, think

for a moment, find a broom, and begin to sweep, knowing as I do that manual labor is the best antidote for anxiety of every sort, including but not limited to performance anxiety.

And I am just beginning to make some progress, having amassed four small but satisfying piles of dirt in the four corners of my space, when my Tea Boy ghosts up.

A Tea Boy, Zimzim, has been assigned to me by the Encouragement Unit. ("The Menial.")

There he is, small and silent, with a bowlful of coffee for me.

"Not much of a *Tea* Boy, are you, Zimzim," I quip, taking the bowl, but he understands neither me nor the jest.

He is perfectly blank as he humbles his way out of the room. I sip the warm liquid, roll it on my tongue, searching for a bitterness which disappears under scrutiny. Everything, including my coffee, is becoming milder, I think. I run the fabric of my uniform through my hands now, slowly, feeling its synthesized smoothness, and I trace the outlines of the stain with my forefinger. I remember Miss Fairfax's words concerning decorum.

I'm stumbling, I feel, right off the bat, and I don't wish to compound my problems by calling more attention to them. I am slovenly. I repeat this word several times, and imagine the word as if it were a projectile, expelled from my mouth with each tongue-catapulting "l." I see the word's clear vector as it arcs out and splinters against the opposite wall.

I'd promised myself that I'd see to the uniform.

Who walks around looking like this?

Time passes.

By the slack hours of the afternoon, I'm still prone upon the floor, in a kind of narcosis. I stare at my space. At its walls, its ceiling. An extension cord slithers around me along the floor. A whiteboard stands to the side of the room, waiting to be written on, side by side with a chair. Here is my desk. I survey my apartment, and I begin to feel my energy begin to return. The place now has the aspect of an apparatus, waiting for deployment to its appointed task. Knowing that everything is being prepared—that even now I am readying myself for such intense mental labor—is galvanizing. It is, in some ways, more exciting than the prospect of the project itself. I feel like a writer with a newly sharpened pencil. I resolve to not be discouraged through the long and arduous process. I will consider today to be the preamble—next, on to the next chapter.

Which is what, exactly? Some company perhaps.

"Zimzim? *Tea Boy*?" I yell.

But he's gone. I look out the window and see my own lit room. It's become nighttime, and Tea Boy must have gone back home by now—home to wherever Tea Boys live; a home replete with long, inscrutable silences and pale pink uniforms.

So, I venture out for a night walk. Down the steps past the empty reception and out. With everything else vacant and murky, I'm drawn to the lonely light in the entrance of the Pleasure Center, and eventually I find my way to the cantina, where I find Dennis Royal sitting alone at the unattended bar, stirring some ice in a glass with another small straw. "Ah, Percy. Pull up a pew. Can I offer you anything?" he asks, holding up his glass at an angle and swirling it up to full chime.

"No—thank you."

"Ah, right. Abstemious, are we?"

"Keeping my head clear so I can work."

"And how is the project kicking off, pray tell? Entrails propitious?"

"It is. They are. I mean: it's fine."

"Is it. Are they."

"Yes, well, if you must know, I haven't quite begun yet, actually. That is, I am not sure whether I have begun or not."

"No judgments from me. From me, least of anyone."

"I'm not worried. Give me a few weeks and I'll have it all wrapped up."

"So you keep saying, Percy. Admirably optimistic of you. But you'd be the first. You really should adjust your expectations."

"Couldn't I be the exception? Perhaps I'm less of a fellow, and more of a—"

"Visitor?"

"If you like."

He smells of hair cream, tobacco.

"What are you doing here so late, Dennis?" I ask, moving away from the topic at hand.

"I'm just attempting to exhibit a little of the proper Institute spirit. Fraternizing with the local population, so I popped over to see what I could see, and it turns out everyone has gone to bed. *Tant pis.*" He brushes his lapels, picks a napkin up from the table, looks at it as if wondering why he has done so, then puts it down again. "And, I was just leaving. Unless—"

Perhaps this is one of those colonies where the residents spend more time socializing than working. I feel a knot developing in my thinking about my project, as yet un-begun, and don't wish this knot to tighten further. Pale Dennis, sensing my doubts, is already getting up and moving toward the door. "So that's *that*, sorted. Glad to hear everything is coming along. Best of luck."

And adds, with a wink: "chum."

And out he goes.

He was rude, I think.

Or I was.

I suddenly want Dennis's company back now, despite his abrasiveness, and wonder if the first person one meets, in a foreign setting, is always important, in some way or other, their actual qualities notwithstanding.

"Wait, Mr. Royal—"

But the door is already shut.

I leave not long after he does, and find myself heading down to the basement levels, walking through the cool, shadowed hallways, down the scissored stairs to the wave pool:

that massive basin of seawater, sloshed by below-ground, hydraulic servos. The doors are unlocked, so I let myself in, find a light and turn it on. *Kerchunk.* Another monumental space, the size of a parade ground, or public park. It is completely abandoned. I walk back and forth on the strand for a while watching the waves come in and in and in. A mockery of tides. I strip down on the sand, not bothering to use the men's changing area, and wade into the surf, jumping as I encounter the smaller rises. I work my way out, slowly past my depth, and continue swimming until I am in the middle of the tank, far from shore. The container surges to and fro. The waves rise, again and again—rise and curl around me. I rise up with them, in them, and fall only to rise again. I feel unburdened of my materiality, uncoupled from the ground. I can think here. I close my eyes and hear the unvarying *thud*s of the crashing waves upon the strand, the strand which bears the scars of rakes—a strand which is raked, every morning and afternoon, by a crew of workers, workers trained over here at birth to maintain indoor beaches. The beach-raking caste. *The caste of the sand-rake.* They have their own flavor of jumpsuit—green. There's one of them now, a jumpsuit. It is a man, with one of those small pikes used to spear garbage. I hadn't seen him arrive. He's a speck on the shore, no more than a sandpiper, from where I sink and swell out in the surf, in the middle of the space. I swim in a little, to get a better look. He hasn't noticed me, I think. The waves are smaller and more restrained the closer in I swim. The water doesn't seem to be refrigerated anymore—not warm exactly, but not quite cool either. The man is definitely alone. His bright green jumpsuit the only color on a dark canvas. (A broad brushstroke of black for the water, a similar stroke of deep brown for the wall behind it, and a little dab of green.) He looks up finally and sees me. And continues cleaning, poking at the beach, spearing it. Now I swim forward a little. And further forward. The entire contents of the tank pushing at my back. I can see his eyes more clearly now, before he looks down.

I wonder if I were to come ashore if he would kill me with his pick. He could. I could perish out here in the Freehold. I could be no one once again. No one and nothing. It would be just like disappearing. He would stab me, maybe repeatedly. The first few thrusts would amaze: more from shock than pain probably. Then it would hurt. Then it wouldn't anymore. After, he'd gather me up, and trundle me into his bin, kick some sand over the blood—my blood—off to the incinerator . . .

A wave launches itself at me from an oblique angle, and I get an earful of brine. The waves are increasing in strength. Has a dial been turned up? Has the worker ratcheted up a little storm for me to founder in? I concentrate on treading water again while the man on the shore continues in his labors.

I could kill him too, of course, I think, idly. If I were to kill him would it even, would anyone . . . No one would care. Or notice. The locals don't have identity booklets, so who would know? This thought does not constitute an inclination, exactly. Killing the local is nothing more than a velle-ity, surfing the foamy, bubbling scum on the surface of my thoughts. But he has turned now, and heads toward the exit and the maintenance sheds beyond, dragging a bin behind him. His bin. The bin leaves two identical tracks trailing behind it in the wet sand, wavering, off, over a rise and out. Whatever.

I never would, of course. But I can't help but feel a lit-tle disappointed in all of it. Furthermore, the whole thing reminds me of something. A déjà vu. A local killed on a beach. As if the fantasy were a mere replica of someone else's. An unsatisfactory copy. The wrong copy. Too bad, I think, it is all just too bad.

And with this, the episode is complete.

(Though, I will add, as a kind of epilogue or addendum, that the sounds have come back again tonight. Those sounds. I was jolted from my sleep just now. I was sure it was that cry. Now I hear it again. Another skirmish. Wait. *There.* No? Listen. Don't you hear the noise?)

7

The noise of a chair, grinding across the gravel.

A man is dragging it over to the shade of a palm about twenty yards away from me, where he drops it with a flourish, and sits.

I assume he is one of us, given the color of his uniform. His skinny legs, knock-kneed; his frame twisted to one side. He is bent toward a small, spiral-bound notebook which rests on his thigh. His back is to me, but his assuming this awkward, warped posture means that though he can't see me, I can make out his face fairly well.

He's writing. He pauses to stare at his work, before looking away from it, blank-eyed—as if in a down-cycle. Now he comes alive again to resume writing. Now his eyes go dead again. I spy on him through several of these "on/ off" sequences, these all-or-nothing phases.

It's peaceful out here: the sounds of the sprinklers of course, but also birdsong. It can't be real, the birdsong, but still. The filtered sun. The perky air. And the endless lawns . . .

A new sound, as the man tears a sheet from his notebook and crumples it. He unfolds an arm languidly, his hand flopping at the wrist, then his fingers open, until the wad of paper falls to the ground beneath him.

It was as if he had produced the trash like a register's receipt, or a printout; or as if he had shat it out. He looks at his notepad again, and slaps it shut, unfolds himself from the chair, stretches vaguely, and begins walking away toward the pool area and out of the recently meticulous grove.

The nerve. The fucking nerve.

"Hey," I say. "Hey." But he keeps walking.

"Hello," I call again, getting up myself, and walking behind him. "You there."

Seeing me over his shoulder, he turns to face me.

He is in his late twenties, pasty. The sun out here could do his sallow complexion a world of good.

"Yeah?"

"You dropped something," pointing to the spot. The ball of paper sits there, oblivious.

"Who are you, again?" he asks.

"Who am I?"

"Yeah. Who are you?"

"Percy Frobisher."

"You the Groundskeeper here?"

"I just thought you dropped something you might need—"

"Nope."

"It just seems sad, with everything so pristine—"

He moves a bit toward me, sticks out a finger and pokes

it at my chest. "You have something here. Look. You've soiled yourself."

My stain.

He sniggers, gives me one more finger-jab for good measure, and strides away.

I notice that some of the other fellows are watching, including the Woman-Whose-Face-and-Hands-Are-Covered-in-Yarn, the Architect, up on a balcony, and I see my foreign-eyed Mysterious Woman too, observing the scene from her umbrellaed deck chair.

Our relative positions to be indicated by x's

     x The Woman-Whose-Face-and-Hands-Are-Covered-in-Yarn
                        x The Mysterious Woman
         x 鼎福, the Architect
    x Me
x chair   --------------------------------> x The Litterer ----------------->

"How rude," I say, performatively, to no one, and now there's nothing left but for me to return to the man's empty chair, move it aside, pick up the loosened ball of paper, and shove it in my pocket.

The park is once again perfect, though my heart rate has gone up.

I root for a tablet in my other pocket and swallow it dry

Move along, folks, nothing to see here . . . when my device abruptly pings.

Time for my two o'clock.

———

"Please have a seat, Mr. Frobisher."

She is all business.

"Ready to begin?"

My first official one-on-one counseling session with Miss Fairfax, and there is a glass of water on the table, directly between us. I reach for it, before realizing that it is actually the feeding trough for one of those plastic, brightly colored, stylized, insatiable birds; a desk toy. It lazily dips its blue top-hatted head repeatedly into the glass, over and over. I watch it keep time, binding our conversation metronomically.

I sit, and she sits, and she crosses her legs, and I cross mine, and she leans forward with a little stretching creak.

"*Ready to begin?*" she repeats with a bit more force. "Okay then, Percy—there are several programs that the Institute is able to offer to our fellows, each of which is custom-designed by our in-house team of administrators to best assist you with your project."

Another little creak. The language of her body, as spoken by the chair.

"These services may be taken advantage of when and as often as is desired. They consist of several types of therapy, the application of which should encourage creativity."

I watch with interest as her lips dilate and contract. And whenever she moves, the room receives a little imbual of perfume and so I now notice the air, which comes at us through two louvered vents, one near the floor behind Miss Fairfax, and another over our heads. (There may be one behind me as well.) I can feel the currents from one vent, softly brushing my exposed ankles, while the overhead vent plays gently with the top-lying hairs of my head. Some kind of suggestive influence is being exerted, alchemized by the combination of woman and space—by the woman in the space. I look at Miss Fairfax, her eyes, her crossed legs; her calves pressed against one another in that double-bind only women can make, and that lithe and comely knot of her body. Parts of her, framed by this "confluence room," are now so captivating, the office becomes an externalized erogenous zone, and everything she touches or looks upon effects a direct referent in my own body, which delights to this contact. So the more she speaks, the more the room seems filled with areas of interest. My eyes sweep over its curves, and explore its cracks and corners. Miss Fairfax runs her hand across her desk, as if dusting it. There is a small invagination on the desk's surface, where a stylus could stand upright, and her fingers ripple over this now-empty nub. Once, twice. Just then, the vesicles and tendons of the room contract briefly.

"Percy, are you with me?"

"Sorry, sorry. Yes."

"Our first program is entitled Personal Efficiency Management, and it is focused primarily on psychic, emotional, and physical well-being. After the administration of a basic Personality Inventory, assistance is proffered in the form of daily meditations, talk therapy sessions, Group (of course), and a regimen of exercise."

I feel the ribbing on the arms of my seat, which is made

out of some kind of Naugahyde. I rub them slowly with the pads of my fingers, to determine their degree of resistance.

"The second coaching program offered is called Organizational Management, and it comprises exactly what you think it would. We help with organizing your project: timetables, spreadsheets, to-do lists, etc.

"The third coaching program is called Feedback, which is technically part of the 'reinforcement' program, and which provides the fellows with the option to receive constant, real-time analysis and judgment concerning a project's wrong turns, impediments, faulty tone, any other foundational inadequacies."

The stylish wall coverings of the office are made of perforated leather. Our "confluence room" seems to have pores. I wonder if the room's skin sweats, if it releases gasses, or expels liquid. I apply continuous pressure on the walls with my gaze. There are exposed pipes on the ceiling, one of which runs down a corner, at which point it brusquely penetrates the floor. The wall-to-wall carpet absorbs the thrust of the pipe, and seemingly grows like a virulent moss around its girth; some of the pile is leaning in toward it, in anticipatory pleasure. Meanwhile the insatiable bird on her desk continues to nod his head up and down, up and down—seemingly faster and faster. . . .

"Of course, there is more to the Feedback program: much more. We provide all kinds of feedback to our fellows. Even certain forms of exclusively negative feedback may be opted for. We've found this program to be unusually effective. Many fellows find the harsher manner of critiques to be quite . . . Excuse me, but this is all for your benefit, not mine."

"Yes, I apologize, please go on."

"Now—there are varying levels of criticism, each calibrated exactly to the participant. We gather analytics from each fellow upon their arrival. Yours are, let's see, right here."

Projecting from her device is a complex and colorful array of data, a dashboard of tools, listing and categorizing all my creative proclivities in a series of compu-glyphs, each in a unique and impossible shape. "You seem at home with a high level of self-directed negativity."

"Yes, that is true," I stammer, finding my voice, "I *am* highly self-critical, but again, perhaps not so much at the beginning." I think back to her comment from our initial meeting, what was it: "Beginnings need nurturing"? and I remind her of this, repeat it back to her verbatim.

"Hmm . . ." she says. Smiles. "Touché. Well, cases such as yours, then, we would wait to initiate this program until the final stage, the final rungs of the Ladder. And, for sure, there arc all manner of intensities here, that can be ratcheted up or down. But you can opt out entirely also. Instead of critique, we can always follow a well-modulated increase or attenuation of rewards. How does that sound?"

"Fine, I suppose."

Has the lighting changed? The contents of the room, all of its membranes, and buttresses, extrusions and infiltrations shine, and everything looks dewy. The whole timbre of the atmosphere is resonant.

"Would you like a full listing of the services sent over to you?" she asks.

"That sounds agreeable."

"Great. It's already done."

"Thank you, Miss Fairfax."

"And we will expect regular updates from you."

"Of course, of course."

"Any missed benchmarks will result in demerits."

"I understand."

"More oversight."

To which I merely sigh.

"'Rigor' and 'discipline' are the watchwords here," she, catching on, sighs.

I sigh back.

"So, good, we are in agreement," she sighs.

Me: nodding; sighing.

"Everything seems in order then. Any further questions?" she sighs.

"No. Thank you for your time," I sigh.

She sighs; I sigh.

The room sighs.

I rise and she rises; we are both still pulsating, slightly. There is a sighing tenderness in both of us. As a result of this brief entanglement. We shake hands professionally, and I leave.

"Don't forget your afternoon workshops!" she sighs after me.

And the door behind me sighs shut.

———

(In the refectory, I'm back again at "the good table." This scene is skipped.)

Outside of the Residential Enclave—which has, imperceptibly, taken on the proprietary and familiar feeling of home and hearth (how quickly this happens)—I stop just shy of the stairs to look at its lit-up swimming pool. The very idea of the pool gives me a brief feeling of satisfaction: of robust (if unearned) good health. But then I see something warbling at the bottom, a blot of some sort or a smudge on the lining. But maybe it now seems that perhaps a thirsty animal fell in and died, sank to the bottom right by the refrigeration inlet. Not an animal, a person? Now I can see that this furtive shadow, slowly bobbing in the depths abetted by the recirculation of the pool pumps, is me. I stand there for I'm not sure how long, hypnotized by the play of darkness on the pool's bottom, and then I draw my attention out from the depths, until my focus surfaces, and as I reach to touch the water, I see my reflection clearly in the water, my hand now reaching toward my shade-hand, and even in the mutating surface I think I can make out the stain on my uniform.

There it is, starting right beside my heart. It is asymmetrical, if roughly round.

Dark, like a lesion.

Nothing I can hide.

And no way is that coming out.

8

I've established a routine. Here is what it looks like.

My day begins when I am awoken by the Institute's morning bell, which rings early. Then I take a breakfast, consisting of the varied, minimalist nourishments our Tea Boys discreetly slide under our doors; each portion nestled in its own unit of an elegant, sectional tray. I linger, eating food at my leisure, listening to the crazed chorus of bird-samples coming from the audio-mangrove. Then, once I am comfortably arranged at a little table, I begin whisper-ing down some new ideas. For me, the late morning is the magic hour for ideation, and so I have to be at the ready if an interesting notion presents itself. After a period, I shower and put on my uniform.

Next, I trod out to my Group gatherings and forms of project-maintenance, all held in an annex of the Residen-tial Enclave or the higher floors of the Arts Pavilion. These are guided by various admins, all dressed more or less iden-tically. These admins are swapped out with such frequency that I rarely catch a single one of their names or numbers. Then comes Personal Coding & Identity Trimming, after which I proceed down the main trails past the contemplation berths and obelisks, all the way back to my flat, watching nervously all the while lest the Director appear unexpectedly, blue amanuenses, orderlies, admins at his side, rounding a corner, dropping from the sky, or popping from the earth. I am left with some time, then, with which to ponder the project in peace. A nice chunk of the day in which I am unmolested.

Lunch.

Then, a postprandial meander about the grounds, staticky with sprinklers. These walks take me all about the park, around the perimeter of the artificial lake, to each of the eight major concrete structures as if completing an obscure constellation.

I do occasionally find myself revisiting my Observation Point bench out at the perimeter, and when I do, everything falls away for a period and I find some peace. I stare at the sand, and this happens to be all I do there. The heat quickly becomes intolerable, so I never last long. The campus has better, air-conditioned areas for reflection. I might loiter at one of the rock gardens, say, or one of the deliberation arenas—pause there to recalibrate my thinking, though I am never alone for long. Mr. 鼎福 the Architect might pop up to say hello, or Miss ☺ the Brand Analyst. And there's the Historian-of-Prosthesis, the Hypnotist, and the Conceptual Artist. The Philosopher latches himself on to me, having immediately determined that I make a good disciple (or, at least, a passive listener). Fellows work alongside me, under the trees, splayed, or sitting cross-legged upon the cool grasses—Disputant 1 and Disputant 2, for instance—or, on a few occasions, various groups of start-up wizards—the techno-mages who frequent retreats such as these—splayed out, quarreling in code; plotting funding. Sometimes I'll see Dennis, and I might pepper him with questions, indulging his testiness, and through sheer perseverance might earn a kind of sideways smile from him—a smile which says that we both know that whatever subject we happen to be speaking of can't matter all that much, at least not to Dennis, and that I have a long way to go before I can truly understand the absurdity of it all; his brand of jadedness having developed flavor over a long simmer. Though Mr. Royal's smile furthermore acknowledges my understanding of all this. And though I don't feel any particular camaraderie with Dennis, I certainly will ratify this feeling in him. And so I might shrug my arms up, as if to say, "What *are* we doing in a place like *this*?"

My interactions with Mr. Al'Hatif are simpler affairs.

I like to visit him in his studio, and observe as he and his fellow conservators unbox the various shards of rock; label the dark red and gray fragments, and begin adding them together. Nothing of the as-yet-unreconstructed statue can be made out—though it is beginning to accumulate. A column of sorts is beginning to form, which I assume will eventually become one of the statue's enormous legs. The process is meticulous and agonizingly slow. I find it soothing to watch.

As it happens, Mr. Al'Hatif and I have discovered a mutual love of checkers, and are quite evenly matched. So, on occasion, we will leave his atelier to play several games at the outdoor tables. We lose hours here. And as we clack and slide our pieces about the board, chatting in our small way, everyone else clacks and slides around us.

I do, albeit rarely, catch sight of the resident phantom, the Mysterious Woman, lingering, melancholic, about the place. Floating around corners, submerging into obscurity. There she is: usually reading; always a book open, and canted out between her hands as she walks, as if to catch something which threatens to tumble out from her lips. And I watch her and think that she promises, perhaps, to be, despite her insubstantiality, a weighty presence in this account. Tbd, Tbd.

Everything here is "Tbd," and I fully inhabit this Tbd; each moment revealing itself to me unpredicted. I have only been here a week—one week only; or is it more? And yet the outside world has begun to seem ever vaguer a notion; more so with each passing day, and I cannot say that I think too much about that life, my life before. Such forgetting is fine though. This is precisely why I chose to live in such an isolated polity. How wonderful to have escaped here, to avoid having to endure that other, meatspace life, the real Irl— where the rubber meets the road, and matter and wills collide. Here there is none of that. Just projects, and fellows, checkers, meals, and walks.

It is idyllic, Imho, and I am just beginning to relax. Because of this, perhaps, I am just beginning to get that sense where life feels, suddenly, as if it *may be seen from a particular vantage point*, and that this life takes on an almost chronicled aspect, where you can see the arc of it, as a yawning projection of *now*; you can see the timeline, no matter how fictive, and you are present as a point in this timeline—in my case right at the beginning. And this feeling is somewhat similar to the feeling of being *dwarfed by large spaces*, as before, when I saw the three buildings, and that chasmic feeling I felt, or like the vantage looking down on the Institute from high buildings as I am wont to do, though what I am now referring to is being situated in time. Of my position in time; not space. That is.

What I do know is that the thrust of this timeline of mine—what the line, my line, is moving toward—is the project.

The project.

The project.

The project, which I only get so much time to complete and which is proving more obstinate than I imagined it would.

Nevertheless, the afternoons are maximized for thinking.

The evenings are for making, though nothing as yet has been made.

And after my strolls, toward the end of the day, I return, alone, to the Enclave, in order to settle myself before the dinner service. The nights, which I spend with my colleagues—in thought-huddles or social pods—are brilliant. And Tuesday nights (naturally) are set aside for the Discourses™.

9

The speaker, the star of tonight's Discourse™, is dynamic. The speaker is charming. The speaker is good-looking. The speaker is one of us (the speaker is relatable). The speaker's dynamic range is mezzo-piano. The speaker is confident, at ease, unruffled. The speaker is merely chatting, which is to say that the speaker delivers the Discourse™ as if for the first time, as if the ideas which comprise the Discourse™ had just now simply dawned upon the speaker. The speaker's ideas are transmissible, scalable, and viable. The speaker's Discourse™ is "a big idea," and "a journey." The speaker erects an edifice; engenders confidence; receives traction. The speaker entreats, consoles, and catalyzes. The speaker carries on two halves of an argument; though the speaker is never argumentative. The speaker proposes an original and surprising solution to this dialectic, as well as to a breathtaking array of other wide-ranging problems. The speaker puts forward—not overtly, but tacitly—the notion that every difficulty should resolve simply. The speaker contends that problems will practically solve themselves. The speaker physicalizes such ideas through a syntax of formalized hand gestures. The speaker uses plosives and pulmonic aggressions and liquid consonants and glottal stops, all to wonderful effect. The speaker evokes contagious emotions—for instance, anger, and surprise. The speaker provides generalized life wisdom, effortlessly extrapolated from their extremely abstruse métier. The speaker packages ideas. The speaker utilizes a familiar rhetoric—that well-worn, focus-tested intonation and gestural choreography we all know and love. That is: the speaker performs a kabuki. The speaker begins softly, then the speaker ratchets up the intensity. The speaker concludes in high optimism. The speaker's optimism—the speaker's *call to optimism*—is the manner in which the speaker fulfills and gratifies us. The speaker sparks within us a sense of wonder, curiosity, eagerness, a galvanizing faith, etc., etc. The speaker will have, by Discourse™'s end, filled us each to the brim with talk-response-feelings. (This rewards packet of talk-response-feelings is not to be confused with the conferral of actual wonder, curiosity, and eagerness, so on.)

Of course, it is uncanny. To be here, in this auditorium, attending a Discourse™, an Irl talk, to be in this singular, brightly branded space; this space I have visited virtually, on-screen that is, so many times. As soon as I heard that introductory music, those triumphalist, swelling, and portentous strains, that synthesized orchestral strike, and the spotlight hit the backdrop . . . well. "Here I am," I thought, echoing Miss Fairfax.

Here I am, though: Do I belong?

Meanwhile, the speaker is approaching the conclusion of the Discourse™, and, strangely, I begin to worry. Worry for the speaker. And as the Discourse™ comes closer to its preordained apogee, this worry intensifies. When the audience, as one, looks up at the final slide, baroque with infographics, does the speaker convey something privately? Sign a word in the air? Point? Silently mouth something or wink? Maybe not. I am not sure. It feels as though the speaker is addressing me personally, confidentially, though not in the manner the speaker intends; which is to say that the speaker of the Discourse™ betrays something. It begins to dawn on me with greater and greater certainty that the speaker is—with smile intact, but with ever-increasing desperation—attempting to communicate an emotion which lies outside the ambit of the Discourse™. Something important. The speaker is making an idea understood, and is forced, it seems, to communicate this crucial message in a channel just above—or just below—the channel in which the Discourse™ is being delivered. Through a prearranged code perhaps—of taps and clicks, or a system of linguistic cues, certain emphases, cryptograms, anagrams, acrostics. Which is to say that the speaker seems to me now like a hostage, reading a prepared list of kidnapper demands while simultaneously endeavoring to reveal hints as to the kidnapper's whereabouts. I.e., the discourse has a hidden descant. There is a submerged intensity about the speaker's eyes, visible, it seems, only to me. Is this another formalized gesture in the Discourse™ itself?

I look around the arena, and see no signs of anything out

of the ordinary on the faces of my compatriots. I presume that, from the standpoint of the other audience members, the speaker's look of solemn intelligence, enthusiasm, and kind forbearance never wavers. But I see something different. That the veins on the speaker's neck protrude. That the whites of the speaker's eyes grow, and that the speaker's dense pupils collapse into themselves. Impotence, isolation, fear— all vibrating on a sub-audible frequency. Amid the approval.

I have to look away. I turn toward the back of the room, and I see, at the far end of the full auditorium, first, the Mysterious Woman, watching the performance. But then, then, several rows behind, I spot the Director, in the very last row, leaning back, arms spread to full and awesome wingspan on the seat backs around him, with his shaved and waxed head, a menacing golem, smiling strangely at the performance. The thought comes to me "This man holds the solution to the problem," and I abruptly turn back around, just in time for the speaker to wrap up the Discourse™.

Applause. Standing O.

In the immediate aftermath of the talk, people are speaking in small groups.

Most of the fellows are here. Pale Dennis is staring out onto the campus. He's sullen and evasive. I follow his gaze and see very little: the semidarkness; a couple of prematurely lit walkways; the periodic flashing red glow atop the metastructure; a canal, catching the last of the light; some pedestrian bridges.

Miss ☺ the Brand Analyst is here tonight, with the

Architect, 鼎福. They are speaking with the Woman-Whose-Face-and-Hands-Are-Covered-in-Yarn, who watches them both guardedly through her woolen mask. Other fellows are clustered elsewhere. It is all very cordial. The Cylinder Maker stands by himself, cradling a new geometric solid in his arms. The Technologists huddle together.

Miss Fairfax, admin5, meanwhile, rests upon a single elbow, legs up beneath her.

As I step toward her, suddenly, the Director emerges from a door, moving through the middle of several fellows, breaching the group, annexing the space. Conversations disband. He's coming toward me.

Miss Fairfax jumps to her feet and heads over to meet the oncoming collision.

"YOU there," he rumbles, the sound of his voice coming out of a face which is more a series of folds than a set of features.

The Director reaches down. He seizes my hand in his own huge one; then he takes my arm in his other hand, so that now I am detained in a three-handed handshake. (Though it's not really a "shake," but rather a very slow, methodical movement: an impressive, quasi-masonic gesture.)

"ALL WELL, Mr. Frobisher? Adjusting to life at the Institute? Taking to it, are you? Found YOUR FOOTING? I am told this project of yours shows great promise."

"Thank you."

"And it is proceeding on schedule, of course."

"I hope so."

"HOPE?"

The Director leans in closer and gives me the hairy eyeball. My palm is beginning to burn and itch in his insistent grasp.

"What Mr. Frobisher means, sir," Miss Fairfax advocates for me, rapid-fire, "is that the project is on schedule, and will succeed. Mr. Frobisher has no doubts on this matter. Why would he when we went to all the trouble and expense to bring him here. Right, Percy?"

"Yes, of course. That's what I meant."

There's one more pump of my insensate hand, and the Director leans farther in and down:

"We expect no less. Speed, intensity, ruthlessness. The PERFECT project and Discourse™. Relatable, marketable, profound, digestible, fun, fresh, smart . . . a masterful theorization of the Now. No effort on behalf of such a project would be wasted and any effort falling short of these standards would constitute failure. We expect TOTAL COMMITMENT."

"Yes, sir," replies Miss Fairfax on my behalf.

"CREATIVITY, in our view," he continues, warming to his topic and straightening again to his full height, "is more or less a technology. One which requires the same methodical application used in developing any other technical product: R&D, ideation, iteration, debugging, beta-testing; market research; analytics, the implementation of a maintenance infrastructure, not to mention an upgrade cycle. Your project will be, Percy, in other words (as I emphasized in my speech at the ceremony), HARD WORK. Of course it will—no one, no fellow—while en-laddered here at the Institute—will be allowed to shirk hard work. But more importantly it will require your complete buy-in. FULL bandwidth. Every aspect of the process running in concert with the seamless integration of your talent/application stack within the Institute's own, every layer contributing. End-to-end; ERROR-FREE channels. Proactivity. Actualization. You see, we—your investors, your developers, your core management team—would like to see this project of yours achieve coordinated, PRIME fulfillment, and it should go without saying that we would like it to reach its actionable phase, an inflexion point, GROWTH, that is— which might, in turn, generate all of the resource-leveling, interoperable meta-services to credibly realize and onboard all of our covalent infomediaries. Simultaneous, PLURI-FORM construction of accelerated global production chains. Rendering: DEFINITE. Tomorrow: YOURS. Maximized provider-efficiencies in networked space. Personalized, multisensory, effortless, horizontal interface fabrication/ consumption, expropriating effective power-patterns in deeply incepted data-noise. Repetition, affirmation, voluntary development of EMOTIONALIZED syntaxes; converting DESIRE into FACT. Harnessing atmosphere, making it serve as a means of instantaneous COMMUNICATION with ALL PEOPLE in EVERY PLACE. So if you find you are WEAK in PERSISTENCE, center attentions upon the instructions in the program entitled 'POTENCY—'"

Luckily, at this moment, a new admin strides up. "Excuse me," he says to the Director, bowing slightly. "I apologize. May I borrow you for a moment, sir?"

The spell is broken.

The Director puffs once, a steam train preparing to leave a station, and then allows himself to be led away. And as I am beginning to feel this modicum of relief, just as he is almost gone, his vast head, above the crowd, turns back toward me and the head says, loudly, between upraised hands: "Mr. Frobisher: we will be WATCHING."

I'm standing there slack-jawed. I think, what a "personality" (the thought containing quotation marks, as in: "The Personality"). Then I see Dennis Royal, observing the whole thing from across the room. We meet one another's eyes, and he shrugs, contemptuously, as if to say: *see?*

Now a tray is borne toward me and I'm handed a fresh drink by someone who isn't in this story.

I make my excuses, and head back, alone, to the Enclave. Just me and the footlights, which illuminate the periphery of the paths. The Institute's fountains, rippling with gradients, crackle in the darkness with watery, white noise. No one knows where I am, and I carry in my throat the illicit nausea of night.

But my feet have clearly decided on a change of plan, because I find that I've arrived at the edge of the property again; back at the periphery; my Observation Point.

I sit on the bench, and try to stabilize myself with the

guided breathing I've been taught in Group. In and out, in and out. I feel ridiculous, until I don't. It is always vacant out here. That much is guaranteed. No one will see me as no one comes to the perimeter. It is incredibly comforting somehow, to sit alone in the presence of the desert's primeval solitude.

I pop a tablet, swallow it dry, and return my gaze to the dark desert. Return to my breathing. I sit there for a while. A long while. (Time passes.)

My mind slowly empties. And I feel comforted.

A gap.

Now, a commotion.

The sounds of muffled unrest. Sounds, coming from the path which feeds my Observation Point. My only means of egress.

Sounds of something moving chaotically through the brush, these sounds broken by occasional grunts. The noises coming from just outside the area's perimeter. I listen, and the noises only grow in intensity. I consider my options.

Then I rise, tentatively, and begin to inch my way forward down the path, and while attempting to do so, I place my feet as slowly as possible upon the uneven, noisy gravel. I'm listening all the while, trying to calibrate the sounds of my movements to those of what surely must be a fight of some kind. It takes several minutes at this pace to reach the edge of the lawns. Thirty-some-odd steps.

As I exit the Observation Point, and emerge into the big clearing, I see the wan, dome-refracted moon again, above the black line of treetops, and below, a tangle of shadows mutating and reforming, a shadow theater, set against the inky palms. A blue-black, liquid spot which transmogrifies into several men, subduing another person, another man, a smaller man. The shadows, the several men, are licking out, grabbing at him—the other man, their victim—assaulting him with their fists and feet. All sound from the attackers is stopped, instantly muted, though their assault is not. The only sounds now come from their quarry, the small, other man, now on the ground, having been thrown there, and he makes low, inarticulate, and clearly inadvertent sounds, the sounds of air suddenly expelled from his body against his will, etc., etc., though he does not actively cry out—does not seek help in any evident manner—and seems to be putting up no resistance to his continued abuse. (I am about thirty or forty meters from them. From the attack.) The entire event is strangely muted, as if performed far away, or under a body of water. I stand there and watch passively as the assault continues. And then redoubles. But soon the assailants cease, as the body of their victim has stopped moving, is lying dead-still upon the gray green. They look down at him, the several men. (It is too dark to read expressions.)

There is an interregnum, in which nothing moves and nothing happens. Then:

Ping!

Shitttt . . .

My device.

Nobody moves.

Ping! Again.

Gah.

Will one of them turn and see me? It is so still in this clearing under the vague moonlight. The stillness.

(The silence.)

The assailants crouch over the body and seem to confer (though I cannot hear voices). I don't move, barely breathe. I feel air from the distant fans blowing behind my ears.

Finally, two of the men reach down, grab the victim's ankles, and begin dragging him down the lawn and away, thankfully in the opposite direction from where I am standing. I'm safe. The body hisses along the wet grass as it is removed offstage. Then they are all gone, as quickly and dramatically as if a black curtain had been drawn across the entire proceedings.

I remain there, pulsing, throbbing like an antenna, an antenna transmitting, and I remain for a time, until I have determined that it is safe to move.

Ping!

Mother fuck.

Without a glance, I shove my device as deeply as possible into my pocket, wring my hands in a hot, slick grip, now rub them on my trousers to dry the perspiration off, the whole time darting looks around me in all directions, and now I scurry off, anxious, back along toward the heart of the Institute.

10

(GROUP)

In the subsequent days, there are no further signs of "the Night Struggle" (as I have begun to think of it). No missing fellows, no marks on the daylit ground—the site upon which the person was beaten and from whence he was dragged.

In any case, the event itself, the crime, is far less compelling to me than my memories of the incident—those imagined, reciprocal incidents which play out in my mind, enacted after the fact. My emotions upon seeing the Irl beating of the man by the gang of nocturnal marauders pales in comparison to the emotions I now feel, emotions about the event, not as it happened, but as I now imagine it happening; aftershock-imaginings in which (for instance) I have stepped in to save the man by fighting off his attacker. Or another enactment in which I imagine that I have been spotted, and thrashed as well. In the first instance, I feel a welling-up of triumphant feelings. In the second: a nauseating wave of anger and self-loathing. In both cases, the feelings spurred by my own creative endeavor overshadow my feelings at witnessing the meatspace, Irl event. What one is to make of this, I can't say.

In fact, I do not think about the event all that much, and actually, I only recall "the Night Struggle" in order to sufficiently establish to myself that I have or haven't imagined the whole thing.

Nevertheless, it does occur to me now that "the Night Struggle" might be of use to my project in some way. The event certainly feels as if it is sufficiently dramatic for such a repurposing. I consider everything, nowadays, in just such a light. That is, as material. As the possible spark which might set my project alight.

Tbd, eh?

The casual chat, the standing and shifting of weight from one foot to the next. The tapping of coffee urns, the sampling of continental breakfasts—the breaking corners off of plastery scones. Vapes. Worry beads. Small napkins. Square, little plates. The stale waiting.

Then, the bell is rung and we sit in a confluence-circle. In stylish chrome chairs. White light coming in through the plate glass. You can see the tops of the palms, in the garden below, fronding slowly in the artificial breeze.

My second Group. Admin17 is leading today. She has the wild hair and beleaguered countenance of a middle-grade art instructor. Nobody in Group seems to respect the authority she has been deputized to wield. But we observe the protocols, for the most part.

We tell our stories to one another—we testify, as we are meant to. We do it of our own volition—ignoring her presence—and she seems savvy enough not to interrupt. The admin takes notes on her device, whispering closely to it. She doesn't want to disrupt the natural flow of the divulgences, but needs a record. These notes eventually are pinged over to the more important admins where they are cross-referenced and analyzed.

There have been some outside presenters—inspirational prompts of various kinds (like, for instance, the kite-flying day, and the day they brought the dogs in). But normally it's just us. Us: unburdening ourselves to one another.

Today, it's me, the Actor, the Sociologist, the Critic, the Translator, and the Miniaturist. Everyone is further along than I am. Higher up the Ladder.

We usually move clockwise around the room. (I'm at nine o'clock.)

The Actor goes first.

Acting, he tells us, is the art of replication, and he believes that if he successfully portrays his characters—inhabits them thoroughly enough—the end result of his efforts will be a performance in which he isn't merely representing his characters, but reproducing them.

For months now, in his small, mirrored studio on the third floor of the Arts Pavilion, the Actor has been preparing his one-man show. In the show, he is to play several roles: a newborn, a pirate, an old crone, a nymph, and a sylvan glade. He has worked tirelessly to perfect each of these personifications, polishing the parts. He has them all down pat. It has gotten to be that, with practice, the switching of characters is, for him, like the effortless donning and doffing of masks.

(He does a couple of these characters for us. Just a line or two for each. They are consummately performed. Perfect embodiments.)

Honestly (he tells us), his project brings him nothing but happiness. After all, as he puts it: "what could be more pleasurable than to be someone else for a while?"

Each workday begins with the Actor performing his elaborate vocal exercises, along with some light facial stretching. This is followed by the most important part of his warm-up ritual, the contemplation of the Seven Questions for Actors. In this exercise, he poses each of the seven questions to each of his characters (Who Am I? What Do I Want? Why Do I Want It? What Must I Overcome, etc.), meditating on how the answers to these questions might differ for each of the various roles.

Afterward, he rehearses the show, meticulously enacting each character in turn.

Yet somehow, the more putatively "real" his characters become, the more he is unable to separate himself from these characters, and the more of himself leaches into them. Put another way: the more the actor reaches out to understand a particular character, and the more real the character duly becomes, the more the character reaches out to understand him, the Actor—and thus becomes like him—rather than vice versa.

And so, the answers to the Seven Questions begin to worry him.

At first, the answers in the exercises come out as expected. For the Pirate, for instance, the answer to the first question, "What Do I Want," was: "riches." And the answer to the question "What Must I Overcome" was: "mutiny," or "a torn and illegible map." But several months into his rehearsals, the answers to these questions have begun to shift, such that the response to "What Do I Want," for his Pirate character, is now: "to better emulate my fellow pirates." And his (the Pirate's) answer to the question "What Must I Overcome" has become "my growing fondness toward my mutinous crew," or "my begrudging admiration for all of my enemies and rivals." He admits that the more he injects these roles with his own empathies, his own neurotic misgivings and actorly sympathies, the more real the characters now seem. Finally, the ambivalence with which he answers these questions irrevocably has contaminated all of his characters—including the sylvan glade—and in the end, the show he has prepared so carefully, which was to show off an unprecedented sweep of characterization, has become nothing more than a monologue about a struggling actor.

(Though it is, as such, we all reassure him, highly successful.) We thank him for sharing.

The Sociologist goes next. She tells us that she has performed a careful analysis of her new data, and, dismayed by the results, has found it necessary to reanalyze her findings.

When she does so, she discovers that certain conclusions are unavoidable. The Sociologist has confirmed beyond a doubt—according to the complex and rich semiotics of social capital which she herself has established in her Institute project—that she is: 1. the exact type of person who would choose Sociology as a profession, and 2. fated, bound by her class and type, to create precisely the complex and rich semiotics of social capital she has, in fact, produced. Furthermore (and more disturbingly still) she draws the conclusion that 3. her very selfhood—not just her taste-profile, or her sets of positions, but her actual self—is pre-determined, encoded inside of her very own theory. Faced with this irrefutable and self-reflexive conclusion, she has decided to spend more time in Group.

We applaud this decision and thank her for sharing as well.

The Critic goes third. The Critic's testimony is brief: but complex. He is stuck in the most excruciating kind of reductio ad absurdum. His particular problem stems from his critical faculties themselves, which are so devastating, so acute, so uncompromising, that as soon as his opinions are transcribed, written down, they instantly become subject to his own penetrating gaze. Which is to say that the Critic's own skill precludes publication, and so his expertise goes entirely unrecognized.

Nobody knows of his talent. But *he* knows, he tells us. He knows. . . .

(We all just smile and nod, as we don't, in fact, "know."

PETER MENDELSUND

But we thank him for sharing all the same, as that is the kind of support we are expected to provide in Group.)

Now, the Translator is hard at work on her Institute project, which is a translation of a work by a prominent fantasist. The work that she is currently attempting to render concerns a great jungle cat; a puma or some such.

In this tale—so ineffably beautiful and strange in its original language—the predator terrorizes all the other beasts of the rain forest. It lives a generally wonderful life, at the apex of its small ecosystem, although it has a single and intractable problem: it finds it impossible to drink from the jungle pool. Every time it attempts to drink the pool's clear water, it is prohibited from doing so by a large predatory animal, which it sees snarling in the water's surface. The cat eventually dies of dehydration.

Unfortunately, every time the translator looks over her rendition of the fable, unlike the original, it seems trite, poorly written, and ends with a dubious moral. She knows that this is because, in the original, the word for "jungle cat" is the same as the word for "translator," and she has yet to find a word or formulation in English which would express both meanings. Thus, she is clearly not doing justice to the work of such a great writer. She begins again. Nevertheless, every time she retranslates the work, something new is lost. She loses either the visceral effect of the cat, or the satirical edge of the piece as a whole.

We point out that, of course, the Translator, the Critic,

90

and even the jungle cat all share a similar affliction, but neither she nor the Critic wants to admit that this is the case. An argument breaks out, briefly—though it is more a display of unchecked snippiness than an argument as such. Admin17 shows her mettle by calming everyone the hell down, reiterating the rules of Group (no judgments), and "moving the show along." Everyone settles again.

A clear sky and hills of sand. A few small rocks. Blazing heat. A bright city. A dome. Wind. The sky is wrinkling. Literally puckering, long veins pipeline across it, bubble up, force it off its cardboard backing.

The paint is drying irregularly. The cutout edges of the foiled city are crinkled, and it is only by squinting our eyes that it begins to resemble its Irl counterpart. The sand is sand. It blows around, thanks to the fan, and the Miniaturist realizes that it will all blow away and she won't have any desert left. She reaches for the scoop inside of the bucket and delicately pours more onto the scene.

(The Miniaturist has brought her diorama in to share with the rest of us.)

She adjusts the heat lamps. The paper had begun to smolder in some places, so she moves the lamps back and away. So that it is suitably hot, but not close to combustion.

Her diorama contains all of us, me, the admin, the Actor, the Sociologist, the Critic, the Translator, and the minuscule Miniaturist, sitting, head-in-hands, frustrated by her project. She rendered herself as accurately as she could, looking through high-powered magnifying lenses, etching a furrowed brow on the figurine with a diamond-tipped needle. Unfortunately, the tiny Miniaturist seems more bored than frustrated.

She supposes that she, the large Miniaturist, is bored as well. Honestly, she tells us, she's just killing time.

Until inspiration strikes.

(Thank her for sharing, etc.)

My turn.

11

Today, they bring animals in. And here are what appear to be: ten large and hairy M's. Tawny camels for today's entertainment.

They are bobbing along in the same direction above the surface of the Institute's sandy Athletics Oval. Brought in from the capital city for a morale-boosting, official event—a camel race. We've all turned out for the spectacle. I've come along, to be a team player, and because I could use a break from the confines of my project's uncertain development. I need to contend with the increasing, claustrophobic sub-jectivity which it has engendered in me. I do this by getting out and about.

There is quite a bit to take in. The M's loiter, grunt, and rear, while they wait for their jockeys to mount them. Some sit abruptly, awkwardly, folding into themselves like umbrellas in order to do so. Though they are now, still, quite far from me, I can imagine them blinking their long lashes and pouting their doughy lips—flirty girls. A long red sash is being raised; this is the starting line. Behind and above the lowing mounts and the sash is the sky, which is deep blue, though every now and again, it is infected by outbreaks of small gray squares, a sort of image-degradation, which blinks in and out, and may last only as long as the image is rendering. Which is to say that the sky today is in progress.

The breeze is strong, and a few sand-devils trouble the surface of the track, along with little bits of litter, which is surprising. A couple of sheets of what appear to be paper, frolicking on the gusts from the turbines. These are turned up higher than normal today, in order to provide proper ventilation for the contest—as the animals are not known for their hygiene. I've just begun to notice that the Institute's bespoke autumnal chill has now faded just a tad, and is now overlaid with a minor yet unpleasant tang; and added to a strong ungulate aroma, the Institute smells Rn like a recently defrosted refrigerator. The fans should eventually dispel it though. And still, it is pleasantly boisterous out here and the crowd's in a great spirit.

I'm sitting on a riser up in the stands. Next to me is 鼎福 the Architect, chin resting on his fist like an allegorical statuary. Beside him is the Theologian. On the other side of me is dear Miss Fairfax, smiling, chatting with the Philosopher. Her leg is resting on one edge along the opposite edge of my leg, connected at our margins. And this co-extensivity is full of promise and potential. In the row just above and behind me is Dennis Royal. He's greasy; mortared up with sunblock which he hasn't really bothered to rub in properly.

There are big smears of white on his nose and under his eyes. Next to him is Miss ☺ the Brand Analyst. She has a banner in her lap, with something or other written on it in the local language. Presumably to fly and wave, once the race begins. She plans on rooting, it would seem.

And oh, there is the Mysterious Woman, that gaunt emblem.

She's across the crowd on another set of benches entirely, sitting alone, way off to the side, taking it all in through her bright but recessed eyes. Even she is joining in the fun.

Now, I see, far away, the Director, whom I have set some kind of internal compass to. Near him is Mr. Al'Hatif. The Archeologist has found some local scholars, and is probably pumping them for information about statuary. Perhaps raising more capital. Among them, he looks more local than ever. He has the talent of blending in. Now I wonder if he is native to this region at all, and perhaps not just a chameleon. Another faker. This group, he and his contingent, are caught up now in the action on the oval, where all the animals are now being corralled into their starting formations, and stand expectantly, twitching and jutting their chins, raising legs, setting them back, attempting to turn, but unable to.

Everything is set. "A dam set to burst."

And even this, now, is reminding me of other races which I've attended or read about, and these other races are now overlaid upon this one, or mixing together like the scent of the Institute and the smell of the beasts, and I'm thinking in particular of that classic novel, not the one I am currently trying to read, but another famous one, where everything unravels at a race, and how the main character is powerless as it all unfolds and it is told weirdly from not one, but two POVs, and everything kind of splits, but then I remember that I am actually thinking of the film version of that novel, the third or fourth adaptation of it in which the whole thing is transposed into a contemporary milieu, though not as contemporary as this one (for whatever could be), when I'm yanked from the slurry of my thoughts by Mr. Royal. Dennis is leaning over my shoulder from above. A delicate gold chain dangles from his neck. He smells like cigarettes and coconut.

"A bit peaked?" he asks.

He blinks, fidgets. Chews his nails.

"I'm fine, Dennis. You? How are the algorithms?"

"Doing what they are supposed to do; make more money, and bully for me."

I once again and as usual begin to fear that everyone's project is going well except mine, and so I reflexively reach in my pocket for some confidence and poise, not that I'll take it here, but just to remind myself that I've got the option, but I don't have the option, because I find the pocket is empty. Did I leave them back at the . . . Ah. No.

Am I out? I'm out. Or I must be getting down to a few. My medicines, my pills.

Though I haven't begun to panic yet, the drumbeat is not far off—I wish I could feel the tablet's hard, little roundness in my pocket. Roll it in my fingers. That feeling would ground me instantly. Instead I feel into my other pocket for my device. Grip it like a stress ball. Hope it doesn't start pinging again.

"You're a cagey one, Mr. Visitor," Dennis now says. He has been watching me. "No fair, you asking about my work anymore. I've noticed all that information flowing in a single direction. It seems that everyone here, but you that is, is just bursting with undelivered narrative."

"I don't want to talk about it."

"Don't worry, Mr. Frobisher, I won't beat it out of you."

"I appreciate that."

"Still, you are suspiciously private about it all, aren't you?"

"I'm sorry, I'm just a little out of sorts today," I reply as flatly as possible.

He concludes the exchange languidly, with the soft, dismissing wave of a hand. "Splendid. I'll just piss off then," he says, and leans back once more. And I turn back toward the track and the race, which now appears to be in progress. I had somehow missed the report from the starter's pistol.

The race is on, and, so far, no more than a cloud of sand, moving slowly around the track on the far side. No details. Though I'm sure the animals are a sufficient distance from one another, they look from here like a single clump.

Everyone's devices are out and held aloft to take videos. I see the race replicated several times over. And on the screen of one device in front of me, I can see now that one of the bestial M's is edging out the others as they scud toward the post from the south. Their bellies heave as they gallop. As the field spreads out they begin to spell out "mmm-mmm" as if the universe were promising good things in ever-increasing degrees of deliciousness. They are now rounding the grandstand, where the pavilions have been set up. The pack thunders around the bend near to where I am sitting, so I now can see all the beasts in their girded and beribboned finery. A merry bunch of careening creatures. They are running fast, each expanding and contracting like octopi squirting through water. Every time the rear legs go back, the neck cranes forward. Each animal is ridden by what appears to be a tiny man, the size of a human baby, but dressed all in black; each whacking away with metronomic precision with a whip-like crop. Mr. 鼎福 leans over and explains: "Robot jockeys. They used to use children for these races, but, what with the systematic abuses—" And so, now, these little mechanical men. Command-and-hit shock-sensor jockeys, built of factory-grade drill presses. Wonderful!

There is some sort of commotion. The crowd is now uniformly turning its attention to a strange event. The camel which is out in front is listing dramatically. "Look out," a fellow in the audience shouts. The great thudding animals are losing traction in the sand. Gripping the track is becoming more problematic, the faster the pack runs. All of the animals are beginning to wobble, gaits becoming uneven. They are tripping on something—too far away to see. The lead beast loses traction all of a sudden, slips a hoof, pitches, and now, suddenly, its far end is rising up as its head points down. It surges and tumbles, and becomes a crazy knot of animal pelts and sand. There is an indecipherable struggle. People are scrambling to get out of the way as the second-place animal runs, uncorralled, toward the hoardings, and rebounds from the side of the official dais. A person pops off the platform: jumps, like a tiny toad. Everyone is scrabbling to get out of the way. I am too far away to do anything other than watch, which I do, glassy-eyed. As the other animals behind the doomed ones make up the distance, they reach the site of the initial catastrophe and halt abruptly, which initiates a chain-reaction pileup, as animal after animal crashes, some of these capsizing, tail over head. There are sustained and distant cries in languages I don't understand (though the basic tenor of these cries is quite comprehensible) as another row of seats across from us is breached by the panicked herd. Now the little mechanical jockeys, who are all newly mountless, are crazily thrashing about in the sand, driven along by their wildly spinning crops-turned-outboard-motors. They seem to want to cross the finish line with or without an animal to ride. One of them makes a mad dash for the perimeter instead, flagellating away like a wayward sperm, and crashes through an advertising hoarding, and is now heading out of the metastructure and the compound itself, in a snaking line, out into the desert sun.

Godspeed, little robot.

Track to be indicated by @'s

@@@@@@@@@@@@@@@@@@@@@@@@@
@   @

START   DENNIS

MR. 鼎福   ME   MISS F.

                             M

                             M

THE VIOLENT
OCCURRENCE   M

                             M

   M
M
     M
M   M

THE
MYSTERIOUS
WOMAN
  M
M

                         M
THE DIRECTOR'S BOX
@@@@@@@@@@@@@@@@@@@@@@@@

100

Wincing in the sun, I turn to say something to Dennis, who is looking in exactly the opposite direction, having not spared the wreck even half a glance, and turning back around again I see the upturned hull of a beast, dorsal side down in the sand, its legs looking for purchase, the sad detritus of its saddle and ribbons. Only one or two of the animals make the finish line. The first to do so is surrounded instantly by men in white robes, trainers and owners, grabbing at its harness, patting it proudly. A bucket of water is brought to it and then it is led toward a winner's paddock.

A hearty shout goes up from the far pavilion. For the winners or for the fallen I am not sure. But then I see the Director, standing to his full and obscene height, all command and joyous competency—he's giving commands of some sort—and the winning camel is led forward, in a foaming sweat (Is it a camel? A camel, Rly? It's dromedaries which have two humps. *Dromedaries* are M's. Idk. Camels are lowercase n's. They don't have those here. Never mind.), and garlands of flowers are played across her floppy, protuberant back. The Director hands a towering golden trophy to the animal's owner, a local man, enrobed, a sheik of some order, and his suddenly frightened letterform lows, loudly. The audience begins to laugh at the base comedy, and then everyone applauds.

While this is happening, several attendants head down upon the sandy track helping the downed animals right themselves. Spasms from feet finding no purchase. Straining, upraised heads. Necks, flopping like enormous eels, dark puddles forming. The animals blink their ladylike lashes and roll their eyes. I'm taping the whole thing, way in close, so I see it enlarged. Also enlarged: the Mysterious Woman all the way on the other side of the event.

"What fuckery," Dennis says, all hot breath on my neck, leaning back over me.

Across the way, the Mysterious Woman rises to leave.

"Dennis, who is that?" I ask, pointing at her, as she picks her scarf off of her lap and starts coiling it about her neck.

Mr. Royal squints.

"What? Who? Her? Haven't you met? That's Miss Chatterton."

"Miss Chatterton," I repeat, "the Mysterious Woman is Miss Chatterton."

And even as I say this, she's passing our portion of the bleachers. She looks up at us shyly, and Miss ☺ the Brand Analyst and Miss Fairfax wave, though Dennis does not; and we all walk down now, the event having officially ended, footfalls twanging on the aluminum steps, and then groups form up, as they do, and then 鼎福 the Architect speaks to the Mysterious Woman, who looks a bit trapped, and then the Archeologist has come over, and I can hear the Mysterious Woman's voice, and it is more girlish than I would have thought, though it is a bit rough as well, though also perfect, really, and suddenly she turns to me and, for a moment, seems to really take me in, and then, looking down, says:

"What did you do to your uniform?"

She has addressed me. This is a fact. A real fact. She's spoken: to me. I stare back at her with friendly surprise, totally inert with shock. People are talking and laughing.

She speaks again and then someone else does.

Time. Passes.

And now she has left.

Workers emerge, and begin to clean—bring a tarp, gather garbage onto it, then haul it off, leaving long troughs in the earth. Snake out hoses, and wet the grounds. A tractor arrives, pulling a long series of rakes, and another comes in its wake with a sand spreader. They make their slow way around the track, in the opposite direction to that in which the animals have just run. A couple of straggling peons clean up the banners and other refuse from the stands. I see a jumpsuited worker with the small spike, just opposite me and Dennis, picking his way around the track. The man from the wave pool? After about ten yards, he stops, and crouches to observe something. Something, even seen from here, is clearly paper. Then, with a quick downward thrust like a heron's beak, he spears it.

On the way back to the Enclave: more trash.

The Institute is beginning to let itself go, I think.

And yet, and yet . . . that paper.

My mind is working on something. Has latched on to something new.

I can feel it.

12

THE FUNDAMENTS OF MY PROJECT

Fundament 1. The project shall have many channels. The project shall have multiple modes. The project shall be polyphonic. Heteroglossic. The project shall be a *total work*.

Fundament 2. (Capaciousness.) The project is commodious. NB this is not to say the project includes everything; the project is not all-encompassing or encyclopedic. But the project is generous. It allows for all material that will be a part of it. Camel. Bowl, palm. Paper. Dream. Preexisting material, even. It pulls many things toward it, from the meatspace into the mindspace.

Fundament 3. The project shall have a visual component (It would be easier for it not to, for it to steer clear of the optical realm entirely, certainly, as the visual aspects of the project are quite demanding, but in this I have no choice. *See Fund.1.*).

Fundament 4. The project shall have a narrative component. Narrative is the key ingredient in all my work, as well as in all work like mine. Perhaps narrative is the key ingredient in all human endeavor. Idk. But I do know for certain that every man-made thing should have a story to tell.

So then: a series of events. Preferably, a series of unstable events in which an agent is confronted by choices. (Narrative is, of course, the component of the project that I have the least facility with.)

Fundament 5. The project shall have dramaturgical components, including aspects of blocking, theatrical movement, stage direction of both a prosaic as well as an extravagantly elevated nature.

Fundament 6. The project shall have a rhetorical component. Rhetoric, here, refers to two separate gestures:
   a) "Rhetoric" in the sense of that which enables the project to convince its audience of something; of the argument being presented, and of my attempts to win you over to the project's conclusions w/r/t this argument.
   b) The sense of "rhetoric" in which the project calls upon a range of stylized movements, shapes, idiomatic phrases, and intonations. These are critical to the work at hand.

Fundament 7. The project shall contain aleatory components. I.e., the project shall be open to chance. (Court it, even.)

Fundament 8. (Communication: there will be none.) Communication is not on the project's agenda. Nothing, here, will be said that can be understood. There will be neither communion, nor kinship. No empathy felt, nor accord reached. All discourse regarding a shared or communicable interiority is undesirable. The project is the enemy of import. (Import is for amateurs.) The project does not recognize putative differences between the creator of the project and the consumers of the project. The project is not some third thing in a triangulation. The project is not a relay. The project is not a megaphone. Rather, the project subsumes the consumer and creator in its own plane of immanence.

Fundament 9. Though the project shall bootstrap its very existence out of its mere possibility, the project shall also be self-liquidating. It seeks, as its ultimate goal, complete erasure. The project proceeds, at first, by building the very material which must, by necessity, be deleted. The project is not to be confused with this material itself. The material is only the raw material for erasure. Especially important is that whatever import—aura, or mystique—which has affixed itself to the project or has accrued in the project must be excised, or allowed to wither.

Fundament 10. Iteration. Imitation; reproduction; duplication. ~~Counterfe~~

Fundament 11. The project should foment psychic dislocation and confusion.

Fundament 12. Appeasement. The project will need to periodically bestow appeasements so as to reward the consumer's continued engagement. The appeasements are sops. Sops to whom? To those who might prefer the project to unfold according to principles they themselves cleave to; those who refuse to interrogate their prejudices, and would thereby, otherwise, find nothing but disappointment therein. (Sometimes this cannot be helped.) "The Appeasements" are apportioned with exactly such people in mind. NB, it is unclear whether this step actually improves the project itself; it most likely does not, but, Imo, certainly, a project which lacks Fundament 12 altogether will be treading in parlous territory.

Fundament 13. Sacrifice. What is to be sacrificed is never known ahead of time. But something must always be sacrificed. Something must be put in, for something to be got out. This pertains to the law of conservation of energy or some such. Sacrifice always comes last.

Etc., etc.

So there you are. This much I know. (Unfortunately, this disclosure has only sapped me.)

13

(A NECESSARY PURCHASE)

What did you do to your uniform?

("What did you do to your uniform?" the Mysterious Woman had asked. She spoke, and that is what she said. "What did you do to your uniform?")

And feeling an almost animal anxiety arise, I'm determined to deal with the stain now, once and for all. No more delays. Pop a pill under my tongue, take a beat until I taste its bitter runoff before gulping it down, and hurrying out to my admin.

"I warned you about this," Miss Fairfax admonishes, her official Institute clogs squeaking on the scuffed linoleum while she bustles, simultaneously shuffling through someone's chart. "Have you tried the residential concierge?"

"Of course I did," I say, "it was the very first thing I tried."

She pushes up her errant glasses, looks away from the garment, and fixes me with distended eyes. "Well, you are lucky—it isn't that bad. I'll give this some thought. But in the meantime, it's really your project you should be worried about."

"I know," I reassure her, hastening to keep up with her. "But I have a new idea now, an idea of how to begin—"

"No time, Percy," she declares, turning abruptly left, and straight out.

"Thanks," I sarcasm at the closed double doors. Pivot, and stride down the corridor in the opposite direction. A quick swing by Mr. Al'Hatif's studio, that is, where he sits at his archeology table, stacking shards.

"It's called 'the Same Same' shop. Nothing could be simpler," he tells me, looking up from his intricate work.

"Some kind of dry cleaners?"

"Hardly."

"What then?"

"A local spot. There are many of them actually. Same Same shops, that is. But you want this one. This specific one. Don't tell anyone. Not even Miss Fairfax. And don't mention that you are leaving campus either. You can go this afternoon, it's perfect timing. No one will see you leave. Everyone will be . . . here." And he hands me a pale green flyer which reads. "Surefire Keys to Achievement."

"But how do I—"

"I'll ping you directions."

"Okay, but . . . in English? *Same Same?*"

And so, a single hour later, sidling behind a palm, I see the last of the dome's denizens disappear into the double door between the Art Pavilion's great stone slabs. I wait until I can hear the lecture begin; the massive, amplified—but now muffled—voice of the Director emanating out, as if from underwater . . .

Transfer value from the body to THE MIND. Hashtag: value-transfer. Inspire with awe, and CONTROL in the avoidance of BRUTE REALITY. Transform mediocrity into GENIUS (through Transmutation). What is your purpose? BOLD STROKES. You must act A CERTAIN WAY. Increasing joy and enthusiasm and results WILL CORRESPOND. Tell us about . . . OURSELVES.

. . . and time to fly. I hasten to the car park, hop in the back of an autonomous vehicle, and am off with a whir—leaving the metastructure vanishing behind me like a soap bubble on the wind. I feel, almost instantly, myself again.

The dunes are flashing by. A scattering of derricks, far off, also moving, but at a different speed. The desert, delirious, stroboscopes forward even as it moves backward relative to my car. I cannot tell which is moving: the car or the dunes. The impression is once again of brightness, save for the matte darkness of the sea lying far off. There is little sign of anything else on this car trip. Occasionally, one or two other vehicles—scarabs which, like their miniature cousins, contain, carapaced within them, the only possible sign of life out here. But no mammal, tree, or dwelling. Nothing else. (Another dead corridor.) It occurs that this may be why the Institute has such an incredibly impressive success rate with the projects. It houses us all in an utter void, and our minds are forced to compensate by repopulating the world with ideas.

But eventually the city approaches, and other roads,

devoid of vehicles, diverge with ours. There are now a few scattered housing developments, partially under construction, probably being built by offshore interests as investment silos. This is the sign that we are beginning to penetrate the outer rim of the urban zone and, before I know it, the car is among bigger and bigger structures, and now I see a truly mind-bogglingly tall tower, which corkscrews as it leans back and away, disappearing into the now sand-filled sky.

The Freehold Crown Spar. One of the tallest buildings in the hemisphere. It is quite famous. Built by yet another influential architectural collective in the initial, frenzied gold rush that was the opening of the region. So very influential were these architects, in fact, that no one questioned their use of reflective cladding on a building situated in the middle of a heat field. Some surrounding objects—none too important really: cars, a crane, a hut, and one or two people (both local workers; helots)—were liquefied on the spot. The building was unclad and reclad, this time with a bespoke titanium, concocted specifically so as to diffuse the sunlight, rather than amplify it.

It is not common knowledge but (Dennis, who has bragged about staying in this building, tells me) it is practically uninhabited throughout the year. All those rooms, thousands of them in the central spire alone, mostly abandoned. The Spar was built to draw, herd, and house crowds; but none came. The site became famous by way of its official photographs—which, because of its indecent height and architectural importance, were so widely viewed and commented upon—and, as it turned out, the images, by themselves, were enough; enough for anyone who might be curious about the Crown Spar, and so no one felt compelled to see the buildings Irl.

And truly, why bother? Such a hassle. So now the adjoining parking areas are all empty as unused graph paper. The skeleton crews which maintain the Spar—the cleaning staff, plumbers, electricians, contractors, as well as that group of locals whose job it is to go room by room through it, switching the lights on and off manually—say that, on occasion, as they crawl through the empty building, like ants cleaning a large bone, they hear sounds; an almost-music. The empty Crown Spar, they say, will hum like an enormous, muted Aeolian organ, pumping out an eerie diapason to nobody, or, at least, no one in particular (especially during the big sandstorms).

My car continues past and I also think: I've seen it too. I've seen it more than most people have. And I wonder if this "more" counts. Or even if I have in fact "seen it more." And then the tower is covered by red dust, sand, and the encroaching sprawl.

Another several kilometers, and we are downtown. The car eases to a stop on a corner and I step out, and it drives away, leaves me there, and this is it.

I am there.

Here, that is. This white mecca, on the shores of disconsolation.

Downtown. The city.

In essence, a city is its history, structurally, sure, but also in the sense of: "Before the bank was the café, and before that was the cobbler, and before that was . . ." Temporal, sedimentary layers. But this city, this city is only a now-city; existing purely now, for now. The Freehold's urban capital has no past, and can't even presume a future, ruined or otherwise. Or perhaps it is more accurate to call it a timeless city: a theoretical city, a conceptual city; no more than a projection, asynchronic; a CAD city. A message city, a city of signs. A model, imagineered by gods from impossible vantage points—looking down a three-quarters angle from on high, and rendering Bézier points and other manipulatable vectors. They thought up these networks of meticulously aligned streets and broad avenues, and when they did, they imagined it all: white. Everything is white. White rock, white cement, white tile, white plaster, white glass, white steel, white sand.

No one is born here, really. No indigenes. Everyone shipped in. For tasks. For color, even. Shipped in for the tourists. Now-cities, timeless cities, exist only for the tourist—those who might compare the empirical evidence with the evidence of the guidebook city and find the empirical evidence wanting. See, down here, away from the god-eye view, the guidebook view, it is different. More detailed, meaning: fraying at the edges. Grainy, and rife with jagged edges. And hot. There is no metastructure. The heat is almost unbearable. Wide avenues, broken up only by the large panes of light, which form triangles, parallelograms, and rhomboids of all angles. The heat comes off the pavement in waves, and it bakes everything indiscriminately, including, it seems, the very air itself. It reimposes itself with each step, and with each unthinking, casual movement. I decide to not move my arms. I wrap a thin cotton scarf which I've brought for just this purpose about my head. Bonus: now I blend in. Quickly scuttling into the shade, which, though less bright, is no cooler, I follow my device's arrow onto an avenue, and then onto another. In the distance behind me, the still enormous hotel tower.

Around the public parks between smaller skyscrapers, tourists in wraparounds and diaphanous windbreakers. Some wear headscarves. Everyone seeking shade. I pass the absurdity—no, banality—of a public sculpture. A biomorphic blob in a rippling silver. There are no public artworks where I am headed though. Not in this next part of town.

Off the main roads now, and I come upon a covered thoroughfare, and then a side street off that. And then a warren of arcades, shops, close in, the relief of small margins, low clearances. It's tight and very warm. Smells of people—broods—and cooking, oranges and cloves, and turpentine, and garbage but also marijuana, Drakkar Noir, patchouli, sweat, Pizza Hut, sandalwood, and Forever 21. A very rich scent, and a very rich picture. Let us see, here, above and all around, some signs, in foreign alphabets and displaying a variety of infographics. These signs throbbing with color, some pulsing with light: gaslight, or neon, or pixels probably—all of it swimming together like a bright and primary-colored finger painting, playing out their colorful subroutines irrespective of who looks at them. And of course, lots of those ersatz citizens. Here's a wash of vibrant and pied cloths, jewelry, etc. Some urchins to pester me, local thugs and bravos, unsticking themselves from darkened doorframes, a prostitute, a witch, a local jolly . . . Tumult, spice stall, tawny people, birds, in bursts. Drab, bereted members of the security force, bearing stubby guns with huge wafer-clips on glossy straps. A real orientalist circus. Why does the whole thing feel put on?

The people themselves are mostly undifferentiated, flat masses. Subalterns, I guess. Strange to see them not in the Institute uniforms, those people who do not belong to the Institute and its culture, who don't breathe its contingent air. People who aren't rarefied or special. Though most do wear uniforms of their own. Uniforms of the Freehold. Ones I don't recognize. I mean, I know the colors, but I don't know what they *mean*. Scarlet, and ocher, and sea green. Gray. There are shouts and a general hubbub. Bustling, imprecations, fruits and tchotchkes, eggs and smoke and rugs and the like.

It's a labyrinth, but I know where I'm going. No one gets lost. Not anymore. And what is this like, to be unable, literally unable to disorient oneself? We take this state of geographical surety for granted, don't we (late times), but it is a kind of hell. Unspooling the same old map—a cartoon's rolling background, a repeat pan—same doorways, same windows . . . nothing new, no stakes. And of course, I've seen all this before—the Street View. So now let us round a couple of more familiar bends, and then let us spill out onto yet another pathway—this, growing ever narrower. Let's follow it until it is time, and it is, to duck into a very specific alley, an alley we have been told about, which our arrow points at, the arrow seeming eager now, almost like a dog, to lead us to yet another maze of claustrophobic corridors.

Then, we are led by a snaking, fenced-in, smutty little street, back in the wrong direction it seems, to beneath a massive motorway overpass. Under the monumental roadway are corrugated shanty homes. Some open on one side. No roofs because the roadway is the sky, and the stacked concrete columns are a forest. Life finding a way at the feet of giants. Several buildings merge directly into the T-columns. The roads overhead intersect and diverge. There are too many vanishing points to keep track of here. Three more quick zags—around a corner or two, and here we are. Our eager and motivated arrow got us here, to this spot, explicitly, and it is impossible in these (late) times to get lost, so this must be the place, beyond a reasonable doubt. And now let us close out our map, dismiss our arrow, just pinch it away, and follow our instincts as the maps do not drill down to a geographic specificity this granular, and let us now see, start to head toward a little unmarked passage on the left; it is not more than a back lane.

Of course, there is no sign, and of course no one would notice it unless looking for it or otherwise spiritually prepared as such is the way of these things.

Let's continue.

Down the lane, which reveals itself to be a cul-de-sac, no windows on the brick walls, but a dense and dank impasto of old posters and flyers, none of which are legible, and the lane gets more and more narrow as if we were walking toward the corner of a triangle, and the end of the lane approaches until it isn't wider than four or five cubits or so, at which point there is a door and a mark or sign above the door indicating commercial status.

The doorknob.

"Hello?"

I am in a shop. Your basic shop.

Nothing exotic. A plain old room.

Could be a defunct post office, or a copy shop, or a banal customer service hub. A gray Formica counter, grotty rug. The room is illuminated by a smoky yellow fluorescence. A few plastic plants. A small metal cash box. A generic ledger book, about a third of the way open. Some chairs, several ratty magazines upon them. No one else is in here, but it looks like the shop must get occasional business: the linoleum is a bit scuffed, and I see a bunch of scrawls down in the logbook. There are two doors: the one I came through, and another behind the counter, leading to the back, and, presumably, to a workshop and an inventory of some kind. No sounds from back there. The indistinct harmonica wheeze of an old metal fan, bracketed to a juncture of wall and ceiling. There's a plain calendar tacked up on the opposite wall. Wrong month. There's no one behind the counter, and no bell on the counter, or on the door. It all seems so very ordinary. I take a few strides over to the countertop, and there's a loud round *ding* and I look down and I'm standing upon a dirty floor mat marked with the words "Same Same" in black rubber. Pressure-sensitive, hence the bell, and now a back door opens, first a crack and then all the way and then a man emerges.

A man. With a long face and wet, expressive eyes.

He looks askance.

I try to arrange my posture to look casual and courteous, and I say:

"Yes, hello?"

He stares at me.

"I was told to come here by an associate. Mr. Ousman Al'Hatif. I need to fix this garment; I mean, to remove a stain from it. I can show you . . . here, see? This. The stain. Ink? It's a funny story, it was my pen, the one I always write with, and so, it kind of exploded. Went *boom*? The . . . I need it removed? Do you understand?"

" . . . "

"Can you . . . do you even—?"

(Nothing.)

The Same Same man (for this is how I begin to refer to him in my head) stands there like a house cat, staring at me; waiting.

"Listen, I have a . . . I was told you could help. Wait—"

I reach for my device, yank it from my shoulder bag, and find the instructions from Mr. Al'Hatif:

When you get in the shop, do not speak with the proprietor. Approach the counter, place the item down,
and say the words: "Same Same." This is the procedure and you should not deviate from it. The proprietor does not, strictly speaking, have to serve you;
to deny you service is his prerogative. But if all goes
well and the proprietor agrees to take your case,
he will nod, and quote you a price. Pay the money
required in cash. Don't dawdle, or stare, or make
frivolous inquiries, as it is impolite. Bow as you leave
(not too low). Exit backward. Relax. Everything will
be fine.

"Ah," I say out loud.

The Same Same man frowns, half turns, and takes a
single step back toward the door he just came out of.

"Hold on," I mutter, and, adjusting my gaze away from
him, I pull everything out of my satchel—all my junk, under
which the garment is buried—and pile it on the counter. I
find the uniform at the bottom of the bag, and pull it out.

Slide it across to him.

I point at it.

And then I say the magic words.

"Well, he counted the price on his fingers, Ousman. I had
no idea this process would cost me so dearly. Not that I'm
complaining, if it works, that is."

Mr. Al'Hatif and I are back at the Pleasure Center,

there's cake, and someone has put on the music, which has been edging louder. Another evening's Discourse™ completed. Some of the fellows are inebriated and dancing with abandon; the Woman-Whose-Face-and-Hands-Are-Covered-in-Yarn is among them. Dissipation and dissolution. Mucky behavior. Perhaps everyone here needs, requires, distraction from their monomanias, their projects. The whole thing is beginning to feel festive almost to the looming edge of disreputable. I see one fellow's tunic is unbuttoned, and some other signs of subtly encroaching disorder. Some fellows go rumbling and giggling off into a dark doorway. Another fellow I don't know weaves about the place brandishing a magnum of champagne in each of her hands like she's about to begin juggling bowling pins. The mean litterbug is here. Miss ☺ the Brand Analyst and 鼎福 the Architect are off by the exit, chatting, keeping to themselves, but looking over at us. Quick little crinkles of laughter. Everyone flourishing, it seems. Meanwhile, Mr. Al'Hatif seems pleased with my Same Saming success.

"It *will* work, as I told you. Now—now you can really focus—no more getting sidetracked, Mr. Percy. Complete the project you outlined for the Institute. They are not infinitely patient here. You wouldn't want that Director breathing down your neck. The Institute is paying attention—don't forget."

"I won't," I say.

(How could I?)

———

Later now, back at the flat, alone again, depleted by the day and night, the trip, the return, the mask I wear for human interaction, I move through the channels of my room screen again. Meme-ified clips, trollish snark, comments eating their own tails, shopping, ads (me finding out more about myself from the ads I have on offer—the ads a pixelated mirror, a portrait of me, holding up my proclivities for me to buy back into, double down on), more football, games, pornography . . . like vaporous messages from another world. But I am only truly arrested by a weather report. Or is it a news report? News of the weather. Overlays of vectors and currents, and his look is the anchor's universal affect of calm gravity. Embedded in the corner of the map above the man's shoulder is footage of what appears to be a vast sandstorm engulfing a city. People seeking shelter, wrapped head to toe, scarves covering faces, leaning into the wind, trees bending, rattling windows, torn flags hastily lowered, tarps sailing loose like wild mantas through the sky, detritus flung everywhere. Ambulances, military vehicles. Glyphs, foreign ideograms crowd the scrolling feed at the bottom of the newscast.

Somewhere there is a state of emergency. Irl. Out there.

I reflexively look out my window, my window which I had left, oddly, open, out past the reflection of the room lamps, and my own reflection, to the calm of the night.

But not here. Not in the Institute.

Then, closing the window and turning, I notice something. The blotter on my desk is empty. Where are my pages?

On the bed? There was a stack of paper here before. Wasn't there? Paper, upon which the Fundaments of my project were written out. Where did they—? Then I remember.

The Same Same!

On the counter.

For fuck's sake.

I'll have to go back again.

Paper always betrays me, I think. One way or another.

And so I worm my way under the covers, and settle in for another night of arduous reading, slicing open the big hardback using its ribbon marker, and begin to make further inroads on this goddam, towering bildungsroman.

14

(THE PAPER)

Meanwhile, deep in the Freehold's capital, at the end of an unlit alley, in a ramshackle building, inside of the Same Same shop's murky back room: a light passes back and forth. Once, twice, in quick succession. Like a light from an airborne surveillance vehicle, sweeping below it for a crime. The light is bluish and very bright. It whirrs with each passage, on a geared carriage, making a flat, blaring sound: *waaah, waaaah.* Not like a baby crying, nothing so needful nor fleshed out. More like an electronic noise. Born of circuitry, of electrostasis, of photoconductors, of motors, of networks expressing functions. Of amalgamation and transference. Gears are whirring.

Each time the light flares, it does so, always, in twos, in sweeps, in pairs, back, and forth—*Same Same*—back and forth—*Same Same, Same Same* . . .

In the room, a man is watching the light. The light flashes upon his face, highlighting his features, before returning him to darkness. Each time the light blazes and moves, the man becomes briefly visible, then disappears.

Then the process is complete and the mechanism is silent; he reaches for the finished article. Examines it. Turns it this way and that. It looks good.

Good as new.

Better than new.

Satisfied that the uniform has come out as he had intended, the Same Same man nods to himself, clucks his tongue a couple of times, and walks over to another table, where he folds the garment and wraps it in plastic. He places this new bundle inside of a small gray box, puts a lid on it, and brings the parcel to the front of the shop.

He takes out the roll of packing tape, and is just about to seal it all up, when he notices something sitting on the far end of the counter.

A small stack of paper.

He picks it up, considers it, and, parting the curtain, returns to the back.

PART II

DOUBTS AND CONSIDERATIONS

15

(SNOW)

"Percy, you have a guest."

I don't believe it; not at first. I am supposed to be the visitor here—and visitors don't have *visitors*—yet here she is, bag in hand. A distant relative, barely known to me. A person who, having some undisclosed work in the region, has shown up unannounced and seems to be intent on staying for a while. Her work is most likely a pretext—I am being checked up on. Someone back home has sent a spy, conscripted to report back. Provide intel. Persuade me to leave, even. Idk. It is futile, and predictably awkward. I guide her about the grounds, just as Ousman Al'Hatif guided me, and I introduce her to several fellows—each of whom my guest finds more confusing than the last. We trudge to the daily open studios; we dine in the refectory. I attempt to "prompt" her several times, though she doesn't pick up on my cues; only looks at me, perplexed. The more time I spend in her presence, the less familiar she seems to me. Could she be an Imposter? Either way, what is she hoping to gain; to discover? Each night she returns to her hotel in the city, and I attempt to retrench, to regain some lost momentum. However, only two days since her arrival, it is becoming clear that she cannot leave fast enough for the both of us.

And on the third day of her stopover, after suffering a desultory breakfast, I find myself watching the back of her head—a pupil in the eye of the car's rear window—as it recedes, down the Institute's allée, and (thank god) disappears. After it is clear she has gone, I stand in the roundabout outside of the Enclave, flickering between old and new lives. I stand here for a while, that is, until all memory of the previous week evaporates. It is as if she were never here at all. Episode skipped. All ambiguous feelings having ebbed, I walk back toward this life, donning fully that Institute persona of mine, gratified in the idea that this relation's visit might have been the very last sign of my prior life I'll need contend with, that life's last attempt to retrieve and reclaim me. A strangely clear landmark I think, on what has been a rather hazy timeline. So little here of note, otherwise. Except for the work of course. After so much hard thinking about my project—its underlying philosophy, the forms it might take, its narrative arc, character, and nature—I am beginning to feel that I have stalled.

I am still the same old me. My predicted personal transformation has not yet occurred. No signs of growth, or molting. Nothing substantially changed. Not yet. I have not even made much progress reading my torturously long-winded novel. (A couple of chapters, at most.) There it sits on my bedside table—dense, deliberately vexing. The ribbon marker falls through its pages reluctantly, and I begin to think of its advancement downward as a measurement of time: sand in a clogged hourglass, a hand of a broken clock. More disappointing still, after several unproductive weeks—a homogeneous lump—I realize, while playing checkers with Ousman Al'Hatif, that I don't even feel any particular urgency w/r/t the project.

"You'd like to complete the work, certainly," Mr. Al'Hatif insists, scrutinizing the board.

"Sure, I would. Of course. That is: I want the project done, but I just don't want to actually have to, you know: *do* it. I want desperately for it *to have been done*."

"Has there been any progress?"

"Not . . . as such."

"Mr. Percy."

"I know."

He shrugs, adding, "King me."

With some benchmarks looming—I clearly have entered a kind of doldrums; become dulled by exactly those longueurs I had previously been enjoying. Namely: the endless meditations on process. Reverie-states which I thought would become productive; a boredom which I counted on turning vital. I should, I think, take the turn toward boredom as a sign that I am now ready, as Miss Fairfax has said I am, for a new rung on the Ladder—a new rung. It does feel, certainly, like it is high time to matriculate out of the "Encouragement" phase of the project, and muscle into the harder phases. And completing the work itself feels as distant a prospect to me now as one of those enormous rococo cloud-gods one sees, way far off at desert's end, not close enough for rain or comfort, but portending both.

How much of the project have I completed by this point? About a third. Bit less. A sketchy third. Rough, and unfocused. Vague ideas concerning vague beginnings. No hard choices made, no definitive decisions, no gauntlets thrown. The Fundaments were pretty much ready from the get-go, of course. They count for something (despite the fact that they, in their actual physical form, remain unaccounted for. They count as unaccounted. *Zimzim, set a reminder for me to return to S.S. in order to retrieve Fundaments*). I am, however, still, merely, investigating the space. That is to say that I have produced less than Miss Fairfax has projected, certainly. Not as far along as any of us had hoped I'd be by now. (I am tempted at this point to say that I am low on inspiration, but "inspiration" is such a shoddy word, isn't it?) I know that I need a prod; some rule of law. Negative consequences, even.

Finding other ways to combat the ennui, I exercise. I am no athlete, but I throw myself headlong into physical contests. At first, I run the sandy track down at the Athletics Oval. Disconcertingly, I am watched throughout these runs by small groups of fellows, standing in the warning area, following my laps in wonder and suspicion. Consequently, in search of privacy, I leave the track and attempt to run the grounds instead. I set off down the palmed alleé, but I find myself, once again, observed: tailed by a mute jump-suit, riding a small ATV at a discreet distance. So much for the running.

I now learn that the most efficient method for physical exertion is to spend an odd hour or two in the Institute's gym. Here, I can strap myself into the stair climbers, tread-mills, walkers, rowers, and various other simulators. This I follow, on odd days, with some vigorous tumbles back at the now-familiar wave pool. And as I bob in the oceanic tank, tangy and bright with chlorine, I keep hoping I'll see that sand-raker again, if only to catalyze some energy in me. But he never returns. Others come in his place, but it isn't the same.

In any case, none of these activities are sufficient to stifle the urge in me to strike out and truly challenge myself. So now, the goal here becomes to climb—to climb the Landau-Schmidt glacier. And so, on this late afternoon, unable to stomach another day at the recalcitrant project, I find myself back at the glacier.

I timed my approach to midmorning, so that all of the other fellows will be at work. I have waited for an all-hands-on-deck—I do not wish to be observed by admins or jumpsuits either—and as it happens, everyone is busy. The weather has turned extra-nasty this week. The Institute has brought in experts to examine the Institute's fans and thermostats. Though it is still significantly cooler in here under the dome, than it is on the outside, there have been moments when I have felt, albeit briefly, the atmosphere beneath the metastructure threatening to rise. Moments of a disconcerting, almost flat, body temperature. It never lasts long though, as the fans inevitably kick back on again and the cool breezes recommence. Nevertheless, a consulting company from the nearby peninsular super-city which specializes in climate control has been contracted, and one can see, now, many new men in bright azure coveralls, scouring the grounds, examining the substations and air-blowers, laying down pipe, threading fresh wiring, and driving their humming electro-carts down the service paths.

I am not too concerned about any of this, the ragged edge of chaos, and, if anything, I am mildly grateful for the world outside of my head to be properly twinning with the world inside of it. NB my uniform was supposed to be back this week; supposed to be back, and I've been laying low. But today, unobserved, wearing my best trainers, sweats, and reclaiming from the closet of my flat the only sweater I own, I walk, unabashedly, to the Mountain House. When I reach the hangar, I first check to see that the observation deck is empty (it is), and stride right up to the foot of the ice, where I am immediately hit by a wave of stale and frosty air. I am amazed by the force and bitter frigidity of the wind. Peering toward the summit—which is barely visible in the fog against a crystalline CGI blue—and with a throb of emotion, I dig my first foot in and begin my climb.

The first twenty minutes of work are invigorating, and my muscles thrum happily—my mind soars, full of promise and exhilaration. I revel in the physicality of the experience and congratulate myself on performing this secret ascent. One foot in front of the other, I am convinced that a struggle against the wounded massif is exactly what I need to propel me forward with my project. That is, rather than the Institutionally approved, metaphysical ascent of the Ladder, I will be ascending: Irl.

Though the smell is horrible. A vision comes to me now of the glacier as a vast beast, confined in its glass cage, eager to slough me, a parasite, off from its stinking pelt. And as the sense of awe I felt at the climb's beginning soon begins to subside, as the morning wanes and my elevation rises, I become so overwhelmed by weariness that I have to sit down on the ice-encrusted snow to rest. Strangely strong, the wind. It is blowing right down upon me from the summit. The blowers, it must be. Cranked too high. Hard going. A gap here. I wonder now, how many other of the residents have attempted to climb the glacier? I've seen none of them even stop on their way to the assembly and recreation center in order to look at it. Everyone is inured to it. Background. Mise-en-scène. But not to me. I'm going to climb this Mf and later, if all goes well, brag about it.

Within a further ten minutes, I begin to believe that the general thermostatic issues might be affecting the low end of the temperature spectrum, or, that the Institute has perhaps overcompensated in an attempt to preserve its captive berg, i.e., it is freezing in here, and this in itself might make my climb problematic, if not dangerous.

My windbreaker is flapping like an enraged crow, my

face and hands slowly becoming numb. Surely this is a malfunction of some kind? Yes, Imho.

Perhaps it is just me, and I'm not up to this task, I think, and I feel a strong wave of embarrassment at my fatigue. Having now attained the lower slope, I have to stop again, as I am completely winded. I am drawing breath as fast and as hard as I am able into my lungs, but the rich humidity of the air isn't satisfying their demands, and I suffer an insistent ache in the middle of my chest. Should I lie down? How humiliating. I was so looking forward to speaking up my exploits this evening. But now I'll have to keep this exploit to myself. Or lie about the result.

I'm just more than halfway, high enough so that the main concourse of the Pleasure Center is completely covered in mists and fog. I cannot see the observation deck, or the outside escalator banks. I could be anywhere up here. The drifts are deeper than my knees now, my sneakers are thoroughly soaked, as are my sweats, as is my sweater (sweat).

And if I were to perish? Would anyone even know where to look for me? Would my body be incorporated into the mountain and only give up my bones upon the ice's melting, millennia from now (if ever)? Someone might stumble upon my remains, gather me up in a bundle, and give my remains to the world, thinking them the last trace of some forgotten human ancestor. A counterfeit Neanderthal. Better keep moving.

The snow is perfectly regular in its consistency. Each

flake recognizable as such, a mirror image of its brethren, at least to the naked eye. Irl, every snowflake is different, one from another. But I doubt this snow is made like that; it should be uniform, being manufactured. A perfect clone army of flakes, mobilized to freeze me to death. I am coughing now, and wonder, on top of the extreme cold, if I am perhaps allergic to the formula used to manufacture this laboratory blizzard. The wind scythes around me and as toes and fingers cease to feel, sentiment wells up—feelings of pity, self-pity, pity for me—me, who thought he could attempt something so asinine—and, as if a corollary to these feelings, I also feel a throb of sorrow and pathos on all our behalves. All of us, we pitiful exiles and isolatoes. Mr. Royal, Miss Fairfax, 鼎福 the Architect, Miss ☺ the Brand Analyst, Mr. Al'Hatif, even the nasty litterbug, but me, especially. Me, especially, as even this episode, once again, feels secondhand, familiar—if diminished.

I see myself clearly for an instant in all of my pathos, and as the veils fall, I have to remind myself to tread carefully, as the way is becoming steeper, the closer to the top I get, the summit itself receding and receding as I rise (though still, I rise).

Until I can't, and I stop. There's no going on. I'm done. Spent. I begin to prepare a hole into which to crawl, kicking the powder aside, pawing at it with my hands, until there is sufficient room for me to burrow. Then, shivering, I climb down into it and curl into a ball, reaching into my pocket to pull out a bottle and pop something to calm myself, I don't even check its color or shape, just ingest the first one I get my numb fingers around. And as fatigue suffuses my limbs:

A dream, in which I dissolve, bodily. I am rendered completely particulate, and scattered. Conveyed outward in a vast dusting, disseminated out over the Institute, over the deserts with their obliterated ruins, out over the glowing cities of the plains, and across the cold, teeming, tentacular oceans, until each perfectly atomic portion of me lands; each particle equidistant from the next. And then the Mysterious Woman appears, walking in her loping and uncertain way, thin as an ibis and harrowing of gaze. She brandishes a long, thin cable. She crouches, plugs it into a console the size of a mountain. I feel a sudden and inescapable jolt—a large sucking—and there is the whine of a printer coming online, the sound of its gears, and monumental spitting nozzles, as it prepares to work, these sounds are redoubled upon themselves as in a plainsong, and suddenly all my separate parts move in the opposite direction, toward one another that is, in a reverse diaspora, drawn in, and up now, and through that same cable, coiling around and around, until—with an improbable and unearthly noise (first a wet spank, and then a metallic ringing) my particles implode, come together in a shrill stream, ejected out of that nozzle, spritzed violently onto an endless white and fibrous surface, in a linear series of glyphs.

I dry, over time.

The Mysterious Woman looks down at me.

I would speak but, as is the way of these things, cannot.

She cocks her head, pulls out a small pencil from behind her ear, and says, *"C'est un rêve bien connu."* I feel an overwhelming sense of gratitude. She winds out the thin, tensile lead, and I am glad that there is no ink here to surge out, spill, stain. In the margins of the printed page, she writes. But she writes nothing but nonsense: *Alterburg, Alterburg, Alterburg . . .*

Someone is poking me. From far away I feel jab after jab.

"Stop it, I'm awake." I say. "Stop it, I am awake."

Standing directly above me is an attendant in an orange jumpsuit. He's wearing a cap, and holds a black plastic tube of extraordinary caliber in his hands, connected to a mechanical backpack of some kind. A snowblower. I recognize this man. I've seen him around the grounds, raking in the rock gardens outside the villas, mostly. He looks at me dully and offers down a hand, which I take. He tugs me to my feet, brushes me off with his enormous work gloves, then silently beckons me to follow him. He is adamant, and points, jabbing his hands over and over, to a spot just behind me.

"I can't walk," I say. "I may have frostbite."

He shrugs, and turns, walks a couple of steps and climbs onto the escalator, not ten feet from where we are standing.

I heave myself to my feet, follow, and we descend.

16

A week (or, I want to say: weeks?) of work. With predictably unimpressive results.

The fruitless hours of work to be indicated by . . . by . . .

Aw, fuck it. Nm.

17

("PROFITABLE IDEATION:
TIPS AND TRICKS")

Miss Fairfax has left this new brochure for me, the most recent issue of what I've come to think of as "The Literature." It lounges there on my pillow, glossy, supercilious. I snatch it up and read it at a sitting, attempting several of the "Tips and Tricks," but nothing comes of it. If anything, the intensity of my efforts has driven away whatever elusive but promising idea was, perhaps, due to emerge. Whatever was there though has now shied away from direct scrutiny—burrowed back out of sight. I'm left with nothing but my own exhausted zeal.

I lie on the floor on my back—one of my preferred work poses—when Zimzim the Tea Boy's head begins to rise, a full moon in the flat's darkening sky. I look up at him; his round little face looking down at me, blank as a page.

"I'm just fine, Zimzim. Thank you," I say. He bends at the waist, slightly now, breathing audibly out of his nose. His face waxing enormous and looking puzzled.

"Yes? Listen, I just need to think. I need to think for a while. Projects like mine require a fair amount of deliberation. It's not just a matter of *making shit*, you know—"

I do not know the extent of his English, but I suspect what little of the language he knows is confined to greetings and farewells. Whatever else I might say to him is presumably beyond his ken. Though I continue nevertheless.

"You see, to create something truly . . . unique—as I propose to do with this project—one has to, one must . . . get lost in a sort of . . . I know what I'm doing doesn't look like much, but—"

(More of the same non-response here from Zimzim.)

"But let me assure you, I am hard at work right now."

He blinks once. Twice. Mouth, a line. Breath, piccoloing in and out.

"The preparation of myself is the preparation of the project. The fact that I am being judged by the Institute (or by you, Zimzim) on my progress, or in any other way in the matter of my project, is intolerable."

He straightens up—he has become bored (I'm guessing, as his features remain opaque) and he eventually withdraws.

Dammit. My Tea Boy was, at least, distracting.

So here, I disappear, stuck in a mental loop, tapping my fingers: *tap, tap, tap*, pondering stains and blots and suchlike. I sit, and get up. Seeking inspiration, I grab my book, the huge novel I've been laboring to read, and settle in, but I only get through a couple of pages before the words begin to blur. The writing is too high-minded and complex for me (though its protagonist, strangely, seems to be a simpleton of some kind). Either way, a chore. *Thump*, it goes back to its spot on the table. Bored again, I stare, and then clench my eyes closed, and then open them as wide as I can. I repeat this. I crouch and open my mouth and give out short guttural howls. I think through the Fundaments of the project. My Fundaments, the ones I can remember. I perform all the necessary conditioning. But nothing comes. Though, for some-or-little-to-no-reason, the word "Alterburg" enters my head, and repeats, over and over. Mr. Alterburg? Miss Alterburg? I don't know anyone by that name. A place? Alterburg. Alterburg? Tbd. Tbd.

Either way, this word and its inane repetition are the only dividend on the day thus far.

By way of acknowledgment of this unfortunate fact, I leave the room, and head up the stairs of the Enclave, arriving at the door bearing the "Roof, no entry" sign and push on through it.

Nothing helps me think as much as a good height.

The roof. The view from here.*

The sunset cools, and now the sky is ashes, and now the sky is ink, and I amble amid the vents and cellular antennae and microwave aerials; in and among the shaftways

---

* The sky is sufficiently uninterrupted, and so attains its truest nature, which is half-spherical; this particular hemisphere slathered in red, in long troughs, though there are some cooler shades too, the holdouts, the last slowly shredding redoubts against an inevitable immolation, which is to say that the sun is going down in a holocaust. Picture perfect. Postcard perfect. Unreal. A *holo*-caust.

143

and ducts, various other structures—forming, collectively, what seem like the reduced form of a skyline, as if the idea of a city reproduced itself on top of the Enclave in fractal fashion. I plop down next to a metal chimney or a water-cooling tower or air-conditioning unit, legs dangling like a kid in a grown-up's chair; and I look out again, and I am, I realize, hoping for a star, but all is black, and everything beyond the planet is veiled and occluded. Occluded by what is unclear—sandstorms, or light pollution, or just pollution as in smog, or perhaps something more consciously man-made, like the metastructure itself, or a profusion of satel-lites, swarming about the atmosphere like bees swarming a hive. But I unveil my device to take a pic anyway—it is pointed straight up at the blurry darkness, and I squint at the sky through the device, through another double set of cataracts, and shoot my photo. The picture comes out a dark square.

On a whim, I post it immediately.

Like   Share   Tag   Delete

Within moments, the device lights up, igniting with approval, disapproval, and commentary—whose is unclear, as I don't recognize any of the names or handles—but all of it relates to my perfectly stupid square.

This square is, though, secretly intelligible to me. For I know that the lights of individual stars shine in that square. They are in there; in its pixels. The special signature of each alien sun is present—their light reproduced, visible but for the noise. And I know that were I to have an instrument powerful enough to edit out this junk, the remaining information (I imagine) would render up a portrait of our original and unsullied firmament as the ancients once saw it. I could make a map to navigate by, and to hope, and to pray by—just as, perhaps, all that we've loved and lost in our lives remains in the tangled circuitry of our bodies, perhaps as bits of color, or small electric pulses, or in the glyphic configurations of our organs themselves, and that all this precious cargo, this information, is equally unavailable to us, though also, always present, hidden within our anatomy's coiled and meaty confusion.

I consider for a moment what it would be like if, with regards to my project, I were to switch it up. Leave the proposal behind and, say, start fresh. Something easy. Tried and true.

But, it is too late for that, I think, and shudder.

My projects are always difficult. It is, perhaps, what makes them *my* projects. The strain that is required to produce them; perhaps it is even the case that the strain *is* the project. (Strain/stain; stain/strain.) Anyway, the opportunity for ease and facility is long gone. If only I could just take a well-paved path. Someone else's. Maybe—

This thought is interrupted by a small white blur, migrating across the sky-black lawns beneath us. I wonder if I'd imagined it. Inhale, and my breath catches.

A ghost. Bird. Garbage.

I let my breath out slowly, audibly.

Paper. That was it. Don't focus on it. Let it gestate in darkness.

I sit awhile longer, then rise, brush the dirt from my bottom, stride out across the microcosmic city of the roof, toward the light that shows me the way to the stairs down.

"How was the day, Percy."

"Not too bad, Miss Fairfax."

"Any more headaches?"

"One or two."

"Concentration okay? Focus?"

"So-so."

"Putting things off?"

"Not really."

"The project is still moving slowly. That's normal."

"Is it?"

"Yes. There is a necessary, initial period of orientation and reflection. Though it shouldn't go on indefinitely."

"Roger that."

"Have you made anything new at all since we last met?"

"Yes."

"Good. Very good, Percy."

"Just a few preliminary thoughts."

"Fabulous. Can you share?"

"About that."

"Sharing is, after all, what these sessions are for."

"You won't—"

"Nothing you say leaves this room."

"Okay, but, that's not it. I don't have my work . . . on me."

"I can wait if you need to go get—"

"No, I can't."

"Why? Where is it?"

"It would seem that it's been . . . I want to say . . . *misplaced?*"

18

(THE PAPER CONTINUED)

The Same Same shop. A murky back room, and a light passes back and forth. Once, twice, in quick succession. Etc., etc.

(It's happening once more.)

Information learned, stored, cached, transferred, read, copied, and transmitted, etc.

Paper.

Paper.

Paper.

More and more of it.

The paper whines and shuffles and whirs then clacks through a machine of some sort, and onto a feed tray, where a hand reaches down to pick up the stack.

The Same Same man reads what's written there:

The Fundaments of My Project

He holds each sheet right up close to him, blocking his face from view. Perhaps he is nearsighted. He reads the whole thing. Each one of these numbered pages.

A little while later, the Same Same man opens the front door, and releases just a single sheet (eight and one-half inches by eleven inches) to the wind, and watches as if it were a trained falcon.

And it flies.

Satisfied that it is properly airborne, he returns inside, closing the door behind him.

The paper flutters away—buzzing, swooping down the dark alleyway, riding the urban thermals. Until it is discharged into the sunlight of the wider street beyond. It enters the complicated currents and cross-breezes of a large intersection. Here, it performs a little dance in the air. Jigging this way and that, up and down. Now it abruptly turns right, up a larger thoroughfare, and, along with a crescendo from the wind—its low tenor jumping up through the octaves—the shape spasms upward, until the wind blows its whistle full bore, and the paper explodes upward further, rattling into the air. It is many floors up, now.

A bleached blur, an obliterating agitation like an eraser taken crudely to the sky.

There it is now: shockingly bright, reflected in the glass of a nearby office tower.

Now there it is in the glass apron-wall of the next building, and the brassier glass of the next, copied from surface to surface, so on.

This sheet of paper.

Now it turns over once, lazily as if to rouse itself, and begins to wamble its way over the buildings, outward, over the city and away on the wind, over the malls and the roundabouts, the casinos, hotels, and mosques, over the outskirts and ring roads, past the gas stations and construction zones which are the harbingers of a sprawl not yet achieved but nevertheless inevitable. It flies ever upward and away. The piece of paper grows smaller and smaller and smaller until it is gone.

Time passes.

(More time passes.)

Where the paper is headed now is anyone's guess. Though it seems to be making a beeline for the bay, and then, it seems, the desert beyond.

19

Anyway, it'll all be fine. It's fine. I'm not worried.

The project will advance when it is ready to. And I'm certainly not worried about the satellite images on my device. The weather bureaus are monitoring a severe front which, though still hundreds of kilometers away, is moving, at least for the time being, straight toward the Freehold. Things could change of course, but still, some sort of disaster-response preparedness appears to be in the works. These provisions, if nothing else, serve to indemnify the local officials from any future blame. Here they are, those very officials: at podia, giving conferences, holding shovels in depots. Back to the map, shortwave infrared images swirl in real time: a bright red, green, and blue smear, spinning in slow motion. Now, solemn looks on the face of our reporter. Gravitas. He does a lot of pointing, which signifies agency and competency. A bright red checklist of precautions takes over the screen's bottom half. These measures could be observed, but seem foolish to me.

I mean, just look at it out.

Here on the roof of the Enclave, I can see all of the sky, unblemished but for the single silver airplane caught by the sun, so far up as to be completely immobile, a staple affixed to the perfect, bright sheet and the embodiment and cause of an inpouring of simply tremendous loneliness. I whisper my device to sleep and walk over to the roof's lip.

I spend a fair amount of my time up here on the roof now; sitting alone between the exhaust pipes and antennae, watching the Institute from this height. Looking down.

Some solitude, literal and figurative perspective.

I gain a kind of perverse satisfaction from watching the tiny fellows—corpuscles in the Institute's vasculature. You can see them now, transporting themselves, but also their contents—their projects, those wet little packets of information—from one space to another. And I wonder, up here, at these times, if perhaps the Institute itself is like an enormous mind, all of us performing ideational tasks within its perimeter which perhaps contribute to some greater process of thought, some collective mega-thought—a thought which, though entirely metaphysical here, might eventually lead to some large and tangible action outside in the world: like an arm, the size of an isthmus, being raised to scratch an itch an ocean away.

These are the kind of thoughts I have up here. Over-arching thoughts. Masterful thoughts.

Regal thoughts.

If only this kind of thinking were profitable in any way.

"You are being given a fairly long leash here, Percy," Miss F. reminds me, "but if you don't meet a single benchmark—"

Ping!

"You going to pick that up?"

I push down, forcefully, on my device's power-off button and shove it deeper into my pocket.

"Percy?"

"No. I get it. Back to work."

But after looking around to see that no one is watching— I settle instead in a long chair by the pool, where I search in my pocket for my special bottle, and find there's only a solitary capsule left. A problem, I think—one I contend with by rattling that last pill out into my clammy palm and popping it into my waiting gob.

"Bit warmer today, Mr. Frobisher," someone announces to me, collegially.

"Quite," I reply, startled (why can't I be left in peace?).

He's right, though, whoever he is. The tiniest thread of heat is now stealing through the dome like a furtive gas, and it does seem slightly brighter out. Looking around with new eyes now, I can see that some of the flowering shrubs are slightly less flowering than they were last week.

The man rolls over in his chaise to face me.

"And do the lawns look . . . *spotty* to you?" he asks.

I squint out at them. "I don't think so . . ."

"The first sign of a general decline, perhaps."

"It's fine, it's nothing," I reassure him, though clearly

some of the neighboring lawns are beginning to show subtle staining, like lightly soiled underarms.

"I wouldn't count on it."

He strikes me as the sort of reactionary who examines the world in hope of its betraying a decline of some sort, constantly on his guard for a frayed edge, moral turpitude, a change in atmosphere and mood.

Conversely, Dennis—walking up to lean against a sun umbrella on the patio in front of us, e-cigarette dangling from the narrow stroke of his mouth—seems to be relishing any sign of upheaval, environmental or otherwise, if only for the novelty of it.

"Hello, boys, did you hear? A fellow, injured on a tread-mill in the gym this morning. They brought him out on a stretcher. The power surged, the belt sped up, he fell. Badly concussed."

"That's terrible."

"The runner whom the race outran," Dennis offers, deadpan.

"Electricity has become as iffy as the gardening," my neighbor laments.

"Percy," Dennis says, looking me squarely in the eye, ignoring the other man, "let's take this as a good omen, you and me. Maybe things will finally begin to get interesting around here."

Though I want to do nothing of the sort, and so gather my work and leave.

The day has listed, sagged under by the time that Mr.

Al'Hatif and I finally sit down to our game of checkers. He appears totally indifferent to these new portents, though he is clearly bothered by something else entirely.

"Mr. Percy, what is that? Is that you?" he asks while I set up the board. He puts his pocket square to his nose.

"What?"

"That odor?"

"It's the heat." I'd been lounging by the pool. Perspiring.

He looks me up and down. "Where's your uniform? Not back yet?"

So, back again at the flat, I search the Freehold directories, but the Same Same shop isn't listed on any of them. If I want the uniform back, I'll have to drive back into town, won't I? Which will eat further into my project-time. That is, unless I just hang on a few days more, then I could wait for another mass event, and sneak off. . . . No, it can't wait any longer. I'll lay low now, but tomorrow morning, I return to the city. Np.

I remove my soiled clothes and let them fall where they may. Man, my room is also getting out of hand. The bed is a roiling sea of salmon-colored sheets, a filthy sock, an encrusted food tray, that mammoth novel I'm slogging through, splayed and broken on the floor—all my leavings from yesterday are still here, my sweat and sloughings, signs and stains . . .

I make a quick attempt to tidy up, myself included. I run up a hot shower.

Once in there, I put off leaving, the hot water feels so

fabulous. I wait long enough that I lose my will entirely. I just sit down on the floor of the stall for a while and allow the water to drench me over and over again; scrubbing myself with the sponge, over and over, staring at the shapes in the tile-work. I spend a lifetime in here. When I'm out again, assured that I am clean as could be—albeit completely bereft of energy—I remember that I have nothing to change into. My dirty clothes from home are smeared across the floor. I do not want to get back into them, thereby undoing all the benefits of the general cleaning. I stand here, naked and dripping, cursing my lack of foresight.

Then I turn slightly, and notice a package sitting on the floor, just inside the door to the room.

A box. There is no name on it, no address, no label.

But I know what it is immediately. As if I had invoked it. Ha.

Neatly folded inside. My uniform.

Well, the stain is gone. Just gone. Totally gone. No more moist spot. There's no remnant of it. Not a trace. There isn't even any of that telltale paleness you often see when a cleanser has been used aggressively on a fabric. Just as good as new. I turn the garment inside out, examine each of the seams. It is pristine, inside and out.

Mr. Al'Hatif was right. This place is incredible.

I put the garment on me, slip it on over my head, step into the pants, adjust the belt, and walk around the room, feeling its weight, its tolerances. It hasn't shrunk. Feels precisely the same. If anything, it feels better. It isn't creasing under my fingers when I pinch it. I bunch a bit of one shoulder together and pull it toward my nose. The fabric now smells like almonds and lavender and vegetable fibers. It smells . . . great. Well, that's one success in a long string of small failures. Maybe it presages good things for my work.

E/o/d, and I'm wearing my crisp, newly refurbished outfit. I am heading to dinner with everyone else, along the pathways. "Hello, Percy!" "Hello!" "Good evening, Percy." "Good evening to *you*," I reply, as the fellows pass, and greet me. And—aren't they all looking, well, a tad . . . shabby? I'm noticing little signs of wear and tear on *their* uniforms. Perhaps it is my newfound confidence, but it seems as though a few of them have allowed things to unravel a bit at the edges. I've detected a missing button, or two, a frayed collar, a thread poking pubicly out from a seam, a slight discoloration . . . tsk, tsk, I think. And it occurs to me that I will be one of the few here under the structure who looks truly sharp, etc. And what's that? I stop for a moment, bend down. A piece of paper someone has dropped. Stooping, I pick it up, roll it, drop it in a bin beside the path.

How quickly things begin to fray. Only a few weeks ago, the campus was totally pristine and I was a mess—now it is starting to seem like the other way around. All a matter of perspective though, isn't it.

And just as I am pondering this, the Mysterious Woman appears on the lit path heading back toward the Enclave from whence I just came. As we pass one another, and sensing an opportunity, I gamely say "Hello!" and try to infuse the greeting with all of the import I can muster. She looks up at me with those exotic eyes of hers, says "Hello, Percy. You're looking very handsome," then walks past purposefully, and is gone past the gate and off down another path. I stand there alone for some time, frozen in place, disoriented, musing on her meaning, her importance, her slender neck and the bones that protrude, noticeably, from it—not, Psa, you know, in some kind of romantic trance, as she is not "for me," not in that sense, but I mean more in the manner of: What is it that this Mysterious Woman *has to do with anything at all*? That is, I suppose, what has she to do with me, and what is her meaning w/r/t the Institute, and why is it that she is so rife with meaning after all? (A gap) And it isn't before long that I suddenly come to, surprised at my own absence from the world, and I shake my head, and now find myself, surprisingly, making my way back again to the Enclave, my feet taking me as it were, and I'm headed back toward the familiar comforts of my bed, and then there is, for some reason, blood on the floor of the hallway.

I stoop down to investigate further, and it is tacky to the touch. This is, indeed, blood Imo. I smell it. No smell. I think of the words: "brown spillage," and then the words "human hydraulics," and then there is another big blank

"Big blank" to be indicated by the space inside of the letter O

O

and it will not be until the next day, *now* that is, that I have begun to wonder (am wondering) about what had happened (then) to all my initiative (then).

Initiative I must protect (now). Initiative I must (now) store up; shore up. Time (then, as well as now) isn't endless after all.

20

(EXCURSIONS)

Gin rummy fever sweeps the place. Now it's backgammon. Charades, dance competitions, shuffleboard, war games, bocce, craft circles (also checkers, obviously, though this is really Mr. Al'Hatif's and my thing), and now it is excursions. A souk, an art exhibition, a football match, an archeological dig . . . educational, fun. the Institute sure does love an outing, and I attend as many as I am able. I do this, mostly, to keep stagnation at bay; and the excursions do serve as a welcome distraction from my project's stubborn refusal to spark. I think of the project now, as almost like a word or name I have forgotten and need to remember. "Think of something else, Percy, and it will come to you," I say to myself. When the project is going well (rarity), it does feel like remembering, rather than making. Strange. But distractions can be salutary under such circumstances—that's the theory anyway, and there's just so much to marvel at out here. Out there in the desert, that is.

Recently, we have been trundled into the sleek glass buses just about every week; off to visit a series of singular structures—follies, always picturesque, almost all of them in the middle of nowhere, always abandoned, increasingly strange, and standing without context amid the dunes. Our first of these desert trips is to an ancient ruin of some sort. The ruin isn't roped off, so we can wander around it as we please. The walls of the ruin list and tilt—what's left of them. The structure is barely noticeable as such. Eroded formations, rough hieroglyphs, lines, crevices, the sand's woven record of all of that wind. You could walk right by this site without even realizing that the whole thing wasn't just a slightly more chaotic moment on the plain.

("Isn't it splendid," Mr. Al'Hatif exclaims.)

The following week we go out to a large limestone sphinx—cryptic and crumbling. That same day, we visit an obsolete lighthouse. No water anywhere in sight. But still, this dilapidated erection in the middle of the desert, its milky eye, impassively reflecting nothing but sand, cloud, and the occasional vulture. We try climbing up to the glass, but the stairwell is too narrow, and blisteringly hot. Also, a large bridge, several hours' drive deeper into the wasteland, all gray stone and wire. Bereft of a river to traverse; red silt creeping up its piers.

One time, en route to a falconry demonstration, our bus sidles up alongside a wall of brick, stone, earth, partially buried, piercing through the dunes like stitching in cloth. The earthworks barricade snakes on and on, for what purpose is anyone's guess, though one would think its use was as a defensive redoubt of some sort. Who knows. Anyway, we are headed elsewhere, and leave the impressive wall behind us.

A month on, we head out to the site of a solitary white marble cenotaph—extravagantly sculptured, its inscriptions smoothed and unreadable. Again, no other pilgrims at the tomb. Just us, we uniformed geniuses; ganged together like schoolkids.

One midday, back on the bus, I look out my window and see a single black line begin to creep up out of the horizon in the distance; it seems to emerge from the desert floor like a mechanical pencil lead. The shape grows taller and taller, taller by far than any gantry or oil rig. It is huge. At least three hundred meters. Is it a minaret? No. More like a crane; though it's black.

It must be an antenna. As we approach it, the structure continues to thrust, obscenely, out of the sand, widening out now at its base. Look; it is growing feet—four of them, separated by huge, semicircular gaps. An obelisk atop a giant metallic quadruped. At the tippy-top, above its bulb, it tapers to a needle point. A communication tower? But no power lines extend from it. No transmitters; transformers. If the scale of the proceedings were different, it would be a sundial; its sharp shadow as clear as could be atop the swelling sand beneath it, stretching out and out.

The giant black steeple seems to have its own gravitational orbit, pulling us in, though when we arrive no one else is there. No tourists, no tour buses, no gawkers, selfie-takers, trinket shops, information kiosks, queues, guides, no restaurant, no trash, no parking. Our bus simply pulls over to the side of the road when we arrive. The tower is entirely deserted. When we clang down the steps of the tour bus, we are hit by waves of heat, vibrating on the electric wind. The heat is amplified by the enormous steel mesh of the tower. Still: we stand on the highway shoulder, idiotically, for several minutes, devices raised like hand mirrors.

And how I long to be up there, perched on the irreducible needle point of the structure. Frightfully high. High as a fever. Alone. But there is no going up. The double-cabin elevators haven't worked for ages. The stairs, locked off and rusting. So we just gawk, until the heat overwhelms us, and so return to our air-conditioned seats.

Occasionally, we go to eat lunch, and visit the shops in town.

The Freehold's capital always makes for a good excursion.

I take one such opportunity to sneak off again.

Does she see me do it? When we first arrive downtown, while everyone else is disembarking, in the bustle of arrival, while everyone buddies up, does Miss Fairfax see me duck and run? I am careful—pretty slick about the whole thing, Imho. The admins haven't been taking attendances lately, so. Anyway, I am not away for that long. Not long at all.

I've gone back, you see. Back to the Same Same.

My uniform came out so well, I've had a few other things taken care of. Small things.

My favorite pen. Had to get that leak shored up.

The peeling sole of my left shoe? Done. It's back on my foot already. Repaired in that indistinct back room while I waited. The seal between lower and upper is tight as could be, and it feels great. The entire shoe looks spanking—the younger sibling to its partner. Shining. He must have polished it up, and now I'm left with this strange (aesthetic, and literal) imbalance between my feet. (I'll have to go back, to do up the right shoe.)

All told, on this particular day, I am probably gone about twenty minutes. Tops. Surgical strike. No one missed me.

Frankly, I can't wait to go back there again, I think, as our bus rebreaches the Institute's boundary, and lumbers onto the highway. We are off again. And this next outing should be fun. It is Venice after all. Yup Venice (or: "Venice"). The Freehold's largest, most frequented mall.

So large, this mall, that from our vantage point in the middle of the huge, open gallery, nothing can be seen of its exterior walls. The building is several stories tall. White canvas and netting hang down from the ceiling, giving the space the feeling of an enormous Bedouin tent. Walkways are tiled in brilliant white, and shoppers—tourists, and those posh faux-locals—parade up and down the concourse, some carrying bedazzled bags, others having these bags carried for them by servants. Cutting in between the walkways are, of course, the winding, swimming-pool-turquoise Venetian canals—placid, but for the small waves made by the silent gondolas which navigate them and transport the tourists to the chain stores. (You just can't make this stuff up.) Many of the people in the mall wear white gowns and headdresses. Most are navigating the promenades blindly, through some innate or coenesthesial knowledge, whispering and cooing to their slabs, or looking through them to capturing the moment. Soft music. Wrought-iron standing lamps tastefully light the arcades; plastic spider plants hang from them below banners advertising everything, and whatever. The perfume from one of the Sephora franchises leaks out.

Unlike the Institute, the air here is comfortably cold. The gondola poles make tiny splashes, like brushes on cymbals. Miss ☺ the Brand Analyst is astern, facing me, her legs crossed out in front of her, looking about her—me, in the prow. "Wow, this is so real," she says. She has a dreamy expression on her face while the electric gondolier punts us slowly, robo-barcarolling us through the channels of commerce.

She isn't really looking at anything specific, Miss ☺, just taking in the general impression of trans-global enterprise, and also perhaps lost in the sounds of the splashes of the pilot's pole, and perhaps also entranced by the Syntho-Oud mash-ups which burble about us. We've snuck off from the body of the group, who were far more interested in shopping than we were. We caught the first boat we could find. And we have the mischievous grace about us that clings to children escaping field trips.

"See?" she says, and points.

"What?"

I follow the line of her sight, from her blue eyes out over her right shoulder, along her slender bicep and down along the gently veined waves of her tanned hand, slipping briefly along her lacquered nail and out. She's pointing over the waters to the mall's arcades and signage, to those bright places in the Venetian Souk, above the generous entrances of the shops where the signs glow: the rows of corporate selling-interests which stake out the mercantile rows of this fake Venezia. Galeries Lafayette, Debenhams, Marks & Spencer, Lacoste, Chopard, Nike, Hershey's Chocolate World, Mumbai Se, Harman, Virgin, Kinokuniya, Red Lobster, Wafi, Scoozi, Vapiano . . .

"Beautiful, isn't it?"

(BHV. Harrod's. Starbucks. Spinneys. LuLu Hypermarket . . .)

"Yeah, just look at them all."

"Everything needs one. We all do; did you ever think of that, Percy?"

"To everything, a sign?"

"Even you."

I put up two Ls with the thumbs and index fingers of both my hands as if to frame a billboard:

"Percy Frobisher: *Mystery Man*."

"Is that what you want? To be a riddle?" (Cipher, on a blank field. Stain, on a field rampant.) "Not a winning look, Percy."

"All right then," I say, "what about you?"

Simple, you'd think. One of these: ☺. But no, no, she's a forward arrow: →. Or, a fingerpost. Better still, just a finger, pointing; ☞. For the jolly little trendsetter that she is: a disembodied finger. A finger with a pretty little pink nail. Pointer finger. Trigger finger; *pew, pew. Digitus secundus.* It's perfect actually—as apical creative and ideation manager at a creative consultancy responsible for branding, systematic trend-watching, scenario development, and visioning. A modern oracle, she is. A roadmapper. A strategic consultant. Sniffs for trends, and then sells forecasts to high-bidding clothing manufacturers, game designers, packaging specialists, fashion conglomerates, entertainment studios, food labs, app developers, and even, ourobouros-like, to other creative foresight consultancies. For a not-insignificant outlay of money she will tell you what that color, that style, that phrase, that cadence, that disposition or humor, that taste will be—the one which will appeal next season, next year, in ten years, as far down the pike as you wanted her to look, all the way to the end of cindered time. Incredibly high success rate: predictions-to-outcomes. Day after day, in her offices, diode-lit by three monitors, tabs open, phone lines on speaker, silent feeds unspooling, networks and platforms auto-updating, page-view by page-view, analytic by analytic, click after click, vibrating with the hum of cooling fans and brushed by the building's ventilation, peering at now's entrails, its wasted wants, its dissatisfactions and refuse, reading in this . .

"... looking for evidence of tomorrow's manias and

mass desires," she explains, ". . . and I should underline: not just mass desire, also yours. Yours personally, Percy."

"What would you know of my desires?"

"Please. And, I would know a lot, actually."

"Would you now."

It isn't a second sight, though she is surely gifted. But she also works hard at prophecy, looks hard, as a gambler looks for tells.

"But mostly it's pattern recognition," she tells me.

She hears trends like phrases on the wind. Hardwired to speculate, possessing a natural gift for spotting emergent phenomena. She is successful. And it all worked for a while. But, but: Don't prophets always get it wrong eventually? Or ignore some critical factor? Isn't screwing up part of the job description? We should all be aware of the long history of oracular failings by now. We should all know the label warnings; the fine print. When the future volunteers some information, something crucial is always withheld. She fucked up quite badly, and was quietly let go. So she ran off to new and distant scenes, freedom, release, forgetfulness—her time in the desert, that old refrain. (None of this is said—I know it all because I looked her up, and found her there, online, in staged photos of her shaking various hands, receiving awards, at various podia, giving speeches, talks, her Discourse™ . . . in and amid all of this was buried the news of her fall.)

She drags a hand into the water, one finger, two, letting them draw ripples which triangulate infinitely behind us.

Twirls the ends of her hair, and kicks the tiny, pointed foot attached to the topmost of her crossed legs, up and down, up and down. She is so bright, but for all her smarts, she seems hopelessly lost. Shunted off to a place which was the last place she'd thought she'd end up in.

End of the territory. Off the map. A Venice which isn't Venice, with the rest of us. "Federation of geniuses," is what Dennis sarcastically called us. Federated around what though? Toward what? The projects, obvs. The Institute's insistent heartbeat.

"So *you* do *me* now," I say, feeling generous, and attempting to prod her from, what is for her, a very unusual funk.

"Well now, I could brand you in, like, three quick strokes," she says, revitalized, batting her lashes at me like a couple of naval signal lamps, "it is almost too easy."

"Go on then."

But just now, as it so happens, we are docking. We bump up gently on the dock's buoys and are helped ashore by the yellow jumpsuit whose job it is to help tourists off of gondolas.

And here comes Miss Fairfax, admin5, a real lack of amusement on her face. She gives a perfunctory hello to the Brand Analyst, which contains within it the full contents of a *Doctrina Armorum,* and then there is a long and equally subtextually pointed hand on my arm. I wonder if this is due to Miss ☺ and me having broken protocol, or is it out of Miss Fairfax's sense of superiority, the cultural divide which stands, definitionally, between the fellows and the admins.

Either way, Miss Fairfax is simply puckered-up with undisguised spleen.

Miss ☺ is oblivious though, or merely acts that way, and so says "Heya, Miss Fairfax, join us for another spin around the canals?"

"No. It is time to go back to the bus," she spits. "And in the future, don't stray from the main group anymore on field trips or you will not be invited out again, understood? We're leaving. This outing is over."

So we queue our way back into the bus. We head deeper, and deeper into the desert's darkening heart, back toward the Freehold's most fascinating landmark—the destination lit up like a lodestar—our glinting dome. An hour of travel away still, but visible, if barely. We should be back before dusk.

The metastructure. At the desert's precise, geographical center point.

We arrive home, driving through the gates and down the allée, and now I see my two buildings line up against the sky again, feeling once more that same sense of remembrance and alien understanding, and now we stop, and leave the bus, and the air inside the Institute strikes us with a new, warm force.

It's becoming just the tiniest bit gross in here.

Me, in time and space, to be indicated by Ps

P (sky)

PPPPPPPPPPPPPPPPPPPPPPPPPPPPPPPPPPPPPPPPPPPPPP(horizon)

P (Residential Enclave)

P (Building 2)

P (Building 1)

P (me_3, having my epiphanic moment)

P (me_2)

P (me_1)

21

(THE PAPER CONTINUED)

Vultures: circling.

The paper follows in their wake, whirling, slowly with these grotesque birds for a while. A vast and ominous mobile high above the plains of dust. Then, as if having received a summons, the buzzards disengage en masse, and the paper is left on its own once more.

A few days later, surfing a downward gust, the paper comes in lower than ever, and it hits the sand hard. It is only a kilometer or so from its destination, so this crash landing is bad news. Now, immobile at last, some writing on the paper can be seen. Words. The words describe . . . But now, the wind begins to pick up again, and now sand blows over the paper. A coarse, grating sound. The writing is covered. Will the sand cover the paper completely? The sand ultimately covers everything.

Anyway, a potentially sad ending for the page.

Sand holds no dominion over

But then, a chain of small movements: the sand is blown about, grains vibrating, relocating, one at a time, then after a pause, in pairs, trios, and quartets, in flights and tiny, mottled clumps, and subsequently in a miniature avalanche, which redoubles into a slightly larger miniature avalanche. The foremost edges of the white piece of paper are revealed.

The wind kicks up, big-time. The paper is released— and it takes to the air again.

For the last time, the paper travels. Picked up by the wind and carried up from the sand; conscripted by the desert drafts and taken off on maneuvers: zagging, diving, spinning, ducking, occasionally army-crawling, over this, under that, in mad cycles and epicycles, from one breeze to another. The paper makes its unpredictable but steady progress out and over the plain, over dunes and rocks, ruins, scree and insects; until it finally penetrates the semi-visible metastructural barrier, and abetted by the turbines, the blades of which it nimbly avoids.

It has arrived.

It negotiates an elegant row of palm trees, skimming their top fronds, and, losing altitude, turns sideways on its pitch-axis as it zephyrs over a lake, several lawns, and now a swimming pool; approaching a building of some sort, before the paper sheet slips into an open window . . .

. . . to settle upon a desk, in the middle of a cool room.

There it lies.

This pioneer. Having paved the way.

Later, with any luck, it will be joined by its compatriots.

The rest of the ream.

22

I've received several prompts today (I think).

The Poet provides me with a prompt when he tells me about a dream he had: a dream of "eating a live alligator." There are many details to this dream which the Poet fills me in on, his forcing the spiked and leathery hide into his stretched mouth, his gagging, how his saliva had turned an awful brown, and even about the acrid and intensely gamey flavor. It is so odd, until I realize that he is purposefully providing me with coded material. That was prompt Number One. Then, I wake up from a brief nap to the smell of burning. Toast? Hair? Rubber? A high palm has spontaneously combusted nearby. I go out to inspect, and the Medium ambles up next to me. We both look up at the crackling fire-bursts; she shakes her head and says:

"Can you imagine the coming world?"

Can you imagine the coming world.

I weigh the question for a moment, pondering a response, and then understand, and ;) at her, so as to say thank you for the prompt.

I will use these two prompts as catalysts for today's work. I am hoping that by day's end I will have successfully transmuted both prompts into something serviceable for my project.

I have zero doubts about my ability to do so.

And here's Miss Fairfax, her surliness of the other day dissipating. I have been demonstrably docile, really toeing the line when it comes to Institute procedures, participation, project management, so on. Overdoing it even. A-student, me.

If only she knew.

I'm getting bolder.

I've been Same Same–ing.

Bit of an addiction now, really.

Everyone at a Discourse™, me, taking a vehicle from the lot and going. No errands. Nothing really to fix or make, though I do toss a red checker into my pocket to bring. I wonder.

Wonder about the Same Same's prowess. Its *extent*.

So when I get here, I put the checker down on the counter, put up three fingers, say the secret incantation, and my Same Same man disappears into the back. In no time flat, he returns, and places three new disks down on the lino, one at a time.

Click, click, click.

My jaw, on the floor. He is not fixing a damn thing. He's making. Maybe. Unless he just has it all at the ready, but . . . He could have amassed a huge amount of junk back there, storage bins from which he plucks (I want to say: *one of every-thing?* Four of everything? Wtf). Or there's a really high-end 3-D printer. A Xerox; a milling machine; lascr lathe, sewing machine; a staff of . . . how many? I keep attempting to see back through the doorway; leaning, craning, peering, nothing doing. I have to be subtle about it, I don't want to inadvertently trigger any cultural sensitivities (I'm clearly in with the S.S. man now and wish to keep it that way). But still: How does he do it? I will take this entire enigma as a challenge. Whatever his methods, I'll trip him up yet. And by tripping him up, find out how it's all done.

And, though the Same Same mystery has only deepened today, I am buoyed by my successful facsimil-izing. There will be more of it. More of it, Tk.

And so, spirits high, I return to my flat and celebrate by whispering up another double, Miss Fairfax's photo, the one I took. Here, this one, captive on my device.

There is, of course, a much higher degree of resolution to the Irl Miss Fairfax than there is to this (still-vivid) photographic stand-in. Yet, speaking of mysteries, there is something truly mystical about her photo, as opposed to her actual personhood. Something mystical about the way I use it. When I've got the pic up, it is like we (she and I) enact a kind of spiritual congress. Not corporeal, not meatspace—metaphysical. Spooky action at a distance. Two souls; two proxies, smelted together. It's an occult wonder.

A minute later and I'm up on the bed, belt undid, device

in hand, ready to begin; device is charged and ready—it, like me, propped up on pillows among the rumpled sheets. I preside like a pale moon in the plumped clouds.

Now, let's get the show on the road.

I'm off. Elsewhere. Easing, oozing my way through permeable barriers. Foreground receding, new foreground emerging. Entering a proxy world of pharaonic scope and wealth, a sensual kingdom, a theater of archetypes which waits upon my whims; one which makes the Institute look like a moron's flimsy phantasm. This new world, which is, even now, opening its own, unmanned, buffering gates to admit me.

Ping!

Pink. Overlapping limbs. Small and sculpted whorls of crinkled hair. Closed eyes, smooth protrusions, red caverns, unguarded mouths. The excitement pushing upward, providing jolts of pleasure and adrenaline, the device, dear device, slick in my hand, rigid, pushing back against my touch even, meeting it with the latest in haptics, partnering in rich and limitless freedoms which are contained therein, deep within its compact . . .

Ping!

Jesus wept.

Sliding back over into Xanadu (close eyes; no, open), the sun edges, and edges, I hit enter: enter. Enter, and thrust. The light touches the rim of the device and creeps further, and Rn the transparent surface rises up, handled, imprinted. But who's that there upon that very same glau-

PETER MENDELSUND

cal plane, amid the material evidence of the device's use, but me; equally smudged; my muddy ghost, there—and yet also within—the action, mixing into these analogous plea- sures, and relishing it, as I am:

Yes, yes.

Ping!

Yes . . .

Ping!

Ignore.

Ping!

Uh . . .

Ping!Ping!Ping!Ping!Ping!Ping!

Rapid detumescence.

Fuck. "What has got into you?" I ask the malfunc- tioning device, though for this, the device remains silent. Anyway, I think (looking down), I've lost it. It's just not hap- pening. (You know when you know.) If only I hadn't been interrupte—

Ping!

The device hits the far wall with a small thud—like the dense life of a bird, meeting a window at speed. It ricochets off, and falls to the floor behind the chair.

Piece of shit.

(A gap.)

I crouch there, tunic open to my belly button. Trousers pooled at my feet. The device has gone black.

Wakey wakey?

I'm such an idiot.

It is totally blank and still. Frozen. Not *cold* frozen, but dead and absent a temperature. I fuss over it, warm it in my palms like a bird's egg, entreat, caress it. Trying all the reboot sequences. Shake it briefly before thinking better of this, then place it on the bedspread and watch for movement.

Time passes.

More time passes.

It slowly, reluctantly shudders back into life.

Ping? (It says.)

A text.

"PROGRESS??"

From the Director.

23

Master of the derivative and all-around financial wizard Dennis Royal sits on his kitchen counter, scrawny legs dangling down, his sockless feet in an unlaced pair of bespoke leather dress shoes. His hair is wet from the shower and he's smoking. He must have disabled the flat's alarms. I'm jealous of his tousled chic, his poise, his critical distance. His not giving one shit.

"Drink?" he asks me.

Dennis insists on calling his Tea Boy, in English, just "boy," which he does now with a wry simper.

(If his Tea Boy minds, he does not let on—his Tea Boy, featureless as a snooker ball.)

Dennis's rooms are like everyone else's. Futuristic and chic. Globular lamps; smooth chairs like lozenges; orange carpets; some small statuary and other mass-produced objets d'art. There are few personalizing touches; but hardly any. It's pretty much shiny and out of the box.

"Feel warm to you, Percy?" he asks. "I can try pushing the AC if you'd like," adding, "It's pathetic, you know. Back before a gazillion of our positions failed, before things came apart that is, I used to live like a king. How far I've fallen, to live in a . . . *unit*."

I sit a couple of feet away on a couch. A football game is on the screen. Dennis slithers off the countertop, adjusts the thermostat, gives the match a weary look. Turns. Takes a long, squinty suck on the cigarette. It glows, but a deep, fluorescent pink. "Have to smoke these now. Admin's orders."

I'm clenching all my muscles pretty damned hard here, trying to keep the shakes off. My palms sweating into my pockets. Dennis seems oblivious.

"In the beginning," he says, looking at his smoke philosophically, "they were too smooth. E-thingies. Didn't burn the throat like the real ones. Turns out people missed that scraping feeling you get from the actual deal; the raspy kick. The pain that is, so they manufactured a chemical which adds the discomfort back in." Takes a long draw. "There's a lesson here. People grow attached. Even to crap. Even to their own suffering. They'll take it, as long as it is *theirs*. Take this place, for instance."

A drink is handed to Dennis by his Tea Boy, and Dennis duly hands it on to me.

I try not to noticeably guzzle.

"A home for masochists, wouldn't you say? I mean, who else could suffer such an institution? I used to have what you might call a 'real life,' and now look at me. Can't even remember what that old life felt like. I vaguely recall its being exciting, even if I can't recall the excitement, *soi-*

même. Now, this dreary old monotony." He pauses for a few moments, looks up to the ceiling, musing. Continues: "You know what people used to say about me?"

"No."

"They'd call me a 'disruptor.' "

Picture his colleagues. In *tableau vivant,* around a conference table barnacled with speakerphones. All of them murmuring about Dennis Royal. The managers and number crunchers, quants, all the hierarchies of greater and lesser money boys—jockeying suits, assemblies of grays and navies; Windsors, Pratts, four-in-hands; who, when Dennis strode up to his designated seat, developed a sudden fascination with their notes, their spreadsheets, their devices, their mail, their bespoke footwear, the mean level of their gaze dropping precipitously; or they'd stare at the smart-board as if at a horizon line—hoping for a distant sail—something. They'd look away. They knew what he was. *Disruptor.* Until the troubles. As all of our tales are tales of the fallen. We fallen.

"The fucking best. Back then my finger was right there on the throbbing vein of the world to come. Counting pulses."

God, I'm feeling really and truly rough.

More monologuing from Dennis. Chitchat. Chitchat.

And this, my latest panic brought on by, of all stupid things, a text message. A stupid effing DM. Why am I so *reachable*? Get-at-able? What does the world *want from me already*?

". . . and everything must come to an end, of course," he seems to conclude.

The bad feeling is now threatening to mount, to become a kind of hellish inscape, but fortunately, nick-of-time style, Dennis pinches from his shirt pocket what seems to be (what looks like) one of my pills, but in a different color (Jesus, yes). Puts it on the table beside my glass. It sits there and sits there. The silence of objects. Okay then—he picks it up, puts it in the hollow of one of two spoons that I didn't notice lying there, takes the second spoon and puts it on top of the first, conjoining them into one big vice. Down it goes on the table. He puts his hand on the top spoon and leans into it, straight-armed. Does this a couple of times. Then opens up his contraption, and shakes the powder out of it and onto the smooth tabletop, worrying the last bits out with a nail. He smiles. I smile. He looks down at the little chalky middens. I do likewise. We both look up. I look away to the game, playing it cool as I can. He walks around beside me.

"Anyway, help yourself. Seems like you may need it. You're a bloody mess, Mr. Frobisher. Shaking like a . . .

"Sure. Don't be shy. Just have . . . one more. For the road. Up it goes.

"The . . . fine. Good. Just takes a moment.

"Now. Who's winning?"

A wonderfully familiar state of ease.

After the familiar terror of the Director's summons, my breathing is finally back to normal, bless you, Dennis.

Bless you for holding; for being the-kind-of-person-who-holds. He who holds; a holder.

Rn, warmth toward my host, albeit chemically enhanced. No more *pings*. Device seems fine. Whatever, none of it was worth the panic it triggered. All of these messages—texts, emails, alerts, reminders, invites, likes, DMs, comments, sexts, trollings, spammings—what do they signify, I mean, collectively? Idk, but I know how they act upon me: like my synapses have been teased out into the Irl, in an infinitely long, endlessly wide, gossamer lacework of live and soggy capellini—a mesh covering the planet, traversing landmasses, transoceanic; a network of gauzy wires, leading from each tiny quadrant, every microdot of the meatspace directly into the core of my mindspace—wires which are round-the-clock open for business; for whatever and whomever. Meaning the *pings* do have a way of sticking the needle in, don't they. But Dennis is waxing on about the good old days, again. Which is, I suppose, interesting enough, and quite a pleasant cadence his voice has, posh, and mean too, but slick, while I simply can't take my eyes off the football. Its angles. Its moods. The eternal skirmish: Blue v. Red, but both teams otherwise interchangeable, Rly. The players are smudging a bit on the screen, leaving little pixelated trails behind them. I'm cascading Dennis's tablets from one hand into another, and then reversing the process, like sands in a perpetual hourglass.

"Back then I had the nicest clothes, nicest car . . ."

A football match is bounded by a fixed time period: ninety minutes in two halves. The game unfolds in real time within that particular allotment. The game proceeds linearly. Tension builds in natural time and then resolves in natural time. But televised football time runs more in loops than in straight lines. Backward and forward. Not to mention variable rates of speed. And with the addition of outside agency—the commentators' and viewer's agency that is, w/r/t instant replay, freeze frame, slo-mo, and the like—time in a football broadcast has become a way more complex affair, hasn't it.

". . . the nicest boys—well, maybe not the nicest exactly, more like the opposite of nice, the least nice, actually—"

Time, stretching out . . .

". . . nicest properties, bronze; steel. Bengali maple. Mirrors. The abundant lure of mirrors. Always loved a mirror. Make the already big rooms cavernous, and multiply the light a thousandfold. But, Mr. Frobisher, I will tell you now that there is no wonder upon this earth so magnificent that one cannot eventually take it for granted. For every palace, there is some prince who is sick of the wallpaper."

The tools of the modern broadcast have made the football more an illustration of narrative than a narrative itself.

"None of it could last."

The score is nil–nil. Both teams probing. Dennis, rimming his glass noiselessly with three fingers of his right hand. These fingers having curiously sharp nails.

"Doesn't matter. I stopped enjoying it at some point. I had enough money. Didn't need any more. Didn't feel need itself, actually."

The cameras look down from a great height. My favored

185

perspective. Up on high. High up. I can see the lines. The possession ratios. The pass completion maps. As if I am looking at the postgame statistics. It's almost as if the game itself needn't even be enacted. But the particulars down on the pitch, the relative slant on a blade of grass, the salinity of the sweat on a player's brow, this is what is truly interesting, and is exactly what cannot be seen on-screen. All that can be seen here are the rules of the game, put into action. Brought to fruition through the ritual. And we all know how rituals end. That's what makes them rituals. Goal. Saw that coming.

"Then, I got the offer, to come here."

Furthermore, the announcers are doing their play-by-play, sotto voce, and the sound of their professional mumbling is so soothing—more than soothing: the announcers are doing something for me, on my behalf. And I realize now what this something is: that the men are relieving me of the burden of having to watch the game. So I watch Dennis for a while. The constant drone of voices tells me while I watch Dennis, the game is being watched by proxy, by someone, and that someone doesn't have to be me.

Dennis gets up, fidgety as a marmot. He returns to the kitchen area, grabs the fifth of something he'd left there, and hauls himself back up onto the counter. Says:

"And then it just seemed preferable to go, to let go, of the apathy. Of the old ennui. I'd come here and that state of affairs would dissipate. Bad there; good here. As if all my feelings were geographically determined."

That goal was writ in the opening of the game, bound and bundled into its code.

"But they are not," he continues. "Geo-tagged. That's the word. I mean, *I am*, but my feelings are not."

I find my voice. "What do you mean: 'I am'?"

"Geo-tagged. My office allowed me this gig, but didn't trust me not to run off, so—"

He pulls up the cotton hem of his uniform's trousers, to reveal his emaciated, veiny ankles, around one of which is a slender black bracelet.

"Had to. No choice. They need me, I need them. But I'd been bad. My nasty habits reflected poorly on them; so, the company, in their wisdom, decided that, rather than give me the heave-ho and lose their cash cow altogether, they would rather that I simply keep up the good work, but kindly do so somewhere else. I've been exiled. Here, that is. Out of sight of the clients. I don't need to be on-site—anyway, the algorithms do most of the work for me. They removed the temptations, see. Dennis can't really get into any mischief out here, or so they think. Aaaand, I said fuck it, why not. Yes, sirs: aye, aye. And I try to behave. We must all be on our best behavior here. Good little citizens. Upright, Institute fellows."

"Must we?"

I'm not worrying about anything, as the chemicals are prohibiting such things. I can feel this protection almost as a woolly barrier, wrapped tightly around my head and chest.

"You are here either of your own volition, or against

your will, but either way, the documents have been signed off on. You agreed to cede control of your life, my friend. The Institute owns your ass. No sense getting upset about it now."

Own what now? What have I agreed to?

"But, Mr. Frobisher—*Percy*—it's not as bad as all that. We all toe the line and all, as much as we are able, but sometimes we slip, and the Institute doesn't know everything, do they. There are some things one can still get away with. See, I am bored. So very bored. You feel it too, the boredom. You are like me. I sense it rolling in waves off of you. You emanate it. A sumptuous . . ." (lingering on each syllable) ". . . nothing."

He's right, of course.

"And I can help there too, I think." Pleased with himself. "I have something you've never tried before."

Now he hops off the counter again and leaves the room.

I'm here alone.

Time passes.

(How does he know what I've tried.)

More time passes.

And then he's back, his closed grin, a little amber bottle in his hand which he shakes like a maraca, saying:

"Yes: I stole them. No: nobody knows. And: you're welcome in advance."

At some point—probably it's much later—I find myself alone in the refectory washroom, standing confrontationally in front of the sink's mirror. (Well, it's now, actually.)

I stick out my tongue, *nyaaaah*, and think: "Who made that face? Was it me? Or *that* guy?"

We both look like shit.

Also, I am remembering that I may have, just a moment ago, thrown up something or other into the toilet. Something troubling. And substantial. Thinking of this makes me want to run back to the stall again, but I force myself to stand there stoically, until the waves of gagging subside.

Gap. Eventually, I unlock my gaze(s), and head out—shaky, joints aching—back to the table.

The good table.

I'm quiet throughout the meal. The Mysterious Woman appears briefly across the room, looks around. Doesn't see what or who she's looking for. The door slams as she leaves. Disputants 1 and 2 hold forth, fractious, uninterruptable. I float on the cadence of their arguments without understanding. No one notices me. I sit there, and I eat.

I eat slowly, mechanically, only to feel now an unyielding shim of paper resisting my molars. I reach into my mouth with a finger, hook it out, sodden, and see that it has words written on it, albeit smudgy ones. Illegible.

Roll it into a small pill, and let it fall to the floor with the other scraps.

Ominous, I think. This paper. Portentous.

Meaning that it does kind of . . . bode.

24

(THE PAPER CONTINUED)

A second sheet of (twenty-pound, five-and-three-eighths-by-eight-and-one-half-inch, felt, off-white) paper dances on a desert breeze, flipping end-over-end, turning in spirals and pirouettes, glissading into the intake end of a fan enclosure at the dome's edge. It is sucked, with a splat, onto the large mesh of the fan's protective screen. DOA.

But shortly after this, a third—twin of both the last one and the one before that—appears, jigs in, before almost slamming into the screen beside its neighbor. It takes a hard right, though, and avoids the fan altogether. It enters the Institute unhindered.

It isn't long then before reams of the stuff start coming in on the wind, out from the desert, sheet after sheet.

The flurry intensifies. A quacking gaggle of white. Ducking, slapping, and weaving in en masse.

Thwack, thwack, thwack.

The turbine's screen, under the mounting paper assault, begins to bend, then buckle. A tear appears in it. Access.

Access for the paper.

It is all coming in.

God knows why.

For better or for worse, the whole catastrophe is on its goddam way.

. . . and I go back there again. I bring odds and ends to the shop: an old eraser from my desk; a pair of my headphones, fraying at the jack; a dulled and scratched-up spoon I smuggled from the refectory. I am continuing to challenge the proprietor's skill. I have become a regular. He never seems surprised to see me. I wonder if it is, in fact, each time, the same shopkeeper (I am not so good at faces) and if, perhaps there are many—though, frankly, it doesn't seem likely. And if there were to be more than one, they all look more or less alike to me (another type: "The Shopkeeper"). I/a/c, my commissions are always accepted. And each time my item is returned to me, either immediately, good as new (whole eraser), or else sent on to the Institute for me, to arrive days later (headphones, spoon). There is seemingly no rhyme or reason as to why some of these things take longer to Same Same than others (a spoon would be easy, one would think). Each new piece of anomalous information makes me crave all the more to know his secret; the secret to his procedures. How is it all accomplished, this arcane monkey business? There must be something the man cannot remake, fix, substitute for?

Last week I dug out a lint-covered pink prescription tablet from the chair cushions back in my room (the ones that flatten me out, smooth the wrinkles, nothing too potent) and I brought my prize all the way into town, trot trot, sheepishly pushing the tiny tribute onto the counter, making the two-times-ten gesture to my man, pushing my palms forward like I'm playing shadow patty-cake, and he squints and picks it up and whatdoyaknow but now I've a score of as-pure-a-hit-of-this-stuff as I've ever sampled. (A chemist? A lab? What the hell is back there? I'm grateful, of course, but what, but how . . . I'll get him eventually. I'll reach the limits of his skills. Find that threshold. And then.)

Is my interest in this silly little native enterprise becoming noticeably close to a mania? Has this mania of mine intensified in direct proportion to my project's stagnation? (The question—of whether the stagnation of my work is caused by my obsession with the Same Same, or whether the obsession is merely a convenient distraction from my work problems—is an open one.) Idk. In any case, I think of ways to defeat the Same Same almost constantly now, and the only impediment to my eventually doing so, at this point, is the status of my quickly dwindling funds. They are significantly depleted.

Of note: on this latest visit, I set a reminder to ask after my missing Fundaments, but when I arrive at the shop, there they are, all thirty-two of them, just sitting plumb center on the counter, as if he knew in advance that I'd ask. And as I am sweeping them up and thanking the man, he reaches out and grabs my wrist. I audibly gasp. (Huanhh!)

After all this time I'd come to think of him as an (I want to say: *insubstantiality?*). But now he's holding me tightly, and it hurts a little.

"*Sorry?*"

Does he want me to pay for them; my own Fundaments, my own ideas?

"But they are mine already," I protest.

He gesticulates wildly.

"And you haven't actually done anything, so why should I—?"

More sign language. Money. More money.

"Here, how's this?"

No. More required.

A substantial outlay.

He insists.

I comply.

And now I'm close to broke.

*

Scratch that. Funds no longer a problem. I am flush, again.

So soon? Just like that?

How, you ask? Nothing simpler.

26

(FROM A GREAT HEIGHT)

In for a penny, in for a pound.

The idea to go to the Freehold Crown Spar was Dennis's. His idea, but I agreed to it; though I am barely recovered from our last get-together.

Here is a solitary receptionist, behind the reception desk, sitting with his back to the street entrance—deeply engaged with something or other, or nodding off even—which is, like, we can't even believe our luck—and so we just inch through the revolving doors and then speed-walk the poorly lit, mufflingly carpeted lobby. No one the wiser.

Anyway, we start on the stairs, and I have been sucking in as much oxygen as I can, inhaling in huge nose-mouth-combos, while trying to keep as silent as I can (neither of us wanting to seem out of breath; to cede that weakness to the other). But Dennis is struggling too, I can tell. I can hear his breathing sure. Also, he is sweating a ton. His uniform, a tiger's pelt of dark blots, big and small. When I reach the landing of the twenty-first floor, half a floor ahead of Dennis, I squint down at him, lagging, and he nods up at me in tacit agreement, and I give an exploratory push on the metal crash-bar affixed to the door marked "Emergency Exit," hoping that it will yield, and hoping it will yield without tripping a building-wide alarm. It holds for a moment before surrendering with a louder-than-expected *kachunk*, and almost mauling my fingers in the process. And then the door swings open. The hallway is dimly lit.

We collapse on the carpet, right there. At this point we are both too winded for shame.

Eventually we have our breath back, and I am about to ask Dennis if perhaps this floor is high enough for our purposes, when he jacks himself up to his feet, looks down at me, and says: "Fuck it."

He walks over to the elevators and pushes the up button. Just like that.

"Dennis—"

"Nobody's here. Haven't you figured that out? The place is abandoned. A ghost hotel."

He's right. I had had the same sense. Of being the only ones. The man at the front desk might be the only true occupant of this crazy fucking megalith. Still. There are always cleaning crews. But my aching legs are complaining so loudly that I can't hear my other concerns over them. So *bing*, there's the elevator, and in we go, and that's how we get up here to floor 187.

The 187th-floor hallway is black. But I can see a door to a single room, facing the elevator. Cracked. So in we go. It turns out there is only one room total on this floor.

A presidential suite, being renovated. Many of the partition walls are incomplete or not even begun. The rooms are separated only by a series of steel framing studs and columns. Basically, an enormous loft space. Wiring tufting out of the wall panels and in some cases hanging down from the ceiling like vines. At the perimeter, all around us, three hundred and sixty degrees of floor-to-ceiling, sheet-glass windows.

The Freehold and its capital city, at night.

Dennis finds a single clamp-on construction lamp, plugs it in, and sticks it up by the vestibule. It is not entirely dark now. We can see a little of the space, but not much. Which means we can still see out of the windows. We walk over to the glass, occasionally stepping on, or inadvertently kicking over various construction detritus. I find a chair wrapped in plastic, and drag it over to the farthest end of the suite and let myself down into it. Dennis pulls up a large industrial bucket, flips it over next to mine, and sits on that. We perch there in silence looking out.

The city is lit, its lights giving the metropolis a structure. An enormous connect-the-dots image of blocks and spires. Don't need to connect the dots actually, as there are just so many of them. Pixels. This time: a high-resolution image.

We hear the hotel groan. It is mournful. Dennis turns to me, makes a series of mock-scary "oogie-boogie" gestures with his hands.

"See? Ghost hotel," he says.

"If no one ever stays here, why don't they just sell it. Or demolish it."

"It's the brand. Doesn't matter if anyone comes. As long as people know it's here."

"But who would know? If they did get rid . . . if nobody ever . . ."

"Good point," he admits.

"Then it would truly be a ghost hotel."

"Faux-tel."

"Quite."

We have a tipple. Drink straight from the bottle, pass it back and forth. Dennis sucking his electric fag in the bottle-less intervals. Feels pretty homey and comfortable. Just two men enjoying a gents' night out. Sitting in almost silence. Oh, and we have his small bottle of pills. The ones he stole. The ones I've heard murmurs of, but never tried. The special ones.

"You've done this before, I presume?" I ask Dennis.

"Once or twice."

"Is it safe?"

"Depends," he replies, throwing back his head to swallow.

"Depends on what?"

"On many things, but mainly, it depends upon how willing you are to experience what you are about to experience."

"Mystical nonsense."

"Nothing mystical or nonsensical about it."

He looks at me, patronizing, places a hand on my shoulder, and pats me a couple of times. Holds out the other hand palm up. Single tablet resting in it.

"Down the hatch, Mr. F. And I'll see you on the other side."

And if it isn't just: The Best Feeling Ever.

I dip in and out, and so, at points I'm occasionally, vaguely, aware of Dennis, shivering beside me, eyeballs spun ceiling-ward. We are conjoined. He's me and I'm him. Both of us no one, and both of us gone. Him, to god knows where; me, to my dreamscapes.

Cold visions. Frozen lands. A steppe, or floe or some such? No, an air-conditioned office. One dream presenting significant personal items, but frozen over and encrusted with a dirty rime. One such frozen item is an old ballpoint pen. And a notepad is another. A tablet. Several vignettes then involving the freezing of a computer monitor. The flatscreen is frozen both literally and operationally. I see through the cloudy ice a crucial notification, a red reminder of an incoming email; a text; a like; a poke; a reminder or rebuke. The incrusting ice prevents my response. Now it is my project which pops up. I can see it—its thin lines of thought—though ice-blurred, as through a cataract. I dream that I defrost the monitor with a hair-dryer, cradle and rock it like a baby animal. After the ice melts the monitor blinks. Just draws down a lazy lid, covers the screen's glossy pupil! Once; twice . . . the lid opens and closes. Languidly, as in a seduction. This stops eventually. We stare at one another, my monitor and I, until I . . .

. . . wake completely, at last, with a jolt, to the chimes of the same device. I'd forgotten that I'd had it. How long had I been out? Rub my eyes. Stretch my limbs.

Find the device.

All the *ping*s I've missed.

I whisper it back to sleep.

Good night, device. Good-bye, *ping*.

Good night, Dennis; good night, e-ve-ry-thing.

Now, later, I hug my knees to my chest and just rock for a little while.

That dream (the cold one, Icymi). What does it portend?

Nothing? I am seeing patterns in everything. My vatic nerve, my interpretational gland, is enflamed, engorged, hypersensitive. Dreams. I don't do dreams. There are no signs here—no omens. The cold is no metaphor, nor is the heat. The Freehold doesn't map. A metastructure is not a signifier. Nothing indexed; nothing allegorical. One doesn't (or shouldn't) do dreams . . . it's facile. Obviously.

I notice that Dennis isn't next to me anymore. I haul myself up. Painfully. Where the . . .

"*Et exspecto resurrectionem mortuorum*," Mr. Royal calls out, emerging from a hallway, uniform gone from the waist up.

"Dennis."

"Welcome back to the land of the living."

"How long," I ask, as it seems the sun is rising. Must have been out all night.

"Eight hours? Nine?"

"The fuck."

"Yeah. Didn't want to wake you."

"Dennis, the Institute, my meetings—"

"Looks like you just played hooky, doesn't it."

(Miss Fairfax must be spitting.)

Dennis Royal sits now on the floor of the hotel room; his missing shirt has turned up as an ad hoc do-rag around his head. His face is looking a tad paralytic; stunned in that post-brain-fuck kind of way. I can only imagine what mine looks like.

He helps himself to the last of the alcohol in the bottle. Giving it a couple of final taps into his baby bird's upward-facing mouth.

"We'll need to make a beverage run."

My head is suffering compression, as if it were a bathysphere at extreme depth, and catching my reflection, I see that the window-glass of my eyes is beginning to spider under the strain.

"I'm not going anywhere," I reply, "at least not . . . ugh. For a bit."

"Not to worry, Frobisher ole pal, I will venture out. Try some lower floors. See if we can't find something we need. Some minibar-jacking is in order, I believe."

"Dennis."

"Yes?"

"The visions I had last night—"

"You get those. That's the whole point, though, isn't it. The weird shit. You should expect some more of it.

Cramps. Shakes. A few other side effects. Btw." (He says: "bee-tee-dubs.")

One hand pats my shoulder again, and he sticks his palm out in exact duplication of thirty hours ago. The same.

"Go again?"

*

How much later I do not know, still periodically surging with cortical excitement, I get up and circumnavigate the suite, a new suite, several floors up. The highest floor in the Spar. We wandered upward at some point. This room, the twin of the last. I find another PVC bucket, one that neither of us has vomited into, and drag it over to the window, place it right up against the glass, where I stand upon it. As of this moment, I am the highest person in the Freehold. Maybe on the entire planet. Probably. Up there, on my bucket. My masterful perspective. My regal perspective. The world is (The end of the phrase comes to me: "on a table." I'm not sure what kind of table, but this is what it feels like. "The world on a table.").

I relish it. I take some deep breaths. Reach up and touch the ceiling. Muse.

I imagine spending the remainder of my tenure at the Institute right here, as a kind of Stylite. An ascetic on the 210th floor of a hotel tower in the desert. Dennis will bring me food and drink—Dennis, my new Tea Boy—but I don't exchange another word with anyone else and I won't set foot on terra firma ever again. I am revered as a saint. *The*

Hermit of the Spar. Plumbing the depths of all of life's enig-mas aided by remoteness and sheer immobility. Pilgrims will come. They will sit at the foot of my bucket—attend my act of extreme sanctimony. "How does one step off of a one-hundred-foot pole?" As the koan has it. (One bloody well doesn't. I suppose is the point.)

My mind casts itself around the space, surveying the vast desert and the city below me, alert to all its details, familiarizing myself with its every nook and cranny, its minutiae, each topographic point of interest like a small rise or valley or clump of buildings below me, preening in the immaculate reflections of their neighbor's surfaces; and behind, the floor of the world, spread out like a series of mismatched carpet samples. From my summit, I look at the distant horizon. I create a mental catalog of all the landmarks, interesting structures, color variations, blem-ishes or stains upon the land, scratches on the glass itself, and other quirks both accidental/superficial and structural/ architectural. I perform an intricate taxonomic, morpho-logical, and geographic mapping of space, overlaying the scene with a cartographic grid. Labeling it all in my mind with type and pictograms, in Helvetica bold, with red lined routes, black circles, crosses, and asterisks. I do this until I am lulled into a torpor, dozing. I lean my head up against the glass. And then my cheek. The glass is cool.

Time passes.

*

A philosophical meditation on Time, its elastic, subjective, and ineffable nature—especially notable when under the influence of certain unprescribed narcotics—to be indicated by dashes

--- ------ - ----- ----- -- -- ---- - - ----- --- - ---- -- -- ------- -- -- ---
- - - - - -- - ---- -- -- ------- -- -- --- - - - - - -- - ---- -- -- ------- -- --
--- - - - - - ------- --- -- -- ---- - --- ------- -- -- ---- - - - ----- --- -
---- -- -- ------- -- -- ---- - - - - - -- - ---- -- - - ------- -- -- - - - - - -
- - - - --- - - - - - -- - ---- -- -- - -- ---- -- -- --- - - - - - ------- - --
-- --- -- -- --- - - - - - -- - ---- -- - - ------- -- -- --- - - - - - -- - ----
-- -- --- ---- -- -- --- - - - - ---- - ---- -- -- ------- -- -- --- - - - - -
-- - ---- -- -- ------- -- -- --- - - - - - -- - ---- -- -- ------- -- -- ---- - -
- - - ------- --- -- -- ---- - --- ------- -- -- ---- - - - ----- --- - ---- --
-- ------- -- -- ---- - - - - - -- - ---- -- - - ------- -- -- --- - - - - - ------
-- - - - --- -- -- --- - - - - - -- - ---- -- - - -- ---- -- -- --- - - - - -
-------- - -- ----- -- -- --- - - - - - - - -- - ---- -- - - ---- --- -- -- --- - -
- - - -- - ---- -- -- --- ---- -- -- --- - - - - ---- - ---- -- -- ------- -- --
--- - - - - - -- - -- - - - - - - - - - - - - - - - - - - ---- - - - - - -- -
---- -- -- ------- -- -- --- - - - - - -- - ---- -- -- ------- -- -- --- - - - - -
-------- --- -- -- ---- - --- -----

I lean forward, and squeakily write a few words in my breath's condensation on the glass with a finger, and then step off of my high watch. First, tentatively with one foot, then, more securely, with the other. I feel my weight beneath me, which feels superb, and, with nothing better to do now, I walk back over to Mr. Royal, still prone. Give him a poke with my still-stockinged toe. I hope he's alive.

Turn around to look out the window one last time and see the city, through gray, blurred, unreadable words, dripping slowly down the large glass pane.

Somewhere, on the other side of these words, deep in the urban sprawl, is my Same Same store. I imagine the proprietor bent to his work, and, remembering him, feel for the wad of bills in my pocket.

I doubted he would do it, but he did.

I doubted it *could* work, but it did.

Just as I imagined it. Holy hell.

I'm in the money now. Loaded, in fact. And the money looks exactly right.

When the blocky package arrived at my flat, I thought I would find only play-money inside, some kind of flimsy scrip. That I would rub on the paper, and it would become transparent. But it hasn't. It's real. Bang on. Right down to the smell of the inks and the texture of the stock. He did it again.

Now, everything under the dome is paid for already. So I haven't any real opportunity or need to pass this counterfeit, other than at the shop itself, which, ironically, could be considered a true test of the Same Same's efficacy. I will try this experiment out soon—to see whether the S.S. man will accept his own handiwork as proper payment for further work.

And if so: well then.

*

Sun is going down over the bay to my left. The building is still moaning. Dennis and I are passing his vape back and forth. Sucking on this glorified thumb drive. I don't smoke anymore, but here we are.

He is sitting in full-lotus back on the floor. I'm trying the posture too, and my crossed legs have cramped up severely. Can't tell which leg is which, here. Which I presume is partially the point. I'm just counting breaths, as I've been taught. In, out. In, out. I listen to the air humming in the air ducts, at first to the soothing constancy of that block of low-level noise, which becomes, over time, not just louder but less constant, patterns emerging, swells and hiccups, overtones dancing around the higher registers. A fighter jet comes streaking smoothly along the sky leaving no mark behind it. Tiny little oil tankers sit immobile out in the bay. A few microscopic vehicles drift along the white superhighways. The clouds take their time. Merge, come apart. Flares bounce around off buildings and lagoons. Every minute the city below changes color, slightly.

I am nothing but an atmospheric density. A field of meaning.

Boredom, and then an outlandish contentment roll through me.

Sleep.

*

Ping!

They are looking for us.

Time to go back.

Ping!

Okay already.

Ping!

Ping!Ping!

Wtf. What the actual fu—

"All good?" Dennis asks, sluggish, levered up onto an elbow.

"Not really."

"What's—"

"Device," I say, turning the offending technology this way and that. "Malfunctioning."

"You really should get that looked at."

"No kidding."

Ping!Ping!Ping!

"There it goes again."

"Calm down, Percy."

Ping!Ping!Ping!Ping!Ping!Ping!Ping!Ping!Ping!Ping!Ping! Ping!Ping!Ping!

*

And so here we are and I am now hitting my device with a hammer which I found in a toolkit in a janitor's closet by the front door. Hit it, hit, hit. Hit it. Hit. It.

Over and over, again, and again and again.

The proprietary structure is incredibly durable and my hand begins to ache before even a dent is made.

Eventually, a dent *is* made—a tiny little pockmark. Not

enough, so more bludgeoning. My blisters begin to scream and the head of the hammer begins to loosen off of its wooden stem and I am out of breath again.

"Percy, what the fuck. You are going to regret this later."

"Shut (Hit) up (Hit) Dennis (Hit)."

Finally, the device succumbs to this brutality and winks out.

Piiiioiioinoinnnkblurp.

(Hit. One last, for good measure.)

Dead as a polished stone. I stand over it, red-faced, sweaty, deshabilled, murderous.

There is a period of panting. Watching. Satisfied that the device is gone-zo, I lie down on the spot, and curl up.

*

"Percy."

"Go away."

"Percy, I think we need to hit the road."

"I'm asleep."

"Get up."

I rub my eyes, look around. Daytime. Though I don't know which day.

I roll over, onto something sharp. Gah! A piece of plastic or glass. Little shards are all around me.

"What's all this crap?" I ask. A disgusting smell from my mouth leaks into my nose.

"That's your device, genius. Get ready. We're leaving."

*

We bustle through the Spar's lobby and push through the revolving doors. Dennis, shirtless, barely keeping up, bleating complaints steadily from behind me, the lobby attendant barking in a foreign tongue after us. The car was there, autonomously, pulling up for us at the roundabout. Shit, forgot about the sun again, which even as it sets is blinding; shades on. Hurl ourselves into the seats and slam the doors.

We ease out of the lot with a slowness which seems designed to frustrate. I kick the seat back in front of me in helpless frustration. I whisper the vehicle up faster and faster, though there are of course controls and tolerances in place for safety reasons and there is only so much recklessness it will allow. Still: fairly fast. Now it takes a wide corner and Dennis leans into me.

"Sorry."

"Don't touch me, please."

"What's your deal with that thing, Percy?"

"It's broken."

"Or you are," he stage whispers.

"Not now, Dennis."

"Don't blame me. If you hate the sound of it so much, just let the goddam thing die already."

"I need it."

"Ah, dependency. An abusive dependency. Well, that much I can understand. And so where is this godforsaken mechanic of yours?"

"Almost there."

The device sits in the hollow of my lap, lies there in a

helpless state. Choked out. Throttled like a small animal. I've hit the power node on it, and it seems to be trying, gamely, to come back to life. It moans, and gutters, and whines with ragged breath. This frightens me somehow more than its total demise.

*

Honestly, worst case, the device is completely fragged, what would it matter? What would I miss out on there, exactly?

My contacts? Who would I contact Rn? There's no more contact to be had.

What would I "like"? Who would I "like"? Whose face and time would I face/time: family, friends? Nah.

(Dennis looking out his window. Dunes easing by.)

But my personal history is in there. Compressed, somewhere in its mysterious solidity. Records. My memory; in its memory. Its memory; my memory. Places I've been. Things I've done. Little things I've jotted down for myself, reminders, prods, thoughts for future projects. Threads. The photos. Those things the device and I have seen. My precious picture of Miss Fairfax. Secrets. The device is the only record of the me whom only I know. My private self. Can I give that up?

Dennis says, absently, to the car window: "You know, Percy, something's not right with you. You've got *problems*, sir."

I am not a monster. These lives—device-lives—are to be lives lived with impunity, in private. No-price, no-cost lives; no-guilt lives. This is where we all do such things, in the whisper-world. And we leave them there, in a smog of willful amnesia. The device is exactly the repository of that which needs to be kept locked away or forgotten—this privacy is the very meaning of the device. Who would recognize the distinction between thought and action without such a space? If such a locale didn't exist? Otherwise these thoughts would be let loose on the world—free to roam the meatspace. We would need a whole new ethics. Everything would change.

(Gap.)

Why is the car so slow?

(Gap.)

My eyes are itching like nobody's business, there is a spot on each of them, in the soft tissue, where the corner of the eye meets the base of my nose, that is on fire. I wedge my fingers in there, and spin them back and forth, one eye after another, trying to alleviate the irritation.

"Let me look at it," Dennis asks, tired of pouting. I hand the device to him in a conciliatory gesture, knowing there is nothing he can see there.

"Poor little lamb," he says, stroking it.

"Give it back now."

The vehicle decelerates and stops, door locks pop automatically.

He places the device back on the seat and I snatch it up.

"Go on, Dennis. I'll find my own way back."

I'm on the run, but I turn my head back one last time to

make sure he's leaving, and I see the car close its own doors before Dennis can utter the bon mot I'm sure he has all ready in the chamber, and now I barrel straight into someone. We tumble to the rough macadam, tangled up in one another.

A woman in a suit, a headscarf, and large sunglasses. She's dropped one of her many bags. A thermos clangs along the ground.

"Look where you are going!" she bleats, rubbing an elbow.

Now the hum of the car, with Dennis in it, setting out. He's probably laughing his ass off in there. W/e. The woman is still swearing, as she collects her effects from the hot cement. She refuses the hand I offer her. I can't stand around here forever.

"Sorry!" I yell behind me, sprinting away.

*

Same buildings, same city, same street corner. Same heat, same walk, same avenues, streets and lanes and overpasses, same alley, same door, same . . .

*

"Hello . . . *hello?*"

There are no sounds at all from behind the wall. I stand in the fluorescence, and then I remember the black rubber mat, set my mismatched feet on it and hear that synthesized bell, and the door opens, and out he comes; the man again. I have a fleeting glimpse of his large and expressive eyes. He moves as slowly and smoothly as an astronaut. Finally reaches the counter, and looks askance.

"Hello again," I say.

He nods once. Points at me.

"Yes, it is me," I reassure him.

He continues poking his finger in the air toward me. Rather vehemently. (Obviously it is hard to see what is going on here as I am trying to look downward, as instructed.)

"Yes, yes. Hello, me. Yes, Again. Never mind. Never mind. But, excuse me, this is a matter of some urgency." I hold up the device in my hands, as if it were a goldfish in a two-palmed well of water. He looks down at it and back up at me. And down at the device again.

"Can you?"

I place the device gently onto the counter, the device briefly lights up, as if in protest, a last plea for me to halt the surgery which will surely take place, before it slips, acquiescing, back into its vegetative brain-death. I look up, and the man seems so familiar to me now, I don't mean from my last visit; rather, it is almost like I know him from before, from elsewhere. I'm suffering from my recurring strain of déjà vu.

But I quickly look down again. I pull some money out, my new money, *his* money. Put the money on the counter, point at the device.

"Same Same."

His brow creases for a moment, but I can't tell what/if he is thinking.

"Can you, just—"

He looks down, and then up at me again.
"Same Same?"

(THE PAPER CONTINUED)

One of the papers which has recently gained egress into the metastructure is currently sailing down a dark corridor. Heading deeper into the Institute's Security Center.

Now (in this next scene) this piece of paper flies through another set of double doors weaving like a swallow, following another turn, and another. It banks right, to swing into a new space, where the Director watches a set of monitors. He doesn't come here often, to the surveillance core. He has underlings, deputies who can perform these tasks for him. (Not to mention the recognition-and-analysis code which takes care of looking out for most signs of trouble—the algorithms are the real watchdogs here.) But occasionally, he will wander from his office, going ponderously down the back stairwell, and waddle into the Business Center's lower levels to have a peek. Especially when he knows no one else is on duty and the screens are unmanned. The spectacle of Institute activity as displayed on the large monitor array is calming to him. All those closed-circuit videos: they provide him with a feeling which is, at its core, deeply ambiguous if nonetheless pleasurable. The ambiguity springs from this: watching the screens provides the Director with a sense of his own insignificance, his "thinness-on-the-ground," his near invisibility. This feeling arises, while watching the monitors, as he realizes that the world goes on without him; that he isn't needed. But simultaneously, and in almost direct opposition to this first feeling, he also feels powerful when watching the screens. Omnipresent! Somehow these two feelings combine to reinvigorate him whenever life at the Institute becomes overly dull.

The paper knows nothing of this of course, and it scrimmages with the ceiling fan above the head of the Director, the Director: who is actually, this time, here on business, not pleasure, and so is especially focused on the task at hand, and therefore does not notice the paper above him.

He is here, it turns out, to watch a particular feed.

Something bad is taking place. Though, frankly, it could be worse. He's seen a lot worse. He sits down in his especially large, reinforced swivel chair, and then whispers up an enlargement of the feed.

"ENHANCE."

The video goes full screen, across all the mirrored, tethered devices.

On it, there are two men, half-dressed, wilding around an unfinished room in an abandoned building they definitely should not be occupying, with a bottle of liquor, a couple of spoons, a credit card, a bunch of pills they definitely should not be in possession of.

The Director stops it, rewinds it, and watches it again.

Meanwhile, the paper flits around above his head like a moth.

(SHAMEFUL SUGGESTIONS)

I don't make it back to the Institute until the thin light of evening. I feel utterly exhausted. And don't even make it to the door without having to sit down by the pool, which is apparently no longer properly refrigerated; algae smudging the late, high-waterline like a green, pastel rubbing. I can't make out the industrious robot vacuum because of the fading light and the growing murk, but I know it's down there, still performing its exploration of the pool's bottom. Despite how unappetizing the pool looks, I kick off my shoes, and sit on the slender diving board which is rough like a tongue, and dangle my legs so that just the tips of my toes skim the surface of the scummy water. As I make series after series of concentric ripples, I wonder once again about the contents of my device, begin again to run through the perverse outings it has accompanied me on, and shudder anew. I am grateful now that my reflection, on this occasion, is lost in the murk.

"Mr. Frobisher."

Miss Fairfax's arms are crossed so I can see the delicate vein-work in her compressed forearms. Dead frown. Grabs my elbow, tugs me, brusquely, in the door and closes it behind us. We are facing one another in the vestibule. In silence for a moment during which I realize that I'm standing in a small pile of paper, which I kick aside.

She looks down, and back again, pushing the glasses rather violently back up to the bridge of her nose.

"Care to explain yourself, Percy? How did you get a hold of those scrips?"

"Wait."

"And trespassing? Destruction of property?"

"How do you—"

"There's been a meeting, the subject of which is your tenure here."

"I'm making progress."

"What you keep making is a mess of everything."

"I don't want to leave."

"Don't you?"

"I lost my head."

"Jesus, how could you idiots do such a thing?"

She pulls her glasses off altogether, and starts poking them at me, punctuating her statements now with little stabs, in what is a hitherto unseen escalation of glasses-based semaphore. I always am amazed at the transformation when glasses come off—how a person looks so innocent, and vulnerable, masks and armor and eyesight removed. She looks at the moment a bit like an infuriated baby owl.

"They've put you on probation, Percy. And you will be handing over your identity papers to the Director."

"But you can't do that."

And I am shocked at her disappointment. At the investment of one human agent in the affairs of another. My affairs; that my affairs, which should have been sealed off, linked up, have been allowed to leak. Me, to leak, to leach. I didn't want for/didn't ask for: this. Never wanted it. We exchanged what we exchanged, Miss Fairfax and I, but there was never a compact of complete forfeiture. Idk. Never mind, it doesn't matter. What does, what does matter quite a bit: is that I am being grounded. What a cock-up. What a fucking fiasco.

"It is private, Miss Fairfax," I plead, "what I do with my time," thinking: at least I get to stay though. At least I can stay.

"What the *hell* are you talking about: private?"

"It's my life. Mine."

She looks at me like I'm nuts.

"Mine," and as the words leave my lips, I involuntarily wince.

27

(ANALYSIS)

"And where do you think you are going?"

Having just opened the glass doors of the Residential Enclave, I feel someone's hand on my shoulder. I turn around to face the resident admin.

"For a walk," I answer, as nonchalantly as possible. I can smell the park and nature trails.

The doors behind me whoosh, then click closed.

"Have you finished that assignment? You're a week overdue. Perhaps you could take your walk another time, Percy."

The hand (firm, authoritative) takes my arm now, and I'm led back down the corridor.

Back in my room, I collect a couple of sheets of paper and a pen from the desk (NB no pens in pockets anymore) and flop down on the bed, ready to begin.

I grab the top of the pen and pull. The cap gives way with a little click, and I flip the pen over in a deft motion, examine it closely to ensure there is no more leakage. It's good to have my trusty pen working properly again. I stick the pen's top on the back end. I now take the thickest of the

Institute brochures from the bedside table and rest it on my knees. I then take the stack of paper and place this on top of the brochure. Now, I place the nib of the pen down, gently, on the topmost piece of paper—about a fifth or a sixth of the way from the top of the page vertically, and inside of the left side margin. Holding the pen in the intersection between my index finger, pointer, and thumb, I begin to curl my index finger, apply a slight downward pressure on the shaft of the pen, using the pad of my thumb as a fulcrum. As a result, the pen's nib begins to drag toward me. I feel the resistance of the paper's pulp fighting the tip and hear a small scratching. A downward stroke of the nib is slowly accomplished, leaving a short blue line in its wake. I have now written the number "1" in the left-hand margin.

(The work I have to do would be easier to write and format on my device, but sadly . . . and now I wonder when I will have it back again.)

I have so many of these stupid-ass assignments to complete; they are meted out constantly. I'm told that they are meant to facilitate my project, but I am beginning to suspect that a majority of them are inflicted on me as punishment. The tasks are small, but it's death by a thousand cuts. If only they'd leave me alone I could crack my project wide open.

Last week, for instance, I was told that I needed to make a list of all my physical routines. Lord knows what for. But as the man said, I'm late on this one.

Gotta start.

Most of my recent assignments are like this. Simple—insultingly so—but mandatory. Generally, I am asked, in these assignments, to account for everything I think and do, and I do so in the form of lists.

The Institute loves a list.

Lists of appointments, lists of accomplishments, lists of failures, lists of social interactions, lists of the foods I eat, lists of the hours I sleep, lists of my variable heart rates and blood pressures. Lists of things I say, lists of my dreams and bowel movements, even lists of the lists I've made.

And now, of course, there is also someone with me almost all the time. Admins, staffers (various). They go with me everywhere—to my Groups, to my workshops. There's one of them presiding over each and every meal I attend. The only place where I am alone is my rooms. Not that the admins threaten or molest me in any way. The admins are just always there. The whole affair is suffocating.

And as if I needed another reminder of what could be in store for me, what perils might be lurking within the Institute's perimeter, last night there was yet another incident out on the lawns—an incident which I witnessed from my balcony—in which a person was confronted in some manner by some kind of dark mob. "That could have been me," I remember thinking, as I squinted out into the night, visualizing the entire scenario, beginning to end, as if it *had* been me, before backing up into the room again, latching the sliding doors and drawing the curtain.

Perhaps I should bolt while I can.

I can, after all, leave. Why wouldn't I?

Funny though, I can't summon the will, moreover: the desire.

What would I do out there, even? Out of the flatlands and back, hidden among the hills. Anonymous again. Who would have me?

Yet the very idea that I *wouldn't be able* to leave, that my passport will be taken from me, that I'll be called to forfeit my freedom at the behest of some shadowy council . . .

What if the answer—the particular answer to this particular quandary—is one which has been presenting itself to me incessantly since the moment of my arrival here, everything inclining me toward it? Every sign, word, every person, object, and gesture pushing me? There *is* something I can do. I am slippery and cunning and . . . I will not be held! Which is to say that they can take my identity booklet, my papers. My passport. They can take it. Fine. Because what if I have two of them?

Tbd.

And the project?

The project?

I thought a lot about the Fundaments again today. Having them back has been nice. Periodically I'll read all thirty-two of them over again and feel, for a moment, confident, as if my life had a program. A runnel through which to move. A channel to broadcast on. It is interesting that I gain a modicum of relief from these documents of mine, given that they are predicated upon knowledge which is, itself, derived from long-standing creative struggle. Pain, in a sense. Without such difficulties, it occurs, these Fundaments would not exist at all. I have sacrificed. There has been a cost, a price paid. But does the Institute take such factors into consideration? Do they commend me for these hard-won Fundaments? No, no they don't. Yet the Fundaments must count for something. I continue to wonder if they are—the Fundaments themselves—the entire purpose of the project. Time will tell, I suppose.

Time will tell.

And I wait for "time to tell" by standing by the window again, as, now, the day marches on, and I am looking out Rn, out and over, and in a palm right above where another attack lately took place, I can see a white shape stuck to one of the fronds, and that white shape hovers between: *whitehawk* and *grocery bag*.

Bag and bird. Bird; bag.

Now trash, now not.

No amount of scrutiny will tip the scales.

Bag, bird. Bird, Bag.

(Paper?)

DAILY PHYSICAL ROUTINES

1.   *Sitting (erect/slumped)*

      ꓮ   peering . . .

          i. . . . at the project itself
          ii. . . . at the middle distance

       iii. . . . at eternity

       iv. . . . at my palm, which is where my device would ordinarily be

       v. . . . down double-barrels of surefire disaster

b. head in hands—common

c. penis in hand—less common (but only marginally)

d. knees in hands—rare

e. feet in hands—rarer

f. at desk

g. on desk

h. under desk

i. on floor

j. in public place (Garden, plinth, Presence Center, Library, so on etc.)

k. in private place (My roof. My regal thoughts, looking down from my regal perspective. My balcony, mostly. Seeing what there is to see)

l. on public toilet

m. up in bed, that influential novel I've been reading, heavy in my lap. I'm trying to add some more pages to my total-pages-read tally. I've promised I'd get a minimum of four pages read every day, and I am keeping up, but I'll be damned if I'm retaining any of it

n.   on floor of public toilet

o.   head in hands, staring down barrels of surefire disaster, on floor of public toilet. The tiles are cool and wet and the smell is faux-lime and atrocious. I cannot even remember now the smell of the tree-limes out in the meatspace

2.   *Walking*

a.   a specific path (on a journey)

b.   just: around (in a fog)

c.   on or near high ledge (in despair)

d.   pacing

e.   pacing

f.   pacing

g.   pacing

h.   (etc.)

3. *Running*

    a.   away (common)

    b.   toward (rare)

    c.   in a pile of paper. I put a single sheet over my face, and occasionally blow on it, and it rises and falls again, gentle. Repeat until it gets too hot and itchy under there.

4. *Lying*

    a.   face upward (common)

    b.   face downward (rare)

    c.   body downward, head upward (impossible)

5. *Standing*

    a.   at desk

    b.   over project

    c.   under project

    d.   back from project in order to assess it, usually through a single squinted eye

    e.   under Sword of Damocles

    f.   before a mirror, in thrall to the uncanny

6. *Crouched*

   a.   to spring into action

   b.   to shield oneself from blows

7. *Hanging*

   a.   out

   b.   ten

   c.   by a thread

   d.   from hands from a bar which is how some people do chin-ups, but I just hang there sometimes

   e.   from feet (gravity boots), which is how I saw someone in a movie once do sit-ups. Jk I don't do this, nobody does

   f.   from neck until dead (not me, obvs, but, one fellow, several weeks ago. In her closet, of all places & you'd think there wouldn't be enough room, side to side, but also, vertically, from the knot of the noose to the, the overripe blueberries which are now the tips of her swollen toes. The admin in his shock at this discovery left the flat's door open and so we all crowded around the narrow doorway, jostling to see, and some got a look in while others craned but no go. This may have been a dream though, Idk.)

8. *Looking*

    a.   Outward

    b.   Inward

    c.   Both @ same time

9. *Speaking*

    a.   loudly

    b.   quietly

    c.   into a jawbone mic, like at a Discourse™. This is speaking quietly and loudly, simultaneously. And though I am far from taking my turn at a Discourse™, I am allowed, periodically, to practice in my room and have even been given guidelines about how to construct one; the timings and intonations, etc. A Discourse™. Sigh. Soon, I hope

    d.   about something, or someone

    e.   about oneself

    f.   to oneself

    g.   to oneself, about oneself (worst case)

10. *Expressing*

    a.   Pensive (chin—>hand)

    b.   Generally dramatic (eyes—>sky)

    c.   Ashamed (eyes—>floor)

    d.   Offended (crossed arms)

    e.   At peace (smile, eyes shining)

    f.   At the edge of a precipice (frown, eyes shining)

    g.   Dangerous (really big smile, eyes shining)

    h.   Inert (. . .)

    i.   Disapproving (hands on hips)

    j.   Confident (steeple-fingers)

    k.   Working through (brow wrinkled)

    l.   Troubled (brow furrowed)

    m.   Lying (dartin' eyes)

    n.   Sardonic (close-lipped smile, eyes rolled back)

    o.   Perverted (wink)

    p.   Etc., etc. (there are a lot more of these)

11. *Misc. Other Exercise*

    a.   Sweating

    b.   Clenching

    c.   Panting

    d.   Tapping on my open palm, as if it contained my absent device; speaking to my cupped palm, as if it contained said absent device

    e.   Fending off (a fellow, recently. He was kind of shuffling down one of the Pleasure Center's nerve-line hallways toward me—the whole thing was so strange Imho—and I thought he was the Media Theorist, but he didn't seem to recognize me, and the next thing I know he's speaking in a loud and borderline aggressive fashion at me and actually kind of physically "in my zone" as it were, so I have to kind of almost wrestle him off, and if the whole attack was in fact a *prompt*, then it was simultaneously too subtle for understanding and too violent not to jar me completely. So: ineffectual)

    f.   Providing and receiving prompts. Every day I learn more about how these provocations function. Mr. Al'Hatif explains that, though some prompts are given intentionally (as in the attack mentioned above in *Misc. Other*

Exercise, Letter e), some prompts occur spontaneously, at random. In fact, any occurrence at all could be seen as a potential creative stimulus. "Let's say," Ousman continues, "that you were to meet someone who is *not* a fellow . . . say, if you accidentally collided with a random woman on the winding streets of a foreign city . . . she falls to the ground, you help her up . . . this could be seen as a challenge to work that particular stranger's imagined life and interiority into your project in some manner or other."

"Could the providing of the prompt *itself* be a prompt?" I ask him. And he shrugs. "Only if your project were a project *about projects*."

g.   Water aerobics (at 4:00 in the gym)

h.   W/ Miss Fairfax: she pushes on me, and I resist, and then I push on her, and she resists, so it isn't all that sexy when I really consider it, and as she's been fairly cross recently these exercises have taken on a more aggressive flavor. Still though

i.   Push-ups. I'm up to twenty. (Jk I can do ten, but plan on rapid improvement)

j.   Apologizing (I do this every day in a variety of ways. Contrition is hard, especially when faked, but I am determined to win Miss Fairfax back over. I have to. I will)

k.   Feeling outrage. I am just tucking back into that enormous (enormously tedious and difficult) novel I am, obstinately, against my better judgment, *still* attempting to read, when I find another piece of paper stuck in between the pages. It must have flown in my balcony window like the others and wedged itself in there. Where are the cleaning crews? Where is the bloody maid? What has become of all decorum here? Pps. "Time Will Tell": possible Fundament? (Imagine the coming world)

l.   Chemical withdrawal (fuck you, Dennis). My right cheek is dull-aching something dreadful both cheeks actually and I realize that I've clamped my teeth down hard, I'm breathing like a saw, cutting a log, and I need . . . but can't . . .

28

(THE PAPER CONTINUED)

The paper is back on the desk. It's come a long way to get here, but it seems content to just do nothing.

A window is open, so an occasional breeze riffles a corner of it. But not enough to budge the paper from its position (parallel to each of the desk's sides and equidistant from all its edges). Disappointing.

Time passes, during which lots is happening *around* the paper. Directly under the paper. Under the desk, to be precise. Here's a man. He's curled up in there, in the desk's dark underpass, hugging himself fiercely, sweating furiously, breathing in shallow gasps, incapable of satiation. Some severe need has seized him up. He's swearing. His eyes look thick and rheumy. His nose is running, and he's yawning, compulsively, like a nervous cat.

He's got a small orange bottle in his fist. It's empty, but he's trying, stupidly, to lick some of the thin powder, the pills' residue, out of its insides. The bottle is stuck on his tongue now.

He pulls it off with an audible *plop*.

(*Plop!*)

He lies back down, and simply moans for a spell.

(THE DISPUTE)

The refectory; breakfast at the Good Table. Disputant 1 and Disputant 2 are at it again. And just listen to them go.

Few people present can follow the dispute: Disputant 1's line of reasoning is confusing, and Disputant 2's equally elusive. But they prattle on and on. It is all agonizingly dense. Not only is the quarrel impenetrable, but it seems intentionally so. One has the sense that these dialogical thickets are like hedge mazes, built to get lost in. That is to say that there is a vague consensus among us listeners that the argument between the Disputants is being presented for our benefit, and that some sort of higher signification is being lent to the difficult proceedings. We fellows who listen in just can't quite get at what that signification is, though it is on the tips of our tongues.

In the end, everyone at the Good Table becomes very, very bored, and simply drifts off, though I stay behind to ponder the eternal argument. After positing (and then rejecting) several alternative rationales, I begin to believe that the dispute between Disputant 1 and Disputant 2 is being enacted not in order to resolve the particular question at hand, nor to draw up ideological battle lines in relation to this particular question, but, rather, the whole thing is performed in order to carry out a theater: a theater of boredom. A performative boredom.

Boredom is the exemplary state for fomenting a hyper-awareness of time. Time: its flexibility; its hazy, labile, variable nature. For this reason (I'm guessing)—in order to turn our thoughts to the passage perception of time—the arguing pair, Disputant 1 and Disputant 2, create and mount: boredom events. (It could, in fact, be said of both of them that they should be called "the Boredom Artists," rather than the appellations they are known by, but, had they advertised their intention to bore us, no one would have attended their events, and the very point of the debates would have been missed.) Once I realize that we are not so much suffering through their arguments as much as we are attending their open studios, I begin to enjoy their fractious company. It can be said that so far, their performances have been very successful, not due to the one (and only one fellow; me) who has understood the purpose of the thing, but, rather, due to that majority who don't understand— those who feel, in their very marrow, the tedium of listening to them—their monotonous dialectic—and who, irritated, leave the field of battle and continue on with their days.

These boredom-susceptible listeners are the work's intended audience, and they have received—if not consciously—the message behind Disputant 1 and Disputant 2's project. I see behind the curtain, now, and so can no longer participate

The admin next to me is not even paying attention,

though. Scrolling her device like she despises it (or the arguing couple).

Or the rest of us? Do they resent us—the admins? Do they dislike their charges?

I'm certainly no one's favorite. Nm, as the big news, here on Team Percy, is that I have successfully pulled one over on the admins with my most recent trip to the Same Same shop. There was a hubbub of some stripe during a meal, and I seized the moment. No one saw me sneak away, and, well, mission accomplished. My identity papers have been properly delivered. When I dropped my papers down on the counter, my Same Same man did not even blink. Swept the passport up, and it is out of my hands now. I will have it back again soon; and when I do, I'll have it back twofold, so to speak, so the risk will have paid off.

I simply need to wait.

I am assuming that I won't need to hand my passport over to the Director in the next few days. A gamble to be sure. But, if I *am* asked to give up my booklet—god forbid—my plan is to stall. I can just stall. Stall, stall, stall. I'm good at stalling. Good at speaking around a topic.

"Yes. Yes, you are," Mr. Al'Hatif mutters.

(I SEE IT!)

Noon in the Arts Pavilion, and the work on display is uninspiring. Self-indulgent. There are plenty of installations—

things flung about in otherwise empty white rooms. A few pieces made of wood and steel, a few made from dust and other forms of debris, while others are made of light: diodes, pixels, videotape. These visuals are so imitative of one another that I wonder if they are all made by the same artist. But no: different works by different fellows, who must all belong to the same school. All of the films looping in the lobby consist of the artists themselves performing their daily activities—eating, exercising, napping, speaking, yawning, kneeling, walking, etc., etc.—but now, framed on the monitors, each of these actions is elevated through being rendered aesthetic. And so we watch the monitors as gallery-goers, rather than (I want to say: voyeurs?). None of it interests me particularly, though I spend what I hope to be the requisite time looking, and asking the requisite questions of the artists:

"How did you arrive at your ideas?" "How long did it take to accomplish?"

So on. (The usual.)

There are also several works of collage, mostly made from tattered magazines, printouts, newspapers, works-in-progress composed entirely of images appropriated from other sources; works by other fellows. Some of these artists had never drawn an original line—not a one.

"Theft? Plagiarism?" I ask, palpitating the notion, and wondering, for a brief moment, if such a practice of collage wouldn't work just as well for a . . . never mind. No one is listening anyway.

Many other pieces are so highly conceptual that I cannot even begin formulating responses. Only one set of works-in-progress truly interests me, and this is a set of intimate portraits, painted in ghostly shades of gray, upon black canvas, with bright primary colors, almost Rorschach-like blobs, scattered over them. The colored-in areas are seemingly random (though occasionally show horizontal symmetry). Bright patches of yellow, red, green, and blue. The portraits are of heads. Just heads. They are lined up on a backlit wall, such that the colors practically jump out of the frames. The artist himself is present in the gallery, white-smocked, and explains in great detail that he is attempting a positivist, rather than phenomenological, interpretation of his subjects; that these portraits are pictures of actual states of affairs, the subjects as they "really are. As they think, that is, the emotions which come over them, while they are sitting for my portraits." It is as if he were using an enhanced eye of some sort to peer into souls, penetrating the visible, the meat, in order to attain and reveal our most personal information.

"What do you think?" he asks me.

It is at this moment that the Mysterious Woman wanders in. As she enters the studio, slamming the door behind her, now looking around her at the art on the walls, I suddenly have the distinct feeling that the membrane around the world is getting thinner, and that the borders between my thoughts and the world are becoming more permeable; threatening rupture. The Mysterious Woman is one such thought. Because I was thinking her, and now here she is Irl, and my mind attempts to find a form with which to describe her shape. Her narrow, northern face; those deep-set eyes. And while I map and index her, she turns, and sees me.

"Hello, Percy. Which one is yours?"

"My—"

"Your portrait."

"I haven't sat for one."

"Haven't you? I thought everyone had."

The artist, noting our conversation, nods to the Mysterious Woman.

"He's right over here," the artist says, pointing at a picture on the wall.

They look at me expectantly as I examine my portrait.

"God, I see it," I say, though thinking that it looks nothing like me.

The man begins explaining the picture to us, and I listen as if in a dream.

"This part is particularly sharp," he says, though whether he is indicating my mental acuity or the quality of his work I can't be sure. He puts a hand on the Mysterious Woman's shoulder, and then points at my milky, color-splotched portrait again, and adds, "rather illuminating actually."

"It is beautiful," she says.

Having her here, examining my portrait—this illustration of my supposed innermost control—is discomfiting, but I grin and bear it.

"Yes, you've really captured my likeness," I say, thinking all the while that no likeness, when frozen in time, can ever truly be a representation. It may replace that thing, but it may never represent it as an occasion of experience.

Meanwhile the artist is nattering away like a spirit medium, channeling my ghost.

"You can see," he says, "Percy's feelings of contentment. Look here, on this schematic representation of the affective circumplex . . ."

"Oh wonderful, wonderful!" the Mysterious Woman responds.

Thankfully, a few minutes later a bell is rung and a new set of fellows are brought in to admire the painter's work and we leave to resume our own.

Out in the hallway, thinking to seize this rare opportunity, I look for the Mysterious Woman, only to find her walking away with an admin I don't know. They seem very friendly. Intimate, perhaps. They are laughing about something. (Me?)

("I see it!" I had said. But I didn't "see it.")

It was a lie. God, that wasn't me, I think, as I wait for the elevator back to the ground level. Nothing about that picture was me. And I'm steaming mad by the time I exit—especially mad that I've misused this opportunity to speak more with the Mysterious Woman. I've only embarrassed myself. And so I commence my sulk back toward my flat. Except I've gotten off two floors too soon, and so double back.

(SUDDEN ENLIGHTENMENT)

Admin Miss Fairfax has come to my rooms again now, where she finds me prone, staring into the middle distance, replaying my conversation with the Mysterious Woman over and over in my mind.

Hello, Percy. Which one is yours? (she said.)

My—? (I said.)

Your portrait (she said . . .)

Miss Fairfax, oblivious, walks over to the vanity and removes a hairbrush, then walks us both to the mirror, sits me down in a chair, and stands behind me. She stays still for the longest time, looking at the mirror, taking me, and herself, in. Comparing, I suppose, this picture in front of her with the one she herself has formulated of us as a productive team. She reaches up and pulls off her glasses, places them on the vanity. Then she raises the brush, and puts it to the crown of my head, my scalp, and then slowly, slowly pulls it down through the thinning thread of my hair, down the right side of my face, never looking anywhere but at our reflection, her head tilting, almost imperceptibly, into a classical assessment pose. The brush is given a little jerk and is lifted, and goes back up, and then back down again, her wrist languorous, like she's bowing an instrument. This goes on for a while. I can't look away either. What does she see there? Why is she so captivated? Then her eyes shift, just a tiny degree,

to one side, barely a millimeter, and abruptly, she's looking at me—looking at her—in the glass. In this shift, in
the abrupt change that takes place, I feel the brush scrape
along my scalp, for the first time, but can't remember having felt this, or any other sensation, while she was groom-
ing me. Though my head now tingles as if mildly and
pleasantly burned. Staff-lines of prickles along my crown.
This touching makes our interactions substantially different from my interactions with the Mysterious Woman.
When someone touches you, a boundary is crossed. On
one side of this boundary, there is no touching, and then,
suddenly there is a moment, perhaps indistinguishable in
every other way from all previous moments, except that
now there is touching. Touching is off or on. Whether it is
lovers, combatants, or some inane manner of therapeutic
contact. Touching is on, or it is off.

Her touching to be indicated by ampersands

&&&&& && &&&&&&& &&&&&&&& &&&&
&&& &&
&&&&&&& & & &&&&&&&&&& & & &   & & &
 &
     & &&&&   &&&&&&&&&&&&&&&&&&&
&&&&&&& &   &   &
& & &   &   &   &   &

You learn things about people from touching. And, once again, I'm not referring to sexual things. What you learn is something regarding their ineffable, secret self. Without touching, you can only guess at the touched self. What is transferred through touch? I'm not sure. Maybe selfhood is like a virus, a species or combination of molecules which, once sloughed off, transmit little bundles of information. Who knows. Idk. What I do know is that Miss Fairfax is less enigmatic to me now, thanks to this transferal, through this, our material connection.

Meanwhile, her mirror eyes are now locked upon my mirror eyes, and the hairbrush is moving back and forth, as if sculpting my head out of clay . . . and I shiver, and come to.

Enough, I think.

Enough of having my hair brushed. (I am not, after all, a child.)

She knows why I have to leave her now—knows as well as I do.

"I have Group."

And, as if it were only for her benefit, I add, "I must be single-minded about my project. Totally ruthless.

"Ruthless," I repeat.

Then I knock the brush from her hand, and rise toward the door.

Openmouthed, she hurries to follow.

And when I open the door to my flat, there's a piece of white paper slumped up against it as if exhausted. I look down at it, then look over to Miss Fairfax, who looks at me as if awaiting the answer to a minor question.

(CHOLER AND WORSE)

Paper, paper, everywhere
and all the fellows stink.
Paper, paper, everywhere
and I am stained with ink.

(THE CONCIERGE)

Later after the Group session is out, it is evening of course, and so we spill from the Annex. There's paper all over, its whiteness instilling the grounds with a generalized luminosity, a dim fluorescence, a glow that is, as if the sheets of paper were magic lanterns, reflectors, strewn there to collect and redouble the attenuated moonlight. The actual moon presides, far off in the sky, foggy and fuzzed at the edges like a tennis ball (and practically the same color), and I think I can see a few stars as well albeit barely. It has been a while since I've seen stars, but there they are, Rn.

Gemini, right above me? Upside down (antipodes, etc.).

On my way up to my flat before heading to the refectory to meet with the others, persistent sheet of paper stuck to the bottom of a

~~the~~ my shoe,

the concierge of the Residential Enclave jack-in-the-boxes out of an alcove, just as I walk past, as if she were waiting for my arrival and had nothing better to do than eject herself out from the darkness at an unsuitable time, as if she has, herself, only exploded into being at the moment that our paths intersect, like a thought experiment in solipsism.

(THE PACKAGE)

The Enclave's ever-vigilant sentinel explains that someone has left me another package.

Left it for me in my flat, on the table in the middle of the living room.

And having conveyed this information, she nods to indicate to me that her part is now played. Though she clearly is fending off follow-up questions, I ask them anyway.

"Who dropped it off?" I ask.

A man.

"Someone from the Institute?"

No. Just a man.

"What was he wearing?"

Just clothes.

"Normal?"

Normal-like.

And she begins to walk slowly backward into the shadows.

I stride the stairs, click open the door. Whisper up the lights.

There it is.

The package.

My device is back.

29

(DRAWING THE VEIL)

There are many rows of folding chairs, set up on flooring panels in the desert. The hum of diesel generators. Smell of gasoline. By the time we arrive—and we are among the last to—the sun is sunk beneath the rim of the world and everything is set with a bluish cast. The world of the desert, cooling for the evening. Another fucking sunset. Another Discourse™.

This one is different though, as it is Ousman Al'Hatif's, and it is to be delivered out here in the sand. Off-campus and on-site. Might as well be off-world. I'm allowed to attend, but barely. Still on probation, obviously, and I've been told by Miss Fairfax that I'm on a short leash.

What I say back to her is: "No worries. I'm a good boy. Model citizen."

Miss Fairfax returns my smile with a look full of fatigue. When she looks away, out the window of the bus, I hold my hand in front of me experimentally, and it trembles.

Our bus, the last tonight, and thus half-empty, pulls up into a car park, which is little more than a series of cordons at the edge of the sand. Miss Fairfax and a few stragglers and I debark and walk between the other cars and the lorries, down a long runway into the dunes, toward the lights, toward the festivities, and I experience that familiar surge of pitiful emptiness which comes from being out on the perimeter of an occasion at dusk.

The rest of the Institute is already seated, ringed around a sandstone platform—the plinth upon which Mr. Al'Hatif's statue used to stand before it was uncermemoniously detonated. There, hiding something large and unmistakably statue-shaped, is a large white covering, a canvas shroud.

We are to witness an unveiling. The reconstruction, one presumes. It looks to me as if we are congregants, gathered to bow down to a gigantic, stylized, cartoon ghost.

Around the plinth and shroud are a series of skyjack hydraulic platforms, each one carrying lighting arrays and speakers. There is the general low murmuring of a crowd held in abeyance. Excusing myself, I edge through the aisles and I take the only chair I can find unoccupied, in the back row, splitting off from Miss Fairfax, who has squeezed up front into a reserved seat between some other admins. There are so many people here; who are they all? They can't all be from the Institute. I now see a party of local officials, sat in a roped-off area toward the front. There is also a group of Institute bigwigs and admins, including the Director of course, who cannot be missed, sitting, as usual, in his two chairs, both ready to buckle like overburdened pack mules beneath him.

Behind the shrouded statue, I can see the Institute's banner, with its crossed motif, being unfurled by workers, spots being trained upon it. Mr. Al'Hatif is atop one of the platforms now, like a conductor on a podium, directing helpers in hard hats. At one point, he turns and looks out behind him, over the crowds, and I think for a moment that he sees me, but he is only looking out toward the distant red glow of lights in the ad hoc parking perimeter, out into the desert, and I suppose he is feeling another form of pitiful emptiness: the emptiness of the partygoer in the thick of things, looking out into the night sky. (The sky waits, but invariably, sensing its moment, it will encroach and extinguish every party, put it right out with a *hiss*.)

Now, there is the nothing-moan of microphone feedback, and Mr. Al'Hatif turns toward his equipment. The Director stands up and addresses the crowd, introduces a rumpled-looking bureaucrat, who, after contextualizing the statue for us—its historical, spiritual, and artistic importance—introduces the man of the hour, Mr. Ousman Al'Hatif. A hot wind blows and briefly delays the heavily choreographed sequence of events. We all shield our faces for a moment until it dies down. Rn there is the familiar lead-in music, applause, and Mr. Al'Hatif strides onto the center of the stage, uniform crisp, headphone mic in place, looking as donnish as ever, but also weirdly assured under the high beams of our collective gaze.

"And at long length did we stand at the end of the col, in the dunes, and look out over the immensity of the Freehold's

Great Bodhisattva, and did we readily wonder if anywhere under the firmament was there a more singular artifact . . ."

These words come booming out from the black speaker stacks behind the platform, taking us all by surprise. The volume is adjusted, duly, downward, and Mr. Al'Hatif, readjusting his headset, continues:

> *Mr. Ousman Al'Hatif's Discourse* ™ *concerning this statue's destruction and reconstruction to be indicated by another text altogether—this particular text having been lifted from a middle chapter of the book I've been reading, the book which rests currently, heavy on my lap, the text of which has begun, without my noticing, to interpenetrate the words of the very speech unfolding before me now, and which will do just fine as a substitute for the thing itself; or, rather, as a substitute for my impressions of the Discourse* ™ *(or of any other Discourse* ™ *for that matter).*

"And what was (he) talking about? What train of thought was he pursuing? I gathered my wits to try to catch up, but did not succeed right away. . . . It was indeed rather odd. (He) adopted a hybrid terminology, a blend of poetic and academic styles; all of it uncompromisingly scientific, but in an ornate, lilting tone . . . which may have accounted for the flush on the ladies' cheeks, and the way the gentlemen kept flicking their ears. In particular (he) constantly used . . . a gently irresolute sense, so that one was never quite sure whether he referred to sanctified, or more passionate and fleshly forms—leaving one feeling slightly nauseated and seasick . . . He destroyed illusions, he was merciless in giving knowledge the honor it was due, he left no room for tender faith . . . and he . . . gave the impression of some fundamental idealism . . . his look . . . rather startling . . . He supported his arguments with all kinds of examples and anecdotes from the books and loose pages that lay before him; even reciting poetry. (He) discussed . . . frightening forms . . . bizarre, agonized, eerie mutations . . . logic . . . looked up and down the rows as he asked his questions, as if seriously expecting an answer from his listeners. But no, he would have to provide the answers himself, though he had already provided so many. No one else knew . . . but he would be sure to know this too . . . (with) his glowing eyes, his waxen pallor, his black beard . . . barely breathing . . . his voice rising noticeably . . . A sigh passed through the assemblage . . . he set his head erect again . . . then he let his arms fall. . . ."

As Mr. Al'Hatif makes this esoteric gesture, there's a billow, and a loud luffing, and a game-show gasp from the crowd (*ooowaaaaaahhh*), and the shroud drops to the stage floor. It is difficult at first to make out what is underneath it, and our eyes need to adjust to the sudden loss of the white sheet, but when we do we see that there is nothing beneath it at all but the platform itself.

Empty. There is nothing there.

A general murmuring.

PETER MENDELSUND

(What is Mr. Al'Hatif up to?)

Now the Disputants, who are seated directly behind me, go at it:

Disputant 1: (A humanist interpretation.)

Disputant 2: (A fanatically nihilist one.)

Just about everyone begins talking now, all at once—but imagine these voices all overlaid atop one another, stacked as it were in a kind of imitative counterpoint.

Things are getting heated.

At which point, there is a large clicking sound and the projectors, suddenly, all turn on at once, everything goes quiet, and there it is.

Wait, what?

Oh.

Glowing in the night, in twinkling reds and impossible golds: the statue.

The statue!

The precise size of the original, which means just looming.

An exquisite hologram. A man, perhaps, though a protean man, with breasts, sure, and other indicators of gender fluidity, not to mention the head of a manga kitten, eyes half-lidded beatifically. A glowing saffron robe, decked out in colorful, vivid emblems adorning its surface, swimming on it like cilia in solution—corporate identities of every stripe, from logos to word-marks to slogans and spokespeople and spokes-creatures, for mobile phone companies, professional sports clubs, fast-food chains, various hieroglyphs delineating political affiliation, a taxonomy of religious symbols, children's book characters, superheroes, fetishistic sexual depictions of outré specificity, the iconography, signifiers, the dog whistles and catchphrase-ology of a hundred forms of mass consumption. One of the Buddha's hands is upright against its breast in a gesture of half prayer; the other is stuck out in front of him/her/it, and it is holding an erect spear which ends in a rudely phallic bulb. The statue wears, on one foot, like a shoe, a gilt SUV; the other foot, bare, is resting upon ten small, straining bright blue dwarves in red, flaccid caps, who collectively hold the foot and leg aloft like Atlas does the world. Meanwhile, the statue's cape flows all around it in a diaphanous tide, silently washing over the stage and over the heads of the audience like runny watercolors. On the back of this out-rushing cape is an all-capped motto I cannot yet make out.

He is a towering god; constituted of naming rights and overlapping consensus polls. An answer to a series of aesthetic-preference research surveys; a perfect being, as arrived at through the application of clickbait questionnaires; a god of the comments section; a god of trolls; extrapolated through data collection using deep learning, statistical algorithms; a god, carefully honed and modulated at the hands of self-correcting analytics, and primed by corporate consultants, a god of on-brand integration and reliable marketability. A god of outrage-fatigue, a god of indolence and ceded agency. A recognizable, commoditized god; scalable; cross-platform. Vertical. Fractal. Nested.

Aura-less, yet awash in a new species of the auratic: emanating flatness like a force. A god of *now*; a now-god for a now-time.

Now God. Our god.

And now I can see, through it all, despite the throbbing lights of the Black Mass, with uproar, its horror vacui, its decadence, its neon contaminates, its grandeur, its barbarism, I see the motto, its back end, just the last letters, and its motto reads "olo," the palindrome which I take to be, actually, "yolo," but might, upon reflection, be a binary code of two noughts and a one, or may be the name "Golo," or a percentage sign, that is a %, or is it perhaps just a blank-eyed face emoji, dead of pupil and unencumbered of affect and appetite.

(What the statue resembles, Imho, more than anything, is the Director. The Director, who is on his feet, hooting and applauding vigorously.)

Mr. Al'Hatif steps back in order to look up and admire his work.

A series of lights begin to flame on in the desert night, as if solitary night-walkers were lighting candles far off on the dunes. It is a constellation of holographic Buddhas. They are all around us. How many are there? Now music swells up from the sound system. A swirl of post-ethnic trance. A kind of Ives-ian collision of gamelan, bouzoukis, bagpipes, and sitars. The audience leans forward, blinking. The work is pretty beautiful. Mr. Al'Hatif's project. Much better than the original statue; an encrusted, grimy, overexposed and irrelevant tchotchke.

(*Chapeau*, Mr. Al'Hatif.)

He walks, now, from the back of the platform to the front of the revamped Buddha, straight through the trans-lucid idol. It seems surprising that he doesn't encounter any resistance once inside. I would think it would be like walk-ing through a molded gelatin. But he passes into its spec-tral body easily. For a moment, he merges completely with his statue and is quintessentialized by the light. The statue warps itself around his features, his curves and troughs, his clothing, oozes about his person as he moves as if it were a cascade of golden oil. He is completely transformed by it, and then he is through to the other side.

The crowd is surging, people have left their seats, some milling about, some dancing, and arguments are breaking out. Shoving and so on.

And here he comes now, squeezing through the crowd, and I'm flattered that he's seeking me out, me of all people, and he smiles at me with what could be seen as a wry form of pride, and he leans in to speak, softly: "You know, this crowd, onlookers, paparazzi, even those local panjandrums, there, are, in fact, bought and curated for the occasion?"

"Pop-up crowd?"

"Pop-up crowd."

"Huh."

"Even this brawl, now breaking out, over there—fake—and so too those fake security forces attempting to quell it!"

Of course the unveiling is the project. Of course it is.

"What about the fellows," I ask, afraid of the answer.

"What about the fellows?"

255

"Are any of them, are all of them—"

"Mr. Percy, that would be mad."

But he is the man of the hour, and so Mr. Al'Hatif is interrupted; whisked off to a reception, where the hired multitude will playact an entire party in his honor. Whisked off by fake officials, before I can genuinely follow up.

As for the rest of us fellows, we gambol and frolic among the dunes late into the night, hunting for more Buddhas—desecrating ruins and trampling brittle bones, shards of pottery and other remnants crackling underfoot in order to find them—many of these Bodhisattvas of light discernible only on our devices, in location-based AR, each Buddha taking a different form (fox, octopus, komodo dragon, clown, so on), each with different sponsors, each possessing different stats and abilities (collect them all), a vast and lunatic Easter egg hunt, the revels only ending at morning light, when the admins came to round us up, and bring us, and all our amassed treasures—finally, home.

But there's one seat empty on the final bus.

Bus seats to be indicated by quotation marks

” ”

” ”

” ”

” ”

” ”

” ”

```
    ,,  ,,
    ,,  ,,
    ,,    <-------------This one is vacant.
    ,,  ,,
    ,,  ,,
```

I'm watching the glow of the party fade into the rising light, as my own small, recently commandeered vehicle reenters the ring road, heading in the opposite direction from the Institute. The city in front of me: a wasted fire, an ember or two still lit deep inside the ashen office towers. The smoke-blue morning mirroring the evening which preceded it. (Sun Rise #1.) My passport, damp in my tight grip. I put it down. Smack my perpetually dry mouth once; twice. Lie back in the car's rear seats. It is so easy to slip away. I am careful, and there is so much going on, so much activity to mask my leave-taking, and so many shadows to merge into. But they should've known. Should have watched me more closely. A risk? Sure. But what choice do I have. It was always going to be bad no matter what. Etc. So I mustn't squander the opportunity. This final shot, Rn. Final shot at . . . at what? Redemption? Lmao. A last chance to get my freedom back. I am spending the last of my capital on this clandestine, emergency run.

They'd take my passport, Miss F. had said, ergo, one more thing left to replicate.

The last thing, I hope. And this is, surely, a crime—another crime of counterfeit, but worse, perhaps. It is one

I must commit, and I do hope my friend the Same Same man will be discreet—his discretion in regards to these plagiarisms being, as far as I can tell, his main selling point. Here's hoping. What other choice do I have but to hope? Without these papers, I am no better than a prisoner.

I slink down farther until my head is level with the bottom of the car window and remain in this crouch as the vehicle drives on. Careful now. Can't get booted yet. What's the point of leaving after all if I have nothing to show for my time here?

But nobody saw me. Nobody saw me. But I see something: and it is a ball of crumpled paper at my feet, under the front seat in the well.

No escaping it these days.

The overpopulation of my inner world is now causing borders to be breached—cartographic lines are being crossed—my refugee thoughts now overwhelming the world's outer space; some of these thoughts dying in transit, as migrants often do, while others are making it, making it out, repatriating successfully, and being granted a kind of visa status in the material world.

Which is to say that even ideas need passports.

30

My reformulated device and I escape out unto the perimeter fence again today. My bench. My Observation Point. Might as well be a plaque with my name on it. I'm alone at last. The desert is out there, as usual. Sky still here. Rocks—yes. Horizon: check. Heat: roger that. Sand? Yup. What season is it? Idk, the Institute is seasonless; the desert burns off seasons like fevers. Nevertheless, the air has changed. It's gotten even murkier. You can feel it, big-time. Even in here. And see it out there. The famous desert winds are whipping up, heralds to the approaching front. Little khamsins and haboobs. Harmattans and siroccos. You can see the effects of the hubbub outside of the metastructure. The desert is encroaching, and odd things are washing up from the sands. Driftwood, animal carcasses, garbage. There's an ugly ring of the junk accumulating around the perimeter. Not enough sand rakes to stem the tide. We are protected, as far as I know. If the worst does indeed come to pass, if the storm from does hit us head on, we always have our dome for protection. We can hunker down here and ride it out. So we are safe, even if we are uncomfortable. And boy are we uncomfortable. The heat and the humidity continue to worsen. The more sensitive of the fellows are feeling poorly. The infirmary is being kept busy. A variety of symptoms. Small complaints mostly. A lot of itchy eyes. Irritability. Tinnitus (and has there ever been an affliction that more effectively blurs the line between the awareness of suffering and the suffering itself)? Also, headaches. Lots of headaches.

In an effort to better the mood under the dome, the Institute has organized even more communal events in the Presence Center—they've brought more of those spirit-raising therapy dogs in to lift our spirits again. We sit in a large circle and watch them gambol on the lawn—happy, spastic beasts. And, at considerable expense, the powers that be have installed a new VR setup. State-of-the-art, full-immersion pods. We jack into its seamless 3-D renders. Fogging, diffraction, caustics, bump-mapping; surround sound. Its smearily beautiful palette. All the fellows have been spending more and more time in there, enjoying the entertainments. I hang back at first, but now, entranced by the uncanny verisimilitude and haptic responsiveness, I grab the experience with both hands, such that I have now become its most frequent client: its self-appointed keeper, and the foremost proselytizer on its behalf. The strange apparatus is not a toy, but a marvel really. A triumph of art, if you ask me. I'm staying up way past my bedtime to enjoy the infinite other worlds which this miraculous instrument, this ingenious sarcophagus, renders up to me. I could spend my life in one of these. Never come out.

So let it storm, Irl. I can just ignore it all: lie down in there, close and latch the lid, and be anywhere else. For as long as I need. (Or at least until the motion sickness sets in.)

This is not to say that I am avoiding my work. Ideas are now popping up with regularity. I am thinking with a purpose. And the work is, fittingly, rendering.

Slowly, line by line, progressively rasterizing toward completeness and identity.

So, a happy report to make. At least from this perspective. That's it. Ttfn.

Wait. Come to think of it actually, there is one other thing to mention; specifically, that I've had another strange and notable dream:

Picture this. Okay. I'm sitting on the grass in the deadening heat of the Cavity Yard when all at once I hear that famous, introductory Discourse™ orchestral hit, which kind of strikes me as strange, that there would be a Discourse™ under way, given that it is, by the sun, the middle of the afternoon. Looking around to investigate, I see something approach from a dark space behind the Presence Center. It is about eight or nine feet tall, and is very narrow, and: well, here's the thing, whatever this apparition is, it is blinking slowly, literally strobing in and out of existence. Here, now gone. Here, gone. So on. Doesn't make a sound. Comes toward me. Quite deliberately. Keeps advancing. I stand inert as the terrifying apparition blinks forward. I turn around to see if anyone is seeing what I am seeing, but I am alone, and so I turn back toward the thing once more, and I see now that it is, in fact, a single line, like a vertical rod, a couple of inches thick at most, but still very tall. An ominous, tall, black, thin line.

As it advances through the yard, here, here is the truly unnerving part: things disappear as the line passes through them, as if they had simply been deleted. How, I can't comprehend, but look: look at the grass disappear (gone!), and now a plinth, and another one, vanished, and now the first row of palms disappears, and now the second, third, fourth. They simply wink out of existence.

I'm really frightened Rn, but as quickly as the line judders forward, suddenly, it now moves backward, away from me, with the same little jerks, which is a relief, as I can't seem to move my legs or feet, prisoner to the proceedings. And as the enormous thing jumps backward, the vanished trees reappear in place, they simply come back (though now they are blue).

Now the cursor moves forward again. It suddenly leaps forward—or rather it swiftly disappears, and then reappears . . . right in front of me! It seems as though (and I know how crazy this sounds), as though, as though: it is *staring* at me. Sizing me up; taking my measure.

I fork my fingers through my hair, close and rub my eyes, look again. Still here (shit!) but even closer now, that tall fucking blinking vertical line (which I will dub, and henceforth call: "Blinky"). We are standing nose to nose.

"Hello, Blinky," I say, not knowing what else I'm expected to do exactly, and tentatively extending a hand to touch it, just to check on the status of its corporality—and let's be honest here my sanity as well hahaha—and as I reach out, Blinky responds by jerking forward again and obliterating me entirely again (as well as the room and everything in it) brb

A gap.

And here I am, now standing in the gardens above the Residential Enclave, because Blinky has just put me down here. I can see that several of the other fellows have been blinkified into existence here as well. There are two fellows sitting on a plinth, and another standing by a topiary. One of them (the Econometrician) clearly wasn't working very well exactly where he was—on the plinth that is—because, abruptly, Blinky moves in on him, bridges the distance in an instant, crosses right over him, and the fellow is bathed in a yellow aura, which is solid for a moment, and then he (the Econometrician) and the yellow nimbus both disappear, cut out, only for the fellow to be pasted back into the world again, this time on the rim of the fountain.

"Okay, Blinky, what are you playing at?" I ask, but Blinky only remains there in place, discontinuous, but not moving, as if thinking, or awaiting instructions.

But now he's off again, blinking his way across the landscape, in and out of frame, over the Institute's landscaped hillocks and vales, rewriting and reconfiguring everything, turning concrete into lawns, lawns into desert, trees into palms, flattening mountains and crushing buildings and constructing others, moving people about, making some things bigger and others smaller, and just about basically changing the color of everything, like a child drafting a landscape with the wrong crayons.

Fellows are running everywhere to avoid it like it's a giant film monster and yes, there is a lot of screaming and mass confusion and the whole ground shakes. It's just mayhem up in here.

And I just stand watching it all, unable to act, no agency at all, passively observing this Kaiju-cursor go about its business writing and rewriting the whole fucking world.

Now finally the Director appears ("our hero!"). He emerges from the Business Center at a trot, meaning loping like an elephant, the medallion around his neck flopping wildly, and he waves his hands, and the monstrous line stops in place, and then everything, the line and the buildings and the people the whole nine yards just up and vanishes. Then the Director turns to me, and without opening his mouth at all, somehow screams:

YOUR PAPERS.
YOUR PAPERS.
YOUR PAPERS.
YOUR PAPERS.

31

(HUMANIORA)

The Institute's Security Center is a high-tech affair. A cramped space, constructed of single-sheet monitors, comprising three of the four walls. There's a single table in the room, which seems to be an interactive viewing console; a command station with a single black rubber joystick, sticking straight up out of it, presiding priapically. Upon the monitors are views of the Institute; uniforms, alone and in groups, studying, building, cavorting, consorting, bathing, exercising, and generally going about their habitual movements. I see, on a screen down toward the floor to my right, someone is speaking with the Sociologist. In another, I see the Architect, 鼎福 , in his full-surround gear. In another, two uniformed fellows are playing checkers. Another screen shows a fellow in a bed in an empty room. On another, jumpsuits with rakes and snowblowers, trying to handle the

~~garbage~~ paper. Bins filled by the truckload

Workers are everywhere. They cannot keep up. That white mass sticking to the turbines grows as the paper grows, and hardens over time, making the blades more or less useless.

An entire party of Institute workers is required to clean and repair the massive fan in Turbine Enclosure Number Two. They have spent the better part of the day there, scouring the enormous screw which presides over the middle of the hangar like the propeller of an old, seagoing juggernaut.

It takes forever to remove the obstructing material. They scour first, with industrial rasps, then with shoulder-slung sandblasters. Ten jumpsuits, with cherry pickers, ropes, and carabiners, climbing atop the blades themselves to better their access. But they aren't making much progress—there is just too much of the stuff to scrape off. The white residue, caked to the metal, is becoming so thick and hard that by the end of their shift, they're resorting to a high-pressure hose application of a proprietary acid, which slowly, but successfully melts the barnacled substance into an ichor, which then can be wiped off and slung into bio-locked industrial barrels. The latter part of the session is spent screwing and bolting the lids of the barrels back on, and mopping up what remains on the concrete floors. The barrels are then loaded onto forklifts and shipped out. To where, we don't know.

Though it might be the lake: a skirt of scum with an oily sheen is gently lapping at the rim of it; the water has turned a soapy gray from the slowly dissolving pulp.

And the smell . . .

It is noticeably warmer inside the dome—inside the

Institute's buildings. The atmosphere is warming to the extent that the fellows' banter now merges with faint, high-treble cracks hissing their way along the length of the Landau-Schmidt glacier, like lit fuses—high notes supported by the occasional basso profundo of its more seismic detonations. *Hissss. Boooom.* The Institute clearly has not considered the possibility of the mountain's structural fragility, and its catchment sink isn't nearly deep enough to contain the melt-off. So now, on the screens, you can see that the main concourse of the Mountain House has small puddles, where condensation has collected. The added inconvenience being that there are now thin fogs, creeping around corners, hovering in the atria, and enshrouding the overhead lights, like a malevolent gauze. The paper has begun to dampen, and stick to the ground, becoming in places a sort of maché, a disgusting, clingy white plaster which one must avoid stepping on, or else have to scrape, at the end of the day, from one's soles.

Things are getting shabbier.

Have we underestimated the storm? Become overconfident in the metastructure's capacities? Either way we have grown complacent. And so, some of the more enterprising fellows are commandeering the paper to make flags and bunting, and there are a few folded paper corsages affixed to uniforms, which could be seen as a bit of can-do spirit here, a "continuing to make the best of things," etc. Look at them there Rn—recorded on all of these screens—doing their level best.

————

Across from me is the Director's great head, behind which are still more live feeds—one showing a very high overhead shot of the campus, featuring various crosses and grids superimposed upon it, like a planetary landing video. One screen is a live stream of the Mysterious Woman in her studio. It must be now—you can tell from the late-afternoon light. She is wearing her uniform, though it is pulled down a bit upon her shoulders. Her hair is unwashed. She is concentrating hard on her device, whispering away. I watch as she peruses the device's contents, casually almost; her face, underlit in blue, as if she were standing in a cool grotto, or swimming in a lighted pool at night. She runs a single hand through her messy hair. She walks across the room. Steps on a scale. Frowns. Goes over to a bed and sits on it. Begins reading again.

I can't help wondering if these feeds were chosen for my attention, strategically, or whether they are just part of the continuous, autonomous viewing.

I watch the feeds. The Mysterious Woman.

The Director watches me. So does his medallion, staring out from its single black-and-silver eye.

"Do you recognize her, Mr. Frobisher?"

It is just him—he has dismissed his aides for this occasion. I've never been truly alone with him, and if this tête-à-tête is meant to intimidate, it's working. We are seated at the barely large-enough table, across from one another, and we have to be conscientious in order for our knees and feet not to touch. The confining situation is especially precarious because of his size. His belly periodically pushes up against the table, which then moves toward me in small increments. I sit almost sideways, and the surface area I am occupying is getting smaller by the moment. The joystick stands at attention between us. The images on the walls unspool.

"Of course I do," I finally reply.

"She is an interesting specimen."

"Specimen?"

"Case study, Mr. Frobisher. You are all my case studies, and as such, fascinating to me. Even you, Mr. Frobisher. Do you resent being a specimen? If I am to assist you in your reaching your MAXIMUM POTENTIAL, I must study you, mustn't I? If I am to help you to lead your BEST LIFE?"

"I suppose, but—"

"And ARE you? ACTUALIZING? Finding your OWN TRUTH? We aren't in any way DISTURBED by recent circumstances, are we?"

"What circumstances?"

"Exactly. That is PRECISELY the attitude to have."

I hardly know where to look. The monitors remind me of eyeballs disconnected from brains.

"Sorry. Can we turn them off?"

"We're rather PROUD of our network, actually. Everyone welcomes it—the grid, the spectacle. It is distributed throughout the program, all the devices, and it doesn't exist without everyone's—without your own—contribution.

Which is to say, Mr. Frobisher, that the grid here is not so much a case of us watching you as you broadcasting YOUR-SELF. Think of it as community building. An investment in real-time, social-validation feedback. Either way, a GREAT BOON to us all."

The Director declaims for a period on the benefits of sharing/volunteerism . . .

. . . to be indicated by "likes"

♥ ♥
♥ ♥
♥ ♥
♥ ♥ ♥ ♥ ♥ ♥ ♥ ♥ ♥ ♥ ♥ ♥ ♥ ♥ ♥ ♥

I look down at my device, and it is just humming away happily.

"You will acclimatize. You might come to enjoy it, in fact. Even your own participation in it all. Especially that. Let us consider this a rung on THE LADDER. A growth stage. Not to mention that perhaps there may be something in all of this participation—these membership contributions—for your project? An idea? A motif? Some sort of idea which properly reflects our core principles here? Our promotion of collectivism as praxis? Toward a philosophy of a COM-MUNAL project? But your work is still languishing on the drawing boards, isn't it—you are still struggling to get it all airborne. Flagging. Still in labor. So disappointing. So DISCOURAGING. Despite everything we have done for you, despite all of our help. Despite our CONSIDERABLE OUTLAY on your behalf. All our attention; all of our investment; all of our CARE."

The Director now affects a kind of grief-stricken expression. "Stuck. It is a little bit unacceptable, frankly. And hard to fathom. Our operating system is proven. User tested, back-end tested, compatibility tested, speed benchmarked, and certified. Where is the gratitude? The humility? The (all-but-crucial) SURRENDERING ourselves to the Institute's higher authority? And, your project is now just one worry among your other concerns, isn't that right, Mr. Frobisher? Which brings me back to THE MATTER AT HAND—the question of your passport."

"Yes."

"Your passport," he repeats.

"What about it?"

"Don't be clever," he says, drawing himself up and extending an open hand.

I scan the exits.

"I may have misplaced it," I stammer. "Give me a day or so to scour the flat?"

"I'm a busy man, Percy, and I think you will find that it WILL NOT serve you to try our patience." The hand closes to a fist.

"Not long, I promise. I do wonder though, if I give you my papers, I won't be better than a prico ?"

The fist opens and raises to become a *stop right there* gesture.

"Allow me to preempt your question," he says, slipping

now into a self-consciously aggrieved and confessional mode which is every bit as frightening as his evangelical one, if not more so. "ALAS, we must keep track of all our fellows' visas, travel and identity papers. The Freehold demands it of us. These are the regional RULES. We are asked by the local constabulary to keep an eye on our fellows' papers for safekeeping. I'm surprised you don't know this, it is—"

"I know. In the contract. What do you mean *keep an eye on?*"

"LAW OF THE LAND, I'm afraid," and he heaves his broad shoulders upward to indicate his helplessness, "you are *our* problem. My problem. Now, we don't always take *physical* possession of a fellow's passport, but in SOME CASES— where we may have reason to suspect that we might have NEED of them, where we suspect they might be handy to have nearby, where we guess that some sort of INCIDENT might be liable to arise between the fellow-in-question and the Institute, or the Freehold in general—in such cases, we ask for them. For SAFEKEEPING, understand."

The back of the huge hand now runs over the monitor which displays the Mysterious Woman, as if in a lewd caress. (Meanwhile she continues on about her business, oblivious, in such high focus I can see each of her pores.)

"I don't know what to think. It is hard to swallow, being kept."

"Always the visitor. Such ITCHY FEET. As I say, Mr. Frobisher, you'll get used to it."

He smacks the hand down open-palmed on the table

and laughs, rises, and the wake of his distended belly finally traps me between the table and the wall.

A gap.

I am being led down the dim corridors (which seem to only turn in a single direction over and over, which would indicate a circle or at best a kind of cochlear spiral) when the Director mentions, casually, "I see that you and Mr. Royal are friendly."

"Not especially. Are we?"

"Aren't you? I could be wrong, Mr. Frobisher. Of course, it is VERY HARD indeed to keep names and faces straight here, isn't it," he admits, ruefully. "So many men and women, so many fellows and admins. And so many of you with a legitimate claim to SPECIAL STATUS. Do you make such a claim, Mr. Frobisher?"

"No, of course not. Not any more than anyone else. I'm just here to do my work. Keep my nose down."

"Your work, yes. Baffling. Can't say I can make heads nor tails of it."

I stand there, mute, not wanting to go down this road again. But he continues, taking a single step closer to me:

"That's fine," he goes on, "just fine. You don't like to speak about it. Though, sometimes, we all need to just get things off of our chests, let it all out. Helps move things along. Don't you think? Otherwise one could calcify. Constipate. Just HARDEN RIGHT UP. And who knows what happens then. If we are alone with our thoughts for too long. People become weird under such circumstances; ESTRANGED FROM THE REAL. They go off the reservation, as one says. Sometimes quite literally; isn't that right? Well, listen to me go on, I've been giving a speech. A Discourse™ of my own! Don't mind me, but I have pressing matters to attend to—minds to PRIME AND CLARIFY; tasks to recenter; connections to refresh; I must hasten to INCULCATE BELONGINGNESS, to render PEAK EXPERIENCES. No time, no time! And you'll get those papers to me then? You've promised, don't forget! TOUT DE SUITE. Don't make me wait."

And with a showily decorous and surreally awkward sweep of his arms, the Director pushes the exit door open with a bang, and prods me out of it.

Make haste, Same Same.

Make haste.

PART III

CHANGES

32

(THE PAPER CONTINUED)

Some of those pages slink into a window leading into a high floor of the Arts Pavilion. They make their way down a flickering corridor, hugging the tiled walls like a SWAT team.

They pass a white room; a room as white as they are. Flutter on in. There's a pale green curtain on some kind of freestanding, aluminum, tubular framing system. The curtain now draws to reveal the Mysterious Woman, who is hard at work on a project of some sort.

The work involves a bag and a tube, and a bed. And several assistants.

One of these assistants swipes at the paper fluttering in front of his face; swats once, twice, and then, irritated, returns to his strange work. Only minutes later, he looks up again, and now expertly snatches the sheet out of the air, and calmly clips it to his clipboard. He begins writing on it. His expression quickly changes from pleased to grave. Then, someone shouts: "Bloody hell—what hit you in here?" as the curtain slashes closed. The papers are blown backward and out of this forbidding place.

(AN ATTACK, AND A REPULSE)

We sit in wire chairs upon the gravel, next to the dead water in the stilled fountain, concentrating on the gray concrete checkers table. My hair is sticking to my forehead and my shirt to my chest and arms. (Hot. Humid.) Occasionally a tiny drop of water falls into the pool, causing identical and concentric ripples to broadcast out toward the water's periphery. Each drop of water that lands in the fountain does so with a noticeable, round little sound, which indicates to me that it has fallen from a great height. Though it cannot be rain of course. Perhaps it is this new, internal heat, causing condensation to accumulate on the interior surface of the metastructure. Idk.

The board is set now, and we begin.

1.	Preliminaries	16.	The Line Holds
2.	Home Rank	17.	Retrenching
3.	Assessing the Table	18.	White's Move
4.	Will o' the Wisp	19.	Volte Face
5.	Etc., Etc.	20.	Forward, March
6.	Misdirection		(A Venetian Salvo)
7.	Poise in the Face of	21.	Vingt et Un
	Great Difficulty	22.	Penetration
8.	Lines of Attack	23.	Out-on-a-Limb
9.	The Stage Is Set	24.	An Opening
10.	En Masse	25.	Price Paid
11.	The Race Is On	26.	High Block
12.	Consulting the Rulebook	27.	Assessing the Flank
13.	A Small Sacrifice	28.	Seeing the Big Picture
14.	A New Salient	29.	Sleight of Hand
15.	Feint (A Snow Job)	30.	Textbook Exchange

"Again?"

He doesn't respond.

I arrange the pieces back on their home stations. Mr. Al'Hatif stares into the middle distance.

Now he leans way forward, and I think for a moment that he will pitch all the way onto the board, headfirst. But he only goes as far as my left ear, into which he whispers:

"No one is safe."

I pull back from him to see if he is referring to the game (no), joking (no). His face remains expressionless.

"What do you mean?" I ask.

Al'Hatif picks up a checker, very slowly, only to put it back where it originated. He doesn't answer me. (He's been lumbering around, my friend Ousman, not, as you'd expect, in some kind of postcoital, post-project glow, but rather with a spent sallowness, a marble-eyed weariness. Some sort of chemical transformation has taken place in him, due to his project and Discourse™ completion, and now he seems quite the different person. Dulled. Anaesthetized even.)

"No one is safe," he says to me again, as I rub the moisture out of my socket with a knuckle, "not even you."

He has listed in his chair a bit, so I shove him on his lower shoulder until he is upright again.

"Up you get. There, there."

Just then, I hear another drop land loudly in the pool, and as I'm looking up, trying to track its source—which I determine to be the sweating metastructure, high above us—another droplet hits me squarely in the eye.

Ack.

Mr. Al'Hatif has fallen asleep. The Styrofoam cup he has been clasping is leaning over and some of the brown fluid is dribbling out. I take it from him and place it on the gravel beside him, pull up his blanket over his slumped torso. He whimpers contentedly, and I leave him to it.

(THE PAPER CONTINUED)

The paper has begun to organize itself. It is becoming orderly.

Back when the paper first began to emerge from the Same Same shop, it did so chaotically. It was rapidly, rudely, evacuated out the door like so much rubbish. But now, the paper has formed long, well-ordered lines. But things are getting tidier.

The papers are now in constant taxi and takeoff, following a protracted and roughly parabolic flight path between the Same Same shop and the Institute.

Naturally, all of this activity raises important questions. For example: Does anyone notice?

Such an enormous event. You'd think someone would . . .

(OF COURSE—A WOMAN!)

Her head is a silk scarf, the rest of her is a beige pantsuit. A low-slung leather handbag—the strap of which is visibly cutting into her right shoulder pad—bulges with a laptop case and assorted peripherals. She lifts a brushed, metallic canister to her lips, and begins to suckle the bitter, antioxidant froth from the built-in, flip-up straw—allowing the fluid to play, coolly, on the space in front of her teeth. A lot on her mind. A lot on her mind. She's en route to the digital hangout she is running lead on this A.M.: a meeting featuring drop-ins from several crucial, far-flung stakeholders in the global consulting firm in whose employ she currently labors, at a desk deep inside one of those crazed office towers straight up ahead, specifically, the one shaped like a cluster of space crystals, this building sitting flat against the sky like the painted background art from the cover of a sci fi magazine, and toward which her feet are being mag-lev'ed by that same caffeinated witches' brew, ten ideas jostling for her attention: two of which concern her

newly updated and shared, multihued, multitiered schedule; four of which concern projected cost (and the reporting
thereof); one, which concerns internal corporate structure
and which requires its own dedicated mental org-chart, one
revolving around a single slight, put out offhandedly by a
reviled colleague, which was suffered during a webinar just
days earlier but which still throbs with the periodicity of an
ingrown toenail, and the plans she is formulating to redress
the pain as well as the insult; the most persistent (suddenly) of her thoughts concerning her spidery but also resil-
ient micro-mesh underwear, the label of which has folded
in on itself uncomfortably, and is now pressing itchily on
her already sore L3 vertebra, the chakric source (the company's lunchtime yoga instructor informs her) of problems
related to painful periods, miscarriage, and bed-wetting—
only the first of these being an actual concern (though with
everything else she has to contend with she might as well
add bed-wetting to the jeremiad, why not, why not; bring
it on), and of course her general back issues would clearly
be resolved by obtaining a new chair from office services
but she keeps forgetting to put in the call—forgets for
obvious reasons really, given her already strenuous mental
agenda—not to mention things would defo improve if perhaps she just carried less shit around every day, and maybe
even switched to some core workouts in order to strengthen
those opposing abdominals, but the important thing here is
that the entire situation—itch, itch, itch—when taken as a
whole (she thinks in her unexpectedly philosophical, ninth

thought) is so emblematic of the Modern Condition, that hackneyed parable—and (thought number ten) so totally modern is our condition here that even the very platitude of "the Modern Condition" itself is now reified into subject matter for even such further clichés as 1. her own warmed-over thoughts and 2. her own running account of these thoughts, and god, she thinks wretchedly, I have become a metaphor—when, stopping to discreetly rearrange her underpants-label situation, she hears a flapping noise, and looks up from the various social feeds she happens to be also absentmindedly unspooling, only to notice that, over-head, there is something happening. Something of serious note.

That is: paper.

A line of it, a conveyer belt of it, now heading out, along the same direction as she is—flying sunward, leaving the city via the air, following an invisible, forceful, and innate logic. It's about twenty stories up—the papers casting a long, snaking shadow, an adumbrating dotted line upon these very blistering sidewalks she is standing upon, though she should be (not sprinting, but at least) speed-walking, so that she can clock in earlier than is strictly speaking necessary, as she needs to run the numbers a third time and rehearse the presentation and recommendations again before having to actually present and rec them—these recs referring to her firm's go-ahead to that consortium overseeing the construction of a spanking new hotel; a hotel in a perfect, exactly-to-scale reconstruction of a famous Bourbon château—one with room upon room of trompe l'oeil, each fantastical, ornate, pastel, Fabergé chamber diverting the visitor's gaze toward its unique series of windows; each window framing a different baroque idyll of bubblegum-clouded skies and nymph-and-swain-thronged parks; windows which, upon closer inspection, open upon nothing, and in fact do not even open at all as they are skillfully painted upon the chalky walls—this luxury hotel theoretically drawing the super big coin—mega-money—not only expected income from tourist occupancy but from the adjacent two-hundred-room conference center, which will assist in recouping their loan funding in a matter of a single fiscal year (or so the numbers suggest, and so she shall claim as the projectors whine, and styluses are twirled and triangular sandwiches calcify into waxwork simulations), but here on the grueling concrete she is honestly surprised to find that she no longer cares much, and furthermore, and more surprising still, she no longer needs her fashionably over-large sunglasses (for the first time in years, for as long as she has been stationed in the Freehold, that is) and so duly takes them off, sticking them on her blouse like she is paper-clipping her various strata together, her clothes, skin, organs, thoughts . . . while others too around her are also taking off their sunglasses; and she sees that everyone is frozen, a line of people like this, all looking up, as in an eclipse (staring counterindicated), but still—the paper leaving the city is a thing to see—everyone in awe of the migration.

The thing itself, the thing moving away that is: ordinary. Only paper: base matter. The movement is the thing. The direction is the thing; the vector. Time asserting itself over objects, nothing stable. So there's raw emotion here, though she can't see anyone else's face in full, visored as they all are beneath the shade of each of their salutes, everyone paying a military honor to the sky; people speaking in mutter-tongue, vibrating with communality. The only times you see events like these are catastrophes. Perhaps this is one too? The great paper diaspora? It is news of a sort. The parade going by up above, sheet by sheet by sheet. The view each citizen is afforded of the paper train, each a slightly different sight line on the event—no different really from how the news of the world comes down for us out of the meatspace, refracted through our portals, each screen also viewed from a unique angle, in a different locale—bar, bathroom, on a bedspread, lap, palm—though here everyone knows that they are participating together in some way which is more real than these other scenarios; secure in the knowledge that each angle on the paper-event will come together like the miracle of binocular vision in order to present a single, coherent whole, a mass revelation; though the truth is that even our cherished Irl, our real here-and-now, is fractured, and individual. Spoked. Watched on that private feed reserved for all of us in our lonesomeness: MeChat, iTube, Moistagram.

She watches the paper trail leave, waiting for it to tail off, which it doesn't. Out, out the paper goes and she imagines that the exodus is definitely heading toward some better place, for sure, better than here—where life isn't tabulated into calendar invites and spreadsheets, the columns and rows of which have long since ceased to stand in for anything except for other designified columns and rows; where life lacks the constant dread of the next incoming *ping*, the stultifying heat-death of office corridors, chaffing of synthetic pantsuits (the fucking rope-burn of her buttfloss), buzzing of network servers and a catalog of performative facial expressions—devoid of sincerity but laden with social significance. It has to be that heralded "better place." And it isn't that she, or anyone else here today, feels a sense of loss exactly, but it is more like a generalized ache, born of seeing (just about anything) up in the sky, anything which moves away en masse, which migrates, which is to say that it is a sadness born of distance, born of a reversal of the work of gravity, born of loss. She, alongside the other onlookers frozen in the city, actually relishes this sadness, relishes the distance, relishes the cool and intermittent reprieve of the stuttering shade.

Will everyone disperse when the papers are gone, she wonders? When the last straggling sheet vanishes? Will she and the other rubberneckers just go back to it all? Will they all remember the feeling of the Universal Family convened here? The family praying together; staying together? Does nothing make a dent? Divert the stream? When it ends, will people look around shyly, feeling a bit stupid, everyone feeling as though they had just tripped over an unexpectedly jutting curb, or belched inappropriately? Will there be that inevitable embarrassing aftermath of the big, communal merging? Will she draw, later, in the margins of her poorly stapled, redundant meeting minutes, a row of rectangles, trailing toward a vanishing point, having excused herself mentally from the deck's time-keeping—sloganed slides, the sands of a commodified hourglass—excused herself for this fleeting reminiscence of the unusual occasion of the great paper relocation?

Doubt it.

Merely a flutter, later, in the space behind her eyes, a brief spasm, then, gone.

33

(THE FULLNESS OF HARMONY)

Two o'clock in the world of tomorrow, and it is whole new terrain out here: landscape of pink rock, blue trunks, a bending river, and gently dipping purple fronds. The sky is egg-yolk yellow, and the air is alive with the barely visible fuzz of small insect life. Blue-gray mountains smudge the horizon. I'm looking around and there is more of the same in all directions. Such a relief to be away from the Institute, among all of this dense flora. This valley; the foothills of a rain forest perhaps. No sign of habitation. Unsullied. One gets the sense that the entire planet may be uninhabited.

We are far from the meatspace—in the surround, being walking through 鼎福 the Architect's new project. We enter in God mode, and just look around. It's pretty amazing actually. Very little lag or latency. I'm impressed. Total verisimilitude. The coding and processing power required must be awesome. It is a real *wow*, obviously, though I must admit that I am just beginning to grow a bit weary of such spectacular moments, out here at the Institute. (We've been privy to so many.) The world, our world, Irl, is not, contrary to what you might hear, devoid of miracles. Spectacular revelation is still possible out there, but rather we've all witnessed enough of these revelations not to care anymore. "Miracle blindness," I suppose you could call it. And here we go again. Dennis Royal must feel the same way—there he is over yonder, affecting total ennui, his appropriately jaded and slouchy avatar slumping up against a polygonal tree, lighting a CGI cigarette and taking a sumptuous and Frankenberry-scented rip. (*Smell?*)

"That's the stuff," he says, still expressionless.

So great, I think again, to be away from the Institute, and its humid cloying fugs and growing general despondency. (And these are the only admin-less trips I'm officially sanctioned to take.) So, I'm doing a lot of this virtual sightseeing now; lots of video; plenty of games, XD, VR, so on. Anyway, I am interested in the Architect's project, of course, but the real reason I've come is to quote-unquote get away, away from Irl and, and, more importantly find a place to talk to Dennis off-site.

The Architect gently pushes aside some spidery vines with the back side of his hand, and through doing so, shows us, me and Dennis, the rules; the physics, etc., etc. I do the same, experimenting with the degree of agency I am granted. A fair amount. We are learning. Some things are possible, others are not, so forth.

We walk, we crouch, we swing our arms. We hit some pose-balls, and duly enact their directives. We follow a river path. A few other presences, bots, prowl the valley, ignoring us. Some of them parade in place, or labor, walking up against a large rock or tree, industrious, dumb, stuck. When one of the more mobile avatars crosses our path, we walk right through it.

"Of course, there are all kinds of glitches and blank spots—places where the kinks still need to be worked out, or where you simply reach the end of the rendering," 鼎福 the Architect says. He shows me one such location, down a ways, behind a thick copse, in a clearing. It is a square of gray nothing. There it is, the nihility. It *is*—so strictly speaking, it is more a presence than an absence, and it stands out from what is around it, but it is inert, flat, dead. And very satisfying. The Architect taps me on my shoulder to tell me that we are moving on.

Most of the area here is pretty fully conceived though, and, the Architect tells me, what I see today should give me a decent sense of the program's capabilities.

"Do you like it?" prods the Architect.

"It's amazing."

"Of course, it won't look like this for very long."

"Why's that?"

"As soon as the product is released, consumers will enter the space, begin occupying it; and they will construct buildings of various kinds. Soon, there will be houses, fortresses, towers, temples, shops, windmills, banks, malls, hospitals, theaters, pleasure domes, bunkers, tree houses, legislatures, hovels, lighthouses, restaurants, apartment blocks, cottages, hobbit holes, stilt dwellings, yurts, tent villages, high-rises, barracks, dormitories, longhouses, pubs, projection rooms, odea, gymnasia—"

I can immediately grasp the appeal of having a place like this to oneself. So quiet. If only one could be totally alone and anonymous in such an untrammeled land.

"The problem is: everyone builds," the Architect explains. "Nobody just walks around and looks. It is as if none of it is real unless it is interacted with. Like I said, everyone needs to get their hands dirty. Every world I've ever designed rapidly became overrun with stuff. I build spaces you see, Mr. Frobisher, and a space is merely a potentiality toward a state of fullness; toward being occupied. Even worse, the stuff we build 'in here' ends up colonizing the world 'out there.'"

"Irl?" I say.

"In subtle ways. But, yes, it escapes. Creeps out. People experiment in here, and that work then becomes a model for work out there, which in turn—"

The simulacrum is just stunning, and quite tangible. I feel like coating myself in it. Grabbing handfuls of it, leaves, sky, water, and clouds, and rubbing it on myself. Would I feel it if I did? Would the world feel like a warm coat? A second skin? We are surrounded by fronds, all reaching up and swaying about us like hands at a revival meeting.

I imagine building a little house Rn, far away inside the virgin forest. Just a single dwelling. I'd stop at one.

Dennis sidles up from behind me.

"So," he leads off, "caught, eh?"

"Mmn."

"I suppose we really fucked up."

"It's not so bad though."

"Maybe not for you, but this is strike three for poor old Dennis."

"What does that mean?"

"I'll go back. I've been expelled. Un-Laddered."

"Your project?"

"As I said when we met, few of us will grab that brass ring."

"I will."

"You seem to mean it, bless you. And good for you."

Mr. Royal taps his simulated cigarette once more, forgetting it is incapable of producing ash. He takes a step back. "Frobisher," he says, affectionately, "you really are a shit-for-brains." Holds out a hand which is so light in my VR glove, and I realize suddenly that I would prefer to just keep holding on to it, even in its insubstantiality. I feel a sudden and unbidden affection toward him, but Dennis is walking away now.

鼎福 the Architect leads us down a new trail now which leads toward an enormous, insurmountable horizon, and you can just tell that we are almost at the end of the landscape. There is another matte gray square, about ten feet tall, in the middle of it. The Architect beckons us into the portal, but this time I insist that he go first, and reluctantly, he does so, and then Dennis follows, and Mr. Royal's disembodied foot disappears, and that is the last of him. So long, Dennis.

I hesitate.

I'm alone. Alone again.

I take a moment here, to appreciate the pure potential of all of this. I look around, 360 degrees, breathing in the untrammeled space and its spacious nothing-air before noticing a small wodge of paper, speared, high up on the spiky edge of a palm made of polygons.

Even here.

I step into the gray portal and quickly flash through several biomes, like cards in a rapidly shuffled deck.

(GROUP)

"See the news this morning?" the new admin asks us, cheerfully.

I saw the dust cloud on the feeds about an hour ago. A sepia filter, drawn down over a photo of the world. Scorching temperatures. Harmful particulates. Work sites abandoned. Ports closed. Airplanes grounded. Day becoming night. Emergency crews everywhere.

"Glad I don't live out *there*," she laughs, treating the whole misfortune as merely another opening gambit. "Now let's get started, shall we?"

———

Once again with the room, the bong-water coffee dregs, the chalky scones, the beautiful chairs, the window. Earnest clasping of hands, half-hearted hugs, general emotional paralysis.

This time we've got the Conceptual Artist, the Theologian, the Photographer, and the Woman-Whose-Face-and-Hands-Are-Covered-in-Yarn . . .

The Conceptual Artist goes first. He tells us that he began his new project, as he begins all of his projects, with a picture. A picture he has made. (He shows it to us.)

After the picture was finished, looking over it, he felt as though he was headed in entirely the right direction. (This was several days ago.) He hung the picture up on his studio wall, then wrote on an index card the words: *"Art Move, Number One,"* and tacked that card up underneath the picture like a caption.

Following this, he grabbed a chair, sat backward upon it, resting his folded arms on its seat back, and stared at the work.

The picture was, he decided then, no good.

It was too sincere; it explained too much! Too much of himself was shown. The work was too revealing—but, you know, in a bad way, which is to say revealing, but not revelatory. ("Don't you agree?" he asks, as he holds up the offending article.)

It occurred to him, to the Conceptual Artist, then, that perhaps the index card, the label itself, was the key. He must begin with the label! The label was everything. The answer to the project would lie with naming.

Later that same day, he duly attempted to generate energy from out of the labels.

He labeled everything in his studio, not limited to, but including: the four walls of his studio; its eight corners; all of its windows; all of the joists and beams; his desks, workbenches, chairs, lamps, whiteboards, bulletin boards, computational gear, outlets, air-conditioning units, floor-boards, cups, saucers, utensils, office supplies, duplicators, art materials, food, hampers, garbage cans, candles, print-ers, room screens, blankets and pillows . . . etc., etc. He had even tied a string to a joist in the middle of his studio and hung a card from it inscribed "Air/Aether." (The string is labeled as well: "String.") The Conceptual Artist's very own Tea Boy submitted to being labeled. The Conceptual Artist was, of course, himself, labeled ("Conceptual Artist"), as was every item of clothing he wore. Everything was named in what felt like a feat of ostension not seen since Adam labeled the garden.

And at the end of the day, as burnt light began to creep around his studio windows, he sat back again on his chair ("Chair; sunlit") and examined his labors with, even he had to admit, some degree of satisfaction.

Until he noticed that the labels were, themselves, unlabeled.

Rats,

———

(We thank him for sharing.)

The Photographer has adopted the use of an enormous camera obscura, which he has successfully rigged up for employment. Here's how it works: "The pyramidal rays from an object receive a decussation, and so strikes a second base upon the retina or hinder coat, the proper organ of vision; wherein the pictures from objects are represented, answerable to the paper, or wall in the dark chamber; after the decussation of the rays at the hole of the hornycoat, and their refraction upon the crystalline humor, answering the foramen of the window, and the convex or burning-glass, which refracts the rays that enter it." So, using this comparator technology, he has attempted a self-portrait.

Unfortunately, the metastructure, even in its reduced state, has been shown to mediate natural light in such a way as to render the camera inoperable. Therefore, he takes it upon himself (despite specific warnings not to do so from his admin, admin12) to move the camera off-site, outside the solar array and the dome's perimeter.

Tragically, though predictably, the camera has melted under the desert sun.

He has, nonetheless, considered submitting the liquefied camera itself to the Institute in lieu of his original project.

(We summarily, and unanimously, agree with his decision to do so. Without reserve. Amazing, we tell him. We, our Group, has perceived, instantly, that the melted camera and plates, his work's scrap and flotsam, its slag, are 1. Also what life looks like, 2. What every project is, ultimately, anyway; that is: what gets made, and 3. He and the Conceptual Artist should probably switch projects.

"Congratulations," we all say to the Photographer-now-Conceptual-Artist, slapping him on the back and raising our cups in a toast to project completion and the final rungs of ladders. He is, after all, the first in our company to ascend, so the whole thing is quite new to us and therefore a bit confusing. Completing a project? In this case purely by accident?

Thanking him for sharing gets lost in a demonstratively celebratory atmosphere. (The truth is though, his fortuitous success has momentarily driven us all, individually, inward, and the enthusiasm is, of course, faked.)

The Woman-Whose-Face-and-Hands-Are-Covered-in-Yarn goes fourth. She has a specific complaint. She needs to complete her Artist's Statement, which explains in detail why she has *covered her face and hands in yarn*. The statement is past due. However, when she sits down to accomplish this seemingly simple task, she finds herself unable to write or whisper to her device, due to the intrusiveness of the yarn itself, which, as it gets more wet, expands, and becomes more and more tangled, until it mittens her fingers and stoppers her mouth entirely, leaving her unable to do more than to scrawl, or mumble untranslatable gobbledygook. She fares no better with attempting to mime her statement. It is hopeless.

(It is, of course, very hard for us to understand even

this story as she tells it, and, in fact, what has just been recounted is no better than my own tentative guesswork.) We thank her for sharing, despite being unsure of what was shared.

My turn.

34

(THE PAPER CONTINUED)

Returning to the deep desert for a moment we zoom on in, over la Tour Eiffel, which is, you will remember, uncoupled from its context. It is stranded in a godforsaken nowheresville. The monument is as hot as an iron and totally useless, except, that is, perhaps symbolically (and even then). Yet here is another strange development: the tower now has something simply massive draped over it, practically covering the whole shebang. This something is, accordingly, paper—but now, to add insult to injury, this sheet of paper has grown to the size of a football pitch, and is impaled on the tower like a colossal newspaper article on an editor's spike. All of which is to say that *scale* is now all fucked up on top of everything else. And speaking of "on top of everything else," there is another of these giant white mantles currently draped over *the entire metastructure* and though, from my vantage beneath it, I look up at the sky and imagine that it is darkest, moonlit night—and this fact is soothing to me, a respite from the anxious confusions which crowd the daylit hours—the situation more closely resembles that of a birdcage covered by a blanket; covered in order to get that restless and compulsively talkative parrot to sleep.

To sleep. Sleep. Please sleep . . .

But I can't. Can't quit my thoughts. Too much troubling information to process. In the Library Annex today, a bit of rubble had fallen from the ceiling onto the beautiful polished concrete flooring—the debris lying there in the path with no one to pick it up. Through the hole in the ceiling, the inner space behind the wall was laid bare, and I saw among the infestation of plantlike rebar, there, stuck to the metal, deep up inside the iron grid—yes, more paper.

It's even inside the walls.

It is everywhere.

Of course, it could be worse. There are still things to do here. Work. Still occasional outings. Presentations. The dogs are still brought in once a week.

We still get deliveries. Supplies. Food. (We fellows aren't expected to have to *eat* paper. Yet.)

But the influx is troubling.

And Psa, the paper is mine, of course. It is for me—meant for me. I am both the cause of and the solution to the paper. (For which I would apologize, if I could. I would apologize for any inconvenience it might be causing. Is clearly causing. I am aware that my paper is just a massive pain for everyone else here. Mea culpa.)

What I will say is that: here the material is. Here it is. Stranger still: the material is—the paper, that is—showing me things; telling me things.

Gives me the sight I otherwise lack.

It shows me wonderful, fantastical visions. But also, I am coming to see that it also betrays difficult truths, all manner of disconcerting sights, events I shouldn't have access to, or be able to witness.

Is it making a picture? Telling a story? Setting a stage? Do facts need to be established?

Wtf.

(PICTURES)

Now . . .

The late afternoon finds me semi-reclined, out by the Observation Point, peering into the yawning void. Resting on my knees, also semi-reclined, is this novel I can't finish, though god knows I keep trying. This is one seriously tedious read, and it's winning the war we are fighting. There's only so much one can take. Hundreds of pages of (albeit transcendent) sick-lit. The protagonist: a real boob. And all the other characters: flat as can be. Worse, they are mere mouthpieces for the author's abstract interests. Wooden, all of them. It is all handled so clumsily. Though I must admit that the book does have a kind of cumulative effect. A nimbus of *late times*—dying worlds, the corrupt breath of the grave. For what it's worth (and apropos of the "cumulative effect," I am beginning to wonder if all of these clumsy characters are meant to form, collectively, a single conceptual apparatus. Idk.) I/a/c, our "main guy" here is, at this very moment in the text, semi-reclined as well. He's lounging about, staring into space—which is all he seems to do frankly—and once again the question arises: Why should I care about this idiot and his woolgathering? Considering the matter, I come to the conclusion that, our specific philosophical commitments aside, this stupid sickling and I—I in my desert, he on his alpine porch—do share an unhealthy preoccupation with time. So perhaps there is some lesson to be gleaned here; I could stick with the story and see where this amateur philosopher's obsessions lead him . . . though I'd certainly rather experience my own tedium than read about someone else's. Tbd. I'll leave the decision for another time.

The air is strangely mephitic today. It's enough to drive one inside.

I put my book back into my bag, and while the bag is open, I root around in there, find my recently Same Same'd device.

With all that's been going on here I haven't had a moment to examine it closely. Some interesting developments.

To wit . . .

The device is good as new. Of course.

Look at it.

As with the uniform, the Same Same man has outdone

himself. The device's outer shell is gleaming—all the dents and cracks are gone. All functions are go, everything purring along, beautifully. If anything, the device is faster and more responsive than it has ever been. As well as having fixed the hardware, the Same Same must have also upgraded the firmware, all the code, etc., etc. New everything, so on. The device is both more efficient and more helpful than ever, and is whispering now at a glorious and remarkable speed and capacity. And most importantly now shows no signs of pinging uncontrollably.

It's been delightfully mute.

Later . . .

I say that the device is as "good as new," but that is not true: it is, in fact, *better*.

I spend some time reacquainting myself with it, ensuring that all the settings are now correct and the customizations intact (they are). I enjoy a sequence of whole new entertainments that were previously unavailable to my old operating system. Some full immersions, various networks, games, platforms on which to game, apps for purchasing clothes and music, food and drugs and pet supplies and cosmetics and companionship and content of all kinds, browsers, various media players, apps for tracking this and that, organizing this and that, recording this and that, so forth. . . , It is only after I look through my pics that things begin to get strange.

———

So . . .

I'm looking for the picture I took the night I went up to the roof, the picture of the night sky. Amid the profusion of photos of the campus, here: fellows, pristine lawns glistening, fountains crystalline, palms swaying, the formidable concrete . . . I find it. There's my dark square. And I notice something strange: the square is now altered; it is white now instead of dark. Almost solid white. Which at first, I think, must be a filter I forgot I had applied.

Certainly, my other photos seem unchanged. Scroll, scroll, scroll. And then I see one (and this is the really strange bit), this one photo, a selfie I took when I first arrived at the Freehold, a picture to announce and memorialize my arrival here.

It shows me grinning, pointing out through a window at a sign outside the airport.

Like   Share   Tag   Delete

And anyway . . .

I took the shot, and I remember thinking, at the time, that the airport, the Freehold Aerodrome, might as well be just about anywhere. Palms and gentle lighting and carpet geometrics and the soft throbs of music. AC so cool. Like a moon base: hermetically sealed. (Soft music: piped in. Fresh air: piped in. Did we all fly in, I thought, or are all we travelers also squeezed out—suctioned through fat-pipes out from some vat of raw hominid sludge and pneumatically forced through conduit systems of subterranean tubes until everything and everyone is plopped upon this terrestrial plane, into, specifically, this airport concourse, with its check-in desks, carousels and lines, etc., etc.?)

Also . . .

The sign "Welcome to the Freehold" proved beyond a reasonable doubt that I was, indeed, there, here, in this crazy foreign place, far, far from home, and so I took the photo then to prove it. Prove it to whom? To everyone, as one does. Idk. But also to myself. To make it real, obvs. But the sign was bright, intense against the desert sky. It was.

The sky in the vivid heat of day.

But hey there . . .

In the photo, in the selfie, I'm there trying to smile—a stab at a Fomo-inducing "look at me and check out how far I've traveled" affect.

There I am, but now: in the dead of night.

Furthermore . . .

I'm not in an airport anymore. Where am I?

I scan the pic for evidence.

———

Crucially . . .

I am outside, and behind me you can just make out that there is a looming mountain, amid the cragged notches of other, smaller mountains, a series of dark copses and vales . . .

And . . .

It is snowing.

35

(IN WHICH I FIND OUT WHAT I AM)

My photos have been tampered with. Or my device. That much is clear. The Same Same shop has screwed up this time or otherwise meddled somehow. An accident, perhaps; it cannot possibly be an act of malice, could it? What do I really know about this guy? What do I know about his methods; his motives? Did my uniform seem changed when I got it back? My checkers, my pen, my shoe? True, the uniform did smell different, but it was otherwise the same. I think. But my photos have definitely been Same Same'd . . . wrong, or something. Shit. Someone else's perhaps? Something has happened, and I realize to my horror that these pics, these memories of mine, could be morphing still. Mutating, even now. The very facts of my life, my personal history, shifting while I sit here doing nothing about it.

Unable to rest, I get up, get dressed, and am off on one of my night walks.

The Institute is empty as could be. I try each of the buildings and they are all dark and locked down for the night. I am the only insomniac in the universe tonight. Defeated,

I head to my Observation Point to plot my next move, but while I'm on the path which feeds it . . .

The sounds of muffled unrest.

Sounds, coming from another path, a path which leads to this one. Sounds of something moving chaotically through the brush, these sounds broken by occasional grunts. Something crunching up the path—a large animal perhaps. Whatever or whoever it is, it is moving quickly and with intent.

I get up, and leave my position, moving at a casual canter. I am just at the point where the trees dilate back out into the expanse of the Institute lawns. It occurs to me to hide, to retreat back into the comfort of the middle of that black wood, but I realize to my horror that it is too late, that I must have already been spotted.

The sounds grow louder and louder and out of the black comes an inchoate blob which continues to resolve further into a group of shapes. And these shapes become men. Heading straight at me.

"STOP," they command. . . .

They are after me—have come for me at last. My mind paralyzed—remembering "the Night Struggle" brings metal to my mouth, and my body twitches to run.

But where could I run to? The hedges are closed-in, there is no leaving the path.

"Hello?"

No response.

They keep coming.

"Sorry!" (I cry, as I finally bolt.)

Bursting through the hedge tears the skin on my exposed arms, but still I push deeper, deeper in until I am through to the other side, and Rn I hear voices rise up in alarm and I'm off running down a new path now but realize suddenly that I am heading straight toward the glacial lake, which means open ground, and sure enough there is the posse on the far side having sighted me, splitting into two parties heading around the water in a pincer-movement, so I dash back again toward the wood and stop, briefly, to catch my breath in a small contemplation arena attempting to keep my breathing quiet and suddenly the path lights up, here they come, through my flinch, I see the bloc of men striding toward me, now in a wedge formation, and I bolt again out of the far egress and onto a lawn, and as I'm jogging away I see the lights on in the Presence Center far off twinkling and beckoning and lights mean safety and other fellows (and where is everyone btw?) and why am I always alone out here at night anyway; but I'm hopping over an ornamental plinth and off round an obclisk and down a third path

The rest of the chase to be indicated by arrows

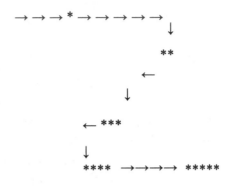

*	Fuck me, another hedge.
**	Have to deke one way & go the other to avoid collision. Ill-judged; barely escape.
***	They have me, but I'm a wriggler, exit stage right. . . .
****	Hedge number 3 and I'm cut up pretty badly, but off I go again.
*****	Wrestled to the ground by five of them, & what's the use in fighting, NB but it takes all five.

. . . of them; five admins.

"Why aren't you answering?" the lead admin demands, brusquely.

"We've been pinging you," the second says.

"Regrettable," a third adds.

". . . as you are already very late" (the fourth).

The rear admin: "We need to leave."

"But where are we going?" I plead.

I find we are heading to the Pleasure Center. Odd site for a meeting. I practically run to keep up with the admins, one of whom has me by the arm in a sturdy grip.

"Not the Pleasure Center," one of them corrects: "beneath. The Wellness Center. Down in the baths."

I'd never visited the spa and baths, on the floors beneath the Pleasure Center, in the bowels of the Institute's general undergirding. We take an elevator down to the subfloors, where we enter a stairwell, and walk yet another flight of stairs down, entering the spa.

I am taken to a small room.

"Please relinquish your uniform. Hurry, sir. You are quite late. Your tardiness has put you at a disadvantage in these matters, right off the bat. Do not compound the problem." He fixes me with a schoolmaster's stare, a look which brooks no contradiction, and I carefully remove my uniform under his scrutiny, and hand it to him.

"*Everything* please," he commands.

What choice do I have?

I pull down my undergarments and remove my socks and stand before them with my hands held out and down in front of me. One of the admins crouches and scoops up the remainder of my clothes, and then they all turn to leave.

"One of us will be back for you."

Ten long minutes later, in which I seriously consider the possibility that a mistake had been made, and that perhaps I should slink away (can't: no clothes), a new admin/orderly appears, wearing a uniform of dull pink. He hands me a towel, which I quickly attempt to wrap myself in. Unfortunately, it is too small for total coverage, so I am forced to merely hold it in front of me. Fig leaf. Better than nothing, I think.

I am led out, and downward, via a grand, open, marble spiral staircase. There, in the artificial twilight, I see several other workers, these also in pink, instructing other fellows, shepherding them in and out of the system of rooms at regular intervals while monitoring temperature charts. Other admins are also present, in blue, for those fellows who suffer from specific complaints (the new admin explains), mostly nervous disorders and other various psychogenic illnesses brought on by creative impulses (palsies, contractions, rheums, cold tumors, affects of the skin, aches, etc., etc.), all of which are to be treated through balneology, hydrotherapy, and physiotherapy. My guide runs through all this in a clipped, rote recitation.

He tells me how the spa works. The primary takeaway is that the treatment consists of an intensely regimented cycle of stations, leading one inexorably out from heat and up through frost.

When we reach the first of the inward spiraling chambers, I am told to hand over my meager towel, which I do without complaint, though with extreme embarrassment. I enter a series of overhead showers. All the spigots are off, and I search for dials or handles and find none. I stand, bewildered, under the vast heads, on the tile floor, listening intently for any sounds, any sounds which might forewarn . . .

The water rains down.

It lasts a short time.

Emerging from the stalls, I get my towel back and am

led into a sauna; the large door is closed behind me. In the perimeter-less room of many tiled tiers, I choose the lowest one to sit upon. I am handed a compress, which has been doused in water, to place around my neck as the heat rises, and so I do this, but in a matter of minutes any residual coolness is gone from it. Large orange heat lamps shine down upon me like demonic eyes. I look over and think I see Disputant 1 or 2, or someone with a similar shape. A baleful gaze from under a towel. Hunched over like this in his whites, he looks like an ancient and corrupt pope— an anti-pope—and, watching him, a drowsiness begins to come over me as I bake in the intense, dry heat, both of us quietly demonstrative to one another that all conversation is inappropriate here. Our near silence lasts through the entire portion of this medicinal cycle; and in the end, I am not sure if it is even him. Or anyone. Meanwhile the heat passes through various points of unbearableness until I almost lose consciousness and only with the help of the bath attendants I am hoisted to my feet and led out of the scalding chamber and into the next station.

This is the "cold room," a chilled, dark space, spiced with faux terpene scenticles, an odor which I am told is sovereign in treating, mollifying, cleansing, resolving a variety of complaints. The roof above me is bedazzled with rhinestones, and in the scant light they sparkle like faraway stars. The cold here is, at first, felt only as an absence of heat, and in direct relation to it, before becoming a positive factor in its own right. I breathe as deeply as possible, and can almost imagine myself alone in an ice cave on some faraway northern shore.

Time passes.

A tinkling sounds through a speaker, and I am escorted out and across to my third environment: steam.

This room is almost impossible to mentally encompass. Upon entering, I cannot see any walls, just endless fog. It is only after exploring using touch that objects (or people?) are found, and, circumnavigating the room in this way, proceeding along the wall leftward all the way to the utmost shore, groping with my hands, I find that it is a great, tiled circle, ringed by an enormous bench. Great gasps can be heard from vents as the floor exhales its hissing steam. I take up my position, and sit, hunched. A new towel is handed to me by a pink shape, and I drape it over my head to catch perspiration. This serves only to lend a further hieratic atmosphere to the already myth-laden space.

A low and accented voice comes on over a loudspeaker, and I am given a short, but interesting lecture on steam, on its ambiguities—being neither aether nor matter—and a lesson on what this intermediary state can teach one about the nature of boundaries. The voice describes the mechanical process through which this vapor is made available to us, and concludes with an informative speech concerning taxonomies of matter. When the presentation has finished, it begins again, but this time in German. (Next, French.)

I listen, and the room seethes, and around this disembodied voice, in descant, I can make out other quiet voices in the murk—no doubt belonging to other fellows—though after only ten minutes in the miasma anything becomes possible, and the vague sounds and shapes of my cohorts could, once again, be evidence of anyone or anything. One such adumbration is so large that at first I think it a structural element of the room, a pillar, or even a small tower in the distance. Huge—though this very well could have been a trick of the fog, a refraction or mirage. I try to reconfigure my sight to accommodate this shape, but it refuses to resolve into anything recognizable. Now it twitches, and I shoot backward in fear. Had it moved? Everything here in this necropolis is uncertainty. As I breathe in the scent of what I believe to be a woodbine air-freshener (for there could be no such thing as the real deal, as a health-giving thermal spring, in a desert such as this one), I think suddenly that the shape is certainly a very large man. When it dawns on me with a sudden, coppery dread that it is certainly the Director, and that I have been led into one of his infernal offices.

"Hello?" I probe.

"*Sdfgiyssisudfibssamècchezzzabìalmiiiszzdfhoss*," comes the response from across the way.

"What?"

"*Vibroskomenotaf blaf blaf.*"

An abject terror grips me and I feel my gorge begin to rise. A series of scenarios present themselves in rapid succession like posts on a diabolical feed: the monster rises and in two quick strides is upon me, grappling me in its immense and naked bulk, slippery and malodorous and inescapable, loose flesh enveloping me, my project incomplete, my corporeal body forcibly merged into his epidermal mass . . .

"Who are you speaking to?" asks the pink-suited admin, suddenly and puzzlingly by my side.

"I thought—"

"Yes?"

The heat keeps falling fresh while he waits for me to finish this sentence, which I cannot, and don't. But then there is a brassy clang from a hidden speaker which indicates that my time in the steam room is at an end, and as the mists begin to dissipate, I see that I had been in error, what had been concealed was nothing at all, except a superimposition of my own imagination upon the blank ground of the shifting white fog. What had I heard? Who knows. But my ears are now both hermetically sealed against the world of sonic frequencies by the water which has infiltrated them. I hop on one leg, and then the other, in order to drain my head, but am unsuccessful.

Out I come, soaked and rubbery, and back into the cold showers with me. Now, I'm led by the attendants into a room filled with tables, each one piled high with towels, and other fellows under these towels. I am directed wordlessly to lie facedown, a semicircular extension cradling my head, a big U, a bed for my cheeks to rest in, so that all I can see is the basin of a bowl placed beneath me for the purpose of catching the sweat and saliva as it falls from my propped face.

The thrashings begin.

The red-coveralled attendants beat me with plastic switches which sting my back, the backs of my legs and arms. And even as I convulse beneath the bright blows, the pain feels most welcome; in direct contradiction to the soporific grayness from which I have just emerged. I am rubbed down with a synthetic lubricant, some sort of sweet glycerin. I am roughly pulled upward onto one side, rubbed along my entire length, and then flipped onto the other and rubbed in a similar manner.

It is at this stage, as I lie here passively, that I begin to feel more at home in this strange underground realm. The world at the apex of those spiral stairs I so recently came down seems so very far away. Compared to this regimented underworld with its Bardos and Malbolges, the outside suddenly strikes me as being a place of hazards and random event. And, just briefly, I find myself imagining that I'd not see the dazzling sky ever again—I have crossed a shore into this land of heat and ice, an almost allegorical haunt, the Institute's inner sanctum (the Institute itself being an inner sanctum of a sort), and I had allowed myself to become a full citizen of these inner realms, surrendering my body and will to them in a manner which I never could imitate up above and outside.

And just at this moment of complete surrender to these regimens, someone whispers into my ventral ear: "The next station awaits you."

So I am once again helped to a sitting position, and

allowed to suffer my head-rushes and reacquaint myself with being upright.

Another cold blast in the shower. And I am shepherded into a winding corridor leading to an impressive door, with a heavy handle. I pull it, leaning back to better leverage my weight against its bulk. Now, I see a series of casket-like tubs, each filled with some kind of greasy mud. I am guided into one, and the churning clay receives me with a series of impolite sucking sounds, like I am being slurped into this coffin for the purposes of being digested by it.

What is this mud? I'm not sure. Perhaps it is dredged by local workers from kilometers-deep wells beneath the hot sands. Perhaps it is cement, or pitchblende, or raw petroleum. I am not told. But its viscous heat firmly adheres to every contour of my comatose body, and I lie there, looking mostly at the stucco hanging down from the ceiling of the dolorous chamber, allowing myself to have a brain as muddy as the deliquescent solids I am now enwombed in, and think of the seminary spirit of minerals, whose prescripts matter must obey; and how they slosh about me, never idle, but always in action, preparing me, impregnating me, with what I am not sure. Visions, perhaps. Something in the slime vapors up and rubs against my mind. Halfway through the action here, between one hill climbed, and another perhaps yet to be climbed, in a delicious middle point of the fulcrum, curled, lazy. Such a Belacquan position corresponding precisely (geographically as well as metaphorically) to that of the Institute itself, a stasis so profound, found centrally, the origin point of X and Y, perfectly inert, between the outside world's ceaseless traffic and the position representing some kind of future transcendence; this is to say that I (and by extension the Institute as well) repose at the moment in a state of utter inaction that only the freedoms afforded by such colony fellowships are apt to engender.

I look beside me, and, perfect timing: there is another fellow (the Poet?) in the sepulcher next to mine, motionless as a statue. Next to him is another occupied tub, a limp arm hanging over its lip. A female arm. Pale as could be. The ashen arm and hand, in direct contrast to the bright and glossy nails. Who, having sepulture in these tombs, makes themselves audible with doleful sighs; a woman? Arching upward, and peering through the haze, I can see that she is turned sideways, practically facedown, in her container. One of her eyes is just above the mud, and is wide open, and strangely unblinking. Is it Miss Fairfax? Miss ☺ the Brand Analyst? The Mysterious Woman? A woman, surely . . . Wait, I thought, how can she breathe?

"Mr. Frobisher."

I sit right up in my tub, peer out, see something; and a struggle commences in my brain to make of it a man, and it is a man, and it is most certainly the Director.

"Sir?"

He silences me with a raised hand. He seems to be wearing a long robe of some kind. A long medallion around his neck, ending in a small, jeweled serpent's eye.

The Director's face like a mask.

Two attendants grab me under my arms and pull me up to standing in my sarcophagus, a risen golem, mud slowly oozing down and off of me.

A bell is ringing. Then stops. Then begins again, slightly more rapidly.

I feel no control over my body.

I am under the sway of some sort of vague command. I feel a strange tremor in my head.

I raise one finger.

Why? I raise another finger. Stop it!

(Am I supposed to speak?)

By now, several other figures have emerged, and are now standing near the Director. There are two people on either side of him, all of them mummified in white cloth, draped in towels. A small parliament.

They have me smell.

They have me taste.

They have me see.

They have me listen.

They have me feel.

They have me work.

They have me read.

They inquired into the content and nature of my thinking.

They put their hands on my cheek, in a slow-motion slap.

Then another man, tall and thin, stooped, second on the right from the Director, steps out of the line to address the others. He does so plainly and professionally, as a lawyer, or an accountant. They confer. He writes down results and consults again.

Finally, he turns to me and says: "It has been decided."

"Decided?" I stammer.

"You will be granted more time; we admit that some headway is finally being made. You are more than two-thirds of the way down the road. But remember that the Director needs to see the benchmarks hit: deliverables."

The parliament nods.

"DELIVERABLES," they intone in a chorus.

The performance, the masque: it confuses me. And the phrase "doubly obscure" enters my head.

"PROGRESS!" repeats the Director.

"ACTIONABLE ITEMS," the chorus chants.

"I'll do my best!" I cry.

"You must do better! ALTERBURG!"

"But sometimes, just sometimes, I can't even recall what it is I—"

"A novel. It is A NOVEL, Mr. Frobisher. Why are you being so terribly coy?"

"What the *actual fuck* are you telling me."

"A novel. Obviously. You are writing one. Now get back to it."

And all of a sudden, a torrential slick of mud tsunamis out from a hole above me in the ceiling above my tub, drenching and blinding me. I am knocked back into my sarcophagus again, rocked by its force. I wheeze and gasp, attempting to breathe, struggling back up to the surface. Finally, I attain the air, and, with two last rude dollops, the cascade stops, and the aperture above me constricts, and I hook mud out of my mouth with a finger. I hear the Director's voice again, but now cannot make out what he is saying.

There is another bell.

At once, my pink admin-and-guide is standing beside me. I am alone with him in the room once more. I look all around but there is no one else there.

Cheap theater.

Cheap theater.

Alterburg.

Doubly obscure.

Cheap theater.

And so I am led out again, along a rubberized floor to a stall where hoses are turned on me, I am rinsed with freezing mineral jets, until I can once again see my own flesh, my face flushed and wet (there's a sepia-tinted veronica of it left upon my last towel), and I materialize from that stall newly christened, and I walk down a short path with handsome potted trees to a series of chaises, chairs which have almost mysterious properties I find difficult to analyze, it is perhaps the most comfortable I can ever remember being, spread out on these contraptions, camel-hair blankets placed upon us, the alpine air siphoned in, and I feel a species of postcoital ease, wherein the body has been recently exercised in pleasure and spent, and so I collapse in heaven among the other reincarnated fellows, holy, arisen, all of us, and after an hour of silent contemplation in which I try and fail to make sense of this episode, a buzzer sounds, and the cycle concludes.

36

THE FUNDAMENTS OF MY PROJECT

Fundament 14. Imagine the coming world.

Fundament 15. I am "the Novelist." (Apparently.)

37

(A WORD TOO MUCH)

Waking Rn to my once-again-suspect device, which is playing a never-ending loop of "Thunder of the Great Cataracts."

"Zimzim: mute."

He does so, and I rise, donning my still-immaculate but now-perhaps-also-questionable uniform.

(This "arising" is, in fact, an extremely complicated affair, as the effects which have taken hold of me since the infernal incident in the Pleasure Center's general undergirding several weeks ago—"*Walpurgis Nacht*," or "the Examination," as I'd begun to think of it—show no signs of abating. Nervous apathy. A chemico-metallic taste in my mouth. A fearful tang.)

Yet despite all of this, I've been wribbing. Writching. Writing. *Writing.*

I've been ~~writzing~~ writing, see. Even as I lie abed. Scribble, scribble. I have been taking the Director and his unholy cohorts at their word. I am a novelist, evidently (despite evidence to the contrary). That is, I am actually writing a novel. I am being, to the best of my ability: "the Novelist."

(What else should I be doing, given the fact that the world is presenting paper to me in an unremitting torrent?)

Writhing!

In some very real sense, it is going quite well. The word count is mounting, the page count is mounting. However, I've noticed that my work is suffering from some sort of as-yet-unidentified infirmity. Something infecting it, I'm not sure what. A kind of confused quality (not to mention a secondhand and warmed-over one), such that I realize that much of what I have concocted here is destined for the garbage. So much of it is utter nonsense. I am new to this, after all, and there was bound to be a learning curve. Nevertheless, I am doing everything as I am supposed to in the hope that something good may eventually come of all this. Each day I compose myself at my desk, and, with a ready wit, reconfigured pen, scissors, tape, glue, my device, my printer, X-Acto knife, pencils, erasers, and an informed air, I begin to work. I make sentences. 1. Things-happening Sentences, 2. Observation Sentences, 3. Affectual Sentences, all of these joined up with 4. Glue Sentences, and there is even an ever-growing pile of 5. "Sentence" Sentences, which don't refer anywhere except to themselves. Most of my sentences, though, take as their subject 6. Characters. Characters are the crucial compositional element here, and the foremost of my nouns. A resource not to be squandered. Characters are not really covered in my Fundaments, and I am really making it up as I go along here, though I have, already, gleaned a few basic rules of thumb.

E.g., the number of characters in a project must be carefully regulated. There may only be so many, and so few. Also, a proper ratio of men to women, youngs to olds, principal characters to peripheral characters, etc. Also, characters should be of a "type." I build these "type" characters using words chosen to illustrate the category of character I would like to evoke—for instance, an angry character of mine will display behaviors which are common indicators of anger: *i. Red in the face, ii. Heavy breathing, iii. Raised voice, iv. Scowling, etc.* (The admins enforced an exercise upon us just the other day in which we were taught to recognize precisely these very anger signs, asked to observe such behaviors in ourselves, and even encouraged to add some of our own descriptions to the general lists which are posted on a bulletin board in our Group meeting room.) Of course, not all characters are angry. Some are overly familiar, or sarcastic. Some are funny; some are warm. Some are flat and blank whereas others are fully formed. In any case, all of my characters are provided with behaviors of a varying degree of complexity, though all of them, at base, behave (in my wriping) the way that people are supposed to behave, not just in the mindspace, but more importantly, they behave the way Irl characters are supposed to behave in the meatspace. E.g., there are plenty of characters in my work who *walk* and *laugh*, and *look* and *think* and *approach* and *depart, eat, smoke,* so on, and when people talk to one another in my work they also do other things, simultaneously, like *pick things up* and *put things down* and *shrug* and *sigh* and whether this is how it's done or not Idk but nevertheless all this behavior isn't sufficient to make a character so information must be provided about the character's past. That is, a character should have a history. The character's true nature, the character's motives, will be located in this historical background. Further to the idea of history, a character should be placed in encounters with the *historical*. Everything should take place in a *particular moment*. We learn about a character through this encounter with the particular moment, and we learn about the particular moment due to the character's moving through it. So: a twofer. Also, Btw, a novel should have 7. Themes. Themes will come back, again and again throughout a novel (I'm told) like a refrain in a song. Though, NB, unlike a song, a novel should never communicate its refrains directly. A novel should beat around the bush whenever possible, allowing these lessons to emerge slowly, in the novel's negative space as it were. It should never simply say such things outright. (To do this would be utterly cackhanded.) Anyway, back to characters. Always remember that the character is the subject of a novel, not the novelist. Characters in novels, as far as I can tell, seem to serve the quite specific purpose of blotting out the author. Not obliterating them, but, rather, distracting you from the fact that the novelist is still, always and forever, *right there*, next to you—boo—their hot, needy breath in your ear. The author's omnipresence is disconcerting, so the more character is built up and put on display, the less one notices the author hovering around. Thus, characters are for misdirection and for forgetting. Characters, as I've mentioned, are made of sentences; specifically, characters are nouns, clothed in adjectives. But to become fully fledged characters, they must eventually, as all nouns must: verb. These verbing nouns are the motion of the text. Its direction and momentum. And direction-sentences, in particular, when taken as a whole, form the rudiments of 8. Plot. Plot is a big one, and I find it hard to see right now quite how my plot will ever truly gel. The construction of plot necessitates, as far as I can see: the author being capable of encompassing the entirety of a novel in his mind at once so that he may build up its architecture. The writer, like a god, observes a sum total. Only then can he turn a book this way and that, and make those very important decisions about narrative tension and release. It is worth noting that when an author gets too preoccupied with the "micro"—the particulars in front of him or her (for instance the nitty-gritty of his sentences)—while neglecting this all-important "macro" component of plot, things tend to bog down and become wordy and boring and the reader will soon wonder where the momentum of a particular novel has run off to, and all goodwill on behalf of the reader will just dissipate, etc. Psa, the novel will be articulated into smaller bits using certain tried-and-true, off-the-rack methods; for instance, the division of the novel into chapters, and the division of a group of chapters into parts (I, II, III, IV, so on). But even so, even using such ready-made tricks, I find conceiving of this complete novelistic gestalt incredibly difficult to accomplish, and that when I attempt the mental feat of holding the entirety of the book in my head, the end portion, specifically—the project's denouement, its *future*— fades from view. The beginning is all clarity and confidence, sure. And even the middle of my novel is available to me (though it is blurring at the edges). The end though, the end . . . Anyway: *plot*. Language. Etc.

Fyi this is not an exhaustive list obvs, and there are so many other important considerations; the question of social criticism, the nature and flavor of novelistic causality, the mandate to exclude authorial motive, not to mention the whole question of what manner of language is employed, and under which circumstances (specifically w/r/t the correct ratio of colorful to workmanlike language [luminous to ordinary prose, so on[*]]). I do hope to return to some of these

---

[*] A BRIEF EXCURSUS ON WORDS.

I've been thinking a lot about them (words) lately; as naturally I would be. Whereas before, before all of this, I would generate language as effortlessly and mindlessly as if I were salivating it—now I am expected (required) to choose my words with the utmost care (attention). This is what writers do, evidently.

But I find it difficult.

For every word (term) I might want to put to use (deploy), there is (exists) another word which might (could) potentially accomplish (achieve) the same semantic, rhetorical, and poetic result (outcome, effect). Choosing between such words is difficult (arduous, onerous, taxing) and now, when composing (fashioning, creating, manufacturing) a sentence, most of my creative energies are exhausted by having to play out just such long lists (collections, catalogs, compendia) of synonyms. The more I am required to contend with the synonymic function of language, the more the very idea of a *mot juste* begins to seem ridiculous to me. No word could ever be the *one* word for a given context; how could it be, when words only mean anything by virtue of their

questions soon and eventually decant my conclusions into a new set of Fundaments, a set of "Post Hoc Fundaments," which will describe the principles I will have employed in order to have completed the project.

Either way, I do hope that the key to all of this, all of it, is my arriving at some real, palpable *feel* for my main character. "My guy," as I think of him (he is still as yet unnamed). It's been explained to me that I should feel him out, get to "know" him.

The key is, clearly: him.

(If I could just see him, or understand the inner workings of his mind . . . If he only weren't so inscrutable.)

Still, the project accumulates.

Every day there is more and more of it. It builds in bulk, the project, strangely, even when I am doing nothing. I remain troubled by this fact: that I've no memory of ever having made some of it; ~~writtin~~ written most of it, that is. I mean written it down, personally. As I've previ-

---

equivalences? (Or small differences, you might counter; though only a cursory glance at the dictionary will tell you unequivocally [unambiguously, inevitably, unmistakably] that words equal nothing but other words, and that these new words, in their turn, equal still other words, and so on.) And I do wonder if my life might be improved if I could only lean upon some algorithm or bot to render my sentences for me. If the platform itself could autocorrect my words: employ its various automisms to change them; throw them into another language and back again, thus creating strange felicities; even predictively choose them, such that they would be granted a kind of aleatory grace, the grace my neurotic overworkings have stripped them of. That is, I wish for someone—or something—to translate my words. Translate them into a better, replacement language. One predicated on . . . on what? On a word's (I want to say: *rarity? Its oddity? Refinement? Elegance? Bombast, or some other species of stylistic force?*). Idk, but Tbd.

ously intimated, there is, undeniably, material that I've created unbeknownst to me. Without my being involved in the slightest. This last bit is a true mystery. When did I? How? By what means? Were the Fundaments employed? Idk. It is all, at this point, anyone's guess. I won't let it bother me. I simply join up this writing-of-unknown-origin w/ my own; join it up with tape, or staples, or string, paste (copy and paste), so forth. All that matters here, as far as the Institute is concerned, is that progress is being made—that I'm ~~wiring~~ (ach, writing) and that the word count and the page count are growing, and I am hoping (vainly, perhaps) that I only require time to shuffle it all about and carve it all down into something a bit more meaningful. Progress is progress; I don't wish to have it interrupted.

Ping!

Okay. No worries.

Take a look: don't get exercised. We've worked on this.

Calm thoughts.

A gap.

(THE GAP)

The dusty glare under the dome is now too much to endure without sunglasses, so I put them on. The world clicks into brown.

Writing time is over for now, so, it is out the door and down the stucco steps.

I find, as I walk the hot and palm-lined paths toward the Presence Center, that all I can think about these days is water. I am constantly parched, and until the Institute's thermostats and turbines are running normally again, it will remain this way. I contemplate the idea, for a moment, of deviating over to the grove, in order to splash some of its fountain water over me, to cool off in it, maybe take a surreptitious slurp of it. Slake this ferocious bloody thirst. But then decide better of it. The water is not great in this part of the world in general, I remind myself—I'd been warned about the water. And certainly, fountain water is non-potable, just swimming with bacteria. I'll have to wait. But water, water . . .

Then I am barged directly into by a man coming down the path in the opposite direction from me, whom I hadn't seen coming. A fellow. (A new one? Have we inducted new fellows, already? And under these circumstances?) It looked as if he had lowered his shoulder in an attempt to body-check me off the walkway.

"Hey!" I shouted at his taupe colored back.

"Dunce," he rejoined. "Look where you are fucking going."

"Excuse me, sir," I said, but he was already gone.

At which point a woman who is equally unfamiliar to me approaches as if to politely ask me directions whereupon I cock my head inquisitively, and she leans in, vivid with grievance, and violently sputters. Some of her words are lost to me, as if she were speaking in a foreign tongue, and perhaps she is, but some of it makes sense including the phrase: "you missed the debriefing."

To which I reply:

"Do I know you, madam?"

To which she replies:

"You are not even being serious."

"I think you may have me confused for someone else."

"You *are* someone else."

(Could this be one of the Institute's "unscheduled interventions" I have heard of?)

"I'm sorry not to be able to receive your prompt today," I say, shrugging with regret and offering the official Institute-sanctified deferral, "but I haven't the time right now."

"I am afraid."

"I'm sorry to hear that, but—"

"I am afraid that my head is a hand."

"Uh—"

"You make me puke."

"Yes, all right, there isn't any need for—"

"I need you to understand."

"Okay, okay."

"Come here."

And she gets up very, very close, and I'm not sure whether she's going in for a smooch, or head butt (either option is horrifying, to say the least), and shrieks.

"!"

Reacting quickly, I shove her aside, hand catching then slipping, briefly, on the shoulder of her loose tunic, revealing one motion-blurred, mottled, and baggy breast, and I scurry away, afraid to look back lest she be following me, her spittle and wormy breath on my neck; and she is gone now.

It's deteriorating. Denatured.

All of it.

(But, I think, but. These unusual exchanges might just work as "scenes" for my project. Tbd.)

I stop in the blue shade of a palm (not the shadow of its trunk, which is narrow and long, but rather in the shadow of its high leaves, which makes a dark, roughly round stain upon the lawn, just my size, trunk trailing off like the fuse of a bomb), and I try to catch my breath.

I'm so thirsty. Where will I get water? Looking up, I see that the sky has turned white in the heat. White even in my sunglasses. The sun reaching the apex of its traverse. I have to get indoors (*indoors*-indoors that is) before I become dehydrated and burnt. The bacteria-laden fountain is seeming more appealing by the minute.

My sweat begins to run into my eyes, blinding me, and I pull my tunic up to squeegee it off of my face, and then I hear a familiar voice.

"Oh god, Miss Fairfax. I have been looking for you."

"It's too hot, Percy. You should get indoors. Poor thing."

And she hands me a glass, beaded with cool condensation.

Water. I drink and suddenly the Institute, and Miss Fairfax, and the project, all begin to mean very little to me. I allow the heavenly cold to dispel the desert, the heat, the anxiety, everything. All of it. As my body contracts into the pure satisfaction of need.

Aaaaaahhhhhh.

Gap.

Later, I'm standing alone by the window of my flat, looking out over the blue grounds, naked but for my shorts, feeling the warm currents—carrying the faintest whiff of disinfectant—flowing over my skin. The bellows of my body does its tireless work. I'm not sure how long I've been standing here. Some of the lights are flickering far off, which could be micro-drones, or malfunctioning lights on the metastructure, or they could even be the strobes of distant stars, though this seems unlikely. Most of the campus outside my room is pooling in darkness. Something is happening at the Institute. "Possibilities are opening up here, lines are just beginning to blur," Dennis said. The evening is blurring everything, and all I can make out is a motley alphabet of possible shapes. It is quite lovely, actually.

There is a very strong wind out of the south. Disturbingly, some sand has entered the Institute. It is the first time this has happened.

Paper, sure, but now sand.

Dennis was right, that boundaries would blur; now they have, quite literally: blurred. The delineation of the Institute from the wilderness which surrounds it is now definitively smudged. Outside, inside; inside, outside.

Outside? We are going out soon. Out there again. All of us. There is to be another outing. Soon. Not mandatory, but recommended. Strongly recommended.

"Team building. Good for morale. Esprit de corps."

Another excursion for the fellows. With any luck.

Get us away from

the paper

our work for a moment.

More souks. A formal tea, in a white tent, out in the inky dunes. Out in the desert, which turns practically lunar at night.

A formal tea—served by women in robes. In the local manner.

White tents. White robes.

Tea.

Out by the massed-up clouds.

Rocks. Blue sand.

Then a group photo. In a couple of days. Or a matter of weeks. Weather pending.

So be it. It will give me something to *write* about.

For now, I hide in my room, between the metal railing of my cot's headboard and the particleboard armoire.

The pilled woolen blanket over my head; listening to the sounds of general movement. Of life going on without me. And I remember it, and wribe it down, record it for later use.

(BACK AGAIN)

Ps. I have begun to develop a cast. A motley assemblage of character types. A scholar, a rake, a functionary, an authority figure, a femme fatale . . . They are all ported into the thing from other places of course, but are performing the work allotted them decently, despite their new milieu (not in the sense that they feel "real," of course. They don't and that is dandy). My protagonist, though. My protagonist. He continues to prove elusive. So I've made a decision. A rather important one, Btw. I've determined that the central character in my work, "my guy," that is—as all novels must, one presumes, have a "guy" in the middle of things; a locus for the material, a hero of sorts—that he must be endowed with some definitive qualities; he must be rendered in greater detail than the others. Moreover, the easiest route for me, in terms of establishing these very granular qualities, would be to settle on an Irl model for my protagonist to take after—a real someone, that is, upon whom his fictional characteristics could be predicated, organized, and grounded. So the decision is this: that I will found his personality upon the bedrock of my own. Physical characteristics as well. As one does. An auto-fiction. The simplest way forward, I believe. Least work-intensive. Most surefire. See, I have no powers of imagination, no resourcefulness when it comes to invention (as things stand). No, I'm resigned to it. I just can't "summon" him. He does not respond to my call. So what better way around the conundrum than to simply perform a small substitution, me for him. (I will even name him "Percy.") I mean, no one will be any the wiser, and at least the depiction I will henceforth draw (of "my guy") will bear all the necessary hallmarks of verisimilitude. Using

this surefire method, I will mimesis the hell out of this protagonist. This "Percy" of mine will simply *drip* with reality.

Starting with his face. Here we go:

Face is variable. Situational. Depends on lighting obvs.
Time of day. Angle of approach. But a thumbnail sketch
would surely include the rather severe narrowness. Have
a bit of a horse-face frankly, all length, escarping precipitously back from the ridge of the long nose. Eyes are close-
set behind thick-framed tortoiseshell glasses.

Hairline eroding; the expanse of forehead gaining
ground with the tide of days. Though I am not old. (Not
young either.) And let it be known that I am not handsome.
Some women have told me that I am handsome, but I'm
not; and there is no accounting for what some women like
or will tell you that they like. I'm vain and I try to manage
my appearance, but I'm not attractive. Objectively I'm not.
Not hideous either. Just not beautiful. I'm not tall either. My
max morning height differs somewhat from my diminished
minimum evening height by virtue of that tariff imposed by
gravity, and of course we all diminish, also, with age, and
it is as if life can only but deflate us; and only an extinction has the power to replenish our stature; either those
nightly extinctions called sleep which elongate us on our
beds, or that final extinction where the constriction of our
bonds, our tendons and ligaments and fleshy matter, finally
releases with a sigh of arrival, and our bones drift apart at
last and we expand out to our acme, a height and breadth,
albeit horizontal, we were destined for.

But despite the variability of me (and him), and the inevitability of my (our) dissipation, you could say that I'm a small, narrow, pointy man. And so is he.

A keen man. A sharp man.

The facts are writ.

Satisfied for the time being, I decide on some R&R, and so I walk several circuits of the room, my arms folded behind my back like a gentleman farmer surveying his grounds, before arriving at a table and idly reaching for my self-assigned reading: my foreign-language epic. Let's get a couple of pages under the old belt, shall we? I cast an eye over its jacket (alliterative title in huge type; handsome painting of a small, W-shaped structure nestled in the hollows of a white wasteland; author's name; blurb) before cracking the binding. I read Rn, as I rarely do, while standing, my finger laboring beneath the words, pulling my reluctant eye along with it. *Now where were we . . .* right. Our simple-minded protagonist has met (while up on the mountain where he is convalescing) a whole town register's worth of characters from all walks of life. He's seen wondrous sights, encountered groundbreaking technologies and all new manners of thought (meaning that he, and by extension we, have been privy to some real, ear-poppingly high-level debate, none of which seem to make him any the wiser, and at the end of the day he seems as featherheaded as he did when he first debarked onto page one). Deciding once more that I *just can't with this,* I put the book back down and now travel the four steps over to my bed. I fling myself onto it, feel its gentle yielding, its expression of its own boundaries and affordances, which awakens a desire in me, and I muse, briefly, on the erotics of objects, before whispering up to full-spin that most intimate of objects, my device. Each time it responds to my call now, I am grateful. The device is throbbing its improved lights and gestures at me, almost showing off, what with its new speeds and sensitivities. Feeling, as it does, the mood in the room, it moves closer to me (or I to it?), and then it pulls up a panoply of images for me to peruse in order to further excite and relax myself into oblivion; the possibilities, as ever, limitless— the device knowing what I require. But now, I find myself looking back at my photos, and Wtf, finding more of them strangely altered.

More and more.

Like the pic of the night sky I took from the roof, now white, now, inexplicably, populated by irregular peaks, which may, I am now thinking, be the result of a bug, some failed data integrity, and, of course, my corrupted photo from the airport, but also, harder to dismiss, is yet another altered photo, the change to it being even more uncanny: my secret, sacred, surreptitious pic of Miss Fairfax, the one I use now, with which I am now intimate, there she is, as she is invariably—at the ready, looking the way she does, glasses, lilting posture, hair bunned up and fraying at the edges—but instead of her chic, bespoke uniform, she is now dressed in a decidedly workmanlike manner, scrubbed and exhausted bureaucratic blues, antiseptic whites, tag, clipboard, cuff, tools of the trade—that is, like a nurse.

PART IV

OPERATIONES SPIRITUALES

38

A nurse?

Get a grip, Percy. You are better than this. So obvious, so tawdry. My least favorite of the sexual iconography as well as perhaps the most perplexing to me personally. How does the erotic find a foothold in such sanitary wards? And what are the semiotics exactly: the administration of health and succor, but the aid administered not by a diagnostician, but by a subordinate of sorts, the subordination being hers, but also then, her patient's subordination to her (or *him*, but classically, fetishistically: *her*), the menial patient beneath the menial helper, she upon whom the patient is dependent and before whom he is helpless, dependency and helplessness being important, certainly—the dependency on that figure who is responsible for a certain portion of violence— violence inherent to the job—the violence to the patient, the swabs, the shooting-ups and the drips, the restrainings, the discipline of the regimens, the cleanings, wipings, and infantilizings . . . so humiliation also (so important, crucial), and then there's the uniform, its sigils, crosses of Christ and blood and deletion; X-axis health, Y-axis death,

Eros/Thanatos, sure, sure—red blood as in lifeblood, or blood which has been bled, vampirically drained, leeched, the patient: pale before the pale nurse, and of course far more important are the white uniforms—white, the whiteness of the nurse, the appalling page-blankness of the outfit, the senseless nothing of it, that nurse's rig of the collective imagination, the colorless field upon which will be, inevitably writ, a language of shit and blood and lymph and green-graying sputum; that canvas for decline, for mortality and death . . . But how is this, is this, all of this, what index . . . of what . . . to what . . . what titillation is there in . . . ?

This picture though. What's wrong with my device now? What is Miss Fairfax playing at? What is with the uniform?

Never mind. It does not . . . never mind. Impossible to analyze. Move on. Get back to work.

You have wrizing to do.

You need some commentary. Critical commentary. An explanation, a mea culpa . . .

Idk, a set piece. An allegory?

(THE PAPER CONTINUED)

A rollicking smack of white, insistent upon entry.

Piles and piles of paper. Clogging everything; collecting everywhere. But is it too much? Can the metastructure withstand the onslaught? It might collapse. The whole thing might come down. (Can that happen?)

Luckily, the Institute has put together a stopgap plan for the surfeit, one they are hoping will be a real morale-booster. So we head down to the main quad and assemble on the withered grasses. Boxes of tools are handed out by admins—staplers, paste, scissors, markers, crayons, inkjet printers hooked up to car batteries, string, an assortment of stickers, sparkles and rhinestones—and soon everyone gets busy, constructing kites. (We are taking singular advantage of the paper, evidently, by flying it.) Most fellows work alone, as kite building is a delicate business and it is well known that too many hands at work on a single kite tends to cause tears or lopsided constructions. The first builds of the day are motley—strange and beautiful, each one sui generis, each attempting to solve the twin problem of aeronautics and aesthetics in a unique manner—a variety of shapes and sizes; each utilizing a different method for navigation, lift, and propulsion. Some are round and some are tetrahedral. Some small against the desert sky, some huge enough to blot it out. (I later learn that the purpose of a few of the bigger kites is to carry a man or woman aloft. Predictably, all of these kites-as-vehicles fail in spectacular fashion, causing, in some cases, grievous harm to their pilots, though I suspect the clear-yet-brief view of the Institute and the desert beyond from on high makes the fall almost worthwhile.) Most of the kites are just for show though. The sky is swimming, spermatozoal with them: they squirm upward, wiggling, juddering, now falling. Some of the early kites are mimetic, resembling birds, butterflies, cats, dragons, etc., etc., others purely abstract, representing nothing but themselves and their own formal relations to the world. There are huge, flapping things, massive sky-spirals, tentacled, wormy super-beasts, and asymmetric space stations. Some: long and sleek; whereas others: blocky and as square as mainsails. Some kites are weaponized—and there are quite a few "kite skirmishes," which everyone enjoys. Some kites—that is, some of the most interesting kites—are made, clearly, to subvert the very idea of flight. These are the "crashing kites," and even more daring: the "ground kites"; those kites which are designed to never leave the ground at all, but to remind the onlooker of the constant and appalling pull of gravity. (Looking at such kites as the "ground kites" which are never supposed to achieve liftoff, and with these, I feel, as we all must, a longing for the air which is all the more intense for its abjuration.) However, several hours into the activity, I see now that many if not most of the kites are beginning to resemble the tried-and-true variety: the basic diamond shape that is, with cruciform struts, and a long, en-bowed tail. The usual that is; the "perennial classic," etc. This shape and structure has been proven, of course, to be flight-worthy over many centuries—and carries the benefit of a high degree of sentimental and nostalgic value (the benefits of which should not be discounted). Say "kite" and people just expect that kite we all know and love, that standard kite which exhibits the requisite modesty, probity. Which is nothing too flashy (above all, a kite should be sensible). Everybody wants to construct one of these "sensible" kites, and the kites begin, slowly and steadily, to shuck off their heterogeneity and converge toward a norm. At some point, one kite engineer discovers that the very paper he is using to build the chassis of his diamond-shaped kite is in fact a loose sheet from a kite-building manual. It outlines, in meticulous step-by-step detail, how to build the "old-fashioned," the classic, using tried-and-true construction methods, and so it is not long after this that *all* the kites, every last fucking one of them, begins to follow what becomes known as: "the textbook build." Prim and proper. It is difficult to remember now, less than half a day on—given how prevalent these classic kites are now—the degree to which they were, in the first instance, a contrivance. How quickly we forget. I cast my mind back to the early hours of aeronautical experimentation on the lawns here with fondness and regret. I already miss the strangeness of the early kites.

Of course all the kites actually work now—which is a major plus, don't get me wrong. There are very few failures. Each kite takes to the convulsive air with a sureness that no experimental kite could ever hope to attain. (True, in a small ripple of last-gasp experimentation, a few fellows begin to paint their kites with crazy patterns, bold colors, dazzle-camouflage, and, most notably: trompe l'oeil of various kinds. Briefly then, it seems as though we might return to the bold and garish times of the early builds, though, of course, we remember all too soon that these wonders are mere effects—that the new experimentalism has yielded truly nothing but impressive surfaces. Too bad, Imho. Too bad.) But as the winches and spools play out their lines, and heads tilt back, everyone seems content. People smile, as though the air were crop-dusted with serotonins; which it very well might be.

Anyhow, at the end of everything, there is a competition for Best in Show, and the judges (admins 2–6, a few representative fellows, the Director, of course) clearly deplore the formal restlessness of those weirder kites (the few holdouts that remain to be judged), and they (the judges) look with distaste upon (what they consider to be) that previous, avant-garde commitment to novelty, and to difficulty. They do not seem to find this new and almost enforced normativity in kite production blameworthy or even remarkable.

However, this reactionary conformism in kite design strikes me as rather middlebrow, frankly. I am no snob, but the more I stand here, neck cramping, watching the hot, yellowing air for a new flying contraption of any kind, any "disruption" at all of "the kite-space," no matter how awkward, immature, or otherwise flawed, I think that we at the Institute may have sacrificed too many species of pleasure in favor of the one, the surefire, the guaranteed, the failsafe. And in doing so have we foreclosed on new ways of navigating the sky? Idk, but I ask this question of 鼎福 the Architect, and he looks at me pityingly and replies, "Flight is what kites are for, and thus also what kites *mean*." The Critic chimes in to say that, in his opinion, "one should avoid at all costs—in kite-construction as in life—didacticism," and that "the only thing more tedious than an argument in favor of one's own tastes is an argument in favor of an *argument* in favor of one's own tastes." I understood them all then to mean that no matter which side of the kite debate you argued, one could not (as in ethics) turn an "is" into an "ought." And I felt keenly sad, though this was mostly because I knew that, were I to make my own kite, it would be one of those that never work properly, that don't even *fail* properly, and I would probably get paste all over myself, crepe paper stuck everywhere, and everyone would laugh at me, so on, and call me a fraud and an amateur and a charlatan (every kite a conflation of fact and fancy; every kite a diary manqué; a crypto-memoir).

Brb.

Anyway, I had thought of the kite projects as a classic case of "nature finding a way"; of our taking the ill fortune that is the paper, and transcending the difficulty through "a conversion of the problematic" (per the admins). I recline on the lawns watching a particular set of kites made from crinkly blue paper, the blue of examination booklets, the blue of fragile paper-gowns. On another note: the last of the turbines has given out, and so all of these kites begin bursting into flames.

39

(Q&A WITH LIVE-IN SUPPORT STAFFER, ADMIN52)

Q: Okay. Let me just make sure the thing is on. . . . So. We'll start out small: Appetite?

A: Not so great.

Q: We can give you something for that.

A: Food?

Q: Very funny, Mr. Frobisher. An appetite stimulant. What about exercise.

A: Not so much.

Q: Take advantage of the facilities. It's what they are here for.

A: It's just that I'm too distracted. I forget.

Q: Forget to exercise?

A: All sorts of things.

Q: [Scribble.] Are you regular?

A: Like clockwork.

Q: Libido?

A: Still have one. Last time I checked.

Q: What about your influences? Talk to that point.

A: Well, certainly I owe a huge debt of gratitude to many who have come before me; those who paved the way. Prepared audiences for works like mine. Done much of the heavy lifting. I can't neglect to mention the work of, say . . . well, I can't think of anyone in particular right now. But you know who they are.

Q: So, there haven't been any more of those incidents? Miss Fairfax reported that—

A: Huh?

Q: The plagiar—

A: NO. Sorry. I mean, I have it under control. I'm taking something for that.

Q: [Scribble, scribble.] Despite that, much has been made of this idea of your project as a—

A: Mirror?

Q: Read my mind. And how does the proposition make you feel?

A: Queasy.

Q: So, Percy, tell us a bit, if you would, about the project's *logo-centric turn*.

A: I am having some trouble hearing you.

Q: Oh. Wait. Better?

A: Yeah.

Q: So, where was—

A: The project's turn toward—

Q: Right. Words. Do you find yourself questioning the efficacy of a visual language? Of an aural mode? Of other channels of meaning?

A: Three times a day, I suppose. Could be more. Should I talk to Miss Fairfax about that?

Q: Yes. Let her know. Could be nothing, but we should track it.

A: I'm having wild dreams.

Q: Also not surprising.

A: In the morning, I wake up depressed and exhausted. Sometimes I cry in the shower.

Q: Ha ha ha!

A: No, I'm being seri—

Q: My next question, Mr. Frobisher, concerns beginnings. Can you tell us: How did you first come to this work? My audience is endlessly interested in origin stories.

A: I can't remember. There was a car. Or a plane. Train? And a mountain. And a hotel . . .

Q: Sorry again, we need to change the, uh, *thing*, again.

A: Of course. Go ahead.

Q: . . . Okay done. Sorry. Any cramps? Indigestion?

A: No. Maybe?

Q: Handwriting?

A: Bit shaky.

Q: Headaches, still? Would you say that you still retain the austerity and rigor which defined, to some extent, your early work?

A: I've moved on to a mode which is far more flamboyant.

Q: Do you take an adversarial position toward your audience?

A: No. No. Why does everyone keep—

Q: Numbness?

A: My toes, occasionally.

Q: Notice any new weird marks on your person? Scars?
       Moist spots? Stains?

A: Now that you mention it—

Q: What about anxiety? Paranoia? Itchiness?

A: My world is growing warmer. Less comfortable.
       Things catch fire. [Scribble, scribble, scribble.]

Q: Okay, well, that's it for now.

A: Really; nothing else?

Q: Nope.

A: Because—

Q: I've turned it off.

A: Okay. Well I hope that was okay.

Q: You were perfection itself, Mr. Frobisher. Just great.
       My readership will love it.

A: Can you send me a copy when it—

Q: Count on it. Someone from the office will inform
       you of your results.

40

(THE GREAT PETULANCE)

"Who wants to begin?"

For reasons which elude me, I've been remanded into the company of a whole new Group.

Who are all of these new fellows? I don't know a soul, but evidently, we deserve one another.

"Start us off, someone," the admin says. "Janet? Miriam?"

"I'll go," says a man I don't recognize who had, only a minute ago, edged another fellow out of the doorjamb in his haste to be the first into the room—to claim a seat in the circle as if it were the last in a game of musical chairs—and whose every gesture told the world he would be the first to speak. "And I'd just like to say this: that I am on to you."

"On to me?" says the admin.

"You."

"Meaning—"

"Meaning that I've seen what's going on here and I'm taking measures to protect myself."

The other fellows are still in pre-confluence-circle-mulling-around-mode here so there isn't much of a response to this guy's fervor, though I think I spy a couple of weary eye-rolls.

"Protect yourself from—"

"From you assholes. I know how you work."

"Whoa there," cautions the admin, "safe space."

"I know what I know."

"Who, even, are you?" asks a fidgety little woman.

"Who are *you*?" the man retorts. "That's a question. I don't know you either; are you one of them?"

"Let's start over," the admin says. "Make some introductions."

"Fuck," another woman says.

"You can't fool me," the first man reiterates, with a shrewd squint of self-satisfaction.

"Introduce yourself to the gang please, Harold."

Harold releases a languorous looger into his empty coffee cup, folds his arms, says nothing.

"Harold is the Cryptographer," the admin fills us in.

("Hel-lo, Har-old.")

"Fuck," says the Woman-Who-Evidently-Swears-a-Lot.

"Miriam?"

("Hel-lo, Mi-riam.")

Miriam smiles.

The little woman now: "This is a joke. Day-in day-out I'm the only fellow here who is making any effort at all to establish parameters for decent behavior for our circle, and I don't see why I always have to be the one who—"

"Janet," the admin interrupts . . .

("Hel-lo, Ja-net.")

"Yes, Janet. I'm Janet. Janet, Janet, Janet."

"Okay, Janet, what would you like to say," encourages the admin.

Janet again: "I'd like to lodge a complaint. That—and it seems obvious—I'm doing the lion's share of keeping order around here, following the rules to the letter and i-it's, it's like no one else is even trying."

"I am the Minimalist," Miriam now non-sequiturs softly, as if the admission costs her.

"Thanks, Miriam," says the admin.

"We did you already," says Harold the Cryptographer.

"You didn't say what your field is yet, Janet," the admin says.

"What does it matter? No one listens," she announces to the listening room.

"Well what about you, Mr. Frobisher?" says the admin.

("Hel-lo, Per-cy.")

"What about me?"

"It's time you introduced yourself."

"Introduced myself?"

"Yeah."

"Yeah."

"So—"

"So?"

"Go ahead."

"Go ahead and—"

"Percy, just introduce yourself, and please stop repeating after me."

"See, *see?*" exasperates Janet, "no one follows the rules. Not one of these dillweeds." She reaches over to tap one of her collarbones twice with two fingers and look up at the ceiling where there is precisely nothing.

"Fuck," says the Minimalist.

Janet shoves her chair back, gets up, and goes over to the table where the coffee urn is, and there she begins violently stacking the empty paper cups and arranging these small stacks into straight rows. "Slobs."

"There is no need for aggression, Janet," says a man I hadn't even noticed who is slumped in his chair at my nine o'clock.

"This is John," says the admin.

("Hel-lo, Jo-hn.")

"Hi," says John. "I'm the clock on the wall."

That said, he nods his head back onto his chest, closes his eyes, and while we are awaiting some clarification, instantly throbs his way, apparently, back into sleep.

"John is the Surrealist."

"John is unresponsive," says the Cryptographer.

"Fuck," says the Minimalist.

"I'm with her, yeah: *fuck*," says Janet.

"Now everyone, please . . ." entreats the admin.

"Incompetent shithcels," says Janet.

"As I've already said, Janet," the admin says, "this kind of response is not conducive to a creative environment."

"I knew it," Janet continues, "no one would help me; no one is ever able to help me. To move this project forward a single inch, and I still have to suffer the goddam indignity of—"

"Perhaps if you tell the circle about your work, Janet?" asks the admin.

"This bunch?"

"Try us," smiles the admin.

"No one will understand."

"Tell us anyway," says the admin.

"I am the Programmer," Janet says.

"Programmer?" I ask.

"Mr. Frobisher—"

"Sorry," I say.

"Go on," the admin says.

"I create executable instructions."

"And what kind of instructions are you writing?"

"Fuck," says Miriam.

"You said I had the floor here," says Janet the Programmer, demonstrably at her wit's end, "and I've barely gotten a word out."

"Did you hear what Janet said, guys?" asks the admin. "Guys? We need to listen better." The admin gets up and writes the word "LISTEN" on the whiteboard.

"We should, we totally should have some kind of system here for who gets to talk when, right? Isn't that what normally happens in these—?"

"You mean like a—" starts the admin . . .

"Yeah. Exactly," Janet the Programmer finishes, getting up and grabbing one of the coffee cups from the stack on the table behind her, taking the time out to meticulously rearrange the stack again so each pillar contains the same number of cups. We watch. She returns to her seat and holds up the single cup. "This is the 'Talking Cup,' okay? I have the Talking Cup right now and so only *I* can speak."

"Janet, it really is my job to decide how this goes," (attempts the admin).

"I have the cup and you will have your turn in a minute." (Janet.)

The Cryptographer, who had stopped paying attention awhile back, but has been, rather, whispering inscrutably to his device, startles at the outburst, scraping his chair backward on the linoleum. The Minimalist looks at the floor again, or never ceased doing so. The Surrealist is sleeping soundly. The admin waits patiently and you have to admire his poise in the face of such anarchy though these are exactly the scenarios they've trained for.

"Okay, Janet. Okay. You have the Talking Cup."

She holds up her talisman, waving it at each of us for good measure, then says, pointedly: "Thank you. Now where was I."

"Executable instructions," I repeat.

"Percy—" starts the admin, "sorry, Janet, continue."

"Don't you see?" asks Janet. "If we don't have the cup, we have nothing. *Nothing*. And I'm holding the cup, and the cup necessitates that I speak."

"The cup doesn't *necessitate* that you speak," corrects the Cryptographer, "the cup *designates* that you *can* speak."

"The cup is the last line of defense keeping us from chaos!" says Janet.

"Keeps us from chaos," I concur.

"Nothing can keep you from chaos," says John the Surrealist, awake once more and grinning inappropriately. "Chaos is the resting state of the universe, innit."

"And why do you think that is, John?" prods the admin.

"Because pancake, pancake, pancake."

"What the shit. I'm out," says Janet the Programmer, rising.

"Part of the process," explains the admin, patiently: "all part of the process. We say what's on our minds. Let it out! A powerful method. Things are bound to get a little wild from time to time, and I know it can be frustrating, and you are right, Janet" (whose hand stops on its way to the doorknob), "we do need to try to the best of our abilities to follow some rules here so as to allow all creatives to feel safe and listened to—but this is a kind of *controlled* chaos, okay, a chaos which allows us to air our positions and unburden our creative faculties; prompt one another, and move the projects along. It's the technique: the Ladder. And it's been proven to work. Our track record is impeccable. Everything we do here at the Institute we do for a reason."

"Obviously," says the Cryptographer, "the 'method.' But what are you really trying to do; what you want is to find out what makes us tick—even steal some of those bright ideas of ours, maybe? *Valuable* ideas. Yeah: I think the only people who are profiting from this creative lab of ours are *admins*."

The admin is shaking his head emphatically now. "Nobody is trying to steal anything, Harold. Not me. Not the Director. Not any of the admins. We are here to help."

"Are you? Aren't you, though? I know what I know," he reiterates.

"I know what I know," I say.

"Maybe we should call it a day," the admin says. Adding: "We've done some good work here." But the Programmer is already out the door and the Surrealist has gone back to sleep.

"Fuck," says the Minimalist.

"Miriam?" says the admin.

"Fuck," I repeat. This is a disaster.

41

(THE CHRISTENING BASIN)

This day kicks up the mightiest of the sandstorms yet. The sky around the metastructure vanishes in a wash of rust. A great brown blizzard, eradicating everything. It lasts for some twelve hours. Attempts are made to seal us in. Nothing in or out. Except the heat, which does not recognize the inside/outside distinction and will not be kept at bay. These storms are becoming more common; at least one a week. They aren't the big kahuna we've been warned about, but still disruptive. As a result of the frequent, wind-induced brownouts, not only am I less productive, but my thinking takes on a dull morbidity. (Though I'm clear of mind once again as soon as the dusts clear.) I'm beginning to feel that there is a purpose to the periodicity of these storms. That is: I can only be expected to create so much, before the world and its whims require me to stop.

Inside the dome, another palm catches fire, this time outside of my flat. Burning embers and charred fronds rain down on the patio. The whole thing exploded in a matter of minutes. I had been watching it. There was hardly any buildup. One moment it is not in flames; the next it is engulfed. A three-story-tall torch. Some of the fellows wander over to watch as well. I see them from my balcony— looking upward at me—as the light dances across their features. The Mysterious Woman is there, but only for a moment. She barely even stops to look at the tree. Though she looks up at me looking at her, and I see her register this looking. Eventually the fire dies down, leaving the tree ashen, several black fronds still hanging down at wrong angles like the ribbing of a broken umbrella. It isn't safe in here, in the Institute, I think, with so much paper about. I turn and walk back into the flat and sit on my bed to take fuller stock.

Worsening conditions aside, I am now continually watched, locked into a schedule, mandatory uniform, enforced diet, required, now, to contemplate an enforced sojourn. The restrictions are adding up. And what they add up to is an imprisonment. You would think that I am, at this point, a captive here. But I must also admit to having been a little cagey. A little sly. I have my own tricks, that is, my own sleights of hand and misdirections. Tbh the Institute knows a lot, but it does not know everything.

What I am saying is that, though I eat the colorful little foods from the segmented trays, though I attend the sessions, though I have been asked to forswear my old clothes, and though I will, assuredly, have to give my passport over to the Institute, I have made my own plans, and must now, in fact, work to maintain the appearance of normalcy. That is, while I wait for my papers to come back from Same Same–ing, the Institute's schedule needs to be upheld. I'm a model citizen once again. It is a performative state.

But I'm getting better at it.

I/o/w, I forget sometimes, and just sink, unconsciously, into the act; into my performance. So, it is a full twenty minutes into my sponge bath when it occurs to me to ask myself why I submit to such things as being cleaned by someone. Such indignities!

(I'm not saying the sponge bath feels bad, per se, but there is some shame affiliated with the experience, certainly.)

The sponge is of the thick, soft species. Not one of those brittle little loofahs that the other admins sometimes employ and which we all despise. Because Miss Fairfax knows what feels good. She knows what I like—as a lover might. She's paying close attention to my naked shoulders, sponging them in generous circles. The warm waters worm about me, filling-in-and-draining-from my clavicular hollows and other bodily trenches, unspooling downward into the tub where the rest of me is hidden beneath the creamy residue. While my admin cleans my body and treats my wounds—those paper cuts which now blight much of my torso—she speaks to me, low-like and soft.

"So what's with all of this paper, Percy?"

I smack the soap out of her hand, playfully.

"*Hey*—"

She reaches in to fish it back out.

"Okay, Mr. Touchy."

She rubs the soap on the sponge and just froths it up nice until the sponge is bursting with lather. Then the sponge goes to the top of my head where it is crushed out like ripe fruit, all the extracted froth flooding down upon me in a torrent, and I scrunch up my eyes. She adjusts the taps. The water's warmth slowly colonizes the rest of the tub in an outwardly moving perimeter.

"How does that feel?" she asks. "Temperature okay?"

I respond with a series of eye blinks, so she hands me a towel to dry my face.

"No more pain?"

"No. I mean: yes. The cuts."

She rinses an arm of mine with a retractable hose attached to the bath's main spigot, then moves on to the other arm.

"Stings? Here?"

I flinch, spasm, and send the soap flying again into the hollow-sounding water.

"Sorry!"

"What is it with you today, Mr. Frobisher?"

"You wouldn't understand," though, by way of explanation, I draw, squeakily on the vapored glass, one of these

:|

meaning not too much pain (though not *none* either) but it all runs together before she can understand my point. "Okay," I say, trying a new tack, "imagine my state of mind was . . ." I grope the reluctant soap off the bottom of the tub

369

and hold it tight, in a two-handed fist, ". . . hidden from you. I have these feelings which only I can think and feel. And I call this hidden thing 'my feelings.' "

I open my hands for her to see now, the soap newly minted, scalloped that is with the inverse of my clasp. I reclench my hands around it.

"Give it back," she says.

"It wouldn't matter what I called it. It could be pain, might end up being red soap, or green soap, or—"

She opens my hands again, folding my fingers back, gently, one by one, and takes back the soap, fully mashed. Haggard smile.

"You have trouble remembering words?" she asks.

"No."

"When did you first notice?"

"I remember words, obviously."

"Do you have trouble remembering in general?"

"No."

"What about names?"

"Of course I don't."

"Can you tell me who is who here? At Alterburg?"

"Wait, did you say—"

"Who clsc do you know?"

"Who . . . dammit. Dennis. Mr. Al'Hatif . . . You, Miss Fairfax. Me, Percy."

She shrugs, and continues to sponge my back, though the tempo has decreased, such that I would describe the sopping and scrubbing of me as "idle."

But I've just thought of something.

"Miss Fairfax, what is the name of the Mysterious Woman?"

"Who?"

"With the foreign eyes; who sits by the lake?"

"Miss Chatterton?"

"Chatterton?"

"Miss Chatterton. Did you forget?"

"I never knew that."

"Sure you did, Percy."

"Ouch!"

"I'm sorry, but we need to finish cleaning these."

She examines my entire trunk, walks to a cabinet. Over her shoulder: "Did you hear about Mr. Al'Hatif?" She takes out a swab and a small vial of iodine.

"Hear what?"

I had not, in fact, heard.

Though the paper was there, and it saw everything.

(THE PAPER CONTINUED)

The linoleum-tiled room. People milling about in various degrees of anhedonia, Mr. Ousman Al'Hatif sitting in a corner at a folding table, a creased and foxed, generally speaking heavily used, box of checkers off to one side, while in front of him is an untenably tall pillar of black and red; an intricate tower of stacked disks, as if a single piece was kinged, over and over and over in a tediously long game. The tower is straining to reach the height of the seated Mr. Al'Hatif's forehead. He's got one red checker in his hand, and he's examining the column closely, as through a jeweler's loupe. He puts a piece on top. You'd never notice him there, engineering this tower with such absolute concentration, off to one side as he is, in his shadowed niche. He is so quiet. Unerringly polite, never bothering anyone. Solitary. Working away. But then, someone does notice; a big, brutish guy with a face like a water buffalo, who lopes over to watch Mr. Al'Hatif work. Just stands above Mr. Al'H. The large man's hands are limp at his sides, mouth slightly open, as he stares down, dully, at the ongoing construction. Mr. Al'H. does not even so much as glance toward this man, but, without his concentration wavering one iota, gingerly places the red disk atop the pillar, moving his hand so very slowly, before, in a flashing instant, removing all his fingers from it. Ta-da. The slack-jawed onlooker continues to watch as Al'H. palms through the pieces in the boxes, picking some out, putting them on the table, sliding them around the hard surface until he finds one that is to his liking, a black one—the tower alternates red, black, red, black—Al'H. picks up this checker and turns it in his hand. Still, no recognition or acknowledgment for the man standing there, threateningly, above him and his fragile tower. The man is so close that his crotch is pressing right up against the far edge of the table, threatening to move it, jar it, and ruin the whole fucking thing. Mr. Al'Hatif takes the new black checker in his hands and begins craning it slowly over to the site, and the onlooker scowls, and, without raising a hand to his mouth, suddenly coughs once. Al'H. halts his progress for a moment, collects himself, and resumes construction. Now the fellow above him is exercised, visibly, and in an act of now naked aggression, reaches out a meaty paw and snaps, right in Mr. Al'H.'s face. And we are all astounded then by the unassailable poise that Mr. Al'Hatif exhibits here, as he continues to lower the black piece slowly, slowly, and then dropping it on the pinnacle of the thing with a tiny little *clack* which is about the volume of a clipped pinky nail. The pillar lists a tick this time, wavers just a millimeter, but ultimately doesn't fall. It's getting to be a simply absurd height. Meanwhile, Mr. Al'H.'s aggressor here, angrier than ever, snaps three more times right up in the builder's craw: snap, snap, snap, but not a blink from Al'Hatif; not a blink. He just selects another red checker, cool as you like, which makes his persecutor totally unhinged, and though we can't tell what's coming we know it won't be great, and as predicted, the man now shouts at Mr. Al'H. not a word but a kind of "Uuuhh!" A quick staccato outburst, followed by an "I'm talking to you," which is intimidating in direct proportion to the slowness with which it is uttered. And we all make mental bets—will Mr. Al'Hatif respond, etc., and, look at this, he does respond! (But almost imperceptibly.) We really have to kind of lean in to see it, but Mr. Al'H. raises one eyebrow, a single one, without looking, up mind you, just that single eyebrow, in complete isolation, up it goes, just, like, a smidge, and everyone is just bowled over by his subtlety, his suave stoicism, though now we all know that the brutish fellow is just going berserk on the inside—you just know it, you can tell—pop-eyed, steam out the ears, etc., etc., so on, and he hinges at his barreled waist that no one had realized he even had, hinges, bends right over forty-five degrees, takes a big and stagey inhale, and then like the big bad wolf himself, just blows (really blows!) the stack right over, and there's a thermonuclear clatter, and the checkers go everywhere all over the table into Mr. Al'Hatif's lap and run all over the floor, some of them striking circumference-side down and thus spin out in all directions ending up under our feet and everywhere really.

Well.

Al'Hatif looks out over the devastation, at the tower's shrapnel, and sniffs a single unintelligible word under his breath, this directed at the brute who he still hasn't looked at throughout all of this (who is this fellow, he must be new) even as this crazy assailant has been seized by paroxysms of mad, joyless laughter, and who addresses himself to Mr. Al'Hatif once more, saying you look at me when I'm talking to you, and adding in a racist epithet I will not repeat, just for good measure, and we all know the incident is going straight into the admin's log, and in fact, admins are coming over even now, and then Mr. Al'H. pushes his chair back with a chalky screech and stands full up which puts him to about chin height on his assailant, and he just walks around this standing man, who is staring at the table as if Al'Hatif were still sitting there, though he isn't, as Mr. Al'H. is bending down onto his hands and knees now to begin picking the checkers up from off the floor, saying, to no one in particular, "I'll just build it again, tomorrow maybe," and one or two of the other fellows, led by the Mysterious Woman, but also the Woman-Whose-Face-and-Hands-Are-Covered-in-Scars, join him down there to help in picking up because no one likes to see such bullying and one has to show at least this kind of solidarity even if one didn't have it in one to confront the aggressor before the violence erupted, the violence which was inherent in the situation all along and which everyone saw coming but was too cowardly to stop but the whole damn thing was inevitable and there was no altering its course at all but then it was movie night and all, so the lights are dimmed and the projector clicks on and etc.

(THE THERMOMETER)

"Stand up for me now, Percy," Miss Fairfax says.

"Ugh."

"Sorry, Percy—I know this hurts, we're almost done."

I feel shaky standing upright, and so suddenly sit back down again, displacing water over the tub's rim. The water sluices around me and soothes the disinfected cuts instantly.

"Well then," she says.

She helps me back up again by grabbing me under each armpit and hoisting.

When I've regained my feet, Miss Fairfax gives me a big fluffy white towel which I use to dry myself and I feel better. It is soft. After, I'm sorry to put my paper uniform back on again. But I do it anyway. We depart the bathroom and sit facing one another in chairs. My hair is wet and feels cool as it air-dries. The slightest movement of the aether is registered upon the small exposed hairs of my arms and neck. For once I don't feel as if I'm sweating uncontrollably.

Miss Fairfax smiles at me and then begins to enter her notes into a device.

(And this scene now feels like it's gone on for too long. I need to move on, Rn. Rn. Rn . . . R.N.? *Registered Nurs*—)

"What's wrong now, Percy?"

"God, can't we dispense with the formalities, the whole admin/fellow thing for a moment, and just be people here?"

"Do you think that I am not a person?" she asks, as she pulls a little plastic thermometer out of its shell casing and launches it toward my mouth.

She has ceased to care about the paper, now Btw. It is all around her. She sits, lopsided, upon a pile of it. The papers cover her feet and crackle at her ankles, etc. But she doesn't appear to notice anymore. She is so collected. She doesn't once reach over to pull one of the sheets off of her, or reach down to brush one away. . . .

"I know you are a person, Miss Fairfax," I mumble, "I know you are."

I try repeating the phrase, that she is a person—a real person—though it is hard to do so with the thermometer under my tongue, and it is precisely during this failed attempt at speech that I suddenly know what my project's final stage will be. And I don't think it will involve any . . .

. . . ~~wriping~~. ~~Ryeting.~~ ~~Riding~~ the writing is proceeding, but I am having increased trouble inventing things in the word-space.

Luckily, I have better ideas for ways to move the project. (The *novel*. The novel.)

Better means in my back pocket.

Last night I began to put some of them into effect, and now that I'm awake, will redouble my efforts.

"Zimzim, turn off my alarm."

"Zimzim, what is the temperature?"

"Zimzim, do I have any appointments today?"

"Zimzim, open the shades."

The shades open, and I am blinded—the sun, fully breaching whatever remains of the metastructure, assaults me utterly, like a blistering shower of lemon juice. I squeeze my eyes closed and blindly, violently smack my hand onto the bedside table searching for my glasses, but cannot feel them. Just piles of sticky paper. Though I *can* feel a lump under one pile, and know that my glasses are in there somewhere, but no matter how much I shove the pile around, there is just too much paper. Instead, I manage to give myself another murderous paper cut in the webbing between thumb and forefinger of my right hand, so this affront, as well as another: I have accrued several of the paper sheets to my sweaty arm, like feathers on a wing. I try to flap them off me, but they are staying on there, riding the bucks. I grab at them with my left hand (my other, unencumbered limb) and crumple one of them up into a ball and try to wipe the sweat off of my brow with it. The paper is not absorbent, natch. So here too I accomplish nothing but spreading the sweat around a bit, along with smudging whatever ink might be on these sheets on my person. Stained again. And to top it off I give myself, naturally, yet another paper cut, this time on my right eyelid, narrowly missing the wet boundary of the orb itself. Opening my eyes now hurts in a new manner, but I keep them open for now, despite the discomfort, and in doing so I see myself in the dazzling mirror, and I am horrified. I am red and swollen. There's a paper stuck obliquely to the side of my forehead in a patch of wetness there. There are two more paper sheets, one on each shoulder like epaulets in a child's game of war. My uniform is off somewhere on the floor, probably under more of it. As it happens there are enough of these sheets plastered to me so that it feels as if I were wearing a robe made of paper.

It is unpleasant.

But I've had enough of this, so I spasm my once-again

prone body in one terrific shaking seizure (up and down as well as side to side). "Aaaaaaahhhhhggghrrrrrrrrrrghghg!" And I manage to dislodge a few more of them, realizing now that each time I move in order to remove a sheet, a new one affixes itself as if I were some sort of allegorical chicken who can never be plucked. I am now winded as well.

Roll over in my bed, as the initial step in rising, onto more—what else—paper, rolling it onto myself like a human lint brush (I never realized how lousy the stuff truly feels), hoik myself up onto an elbow and now to sitting.

Shit.

Time to wade through the tundra and make some sense of it all.

Fiction goes into the "Fiction" pile, nonfiction in the "Nonfiction" pile. I put crime in "Crime," sci-fi in "Sci-Fi," poetry in "Poetry." Etc. I find a crossword puzzle, and try for a period to solve it. A coupon: clip and save. Pictures of any kind go into a single pile entitled "Imagery," and one should never neglect stray images especially if they are old, and belong to someone else, as there is plenty of memory jammed into them that can be reused and reapplied and why should any memory ever go to waste. The site of the piles matters, which is to say that genres which are related to one another are located in geographical proximity. Also, the location of the piles is proscribed by personal preference and habit. For instance: "Horror" and "Disturbing News" go next to my desk so that I can read these during the day—not after sundown, for obvious reasons—and "Obscure Philosophy" goes by my bed right next to the pills in order to render me up unto Sleep, Daughter of Night. "Self-Help" goes in a pile in my closet, where I keep such things hidden, because I am embarrassed that I find some of it useful (and the same goes with the "Sexy Stuff," obvi). I also leave some personal piles of paper out in the middle of my rooms—and, as with "Obscure Philosophy," I leave the impressive, difficult pieces on the tops of my piles in case someone is to look at these piles and judge me accordingly. I am, I realize, constructing somewhat of a persona which is predicated on the "tops of the piles," one which differs in substantial ways from the "bottom of my piles" or the "underneath-my-bed piles." In this way, through my curation of paper, I may lay some claim to ownership of it.

Fully standing now, I shuffle my way slowly into the mounds, trying to make it toward the particular hillock down there, under which must be my uniform. Kicking out rather than walking, and earning myself more cuts on the prows of my shins. When I reach the pile in question, I dig down with an arm, reaching waaaay in there, groping, groping. But all the hand encounters is more paper with all of those stealthy edges.

An hour later, I am seated at my desk, naked from the waist up. I have a large pair of shears, a stapler, and a black grease pencil, and a big roll of tape. (And lots of paper, obvs. There are drafts and revisions galore, mostly futilities: false starts, dead ends, and outright toss-outs. Lists, maps, and charts as well. The project's debris.) I've been hard at work. Many of the sheets of paper now have dotted lines drawn on them. These are clothing patterns. I have already made myself a natty pair of paper trousers in perfect facsimile of the uniform's own pants, they are finished and currently being worn, and I am just putting the finishing touches on a tunic. Some cutting, some stapling . . . When the two sides of the shirt are affixed together, I pull it on, gingerly, over my head (it is rather stiff, like a sandwich board—should I write something on it? A motto of some sort?), and then, the paper pipes of the sleeves go on like oversized bracelets. A little tape here, a little tape there . . . the stapler goes: *kerchunk! Kerchunk!* And my uniform is complete. God it is uncomfortable (and hot). But it looks okay.

Imho.

I grab the grease pencil and draw in the appropriate spot a fairly decent approximation of my original stain.

Great.

Suddenly—

Ping!

I root for my device. Luckily it is in the white shallows by the bathroom, and I dig it out without too much trouble. Good. I'd hate to have to build one of *those* out of paper (it's only a matter of time, probably).

The message on my device is from Miss Fairfax, and when I v-chat her back, she does not seem taken aback in the slightest by my new duds.

"Don't I look handsome?" I ask.

"Tip-top," she replies, writing something down on a pad, and leaving the hangout.

I plow my way like an icebreaker over to my balcony and

now I sit on it, surveying the scene before me. The Institute. Under the thinning membrane of the metastructure.

A white world. A flapping world. Slippery and sharp. The grounds area covered, the trees bedecked. Way off, by the perimeter, by the solar array and turbines, there is a wall of white built up along the edge of the metastructure, as if a giant wave has come from all directions, collapsed, and a tsunami's worth of foam was left in 360 degrees. Down below, some of the fellows are leaving for Group. I can see that several of them have, themselves, constructed paper uniforms as well.

"Hello!" I shout down to a fellow, who seems to have used some kind of paste to assemble his getup. It is coming apart along two of the seams, and some of his fundament is exposed to the world. Nevertheless, he has also added a paper tricorn hat to his ensemble, which lends him a formidable and military air.

He hasn't heard my greeting from all the way up here, and so continues his trudge.

I hear Zimzim the Tea Boy behind me. I spin around, and he is standing patiently in the mess, dressed in pale pink as ever.

Me: "Zimzim, do I have any calls today?"

Tea Boy: ". . ."

Me: "Tea Boy, you really are quite something, aren't you?"

Tea Boy: ". . ."

Me: "I told you the project was coming along, and just have a look at me now!"

Tea Boy: ". . ."

Me: "Up to my eyeballs in success."

Tea Boy: ". . ."

Me: "I think *somebody* owes *somebody* an apology."

Tea Boy: ". . ."

Me: "Still, with the accusations; the condemnations?"

Tea Boy, bored, salaams, turns, and goes.

Will I see him again? Will anyone? Doesn't matter. I don't need him anymore. Just see if I don't. And by the end of the work period, I've made a pretty good Tea Boy out of paper, drawn in graphite, in variable, perishable intensities of sooty gray, using the control rods from my window blinds as an armature, a skeleton. They are tied together with bailing wire. The paper Tea Boy is a bit smaller than meatspace Tea Boy, but not by much. I think I've captured his blank affect pretty well, actually. Though I'm pretty sure that the paper version won't be able to serve me beverages. This saddens me, briefly, but now it also occurs that I could simply add a couple of "stories of tea service" to his white and wavering trunk. In this way, I could just read about drinking coffee out of bowls. Actually, I have changed my mind, and I have decided and it is that in these stories I will have Zimzim serve me some fucking *tea* in a fucking *cup*. See, it's up to me now how this all proceeds from here on out; my way or the highway. Take that, you uncooperative peon. Tea it is. In a cup.

Sketches for Stories of Tea Service

So, one story would be about obedience actually, and the tea will only be a device, a metaphor, the vehicle through which the lesson about obedience is learned. The story is one in which a young Zimzim is taught the order of things, the ways of the world, by a wise and compassionate (if firm, and uncompromising) master. A bildungsroman. His. This will be the first of my Tea Boy stories.

Another story could be about the actual experience of drinking the tea itself, about enjoying tea, its sensual aspects, its tannic texture on the tongue, its earthy tang rising off the palate and imbuing the nasal passages with a kind of smoke; the feeling of the heated porcelain in the hand, the sweet warmth creeping down into the belly, suchlike.

Maybe another story would tell about my adverse reactions to not receiving tea? About (I want to say: *frustration?*)

Maybe another story would be someone else's story of tea. I've heard a few. Maybe I'll pass some of these off as my own.

Nm. I can work out the details later.

"I've made real progress today," I tell the duty officer, admin18, at day's end, and I'm fairly sure that even the Director and his other cohorts would agree. Miss Fairfax will be so pleased. Though I won't tell her yet—I'll make her wait. She'll have to tease it out of me.

But no: I've accomplished *tangible results*. It is *coming to life*. I am *creating*. Really *making things*.

To wit, I now have, aside from my paper uniform and paper Tea Boy, made a paper Dennis Royal to keep me company and amuse me with his wry asides. Paper-Dennis is the very picture of the louche and disaffected lounger, and I've perfected, after many attempts, the exact sardonic slant of his mouth. There he is, slumped up against a structural column off by the window. (There is nothing that the meat-space Dennis won't lean up against.) This Dennis looks as if he will be saying something to me any moment. A quip of some sort, or putdown. I haven't yet determined what it is he will be saying. Perhaps it will be something like "Oh, well done, Percy." (Sarcasm.) Or just "What an effing mockery." (Derision.) But I feel like, at this stage, even mute, the new Dennis is providing decent companionship.

Also, I have constructed a map of my rooms, in a 1:1 scale, made out of hundreds of sheets of paper all hot-glued to the floors and walls of the space. The flat is now a map of the flat. (Listen: it had to happen.) I've even papered over the windows and have drawn a serene scene upon each of them, a tableau of the Institute at rest, fellows out in huddles and conferences, swaying palms (you can tell they are swaying from the movement lines I've drawn around them), various rectilinear buildings in the distance, lake, Pleasure Center, Mountain House, a tiny desert-viewing bench, and that clear, clear sky, which I've almost finished indicating.

It should all be over soon, I think.

43

(HIGHLY QUESTIONABLE)

A break in the weather, unexpected, blessed. A boon. Though who knows how long it will last, as it all, everything that is, feels as though it is building to something. Is this the proverbial calm then? It must be. And so, it is out to the souks with us, right away, while we can, all of us, practically the entire Institute, to get away from ~~the goddam paper~~.

We visit the Gold Souk, and the Spice Souk, the Rug and Tapestry Souk, and, just past the Digital Services Roundabout, the Perfume Souk. Enthusiasm about shopping has, for the fellows who have been bused out to the bazaars, reached an all-time high. Enthusiasm, or competitiveness. Fellows run the souks like obstacle courses; alone and in small groups. Baskets fill with trinkets. It's a spectacle. Everyone eager, trying out their skill with the local language. In the Souk D'Adidas I speak to a man who sells shoelaces. He is drinking surreptitiously from a small flask, and he nods as I speak to him, but never speaks back. All the streets in the various bazaars are crooked. Some by design. But the place is alive, just thronged with vendors and shoppers. And children, who beg insistently for coins, and who offer up wide and genuine smiles for us. Some are shoeshine boys. Some are musicians, or acrobats. Some are selling small items, foodstuffs. They paw, lightly, at our arms and legs like seaweed around a swimmer.

We have a traditional sweet mint tea, in a tent inside one of the stalls. The famous mint tea at last. The vendor pores the hot liquid from a virtuosic height. Then we sample it. Then eat our energy bars, and drink our juice boxes, the ones which were handed out to each of us by our admins. We eat and drink in silence.

Then there's a brief moment out in the glare, in the car park. Wind from the north, dry irritants. Nothing to look at but the desert's rim: a faint waving line. Just a line. Merely. Wavy lines are everywhere, frankly—a dime a dozen. To prove the point, I draw a snaky line with the toe of my shoe in the sand of the lot's divider. And I draw another. Three. I could make twenty. A thousand. Who cares.

Then the admins call us back.

We are organized for a group photo. Many, many rows of us. Institute support-staffers as well. We stand in designated spots. Takes a while. It's hot but we persevere. The admin who whispers up the shot takes a long while to get the settings right. The brightness is through the bloody roof. Everyone is sweating; squinting. But we get there—the photograph is taken. And now, of course, other devices are passed forward. Everyone needs a pic on their own device. (Though of course the original could just be pinged out to everyone. Sure, but it's the principle of the thing. Everyone wants ownership. Even if it is merely ownership over whatever filter they've scrupulously elected to use.) Later, I might look at this photo on my own device and notice that we—all of us; the Cryptographer and the Sculptor and the Philosopher, the Psychologist, the Actor, the Translator, the Set Theorist, the Miniaturist, the Critic, the Sociologist and the Composer, the Developer and the Astronomer, then the Humorist, the Philologist, the Theologian, the Urban Planner, the Percussionist, etc., etc.—each of us has been arranged so as to form a meta-picture, a picture of a head; a giant head, that is. Perhaps it is the head of a single fellow, an everyman fellow, or perhaps the perfect, idealized fellow, whose very existence is predicated upon the presence of all of us; whose project depends upon leveraging the skills of all of the others; a fellow who doesn't exist except in aggregate. If only I were high enough to see!

Everyone is here; everyone but, again, no Mysterious Woman. No "Miss Chatterton." I've lost track of her, I realize. And wonder how she avoids having to come on these group outings. She is always apart. Always keeps apart. And why deny her the pleasure of solitude, Percy? Idk. Because it is denied me? W/e.

Me: I'm assimilated now, a piece of the large head. I can't ever manage to be alone. Or, rather, unobserved. I'm always watched. So no more Same Same sneakaways.

I shuffle off with the rest of the brigade, obeying the loud but cheery exhortations of the admins, and now it is off to "Aladdin's Cave."

"Aladdin's Cave" is a souk which sells I-don't-know-what-exactly, but once I part the diaphanous curtain and enter, I can see that there are oil lamps which contain lightbulbs in lieu of ancient and bonded spirits. Brocaded red vests, and fezzes too. Necklaces of bright turquoise, scimitars (plastic scimitars), key chains with a wide-eyed cartoon monkey on them spelling out names from Aaron to Zinedine, as well as signs from Aries to Virgo, and there is jasmine but not the plant but rather the T-shirts bearing the word "Jasmine," in a faux-Arabic script, and baseball hats upon which are emblazoned the word, in gold thread, "Aladdin," plus rows of Blu-rays and DVDs, water bottles, snow globes, plush dolls, USB drives, figurine play-sets, flying carpets, stacked like pancakes, hookahs which are actually coffeemakers, and an animatronic purple genie who takes smart chips, credit cards, or Apple Pay, and who grants wishes. A song is currently emanating from a perforated speaker where his mouth should be and I just catch the words ". . . where it's flat and immense and the heat is intense . . ." this followed by a tinny rendition of "The Old Bazaar in Cairo," followed in turn by the title track from *Follow That Camel!* (There's a touchscreen playlist.)

The Brand Analyst is here, but she's done with me. She hangs, proprietarily, on the arm of 鼎福 the Architect as they travel from stall to stall, picking up wares, turning them this way and that, looking for prices underneath ceramic bowls, and smiling at one another like they are standing at the glass looking into a nursery. I am tiring and hot so I sit down on a stack of velour rugs.

"Intending to fly your way to safety?" It's Mr. Al'Hatif.

His previously smart beard has gone wild and untrimmed, and his skin now seems yellow and hard. He remains more or less affectless since his presentation, though there is, now, a tiny glimmer in his eye, a light on the far shore, and I wonder what this encounter of all things has catalyzed in him. But as soon as it flashes, the lantern is snuffed.

"They don't have any 'Ousman' key chains," he reports, glumly.

"Not surprising, really."

"There's probably a Mr. 'Percy,' if you want me to find you one."

"No, thank you. I'm fine."

"I've brought you something," he says, digging into the pocket of his uniform, and coming up with a balled-up handkerchief which he extends to me. I reach out, cautiously.

"Go ahead," he says.

I unwrap the bundle, and a series of small, worn red plastic disks spill out onto the floor of the bazaar, which he hastens to sweep up and put back into my cupped hands.

"What is this, Ousman."

"Isn't it obvious?"

"Aren't these—"

"Yes."

"Checkers?"

"Fragments." He raises one brow as is his manner, and leans way in.

"True fragments. Of the Great Buddha. Authentic. The last of them. I saved a few. Just for you."

"What an honor, Ousman, thank you."

I cascade the synthetic rounds into my uniform's pocket, and clasp his hands in mine. He looks at me, his face devoid of strain or effort. Permanently off-Ladder.

But admins are beginning to hustle us toward the vehicles. There's a barely discernible uptick in their urgency. Faintly now, I hear sirens again. Sliding up and down like soprano trombones.

The storms are back again.

44

THE FUNDAMENTS OF MY PROJECT

Fundament 16. In the beginning, a character arrives in a strange, new environment—on the page that is—devoid of characteristics. But he should, eventually, come into focus (as should his new milieu). In order for this to occur, the character must be placed amid other agents. Interactions are vital. Through such interactions, a character will find himself in opposition to something; he will overcome that something; and finally, through this very overcoming, he will learn something crucial about himself, so on. In other words, he cannot remain static, the environment cannot remain static, and the project itself cannot remain withholding throughout its entire duration.

Fundament 17. Psa: meteorological symbolism is to be avoided.

45

Catastrophe is binary; it either mounts, or is averted. In this case, the former, and the Institute now resembles a disorganized archive, the confettied aftermath of a parade; the floor of a stock exchange when trading closes; a beaten piñata; a leaflet-strewn battleground; an unflustered snow globe; an ashy fireplace . . . images, analogies, metaphors curdling on my tongue before I can commit to them, piling up like so much paper trash. And now I only recall my reluctance to think along such lines with a kind of wistfulness. I am resigned to softly yielding to whatever is undeniably transpiring around me.

(THE PAPER CONTINUED)

Meanwhile, four pages fly low over the lawns where one or two fellows mill about. They fly past broken park benches, over cracked pavement, mud patches, grass (sparse), half-empties, stubs, wrappers, albino dogshit, whatnot—over the yuck of it, i/o/w—and, understandably, the papers hasten off. Straight on through Gate 22 and through the double doors to the Mountain House.

They now follow the airstreams about the building, swirling around hallways and dipping in and out of doorways. Now breezing past and over the sad, mostly melted, once-iceberg, they enter the cantina, where two women yell incoherently at one another. A lot of hot invective and spittle—a mess of intimidation and fronting—charges, bellows, dominance displays. The women come together. Claw at one another. Hair grabbed, thumbs digging for purchase, eyes scratched at. Punches landing. Elbows, knees too. It is raucous, shrieking, fugal. That acceleration of time that violence provokes. Chairs flipped, Dixie cups and cutlery clatter to the floor.

One of the sheets of paper peels off, gets in close for a better view. Its approach is low, via the ground, but it comes in much too close. Pull up! The smaller of the two women backs up onto it, and trips—the paper is wrecked; crumpled and torn—and the woman falls loudly to the floor. The standing woman gets right to it now, straddling and subduing her adversary, and just pounding on the fallen woman, whose uniform is tangled, riding up—no dignity in these things. There are ugly, damp sounds. Admins running. The straddler is pulled off the straddled by her armpits, the prone woman lifted by her feet and hands and hauled away. The papers leave now as well, though not of their own accord; they go where the gusts take them.

Another set of papers (about a short story's worth) is shooting down a different corridor, the walls of which glint with laminated schedules, invites, cheer-me-ups; a rainbow alphabet: "Don't backtrack!" "Strive for a new life!" "Journaling can help!" (If the papers could laugh at this last one, they might now.) Instead they sail past the shiny and cigarette-blistered couch and follow the scuffed lines running centrally down the tiled floors like runway markings. Beneath, more fellows mill, and fragments of conversation can be made out. Taken together, these fragments coalesce to form news: the news that "5B is freaking out," and that there is going to be a "six-person lockup." The papers, sensitive already to the smallest vibration, feel alert; exhilarated.

And here's 5B, in front of which the night staff has duly assembled.

Meanwhile, a fellow—whose scrawny, pale arms are being held behind his back by two admins, one admin per arm—dances violently in place.

One of the admins says to the others: "He needs to be sectioned, I keep saying."

Another fellow, a bystander, walks by, holding a single folded bedsheet under his arm, and a single thin pillow in that same hand, like a commuter, managing briefcase and newspaper. The fellow rubbernecks the scene. Other fellows shuffle over to watch as well—it's exciting. The commuter and the other onlookers are encouraged by the staff to back away.

The already restrained fellow is now grabbed by two more admins, though the man continues to judder in their grip. He's slight, but putting up an impressive amount of resistance.

"We're bringing you back to your room now."

"It's not time."

"Time's up."

"Actually, fuck right off."

"Now."

"Who appointed you, sir?" he asks, sardonic, even (especially) in his bondage.

"Easy does it."

"Unfh."

"Easy, there."

"Bastards."

"Easy, love."

"Imbeciles."

"Take it slow."

"Nobody appointed you, asshole."

"Nope. Nobody appointed me. Ha, ha, ha."

"Don't laugh at mc."

"Easy."

"Shit."

"Get his ankles."

"What did I do?"

"Be calm."

"I can piss where I damn well like, it's a free country."

"File a grievance."

He writhes again, in their grip, massively now, manages to free one of his hands, and grabs the tie of the laughing admin.

A clip-on. Still holding the tie, the fellow slips to the floor.

"Ha, ha, ha."

"Stop fucking laughing."

"Turn him over."

"Get off."

"Going to remove the shoes now."

"Get off."

"Facedown. Easy. Elbows, we've got knees."

"Frrrrk."

"Relax."

Facedown on the linoleum.

Six admins holding him, one brandishing the hypo.

"Ahngg."

"There you go. Calm."

Time passes.

Now carrying the fellow between them like a bag of water they don't want to spill.

Through the door, lights on.

He's in.

Turn him around. Lying on his back now, feet away from the door, crown of his head pointing toward it. Rocking gently in the narrow bed, restrained by twelve blue hands. They form a symmetrical figure; lines, restraints, relays, sephirot. A Vitruvian prisoner.

Admins release their grips serially; one hand at a time. The last admin to leave the room is the admin who is holding the head. The head is freed at the very last instant by this admin who is also the admin closest to the door.

Everyone clear, the door is closed and locked. A small card in a scuffed, wall-mounted, Plexiglas holder next to it reads "ROYAL, D."

Through the door, weakly: "Who appointed you, you mutherfucking peons?"

The onlookers disperse now back to their own rooms.

Above, up in the cantina, the admins are mopping up: retrieving all those wrinkled little white cups, the floral printed, embossed napkins; the beige plastic sporks. These admins also wear chic pale blue gloves. They count each utensil before returning it to the locking bin. And then they tally up the sum. One missing. Not too bad.

(PURE, THRILLING)

The work today is pure, thrilling. I can feel myself ascending, transcending, disappearing almost, into free-flowing gavottes of creativity. Now that I have found my legs in the project, there's no stopping me. The sheer inventiveness is overwhelming. Power and thrust. Energy and movement. Goddam, it feels great.

I'm naked to the waist, sweating like an idiot, hair a nest. *Sounds from the Ocean Floor* is on loop, blasting full volume. The flat is now entirely covered with my renderings, including a precise picture of the very walls on top of which these renderings sit. (All of which will be obviated when I've completed my rendering of the building itself from its exterior, the rendering which will supersede all this, etc.)

Other of my renderings include life-size ones of several admins, as well as a sketch of the Director (incomplete), some elevations of various other buildings, a map of the entire Freehold, the renderings of (as previously mentioned) Dennis and Ousman Al'Hatif and the Enclave's concierge, Miss ☺, the Philosopher, 鼎福 the Architect, some of the other fellows (though most of these are drawn in groups, roughly indicated through a rush of strokes, two-dimensionally, scribbled rather than accurately depicted in detail), and now: we get Miss Fairfax. Miss Fairfax, admin5; here she is, coming into being, into focus, disparate lines finding meaning in juxtaposition to one another, multiplying into life on paper. I have exercised my happy skill, such that Miss Fairfax's body—its S-curves, U-turns—is coming into palpable existence, her dancerly, turned-out feet, her buttery calves and strong legs, her proletarian arms, now her alabaster neck (isn't that right; alabaster? Idk) and finally the face, always the most difficult, but here I have help in that single signifier of her black-framed glasses, which I illustrate in darkest lines upon its own sheet of paper and then carefully (carefully!) cut with scissors along their outline. They are perfect.

And what of the mysterious Miss Chatterton? I'll make her too.

And I do. Make her through patchy memory and guess-work. An hour later and there she is, though I can't remember clearly what her foreign eyes look like, so I just punch two ragged holes with my pencil in her face, where her eyes should be. I now try to prop her up on a chair so I can get some perspective on what I've made, but she keeps sliding down again, and as I am holding her up, one hand under each of her sharp-edged armpits, I briefly get a glimpse through those pencil holes, and see what she sees, as it were. And what *does* she see? Well that's just the thing—I can't decide. It is up to me of course, it all is now, which is wonderful but also a burden, and the possibilities, the infinite possibilities, lead briefly to a creative impasse. Standing behind this 2-D manikin, the back of her head scraping against my occasional lashes, I contemplate what it is like to be Miss Chatterton, that is, what it is that Miss Chatterton experiences and how she experiences it, what she contemplates of this seeing, and finally I come up with an obvious answer and go back to work with my trusty (unleaky!) pen this time, take it out, denticulate, from my mouth where it was clamped during the scissor-cutting and contemplation, and I begin, on another sheet of paper, to render myself.

Percy Frobisher. Self-portrait.

Ping!

A message on my device and you'll never guess who it is from. . . .

(Shershay la femme.)

46

THE FUNDAMENTS OF MY PROJECT

Fundament 18. The project will turn out less wonderful than I had hoped on my best days, yet not as nerve-rattlingly terrible as I had feared on my worst.[*]

Fundament 19. As the project nears completion—as it begins to take a final shape, find a more or less permanent form— my attachment to the project will fall off. The project will ease its way out of my thoughts; no longer dominate my internal conversation. What this new detachment will lead toward, only the future will divulge.

Fundament 20. What the project is, only the project knows. It reveals itself, not the other way around. My job here is to

---

[*] If the state of happiness serves to confirm the inevitability of joy, and the state of sadness reaffirms the inevitability of sorrow, then the only intermediary positions left to one are *worry* and *hope*, both of which are delusional disorders. Therefore I bind myself to nullity and flatness, so as to reaffirm a total commitment to the present moment or w/e.

remove anything which is "not project," i.e., to clear a path for its arrival.

Fundament 21. In the end, no one will care. (Caveat) Unless the project incurs general disfavor, which it undoubtedly will. People will just hate it. I know it, you know it. The project will be poorly received. (Best to separate oneself from a project sooner rather than later, so as to suffer less from this inevitably poor reception.)

Fundament 22. The only things which will matter are those things which the project will leave completely as they were. Untouched, unmolested. (The project does not, will not: edify.)

Fundament 23. The whole "Alterburg" (*sp?*) thing continues to plague me and I do indeed wonder if there are natural receptors in our minds to which certain ideas—phrases, words, gestures, phonemes even—adhere. The word has set its hooks in, and I can't manage, no matter how I try, to distract myself; to dislodge it. It's like that song, you know the one, which is always playing, which everyone loves; playing, even now, somewhere, on a device, a radio, or leaking from someone's headphones, faint, metallic, from out past the windowsill, far away . . .

Fundament 24. Okay, maybe not *everyone* will hate the project. Someone might actually like it. Let's not fetishize its awfulness. If, say, maybe, a small fraction of the project's potential audience finds in it something to recommend, then this should be deemed a success! (Take some damned pride.)

Fundament 25. Anyway, is success not synonymous with the concession of defeat? (*Vide supra.*)

Fundament 26. The project shall comprise a series of representations. The project's ideas, sounds, words, images, etc. shall replace other, meatspace ideas, sounds, words, images—much as :) stands in for delight, and the words "et" and "cetera" stand in for any and all manner of things. But more than this, the project shall comprise a series of transformations. These very ideas, sounds, words, images, etc. will be redirected, projected, distorted, *denatured*, merely by virtue of being presented in the form of the project. These "project ideas" cannot replace these other Irl, "non-project ideas" without altering them indelibly. So rather than thinking of this subject matter as being replaced, or even represented, I think of it all as being recast.

Fundament 27. Even the project itself will eventually become fodder for, and duly enter into the body of: the project. Viz, the accumulation of paper is now mapping exactly, one-to-one, with the project's advance toward completion. And, not coincidentally, I have become simply replete with ideas. I cannot stop them coming. Is this what a project is? What it feels like? This cacophony? What is happening to me? (Time will tell.)

47

(HE PRACTICES HIS FRENCH)

My meeting with Charlotte Chatterton aka the Mysterious Woman takes place on the fourth floor of a special housing unit set apart from the Residential Enclave. I arrive at its double doors promptly at the appointed hour and climb its stairs until I begin to see a small, shod pair of feet, a loose pair of socks, bundled into a ragged foreskin around the ankles, out of which arise a pair of spindly legs—yellowed, taut, spreading at the knees, knobby and veined like a giraffe's. Then a white tee, comically oversized but flat all the way up (if not concave) until the hugeness of the garment reveals the brutal wings of her clavicles, an uneven fringe of hair, a ropy neck, set jaw, long nose, the valley of the face—full of sorrowed dells and hollows. The full (albeit thin) aspect of a woman. Younger now, it seems, seen up close. Younger than I thought she was. A young woman, prematurely aged.

Also, her eyes. Now that I am getting a long look, they don't seem so "foreign" to me, at all. Nothing so exotic. Just "regular," if active eyes, perhaps made brighter by an encaved, shadowy context.

She's looking me up and down, her face moving rapid-fire through a series of expressions: 1. Quizzical, 2. Alarmed, 3. Angry, 4. Doubtful, 5. Resigned, 6. Resolved. Having settled on "resolved," she gestures to me to follow her, leading me along the elevated pathways above the main atrium. She moves gingerly, as if recovering from a procedure. She concentrates hard on walking upon the sticks of her legs— a concentration which forestalls conversation. We walk through a set of double doors into a hallway I've never seen before, a hallway which is a kind of catalog of cheap tile— linoleum, ceramic, particleboard ceiling—past more doors with external locks and windows, and finally we arrive at what is, I suppose, her project studio, Miss C. kicking aside a largish mail-pile of white paper which paws up like a dog against the door; a door which like the others contains, at head height, a single, fine-graphed window, and I am shown through it, and into her work space, and we close the door behind us.

I turn to look back, and see another fellow—someone I don't know—look in from outside of the door's porthole. He points at me, tapping on the glass, laughing his ass off, before moving along.

There is only a single chair, and a little bed. On the bed, some pillows, and a stuffed bunny, tucked down tightly in the coarse white sheets.

A pretty small, barren set. The walls, the floor, the ceiling: all white(ish). Light comes in through gray glass window. The only color in the room is hanging on the wall above the bed: a decorative quilt in depressing pastel panes.

"Can a quilt discourage strong emotions, do you think?" she asks.

"I'm not sure." It is so miserable. Full of disappointment.

She slouches on the bed; I sit in the chair.

"I suppose it is supposed to encourage docility, but honestly, it's hideous and I find it quite disheartening. If anything, it makes me want to scream and tear it off the wall. But I can't speak for anyone else. There is, perhaps, a fine line between innocuous and repressive. Do you have a pointedly inoffensive tapestry on your wall, Percy?"

"I don't think so."

"Well then. Lucky you."

"Lucky me."

"I've seen you watching me, Mr. Frobisher. It spooked me, to be honest. I keep to myself, and people mostly just leave me be."

"You piqued my interest. I didn't mean to scare you."

"There isn't much to learn I'm afraid. Anything specific you wanted to—?"

"What do you do? What's your project; I never see you working at it."

"Project?"

"Everyone has one here."

"A project, really? Self-improvement, I suppose. Does that count as a 'project'? Some kind of recovery. With a little luck, maybe a discharge—"

"No, no. We all have a project," I insist. "A real one."

"Then I guess I don't know what you mean by 'project.'"
She's grabbed a loose thread from the offensively drab quilt
and is slowly teasing out the bottom row of stitches.

"Come on, are you the, the what? Weaver? Cosmologi-
cal Modeler? Larper? Data Mystic? Bibliographer? Hagiog-
rapher? Hunger-Artist? What?"

"You mean, like, a profession? I don't work anymore.
And I certainly don't work here."

"But then what, what are you actually *for*?"

She slides a bit away from me, and the bed whinnies
under her.

"I'm sure I've no idea. What the hell are any of us 'for'?
What the hell are you 'for,' Percy?"

"I'm the Novelist."

"Oh?"

"The Novelist."

"Yes, well. A novelist. That explains a thing or two."
(Laughs. Laughs turn into coughs.) "Kind of figures."

One last tug on the thread, which snaps off. She wraps
it around an index finger. Indicates that she would like to
stand. Holds out a hand. The gentle weight of her pencily
fingers. And I notice again how young she is. Younger even
now. And that huge uniform: she's swimming in it.

*Disquisition on the symbolic resonance of the small woman in
the big garment—swaddling blanket/daddy's jacket/boyfriend's
jersey/ husband's dress shirt/grandma's shawl/corpse's death
shroud etc.—to be indicated by carets*

∿∿∿ ∿∿ ∿∿ ∿∿ ∿∿∿∿ ∧∧∧∧∧ ∿∿∿ ∿∿ ∿∿∿∿∿ ∧∧∧∧∧
∿∿∿∿ ∿∿ ∿∿∿∿ ∧∧∧∧∧∧ ∿∿∿ ∿∿   ∿∿∿∿∿ ∧∧∧∧∧ ∿∿∿∿∿
∿∿ ∿∿∿ ∧∧∧∧∧ ∿∿∿∿ ∿∿∿   ∿∿∿∿ ∿∿ ∧∧∧∧ ∿∿

Holding hands is nice.

"Miss Chatterton—" I say.

"Charlotte."

"Charlotte."

"Yes?"

"Are you a guest here?"

"Obviously."

"What brought you?"

"My family."

"Is your family here too?"

"No. No, they are not. Are yours?"

"No."

"Of course not."

She cranes to look at the door; the knuckles of her neck. She chews her nails.

"Where is your family?"

"Back home."

"You left them?"

"They left me."

"Why."

"No one knew what else to do with me."

"I'm sorry," I say.

Someone else appears in the door's porthole, sniggers, and leaves. (What is it about me that's so goddam funny?)

"Jesus, stop apologizing," she says. Sucks her teeth. "It's actually pretty nice to have someone to speak to."

"For me too, Miss Chatterton."

"Do you want to tell me about your novel? It would be nice to hear a story."

"Not particularly. I don't want to. It doesn't really, it's hard to . . . well there isn't really a story, not in the normal way. No real 'short version.' And it isn't really, like, 'a novel,' not in the traditional sense. It is kind of a grab bag. There is little in the way of development. No dramatic turns of event. And the narrator may be unreliable."

"Too bad."

"You're telling me."

On the windowsill of her room are some crude pots. None of them symmetrical, all mottled and unevenly glazed as if covered in thin layers of toothpaste. I pick one up. Nothing in it. Turn it over, as one does, see her signature etched on the bottom. *C.C.* Oops there was a paperclip in there after all. Pick it up.

"The pottery is nice," I say.

"Big on arts and crafts here, aren't they. It does help to pass the time. I get so bored."

"We could head over to the Recreation Center if you'd like," I suggest.

"The rec room. God that place is so unbelievably shitty. The smoke . . . and you'd think they'd get a net for the Ping-Pong table at least."

"We can stay here, too. Checkers?"

"No thank you."

"What about a short walk?"

"I don't have much energy these days and don't venture too much farther than the end of the hallway," she tells me, and droops her shoulders, her eyes reflexively and wearily heading toward the window.

The windows don't open here. Not in this wing.

We look through it.

The view: Fellows walking below. Fellows speaking to one another. Fellows alone. Fellows smoking. A few sorry, leafless trees. Pale. Brown strokes. Brick wall. Trash, blowing.

Paper.

Time.

Time passing in this manner.

"Do you write about this?" she says. "All of this?"

"No."

More time now.

Later, at some point, she says, "I almost died on the drips."

"Terrible," I reply, thinking this is what is required.

Miss Chatterton coughs some more.

We look again at the down-below. She smiles a dead smile.

She says: "It's so ugly, isn't it? I've seen you collecting all the garbage around the grounds, which is generous of you. I like that. It's one reason I asked you to visit. I wish others would do more to help out around the place. It is all so grim."

Wind and scattering paper. Distant rattles.

"I am not cleaning, Miss Chatterton, I am making something."

"With trash?"

"No. I'm making a great collage. A *bricolage*. That is what the novel is, sure—but it's more than that. It's hard to explain, but there's all kinds of stuff in it. And you are part of it, Miss Chatterton. You are part of it. An important part, in many ways—ways which will most likely only become clear toward the end of it all. But it will make sense. I'll figure it all out, and I'll figure you out too."

Her focus finds my eyes, and then darts around.

"I suspect that you won't, in fact."

And just now, the door swings open.

Her admin has come in. Her admin looks angry.

Miss C. and the admin confer.

"No, I'm fine. Really. Michelle, I'm *fine*."

The admin is now pointing me back toward the elevators. The admin gives me a kind of "don't fuck with me" glare. The admin is calling someone on her device. Time is up for today.

The M.W., Miss Chatterton, tilts her head, takes me in one last time.

"Well. I guess it was nice to have met you, Percy. It is important that we become helpmates to one another. That we care for each other. Or at least that we show an interest; a little humanity. Which you've done. So."

"Bye, Miss Chatterton."

I see another man, backup, coming up to collect me now. Miss Chatterton holds him off for a moment. I hear her say the words: ". . . and is completely harmless." The staff member backs off a step, and Miss C. turns toward me again.

"Thank you again for cleaning up around the place. You are a kind man. If a bit confused at times."

"I'll come back then and visit, Charlotte?"

"That would be fine. That would be fine."

The new orderly, given the nod, walks over now and takes my arm with intent.

"Good."

"And Percy?"

"Yes, Miss Chatterton?"

"Next time, could you try to remember to wear some pants?"

The day finishes off with another meal in the refectory. Many of the fellows are here tonight, I suppose no one wants to contemplate the specter of being alone, given the conditions—alone atop or inside of a pile of paper, with the stifling heat, heat made so much worse by the almost contradictory darkness of the campus. There are no more Discourses™. They have been suspended for the time being. The broadcasting tech is broken, wires melted, fused, short-circuited. No one outside the Institute can watch them, and it seems ridiculous, the admins tell us, for the talks to take place just for the benefit of the fellows. And anyway, the

Presence Center has been stuffed to the gills with paper. So no more Discourses™.

A shame, as I was due to give my own. (Picture it: *me*, on the top rung of the Ladder. The Ladder of Perfection. The Ladder of Completion. Spotlit. Jaw mic. The Fundaments up there on-screen, each given its own steel-blue, glowing slide. My bantering profundities, my ROADMAPS to THE FUTURE. Betterments FOR HUMANITY. My touchingly personal yet broadly applicable anecdotes. Me: ACTUALIZED. Applause, applause. Viral sensation.

But nope. No final stage, no valedictory moment. No Discourse™. No platform from which to give it, no tech with which to broadcast it. Not for now, anyway. Bad luck.)

The dining hall is a hot mess of sensation. It's local food night, so we are back to the *sudsas* and *tagines*, and palm *this* and date *that*, all uniformly disgusting, but you can't fault the Institute for attempting some regional flavor, now can you.

Now I am on the way home, knee-deep in beautiful blooms of crumpled paper. Ruined flowers. I've fashioned gators of tape, so no more paper cuts on my ankles, no sir, though the going is still tough, slow, and surpassingly loud (*crinkle slap, slap, slap*) and who should pop up once again like a demented cuckoo but the Enclave's concierge.

Hello, madam.

There's a new package, says the Enclave's resident hobgoblin.

(My identity papers, my passport booklet: back!)

"Who dropped it off?" I ask.

A man.

"Someone from the Institute?"

No.

"What was he wearing?"

Just clothes.

"Just normal clothes?"

Normal-like.

"When?"

Several days ago.

"Several *days*? Well why didn't you . . . N/m. Anything else?"

"Yes. Someone else has been up there," she says.

Not a fellow, not an admin. So, some *outsider* has been in my rooms? There have been movements. A door was left open. Noise. Rustlings about. The other residents complaining. No-guest policy in place. Rules. If you can't live by the codes of conduct . . .

"Who, who was up there? Who was the man with the package?"

"You don't know? Hmph." She winks at me as if we share a sinister secret, then begins to recede, slowly, backward, into the shadows.

I stride the stairs, click open the door. Whisper up the lights.

The place is empty.

He's long gone. The Same Same man. Or one of his

minions. Must be. What this all means is that the passport is back, surely. But where is it now?

Under the paper. Of course. Buried.

I tunnel once more through the piles, glancing, occasionally, at what is written on the sheets. An ungodly slumgullion of texts. Dig, read. Dig, read. Dig, read. It must be here! Walking room to room, reading/crumpling, reading/crumpling, kicking piles, until finally I see it (I see it!). The corner of the slender gray box.

Shove both of my hands into the bank of white, and papers erupt everywhere. One last tug, one last geyser, atop which rides the parcel.

I tug off the packaging, and inside of it there is mostly wadding. In this, an envelope. In the envelope: the passport. My identity papers.

The original pebbled blue booklet.

Under this, a pristine, new one.

Name. Passport number. Photo. Visa Status. D.O.B., S.S.N. Purpose of Visit. Length of Stay. Signature from Sanctioning Officials. Fingerprint. Security watermarks. Signature of Holder . . .

Looks good. This golden bough, my beautiful new set of identity papers—provided by our local neighborhood Same Same—that very same passport which I will, in due course, give over to the guardians who await me at the border, at the threshold between inside the Freehold and outside of it—those papers which I will slide, with only the slightest promise of their return, through the window of the bullet-proof booth as requested. The papers which that official (whatever custodian of the border my number has called up for me) will scrutinize. I will watch as he reads the booklet, looking back and forth between its pages and me, then looking down again to flip through more, examining my stamps, my ideogrammatic footprints. This frail little book, which he will spatchcock and grill under his red-lit scanner in order to confirm my prints, my biometrics, to cross-reference my materials with those of known agents of discord; these papers which are all that stands between me and . . . not me.

Yes. It's back. My passport. And everything is in place; everything in order.

(THE PAPER CONTINUED)

. . . while out behind the Residential Enclave, a set of twin doors have just sprung open automatically. Here comes a new sheet of paper on the wind, followed closely by two gentlemen, transporting a gurney between them.

On it rests an impassive Mr. Ousman Al'Hatif. Coming around now on either side of the stretcher, the men collapse and slide it, and him, into the back of a long, long car.

The paper slips easily into a clipboard, which one of the men now signs. The other man takes the clipboard, mechanically, comes around to the driver-side door, gets in, and drives away.

Several hours later, if you were listening closely enough, could you hear a barked order, and perhaps three sharp volleys, which splatter a flock of birds into the sky? Or maybe, instead, the sound of a large drawer, sliding into a wall, and clicking closed? A gas jet?

You wouldn't hear. Not a single one of these sounds. Though the paper might.

48

(DANSE MACABRE)

The admins all wear masks now (occasionally gloves as well). The air smells of carbolic acid. And as the front advances—and with it our cabin fever—we gather in the buzzing gloom of the Arts Pavilion for testimonials. But before we spill our guts, we recite the Institute's oath. We all do it, though no one wants to. Either way, nobody has to look at the sheet anymore. We are all pros, old hands, we all know it by heart. So we deliver the thing in a reluctant chorus, like kids muttering pledges of allegiance, or athletes a national anthem—mouthing the words mostly, sometimes just na-na-na-ing through it all, making just enough sound, collectively, to constitute a full(ish) rendition; meaning each of us only takes a word or two for each line. So, though our recitation may be made up of indifference and incompetence, the oath is, despite us, a truly collective thing.

I need grace because
Things can't be changed.
Courage; you super-duper need it.

Intelligence. Cunning. But also blind luck.
Because we admit here and now
that we are powerless.
Can't do shit.

One day happens after another.
And another (identical-like).
The moments are lined up
In a kind of catalog of hardship.

Pathway to serenity? Nope.
It is what it is, and it is getting worse.
Meaning that "the world to come" will be pretty awful,
*   probably.*

So be prepared.
We will all most likely drown in something.
Could be fire, paper, blood.
Or radioactive sludge, or our own filth.

Or the whole thing might go down like in that book, the
one which was made into a movie in which all the insects
have become enormous and tornadoes spawn out of the low-
slung sky like stalactites and the only sounds are booms of
ordnance, the constant crackles of fire, along with grace notes
of lightning and faint whimpers from the wounded and
despondent—and our faces will be soot-blacked, our clothes
rags, and we, the living dead, will shuffle our broken shop-

*ping carts around, will avoid the major arteries of course as
the biggest threat to us will be—as it always has been—one
another, and one more thing, this is because we will probably
be eating human flesh for sustenance by then and Ps. no water
left. Which is to say, yet again, that the world is what it is,
and also what it will be, and not as you would have it.*

*So make right all those things you are able to.
Square 'em good.
Draw up wills and testaments.
Surrender.*

*What? Yes. Sure,
a kind of measured and reasonable happiness
has been known to occur (terms and conditions apply),
but most are living one day at a time
accepting hardship as a pathway to a distant, mythic peace,
blindly trusting that somehow things might be made right
      again,
And that eventually they, that is, we, may be happy, if not
      in this life,
then who knows, perhaps with Jesus almighty motherfucking
      Christ,
forever, in the next.*

*Alterburg, Oh Alterburg!
Liberty, Equality, Fraternity,
So on. So forth.*

We do not look at one another during the oath. It's embarrassing. The recitation (blessedly) over, we observe a moment of silence.

Then we do the testimonials, then we file out, shuffling like a chain gang. The recitation, for whatever reason, has irked me—the sentiments, tonight, grating more than is normal. Maybe I'm sick of being subsumed in the collective. Of being just another fellow. I mean, just look at them there, loitering in the atrium. The Woman-Whose-Face-and-Hands-Are-Covered-in-Scars smiles at me grimly, and inserts a cigarette into the dense warp and woof of her mouth. Lights it. The ember glows, and the yarn does not ignite. She exhales a plume with an exhausted, but satisfied moan. 鼎福 the Architect and the Branding Expert scamper off like schoolkids, and here is the Cosmetic Dentist, speaking with the Plastic Surgeon, and here is the Camouflage Engineer, and the Man-Who-Collects-Commemorative-Snow-Globes. I'm left with the Minimalist, and Disputant 1. (Where is Disputant 2?) Evidently Disputant 2 isn't here anymore, and I'm not sure why. Did things get too heated? Was there a duel? Some positions in a debate are only that—positions—but some positions are beliefs, ingrained, and harder to slough off. Which is to say that perhaps I have misread their argument and its purpose. Either way Disputant 1 seems heartbroken. When did Disputant 2 leave exactly? Disputant 1 doesn't want to talk about it. Okay, but. He left. Begging the question, should I simply . . . leave?

And going back to the flat, I find instead that I'm walk-ing to the car park.

I mean, what if—what if I were to go? Just up and depart this noise. What then? I now have the means again. I could leave the Institute. Head into the wilderness, Absent With-out Official Leave. There might be a place in that desert for me, a shanty, a fleapit where I could live out an anchorite's life—my own patch of earth, outside of the dome's forum of conversation and commerce—I would be dead to the world, sure. And living at sea level; the flattest of the flatlands. So no more of my elevated perspectives. But I'd be content, perhaps. With no more scrutiny, no more *ping*s, no more pressure. I'd live, albeit frugally. Simply. There's a vehicle right there. Totally unattended. Why not?

I find I'm flushed with excitement, heading toward the car, hearing the urgency of my blood, and the road crunch-ing under my feet. I just could hop in, now. Tell the car to set the GPS randomly, drive until we stop. Exit the vehicle wherever it happens to run out of juice. Who would miss me, eh? No more groups, no more oaths, no more Ladder of Completion and confluence units . . . ah, but then, Percy, then: How would the project be completed? There's the rub. Without the infrastructure, guidance, admins, the pro-gram: How would I finish? I wouldn't, and that's the Mfing truth. I wouldn't last a day on my own. And would I survive the storms? Sand and soot? The swirling paper and other debris. Good questions all. And the project is getting made. It would be so foolish to leave, a yard from the goal line. But

think of the freedom, the anonymity. The death of ambition (the peace). To vanish . . . and perhaps there are more
radical ways in which the Same Same can help. Who knows?
And, my hand *is* on the car door, so I might as w—

Several bodies slam into me, and now it is lights out.

(. . . AND OF YOUNG HANS'S
MORAL STATE)

Darkness. Total darkness.

I need to concentrate. A new room, now. I've been isolated. It's so black. Can't see a damn thing, though the situation could not be more apparent. Which is to say that,
perhaps, a great honor has been bestowed upon me. Hasn't
it just? Retreats such as these are only granted to those
most promising of fellows (I'll have you know)—content
providers whose work will be of enduring value. So the
great, clandestine peer committee must have assembled
on my behalf (I'd imagine), my project scrutinized, and
then the go-ahead given—given (again: presumably), with
the resounding *whump* of a great rubber stamp hitting the
proper forms. Then a cheer goes around (I can practically
hear it), handshakes, so on.

I must be equal to the honor.

Though endings are the most difficult, and so require
the most solitude. But it is hard; a hard row to hoe—this
loneliness.

Think, Percy. Think. So close to the end. You've got this.

Hard too, when my cloister is completely dark; darkly, dark. Though this darkness is in line with the mission, after all. No disruptions; not even in the form of sense-data. No empirical input. And obviously, I am not to interact with my peers. I am not told how long this specified period will last.

(FAQ: Has any fellow remained in such creative isolation forever? A: Idk.)

I am granted ocasional breaks for solitary meals, naturally, pushed under the door by silent Zimzim, my Tea Boy. But that's it. The main takeaway is: no distractions.

This, the new austerity.

Btw I think I've passed some sort of anniversary here in my solitude. No one celebrates these things here, but I am pretty sure yesterday was the date of my arrival at the Institute. A year. One whole year. Amazing. Amazing that it has been two years already. Hard to believe. I landed under the metastructure only (I want to say: *five?*) years ago. Idk.

I will leave. Soon. But I will only leave with more pages under my belt. The final pages. More paper. This is what my confinement must signify.

That I will prevail.

But only with no input.

Only output. Only output.

A second meditation on time, on my crippling awareness of it—the unending stretch, alone with myself, with nothing but whatever threadbare inner resources I may possess.

> *My own poor company; imagination; impoverished nar-*
> *rative skills; so forth—this meditation to be indicated by a*
> *solitary word:*
>   *"Etc."*

Days pass.

Moan. Roll my neck.

More time passes.

Scream a little. Cry a bit. Grunt.

Feel around in the darkness.

Cry more.

Purgation, illumination, unification. Am bored.

Being "all cried out" is the only novelty.

Though I've developed some techniques for staving off despair, e.g.: certain fantasies I'll unspool, certain songs I croon to myself from time to time. Also, I perform occasional physical exercises (see under: Daily Physical Routines).

I add a new activity to the list, that is: the fine art of tapping my fingers.

Tap, tap. Tap, tap, tap.

Repeat.

While tapping my fingers against my legs in the darkness, something new happens. I.e., a light flickers. Not inside my head that is (pretty sure). But an actual light. (Tbd.)

Tap ta—

Light.

I freeze, and look up to see from whence the light comes, and just like that: the world goes dark again.

Sit in the darkness.

Am frightened.

More crying/singing/self-pleasure/etc. Blah blah blah.

After waiting awhile (I want to say: *days?*) I try again, experimentally. Tapping my fingers once more, and boy howdie, the light twinkles back on. It's just a glimmer, mind, but after the blackness it is disturbingly bright.

I stop, and the light winks out, as before.

Conclusions:

Drum fingers—light goes on.

Stop drumming fingers—light goes out.

Cause/effect. Qed.

Tapping my fingers again, tentatively of course, but slowly accelerating, and the light dilates, and I am becoming a bit acclimatized to it now, the deepening glow, and so continue tapping until the light gains enough strength to begin illuminating some of the space I now think of as my home (albeit a lockup). Square. Single room, small enough to be covered, wall-to-wall, in four strides. More finger-tapping and the light oozes out to the very perimeter, to the room's corners, brightening. Spreading. There's a bed, and a bedside table with bright objects on it. A sink, a steel mirror.

Tap, tappety-tap, tappety-tap-tap.

While I drum away like this, I consider first causes.

What is the light's source? Is a window being opened— a possible egress? Idk, but the more I fiddle with my fingers the livelier the light, so I just keep at it because I have nothing to lose, honestly. So I'm really getting into it now: whiz through some paradiddles, a couple of trills, roll a few chords, add some five-fingered arpeggios going up and down, lots of grace notes, flams and drags, bunch of Swiss Army Triplets, and that light—which is just overhead but aggravatingly just out of my line of sight no matter which way I turn—swells way, way up. Brighter and brighter.

Both hands now. "The quick brown fox jumps over the lazy dog!" "Pack my red box with five dozen quality jugs!" Etc. The light—which is a crazy kind of fluorescent teal: nuanced, bewitching—responds, and jigs along.

The unsung—purely tactile—pleasures of this mode
of finger tapping to be indicated by letters in formation

Q W E R T Y U I O P
A S D F G H J K L
Z X C V B N M

Swelling, warming, and, frankly, burning a little. Just a little. My skin is starting to itch. Don't care. W/e. I'm no longer tapping out of fear, see, but in hope rather, and kind of, just a little bit enjoying myself really, despite the itching, and despite the fact of my reddened, irradiated skin, which is—matter of fact—beginning to actually flake and peel off a little now, little bits of hair too from off of my head and arms. My hair is all kinky, pubed up from the now-withering heat—it has tumbled to the floor in front of me in little ashen piles, and what is this but, yes, great big wounds; my skin weeping and opening and then miraculously scabbing over, in an accelerated, stuttering, stop-motion time, and I am just, like, shedding. Rapid-fire. My body molting, and it (my body) beginning also to reek like (disturbingly) a backyard barbecue—and though I am in exquisite pain and itchy as an ant farm, *tap tap tappet-tip-tappy-tap* the feeling is ecstatic. And my fingers keep going: whirlwind air stenography, faster and faster, fingers as wild as all get-out; virtuoso stuff coming out of me, a real barnburner, just riding this excitement to swelling ovations while my body now expunges its fluids, deliquesces in ecstasy (and the light really goes incandescent at the word "deliquesce"), and I'm doing it compulsively now, unstoppably, *clickety clack, clickety clack*: "jackdaws love my big sphinx of quartz," so forth, and I can feel so much pressure building, the brightness mounting, the acrid stink filling my throat, the light is now so bright, my head, as to actually have a sound, a pulsar-noise—electromagnetic, crystalline, purring—and my head, my head, *tap tap*, and *TAAAAAAAPPP* as the light finally goes nova, and all the walls, my head, seemingly collapse, I'm blinded by white as the light peaks.

And must stop.

The light fades rapidly. And, Rn, though the room is darkening again, and though my eyes are blurred by the auroras branded into them, I can still make out the basic shape of the space around me, unchanged by the recent photic detonation, and I look straight up, finally, toward what seems to be a fancy chandelier, an insectile ceiling fixture on a long and articulated steel arm.

The bulbs: space-age, and tessellated like a bug's eye.

Men and women are gathered around me in a circle. Men and women who were always there, looking down at me. Gathered like druids for a sacrifice; to violate me with a ceremonial blade, and to read the coming world in my convulsions.

And then, just like that, it's dark again.

Wait!

Much later, a door opens, and I'm wheeled out.

In the next room, an antechamber of sorts. In it, the Director.

"Ah, Percy. Good."

"What gives you the right to do this to me?"

"You did, my boy."

"I demand my papers back."

"I think NOT. We are making such progress."

A gap.

(MESSAGES)

But on the other hand, the good news is, following a lengthy convalescence and recovery period, I'm back in the flat; my original Institute lodgings. Good old Room 34. In my own bed, thank the Lord. I've had some visitors, who sat in the chair beside my bed, or who just stood at my side looking down at me. I don't know these people. Eventually they stop coming. So, I've been using the device to reach beyond the

Institute. I've sent several messages. Searching. Scanning. Probing. Feeling my way outward. Some of these communiqués have been long. As in, full-blown missives. Others are no more than a quick ping:

—*HOW u*

—*u out there dennis?*

—*Ousman? Uuuuu's-man?*

—*fkkkk it sinks here*

—**sinks*

—*Autocrrct FUCK it *sucks here*

—*Dennis*

—*U there?*

—*How u*

—*Where u*

—*Ansr pls*

—*Dennis*

—*Kk*

—*L8tr*

I've been lobbing such pings—my carrier pigeons—up and over the walls of my confinement, hoping that they'll flutter their way out, and then alight on the correct windowsill. Rapidly firing them off, hoping for replies, for information, for some proof that, indeed, the world is continuing, unabated, elsewhere. That life exists outside of the increasingly radical insularity of Institute life. Hoping that, even if the messages don't make it to their recipients, at the very least, one of these aimless messenger-birds might just shit on the world outside of this one, thereby confirming that world's existence. That world without domes, without Discourses™, without projects.

 —*hello*

 —*any1*

 —*It's been a while.*

 —*??*

Though I haven't heard back from a single soul yet, darned if I don't keep at it.

 —*Yo*

 —*still here. Where is u*

Meanwhile: so many white servants, so many dark charges. So many doors opening and closing. Footsteps. Boundless echoes reverberating in glazed corridors—so many echoes outside my room. (The admins of course. They have the brightest shoes. Shoes with laces even.) I hear them talking through the door, from my bed, from the cold tiles of my floor, from the bathroom, even over the running taps; these echoes without source, each echo slipping down an endless chain of sound whose center is nowhere. Not *Midnight Rain Forest*, not *Maternal Heartbeat*, or *The Great Cataracts of the Far North*. But echoes. I tried counting them and I simply cannot NEmore. Tried counting all sorts of things. Years, eons, minutes, months, heartbeats, eye blinks, loops, echoes. Can't tot any of it up, Ffs. Can't make a total. I thought I could tally the days in garbage. In paper. In pages. But no.

 —*Can someone please come and get me now?*

 —*srsly*

—*I'm super serious. Really.*
—*I'm sorry if I did something wrong.*
—*for wtevr I did*
—*Please?*
(No reply to this last one either though.)
W/e.

My words are clearly no longer working here so next I send along this:

:(

Which means: "It all makes me sad."

And time passes.

Even more time passes.

Much more of it.

And now I don't wait anymore. No one answers back.

Is it that the churning front of wind and sand cannot be breached?

No matter.

No matter.

No matter: there is still work to be done. I'm succeeding at this. Me, Ftw.

By hook or by crook: me, Ftw.

49

(ENCYCLOPEDIA)

I pass another (I want to say: *year?*) at the Institute. The desert continues, throughout this period, to provide fodder for my work in the form of pages of text. Given that all of these texts, though superficially random, are, upon closer inspection, quite germane to my project—all seemingly relevant to me and my labors, as if specifically curated for me, on my behalf—I can no longer doubt the papers' provenance. That is, I can no longer deny the obvious: that the source of this great in-surging of material is my Same Same shop, and that the organizing principle behind the deluge must be my very own Fundaments.

Perhaps I've always known this. But what does it matter, now? What does it matter where the paper comes from; its provenance? Who cares where my bricks are made, or what they are made of, so long as the edifice I am constructing continues to rise up? What matters is that the material is coming in, and who am I to impede its progress.

Conditions under the metastructural vault have—incrementally, if steadily—continued to worsen. Yet, despite the depredations, despite the fact of our collective enterprise having been hermetically vacuum-packed, despite our submersion inside of this bubble—our dissolute Atlantis under the seas of red storms and white papers—despite the disarray, the stench, not to mention the slipping mores, nosediving ethical standards, the sudden sartorial and ethical wildness evinced by our environmental catastrophe, this Anthropocene nightmare, despite all of this, life at the Institute has not, in fact, changed one iota. By which I mean that despite my progress, despite the outward chaos, the daily rhythms remain unaltered.

I still attend my clinics, my guided meditations, my creative-dynamics workshops; still read the info-blasts and reply to the subsequent online questionnaires demonstrating my having read them; still have it all to do. Everything the same. And you could say that it is all working: the project, my novel, is rounding the corner into a final lap, with a fully completed and polished, sacred nine-tenths of the work all locked up.

I can hardly believe it.

I simply cannot (believe it). After all of these years. So many false starts. So much fruitless ambition wasted on aborted works. But I am, now, demonstrably, "getting it done." I am rising above the ranks of those whose destiny does not include a finished project. Those whose aborted, malformed, inertia-laden, or otherwise thwarted works will never see the light of day.

I will finish. (I think.)

And it seems (I think, again) to be happening quite of its own accord. I/o/w, despite me.

News of my impending success has no doubt got around, as Miss Fairfax is back at my flat, checking up on my deliverables, no doubt. She has trouble getting through the front door.

All the surfaces are plastered with pages; a world of pallid, but mottled whites, yellows and browns, pinks, and occasional blue or green, but mostly the spectrum which ranges from *tooth* to *Caucasian*. Each page here, here in my studio, seems unique, unique in height and width, in color—each page a distinct shade—each marked by a different typeface and margin size . . . in short, as if every page were a page torn from a different book. As if it were book litter. Book trash. But I know better. This is material for a great recycling.

Some are blank, most are written on. Some drawn on, some folded or sculpted. There is an order to it all, here in my flat. Unlike on the dumping grounds of the Institute, the paper in my room is tightly, intricately, deeply structured. One page leads to the next. There are diagrams and charts and even sculptures, paper facsimiles of just about everything and everyone present in Institute life. There are now lines of thread, in bright colors, connecting all of the pages; the whole thing forming a vast web, an overlapping, doubling back, tangled-up network of coded lines.

She tiptoes toward me like a crane through a marsh, tutting and sighing disapprovingly. As she seems lost in it all, I take her arm, and begin to guide her through, cautious around the threaded matrix, the piles on the floor. It is slow going. We have to stoop, and jump over heaps; step through the threads and stacks. She stoops to examine some of the paper more closely, and seems surprised that the first page she pulls up is a travelogue.

"That one came in handy," I admit.

We wander on through atlases, cookbooks, works of literary criticism, philosophy, seemingly random lists of objects and names, various registries, printouts of social networks and feeds, minutes from board meetings, manifestos, medical references, thrillers, feuilletons, puzzles, murder mysteries, religious tracts, shopping lists, poems, newspaper clippings, biographies, postcards (boats, buildings, deserts . . .), paranormal testimonials, sheets of note-shot staff paper, abecedarians, classics, memoirs, diaries, classified ads, marginalia, pornography, assembly instructions, children's board books, building directories, architectural elevations, suicide notes . . .

"What the hell is all this?"

"My project. In these pages. Yes. This is it. I arranged them. Just like so."

She just stands there, hands on hips, the very picture of . . . what exactly? I, meanwhile, continue to navigate my network, trying not to upset the delicate ecosystem, chary of tearing the web around me. Miss F. looks down at the apparatus, and then over at me, then down again. Though I wish I could read her, I cannot; I can't tell what orders her

PETER MENDELSUND

features as she assesses my work, but it might be maternal concern, or weariness, or anger, or perhaps the patient sufferance of the chronically unheeded. Idk.

"The desert has provided," I continue.

I sweep my hand around in a generously arcing, grand gesture, scooping "it all," the room, its contents (a room which, to the untrained eye, would resemble a hoarder's den), all of the paper, and the discourse contained upon it, even her, and I gesture it toward myself, encompassing with the gesture all of it, all of it. I bring it all toward my bosom.

She turns away from the jumble of my work and says, "These are the books we brought you? Jesus Christ, Mr. Frobisher, do you see these stamps? These are property of the Institute library. They are not yours to destroy."

Brought to me?

"We do not tear up books, Percy!"

(Admins, with rolling carts, carrels full of them, a muted rainbow of bindings—buckram, canvas, cloth, paper, board, their smell of time spent, these books—and the reams of paper too, in crisp, glossy wrapped blocks, the room filling with them . . .)

No. No. The desert. Either way. Tbd. Doesn't matter. What truly matters is that I winnowed them.

I cut them to pieces. I made sense of them. *I* did.

"You cannot say that of what I've made here, that this isn't a project. Of a sort."

Looking around, she seems angry I suppose, but also a bit moved, perhaps?

"Good Lord, who is going to pay for all of this?"

"A *novel* of a sort," I repeat, undaunted, "if nothing else."

"I'll have to speak with the Director." Not threatening, but resigned. "I'm sorry, but—"

After she's gone, I take advantage of the solitude to do a little more pruning.

I continue through my maze, following a particular thread which winds through Crime and Self-Help, through Cybernetics and Media Theory. This page here carries at its top the title: *History of the Arabic World*. Another reads as though written by some contemporary humorist. Here's an ecology of deserts. Several pieces of critical and literary theory. Not to mention that many of the pages here bear more than a passing resemblance to the monumental novel I've been trying for years to finish reading; the one I lugged with me out here; that modern classic we all know and love; canonical, colossal. Here are its pages, sacrificed on the altar of my project. Cut in. As if my own novel were nothing but a prismatic version of this other book—as if that great work had been thrown in a wood chipper, its chapters, sections, sentences, words even: mixed willy-nilly. Its names, themes, locations, all kaleidoscoping together into something approaching randomness, though still making a (faint yet decipherable) pattern.

I continue to follow where the thread takes me. To me, at least, there is the hint of a coherent narrative here now. But as the one thread begins to run out, leading to another to which it is loosely knotted, the tale becomes a bit clearer, my tale-slash-collection. At one point in the traverse, I notice how dark it is outside and realize that I have just read close to (I want to say: *three hundred?*) various-sized, pied pages. As I wade on, there are a few things I can say now, definitively, about it. About its plot, about its principal players, so on. I could make certain reasonable assertions concerning the novel's structure, about its general themes, its overall aims and underlying meanings. A competent reader could even tell now where it is all heading—as, of course, I myself can. And though I am still quite far from the (final) thread, the finish line that is, the last of my strands, it is just the most obvious thing in the world to me what I am doing here and how it ends.

Brb.

(THE THUNDERBOLT)

Breaks. Much needed breaks.

In order to relieve my mind a bit from the intense labor of my project's final chapters, I spend much of the next span in relaxed preparation. I.e., a dissociative fugue-state of game playing. There are puzzle games and mind teasers and crosswords and platform jumpers and races, but I love the first-person shooters the most. *Frontline*, *Festival of Death*, *Over the Top*, and *Attrition* modes of Passchendaele Multiplayer FPS™. Mud and sandbags. Vertebrae of burnt trees.

Barbed wire. Bomb craters. Tracers. The whole thundering, smoking, quagmire-of-no-man's-land deal of it all. Fokkers droning overhead, Mark Vs, grinding their monstrous treads over body piles. Gas attacks in a wide range of beautifully toxic shades. State-of-the-art particle effects. I bob around, hand on the stock of a bolt action mauser, locked into my own, red-misted line of fire, looking through the dual rose windows of my virtual gas mask. Screams. Bones snapping in the headphones. Going over the top, ducking and weaving, mowing down the enemy, one bullet at a time, or in bursts. Killing with my knife, killing with my bayonet, killing with my trench shovel, killing with a grenade. Death throes with lifelike sound effects. Enduring the tedium of cut scenes and death marches. Maps. Orders. Digging in. Eating a rat. Contracting cholera; Spanish flu. Being shot, stabbed, dying in every which way but always rejuvenated, procedurally regenerated for long enough to reach the kill screen. Going again, and again, new lives, new me's, from the beginning each time. Repeating this same solo campaign, over and over and over, reborn, etc.

It feels like a rite. A celebratory ritual, perhaps.

And there is much to celebrate: I am out of administrative segregation and back among a better class of people here, a better class of artist, back in my old Group. The admin reads the roll off of her device. We grunt when our names are called. *Here, yup, yes*. All present. We are all here. And we hear, from outside, the rattling of the dome. The room sways slightly.

PETER MENDELSUND

Unfold the chairs. The men sit wide, elbows on legs.
Heads bowed. The women cross and uncross their legs nervously. Someone rapidly whisks something off their shoulder. Someone else coughs. Admin11 calls us to order.

Today's participants: Mathematician, Puppeteer, Astronomer, Painter, Set Theorist, Composer, a bunch of newly
inducted fellows I don't recognize, and me (obvs).

The Painter goes first and tells us that he is a highly
respected and well-paid society portraitist ("I've seen your
work," I say, but am hissed down by the mob. *Don't interrupt.*). Actually, he *was* a highly respected and well-paid
society portraitist . . . until . . . until each painting of each
distinct patron slowly, almost imperceptibly, sitting by sitting, began to ressemble a painting of the Painter himself;
the sitter's features dilating or contracting to mimic his
own morphology, their genders, ages, ethnicities erased and
overwritten . . . Okay. Well. *Yup.* His portraits all became
self-portraits . . . *Aw fuck it, fuck it* . . . followed by the Composer, whose massive fugues set new standards for contra-
puntal complexity; so impeccable were his works of species
counterpoint that his colleagues folded up their books of
staff paper, broke their quills, abandoned their organ lofts,
and shunted their clavichords down to basements under old
blankets, yet, yet, the Composer is still reaching for new
heights and keeps adding more and more chromatically
difficult counter-subjects to his compositions, but always
(again, of course!) ending up, ending up with the same final
theme, the only theme which can function in his clockwork

442

musical puzzles as an ultimate motif, the only one which works against the inevitable movements of all the other parts—over and over again, that theme being the notes which spell the *letters in his own fucking name* . . . ugh . . . then, then, then, the Mathematician who keeps finding paradoxical self-evidence (sigh) in all of his closed systems . . . *shit* . . . and the Puppeteer who keeps making little puppeteers, who make smaller puppeteers, in dangling-down family-tree-like skeins, cladistics of fraying tapestries in ever-increasing fractal self-similarity and inbred corruption . . . and a certain man who rewrites another man's book, line by line, word by word, thereby imbuing the old text with an entirely new set of meanings not contained in the original, we already know this one don't we . . . uh . . . etc., etc. and suchlike, so on, but then here's the Set Theorist whose *set of all sets that do not contain themselves* drives him around the bend and, and, and the Astronomer who sees nothing but the glint from his own eye reflected in his telescopes, and the Philosopher who only believes in the surety of analytic propositions—propositions which take the form of tautologies, and the Neuroscientist who tweaks his own angular gyrus in order to record a series of dissociative OBEs, all of which contain (sigh) himself, and every difference everywhere is only one of scale, if even that, suchlike; and then it's my turn, and so I begin, but, in the middle, in the middle of what (I should add) has become an increasingly triumphant account of my project, of my various moves up the Ladder, of my victory, I have a memory—bright and stark.

It arrives obvious as could be, as if it had stridden in during visitation hours on a predetermined day, stomped through the main glass doors of my conscious mind and signed the registry at its front desk; *ding ding ding*. And stood before me in all of its simultaneously accusatory and frightened facticity. This memory which will be the beginning of my story.

A memory of my trip here. My trip to the Freehold. To the Institute. (Listen, it is plain as day.) A single lurch forward, and I was gone. Flight. A gap. Then: the desert as I first saw it, that is, from the airplane. No, earlier. A monitor on the seat back in front of me. There was an icon: a miniature white cross, trailing a red dotted line behind it like spoor, that's us; our path growing imperceptibly longer and longer, the plane set against a sea of desaturated blue, entering and despoiling it; we are turned at an impossible angle as if flying sideways, plowing toward a promised-land green—which wouldn't be green of course, but tan and brown and also blisteringly, ascendantly white; but there, then, on board the plane, it was green, an impossibly beautiful, transcendental green; the green of aspiration, and fecund possibility—an LCD world. 7,000 miles. 6,999 miles . . . the roar like a silence.

6,998; 6,997 . . . This memory one step more toward the source. Backward I mean. Idk. Crucial info, though, Imo.

Leaving the Group and the complex and heading out onto the sandstorm-wavering, darkened, and polluted grounds, I think: though we departed from our own, disparate homes, we all saw the same seat backs; were all represented, somewhere on that screen, buried deep in the pixels of that map, in that white cross, flying, flying over the blue ocean toward the falsely green land? We all flew into the same hub here, didn't we; were all driven along the same endless roads. We suffered the same thirsts, hungers, disorientations. All of us, perhaps, even sharing the same affliction: that need to make; to create and perfect our idiolects. I feel now, a true member of the community, and wish to play my part here. There is so much to share, so much I can contribute.

"You will see, Percy. It all seems strange at first, but, when the coin drops, it can feel like an awakening." This is what Miss Fairfax had said, and I had scoffed at the idea. But just look at me now.

It is a free period, and everyone is emerging from the buildings at once, some chatting, some lighting cigarettes, others clutching notebooks and other project-work, in twos and threes, a group of ten, and some solitaries, all in their uniforms, their beautiful, if ragged, uniforms. Where is Ousman Al'Hatif? Gone already? I look for his beard, his tam, his scarf. Not here.

I go to his little room—there is, now, just a sad, stripped single bed, his drawers are pulled and void, and in the brown and dingy bathroom there isn't even a toothbrush; all traces of him stripped, not a thing left, except wait—I see now that here are a couple of his photos, from his home maybe, still sticky-tacked up there on the far wall. His family—two Al'Hatif parents and an Al'Hatif son—and a desert, and a souk, and a city, a postcard of a statue, camels. He must have forgotten to take them, so maybe he will come back for these personal effects, though somehow, I now doubt this, and look, there is a single red checker on the floor right there in the corner by the bed. I leave the residence, and head out into the garden again, and where is Dennis—oh right, Mr. Royal has left too. They'd be the ones; my friends and confidants. *Have you seen Miss ☺ the Brand Analyst?* I ask a group of fellows, promenading arm-in-arm out of the Science structure. "Who?" *Never mind. No worries.* I have to . . . *Hey, hey; excuse me! Do you know where the Philosopher might be . . .* I'm sorry I don't understand. Where the hell are all . . . *Pardon? So sorry, but I'm looking for* 鼎福 *the Architect . . .*

I can't find anyone I recognize. *Where is? Where, where . . . is . . . gone, gone.*

Gone.

My clique. My tribe. Everyone: elsewhere.

Charlotte Chatterton, my Mysterious Woman. She, at least, is still haunting her usual spots . . .

I bustle over to the glacial lake—now a decidedly unglacial landfill. It smells to high hell. A pulpy morass of sodden shit.

Circumnavigating its perimeter until I reach her bench outside of the Mountain House, the spot where I saw her from the car, reading, all of those (I want to say: *six years?*) ago. And it is empty.

What now? Achy disappointment. I plop down.

The bell is ringing—faint as it is from out here—ringing for another Accessional Moment. Soon, everyone will be back indoors. If it were another day, an earlier day, I'd be scrambling toward my flat, hustling to make some progress. Up the Ladder. Up and up. Instead, I sit here quietly, observing the ghost town, the gray structures, the kaleidoscopic metastructure, the clogged allée, the Institute's cooling, wasting body, listen to the hiccuping breezes from the malfunctioning turbines as they disturb the papers with their last, choking gasps, rustling them like grasses on a savannah. What now? I idly tug a single sheet up from under my resting thigh, and examine it. There is writing on it which I can't read so I snatch another sheet, its neighbor:

An unassuming young man was traveling, in midsummer, from his native city of Hamburg to Davos-Platz in the Canton of the Grisons, on a three weeks' visit.

I pull up a handful of the sheets now, some pristine, others crumpled into balls, or folded, sometimes haphazardly, other times conscientiously according to principles understandable (paper airplane, tricorn hat, lady's fan) or not (arcane origamis).

I unrumple them and read. One says:

They have been called up, these comrades here, for a final push in a battle that has lasted all day . . .

A war narrative of some stripe.

As opposed to the next sheet, which, though it is numbered at the bottom, is otherwise blank . . .

And another paper, from a small pad perhaps, which bears at its top, like a letterhead, a picture of a tree. A palm? Linden? Or a ladder? Flagpole? Two snakes slithering up it, the structure ending unnaturally in a pair of brazen wings, spread confidently broad, as if the whole nightmarish, chimerical contraption could rise up, an unholy airscrew in a fever-dream of flight. Crumple, jettison. More pages. Written in German, French, a tale of illness, racking coughs, blue bottles of sputum, thermometers, straight razors, an argument, a duel, a phonograph, a suicide, a Tatar beauty, a sharp-nailed, malarial superman who is unable to finish a sentence, his wordless manservant, a doomed young Samaritan, a grieving mother, a rationalist, a Jesuit, a blustering director, a soldier's duty, a love unrequited, requited, then unrequited again, then dropped entirely, discontent, philosophy, lectures, hikes, alpine fevers . . . a spiritualist too, and a ghost. And look who is coming toward me now, but the Medium herself—the Institute's youngest, most precocious talent—a fellow with a knack for showing up late, at the eleventh hour, in order to disrupt the proceedings with unwelcome clairvoyance. She always promises a little final-inning drama. Her mysterious, occult powers crackling about her, a visible nimbus of ectoplasm, her glazed eyes in constant intercourse with the beyond, and at this moment she is sleepwalking toward me, holding out a new sheet of paper.

But, but, but oh boy, look at this, will you.

Just look at this one . . .

(THE PAPER CONTINUED)

One lurch forward and, and we were gone.

The highway runs straight through deciduous northern forests. Isolation is part of the promise and the cure. I have a single, faxed sheet with the intake info on my lap. There's a map and a schedule and a picture of some of the employees smiling. The car's otherworldly chill.

I spend the night in a motel. A no-place. There is nothing around it. I stare at myself in the mirror in the morning for some time.

It's leaden out this morning, dark, but the drugstore glasses stay on. Step away, they say, by reflecting you back at yourself.

I go through small industrial towns on their last legs. Passing through streets, ramps, ramparts, overpasses, roundabouts, convergences, and divergences. The fog of transit. Gone through green. A roadside green. The green of dying. On and on. Everything proceeding along a line, spooling out more and more, trees now broken by off-ramps and shopping centers and weigh stations, everything wiped, smudged along at a single speed. This maintaining. This attempt at maintaining continuity. This, despite so many new surroundings, one after another, which cumulatively threaten to unhinge and dismantle the calm. And now I'm sleeping. And waking and sleeping again. And then my body, alert to new forms of motion as the car slows and stops. The car only speaks the language of motion and it is saying that we are getting closer, and closer still, and the car is saying all of this to me through relative speed.

Slowing. Going again. And slows and stops again, and accelerates again, so on, which must mean smaller towns, smaller roads, smaller and smaller roads. And then I sit up. Sad exurban ghettos now. The row houses, the clone houses, overlooking the highway's ravines whiz by, though I inhabit them mentally—their vinyl siding, drab stucco and brickface, linoleum, blowcrete, wood-paneled grimness—I live in them for just long enough to smudge the passage of time. "Bear right in five hundred feet onto Interstate Twenty-three." Corporate parks, no-man's lands, depots. Piles of gravel. These derelict gas stations. That scrub and waste. Occasional tracks and platforms. This blank passage. Once-Drive-In-Movie-Plazas now unofficial parking lots, stubbled with broken speaker stands. These shoulders, embankments, culverts, off-ramps; rest stops gone to despair. Industrial structures webbed by power lines. Factory chimneys: those sad sentinels. Marsh reeds; roadkill. Rail yards—railway trestles; lines of cars, obsolete for passengers, but a brute force method for transporting what? Solvents, plastics, wood gums, pesticides, industrial resins, potassium chloride, polyvinyl chlorides, polypropylene, polyethylene, sarin, mustard gas, cyanide . . . production lines of oversized capsules, mobile Bhopals poised to move these varieties of fatal medicine to a world always-already laid waste. This thin, crepuscular light which reveals geometries hidden in the facades. Dandelion is here; crabgrass. Wrappers and remnants; rags, cans, frayed tires, rotted food, sloughed-off mufflers. Flashing constellations of obliterated glass. A latex glove. Whose? This grime. This rot and ruin. This roadside garbage. Our common debris. "In two miles, take a right onto Exit Fifteen."

Later, a thought: Doesn't every trip undertaken alone bear a trace or foreshadow of that other trip necessarily undertaken alone? Shut up. Shut up. I see a water tower off in the distance, a fixed point to focus on. In the foreground, though still far off, are power lines, attached to huge stanchions. I watch the alien and bulbous water tower move slowly through the power lines like a series of whole notes through a grand staff. The triangulation of our car and the two large objects far off awakens something in me, deep in me, though I am not at all sure what. And then the forest scrim overtakes the scene.

The landscape tilts back now, and our car reclines into higher precincts. The air, a bit colder. "In one point five miles, turn left." We've entered the near country, the dingy foothills. Through fogs and rains, and hail the size and shape of pencil erasers. Cold winds. The various slow-motion undersea sloshings of the maples and elms in the wind, the anxious shiver of asters, fewer and fewer cars, box stores, "no hunting," then we are going up farther, and there is a ridge of sorts, which we follow. When I first see it I think "What a grubby little mountain," as it's pathetic really. But I guess it is as near to a peak as we get out here, and at least there's a view, though not of much, and then a bit farther on still and then I see a gate right at the hollow of the mountain's throat, and then here now is a small chain-link fence, and the roundabout, and then the sign, the sign reading "The Alterberg Institute," and then onto another gentle upward, and then a subtle leveling-out which leads to another roundabout, the perfect little lawns of hell, the hedgerows of Hades (smelling no longer of citrus but loamy with mud and dead leaves, nettles and burdock, dog excrement), and oh ye gods the facade, the white glazed bricks, the bricks, the horrible white bricks, the building blocks which make the world a toilet. And then the little sculpture, please no, that perfect, plaster, vaginal hood with the pale blue Virgin's dumb, grinning head at perfect clitoral height, hands outspread to admit, to admit all of us, willing or no, and subsequently the little windows, the dark mullions, the shitty little concrete sidewalk, weeds pushing up, escaping like errant pubes, the scratched revolving glass doors, the sound of gravel under the tires, "You have reached your destination," stopping, catch of latch, clunk of trunk, and, the lobby, the smell, of petroleum, talc, wintergreen, B.O., antiseptic, the admittance, the desk, the scattered, dead-eyed loiterers, those scaries, those saddies, those wounded, the . . . and the . . . fucking untold. Sorrow of it all. The fathomless lonesomeness, the why, and the oh, and . . . I don't think . . . really? And . . . It was the best of times it was the worst of families is unhappy in its own truth universally acknowledged that a single Ishmael is a hot weary

dead man a wicked man exiled by fate in long *longtemps* ago
woman est morte also father died last year just gotten over a
serious illness that I won't bother to talk about except it had
something to do with the heat closing in on the dotted line
but in my arms and the child he is pale and thin he wears
a miserably weary world as he stood on his balcony gorging
himself in the correction of the correction of the correction
of gloom no love was left all earth and that was bottom-
less perdition there to dwell in the present tense though he
may use the past because a passive voice depends directly
upon the exterior form of a rupture and a redoubling for
the straightforward path had been lost in that place whose
name I do not care to remember that someone must have
by a vicus of recirculation led us borne back ceaselessly to
the lower frequencies on which I speak for you as his soul
swooned slowly spoke aloud to the large crowd of specta-
tors the day of my execution now everybody along a way
a lone a last a loved along the ecstasy of extreme fatigue
which I have borne what no man the fallen wonder one of
the best of its kind I ever lived faithfully a hidden life and
rest in unvisited tombs so all things limp together for the
only possible

PLEASE RELOAD LETTER-SIZE PAPER IN TRAY 2

50

THE FUNDAMENTS OF MY PROJECT

Fundament 28. ~~Write what you kn~~
~~Complicate traditional notions of authorship through deploying strategies of~~

Fundament 29. The project—and what makes up the project—may, in fact, turn out to be a contrivance. Okay. But claiming something is a contrivance doesn't absolve one of the responsibility of having to construct a fucking decent, readable one.

Fundament 30. ~~On this _____ day of _____ the Alterberg Institute took up the involuntary detention and treatment/ rehabilitation of the respondent herein. That the respondent was present in person. That having had the matters submitted, the Institute found upon clear and convincing evidence as follows:~~
   ~~1. That the respondent should be detained and involuntarily evaluated and treated/rehabilitated 2. That the respondent had _____ illness or was a~~

~~——————— or ——————— abuser, and by reason of such,
presented a likelihood of serious harm to himself
or others, and was thus in need of continued detention and treatment/rehabilitation 3. That detention
and treatment/ rehabilitation in the least restrictive
environment, as defined in Section ———————, was to be
provided by the Institute. That the Institute would
appropriately handle the respondent's condition
and had agreed to accept respondent. It was, therefore, adjudged and decreed that the respondent was
to be thereby placed in the custody of the Institute
to be detained for involuntary inpatient treatment/
rehabilitation for a period of~~

Fundament 31. Consider that the paper is not, in fact, white.

White? With all the words that have been written already, down the eons, by all those others? Nah, the paper is all filled up, and so (I want to say: *black*?). White would be easy, Imho. If I could just find a glimmer of it—a little glimpse of that pallid promise; i.e., some room to write my own thoughts down. But I can't. Lord knows I've tried.

51

(RESEARCH)

I pass yet another year at the Institute, in which I continue to study the novelist's art and apply what I've learned to the construction of a traditionally plotted novel, or at least what I hope is a passable approximation of one. (Or not, Idk.)

Time passes.

52

(A STROLL ON THE SHORES OF TIME)

"Time passes" is an odd thing to say. Gratuitous, certainly. Passing is what time does, and time is nothing if not an obvious precondition for anything and everything. Aside from the blatancy of the statement, there is its obvious facility. An easy pronouncement; one which replaces a lot; a thoroughly dismissive &tc to stand in for a rich field of occurrence which one could otherwise report on. It is the temporal, storytelling equivalent to that cartographic problem in which a coast may only be rendered when its fine details are ignored. The truer the map of a shoreline, the longer the shoreline grows, and the closer to impossible it is to execute. Me, I don't have the patience for infinite shorelines, so "time passes" has to suffice. And, in my case, there is little in the way of this fine detail to report.

All of this being a rather baroque way of saying that it is now time for me to call it quits, as the project has more or less shot its bolt. I've only just now added the last bit. Meaning that I will, soon, perpetrate my work upon the world.

I merely have to pack it up and pack it in.

Time to leave. Mind's made up. Friends fled, nerves shot, games played out, cut off entirely from the Irl . . . the hour has surely come. I'll leave, and won't Brb. It's all been a farce, tip to tail. (Let's face it.) Many a poor soul would have stayed longer of course, but some braver ones would've left a lot earlier. Me: In trying not to underappreciate my welcome here, I have overstayed it. I have *malingered*. What a dreadful show I've made of it all, but it isn't too late. All I need is the courage to submit to the obvious—courage I will summon with a little final-inning *amor fati*. Thus, with little in the way of personal possessions to account for, but much in the way of a giant network of paper to fold up and put away, I now get to work—striding around my project, thinking resolute thoughts.

Specifically: How to carry it with me?

I will have to clean the thing first. All manner of junk has landed in the web and become tangled up: dust, sand, dirt, food wrappers, orphan socks, toilet paper, newspapers, receipts, and other general trash. (I can't open the windows anymore to air the project out, as doing so might jeopardize the delicate structural integrity of the total contraption.) So Phase One will be a manual cleaning. Then, I'll need to track the various guidelines to their proper anchors—taped to walls, floor, various spots on the ceiling. This could take days. I'll have to detach all these anchors and furl up the string according to some kind of strict (and most important, reversible) methodology. Then, parts of it will need to be folded. The project was built in three dimensions, so I will need to create some guiding principle with which to collapse it into two. A manner with which to collate one stack of paper with another. It hurts my head to consider how this will be accomplished. It occurs that maybe I should just crease and bend the entire thing up into a rough taco shape? Fold it again into a pie wedge and then into a smaller pie wedge? But, no. It is too flimsy to survive such a brute-force operation. I'll have to take the project apart one page at a time and

(This realization causes me to become so overwrought that I have to take a breather, Brb)

so I now turn my attentions to my more easily packable items. Clothes, for instance.

The uniform.

It hangs there on a hanger in the closet, a limp and suicided version of myself.

Though I'll miss it, I think that it must remain with the Institute that spawned it, and so I hoik on my ragged civilian clothes, musty from a bottom drawer.

Next, I pinch my toothbrush from its bathroom glass, and a few other items are tossed into the vivisected suitcase on the bed . . . but what am I neglecting? Ah, right. And just as I pull those crucial identity papers out from the closet safe, as tenderly as I would a splinter, something stops my hand.

A question; a hunch; a throb of dread. Of excitement.

An idea for the work? A coda.

I vaguely hear the safe door clang shut behind me as I

spasm over to the desk, clutching out at the scissors, the knife, the paste . . .

And here we are.

Rn, I lie in and among a tangle of pages: that jumble of sheets which includes, yes, a library of other works but now, also, my precious traveling papers as well. The passport now belongs to the final mess. Its excised pages dangle right above my head in my current position. There they sway—tantalizing pale leaves—from the virtually invisible threads to which they are crudely taped and stapled, and from which they connect to the work as a whole.

My passport? So lovingly Same Same'd? It is now completely minced up, pages redistributed. Thoroughly worked in. Voluntarily. The breakthrough. The missing bit. The final impediment: conquered. Last puzzle piece. What had been missing from the project was this small tribute: this little piece of myself. And it comes at a cost, to be sure.

But now is not the time for second-guessing. Now: time for a return back over the old material. A last read. This, the final agency available to us: a determination to inspect what we've already made. Of course, this is a choice. Some ends are unreflective; some eyes, at day's end, fix themselves steadfastly forward. But many ultimacies (I want to say: *most?*) are retrospective in nature. Nostalgic, even. Nostalgic and so: kitsch. Mine is. Or will be.

So, let's see what this last bit has to say, shall we?

It's not like I have anywhere to go, now. That door has closed.

A little light reading before lights out?

I reach up and pull down the dangling pages from my passport and begin.

(VIATICUM: THE PAPER CONTINUED)

Name.
Can we talk about the name? Percy Frobisher? Being, self-hood, are built upon names. Names should not be arbitrary. They should be, above all else, naturalistic. Mimetic, sure, yet also intentional in some deeper sense. That is, one should also learn something from names, without realizing at first that there is anything to be learned. Given name: Percy. Surname: Frobisher. (Why am I this name?)

Country of Origin.
Where is home? And who would we find waiting for you? Just who are these people—your people, Percy, the people back home? Background pls.

Date of Issue.
When are we, that is. The future? The not-yet-to-have-happened, certainly. On the face of it, yes. It would seem that way. But, is anything—environmentally, technologically, culturally speaking—presented herein, *inconsistent* with the present moment; that is, in evidence, available, even now? Has time itself collapsed? But, we've had enough of time, have probed the notion enough, so, n/m. Moving on.

Certificate of Good Health.
Go on. Complete Medical History. Less elliptical this time.
By which I mean don't omit performance results on a series
of exams: multi-phasic personality inventories, word inter-
ference tests, house/tree/person projective tests, attention deficit scales, color word interferences, etc., blood and
urines, MRIs to rule out structural causes, EEGs to rule out
seizures. A complete case report with mental-status exami-
nations, Axis diagnoses, the all-important medication list,
so on. Throw those on the pile with the rest.

Occupation.
Idk. "The Novelist" hasn't really worked out so great now,
has it?

Photo.
Look at me. I seem to be in the act of spinning away from
the camera. Just at this instant having had the idea to turn
tail. See, I'm headed out somewhere. I'm on the go. Leaving
the flat, closing the door behind me. Going where? Where
are you going now, Percy?
    I am going (I want to say: *out*).

Purpose of Visit (business; pleasure).
Both. Business and pleasure. My business and pleasure
which were, once, the creation of this project, my project,
and the subsequent delivery of my talk. These: my everything. I'd imagined it all so often, this climactic experience.

So often, with such clarity, it was as if I've already done it all; the fulfillment of this dream being the dream itself.

You see, I'd arrive via the main allée, in a grand, but solitary processional . . .

. . . and instantly, the mercury would drop. I'd smell the crisp and palm-blessed air, notice the quiet, and would realize that the place would be empty—that I wouldn't have seen a single fellow yet—i.e., that there would be a hushed expectancy about the place, and I'd note that the copses and nature trails and even that bright blue artificial lake would be collectively giving off a feeling of taut eagerness; and as I'd round the first buildings, the Mountain House and Pleasure Centers, amid their finely carved shadows—I'd open the car window and fill my chest full of that rarefied oxygen provided by the air circulator/amplifiers, and I'd see the just-greening lawns, the newly dredged, refilled and purified glacial lake, the copses so recently spritzed with their first growth of tender buds, the concrete spatulate column, the distended cloudlet, the conjoined volumes and recto-linearities, the grid-sleeve and arbitrary torus. Leaving the road then, I'd take a hedged-in garden path around several plinths and obelisks, up a knoll and down its far side. I would be a solitary man, walking in a vast playground of dwarfing structures, a man who would be heading, inevitably, toward the huge double doors of the Presence Center, the doors of which would have been left wide open, it would seem, just for me.

There'd be no need to psych myself up for what surely would happen. I'd be ready.

Bells, far off, would be pealing.

Ding. Dong. Ding . . .

And as I'd reach the threshold, in the brief moment before the adrenaline would kick in and unconscious expertise take over for conscious thought, I would muse on the fact that I had always known where the paper would lead, that this was the first thing I knew, and that I had followed the thread anyway—though whether it was a profitable direction to follow, only time would tell. But then I'd think, "This is how it all spooled out." The end—that is: this end— which would be the best and only end there could be, and there it would be, right in front of me.

Would regret be in order, then? Apologies? So on?

I would surely realize that it would be too late for all that as well.

(Late times. Late, late times, I would think. Too late!)

So I'd walk through the doors, my work polished and ready—boiled down to a neat fifteen minutes, a swift, clean nine-hundo seconds, a real demi-glace of a thing; simple messages, nothing cryptic or overwritten, no spastic grandiosities, everything bright and obtainable; my manifesto, my inspirational, creative guidebook, my deck, my manual, my diary, my brilliant act of creation—and I'd see that an audience would have assembled—assembled there for me, and I'd stride on past the rows of heads, none of which would crane to watch my journey down the center aisle of the auditorium—faces forward—they would be as immobile as an audience in a dream—and as is the way of such things, everyone would be there, all the fellows, Miss Fairfax, Miss Chatterton the Mysterious Woman, the Cryptographer and the Sculptor and the Philosopher, the Psychogeographer, the Actor, the Translator, the Set Theorist, the Miniaturist, the Critic, the Sociologist and the Composer, the arguing couple—including good old, dearly departed Disputant 2—the Woman-Whose-Face-and-Hands-Are-Covered-in-Yarn, the Brand Analyst (Miss ☺) and the Architect (Mr. 鼎福), the Man-Who-Assiduously-Tracks-His-Own-Life-Data, the Poet, the Philosopher, etc., etc., and the Director, of course, presiding over everything, always, and, of course Mr. Al'Hatif and Dennis Royal would be there too, those fellows, who, like me, had acclimatized so thoroughly to the Institute that there would be no way back now, no life outside of the place, no way forward except back to it, always back, returning not as visitors, not even long-term visitors, but as permanent residents, and so there they'd be, among all the others, everyone looking fixedly ahead at the luminous stage, at the white scrim with its Institute logo emblazoned upon it, which I would walk toward like a clear signal cutting through static, noticing the slight rake of the aisle, and as I'd complete the final few feet of carpet and take the (four) stairs up to the platform, among the almost-canned-sounding crowd (murmuring, whispering: *Percy. Mr. Frobisher, Percy . . . It's Percy,* etc.) with the love (yes, love) rising from the ranks like a fever, they'd all settle down in a rapid decrescendo from *mezzo-forte* all the way down to *pianississimo*, the new silence broken suddenly by the bright and brassy, synthesized heralds, that introductory theme song heard round the world, the tune we all know and love, and in a few more bounds I would be up there, ready to provide; ready to articulate my insights, breathing deeply and calmly, arriving at my designated spot, X-ed out on the floor of the stage, the clicker comfortingly in my hand, though having never been handed to me, the lights in my eyes, the music in my ears, my mic upon my jaw, my feet planted, and I'd look out, straighten my spine, and then I'd be talking . . .

But.

But instead, now, now, I couldn't care less. Not a fig, not a farthing, not a whit. Not for any of that.

How could I have wanted such a truly vapid end to it all?

I now have other, deeper mysteries to plumb; more insistent itches to scratch. Certain mysteries which lie on the far side of the Freehold's bounded life. These mysteries are, from here on out, my "business" and my "pleasure." Finding answers won't be easy. No. But still, out I go.

Port of Embarkation.

There's no light and where are all the stars? They are gone and instinctively I know that the paper has covered everything. I am buried completely. But still I go forward. Down the steps, past the swimming pool, shimmering with water browned with pulp, down the lane, across the downs, up

467

the narrowing path, past paper towers, edges crowding in, accosting my face with a special predilection for eyelids, stabbing out like dried branches, the way growing darker and darker until the lane opens out, widens into a circular area surrounded by a wall of silent witnesses—all the true palms are gone, burnt, felled; only these fake ones left—the cell towers masquerading as palms, gone are the trunks of the truer trees, with their sere, aromatic bark peeling down in slender belts, I miss the smell of them, but there are no more now. No matter. I walk on. The sensation of walking on the paper is like strolling along a wooded lane in deep autumn, after a rain.

I can see the bench at my Observation Point, though, some little ways off. I could imagine resting, sitting and taking stock, thinking for a beat, perhaps then deciding, upon reflection, at this late date, that I should take a more prudent course than the one I am currently pursuing; that I should try to avoid whatever fate is fast approaching me; that I should swerve away from danger. But there is nothing to consider here, nothing to observe at the Observation Point; nothing inside the Institute but filth; nothing to see outside of it but squalls and gloom.

An echoing growl.

The world rocks for a moment, and I lose my feet as something hits the Institute and knocks the wind out of it. Sirens. I hear the sirens again, as well.

I pick myself up and cover my ears.

The wails: louder and louder.

The dreaded front has finally arrived in all its force.

Everything shakes. The piercing and melismatic soprano of high winds. Sizzles and explosions. Looking up in the tumult, I can see, between me and the dangerous sky, a red warning light, one of many on the Institute's sensor-array—all the way right up there in the dizzying heights of the metastructure's central vault. It's blinking. Warning us of something? Has the dome reached its maximum load, given all of the paper piling outside, and given the beam's particular tensile strength? Is the beam losing cohesion? What if a particular column can no longer bear the weight of all this paper anymore?

I hear the sirens. I hear the sirens.

But it couldn't possibly . . .

And even sooner than I would have imagined, right away in fact, there is a wrenching groan, as of a massive, old wooden door opening, and then the beam gives way. And indeed, the northeastern buttress, of which this I-beam had been a constituent part, folds. There ensues a cascade effect. The groin-vaults buckle, one after another, the entire dome begins to sag like a soufflé before falling away entirely. After this, silicates shower down, and there is the briefest moment where it seems beautiful, the glass particles and shards look to me surprisingly like rain, glinting at the exact same angles as would a sun-shower, a shower which would have been very welcome back when all the fellows and admins alike were convecting alive within the Institute like hatchlings in an enormous incubator. The

downward shivering glass, happily, does not injure me, I
don't feel it at all in fact, as I am buffered by almost twenty
meters of paper baffling, though the glass hitting the paper
still makes an impressive noise. A noise like an immense
sizzling.

No more metastructure.

(More sirens.)

Paper raining down, billowing up.

A long, long (very long) gap.

Local Address.

Cowering. Fear.

Vandalism and riots. Mob violence. Flats and studios
ransacked. Fellows attacked, beaten, humiliated. Then.
Martial law. Police actions. Admins in masks corralling the
fellows, putting up cordons. More red lights. (Not flares
though, as the whole paper world is now thoroughly com-
bustible.) Fellows herded into safe areas. The admins in
hazmat attire, waving, pointing, yelling.

Time passes in just such a state of emergency.

More time.

Now . . .

Citizenship.

The world is white.

But order is restored. We are now deep down under the
paper, inside hollowed-out areas of it. We become mole-
people. The Institute: a warren. Rooms, large and small,

mined-out. The bigger volumes, small halls, dining areas, cloisters, are constructed through stacking paper reams, on top of one another, to form restraining walls, colonnades, and other structural supports. Rebuilding the entire infrastructure underground (as it were) is quite a feat of collective effort, a great "pulling together" of admins and fellows, and during the process, many of my fellow fellows continue to live and work exactly as we once did, back before the paper "just came out of nowhere" and swamped us all. They do so with renewed purpose, almost as if to prove a point, as if still carrying out an argument with a respondent who had already packed it in and left the debate (there is also, briefly, an Institute-wide dispute concerning the derivation, nature, and meaning of the paper, and naturally, these hypotheses and opinions vary wildly according to our commitments—the Philosopher providing a philosophical account, the Ecologist providing an ecological account, the Poet a poetic account, so on; I may even provide my own— but the meaning of the paper is obviated and overwhelmed by the sheer *fact* of the paper, its presence becoming confirmation to us of its necessity, all of us, every one, caving in to this *new normal* and making necessary adjustments . . . no one surmising that I am the cause of it, was, all along, and as such, must soon move on and take the paper with me. But yes, in this newly built ecosystem, order is more or less maintained: fellows and admins alike, dressing exclusively in paper, breathing pulpy air, and eating sketched-out meals. The paper becomes fungible, commoditized.

My counterfeit is openly circulated. Companies of paper-holders are formed. Ledgers of ledgers are kept. Some fellows form mini-collectives, small, independent city-states which proceed with their own Groups and Discourses™. (Sure. Sure, why not.) The various collectives cleave to their own schedules, and their own rules. The codex of suggestions, rules-of-thumb, and other generalized wisdom known as "the Ladder" is also maintained, but over time, these various will begin to interpret the foundational document differently from one another, such that, in the end, the text seems almost like several separate and contradictory documents. These various subgroups, the various "Sects of the Ladder," coexist for a period, though eventually, under the harsh, sharp, and bright conditions, internecine turmoil arises (as it inevitably does in such closed systems). Other fellows—and one might say wiser fellows—disappear, one at a time, alone, down into the narrow passageways and tunnels (I will be one of them), paths most no wider than the width of a man, these spelunkers deviating at various points from the marked routes, bushwhacking their own roads into the paper-mass like they are walking into an endless white cornfield, pushing the sheets away with their sliced-up hands and forearms, merging into it all, as more often than not the paths they blaze cave in behind them as they travel, and these solitary adventurers might, when deep enough into the paper, carve berths for themselves, berths just large enough to fit their prone bodies in, little dens, in which to snuggle up, sleep, eat, live, read, and die. But not me. I keep heading out.

Travel Route.

Now, in the heat of the morning, I plow my way to the perimeter. By the time I reach the edge of everything, the old dome is good and broke—crenelated, shards of the meta-structure sticking up into the sky like pickets. For some time now, while we were persisting on with our lives inside of it, the Institute has become just another ruin, another of the desert's follies. But this is no longer my problem. The storm has passed on. Cloudy skies are clear again. The world around the ruin is healing. Closure: the order of the day. So I clamber up what is now a ridge of paper, slippery with pages and sand, and now find an aperture between two ragged shards of dome-glass, which I slip between, heading always outward, and now I am upon the sands of the desert.

The sand radiates warmth—even through my shoes. I struggle to find purchase upon this new and uncertain surface, though I am happy that I am Irl again. I realize that it is the very first time I've walked in the desert, can you believe it, having previously only looked at it—looked at it from peripheries, from my observation bench, from towers, from classrooms, parking lots, sides of roads, vehicles, my wall screen, from afar that is—having abrogated my every tie to the thing itself. I am now just so thrilled to be participating in the desert as opposed to merely witnessing it. Participating; crest and trough; crest, trough, so on.

Out I go, still. The desert world becoming more visible as the sun, sweating with endeavor, chin-ups above the horizon. I take a step, and then another. I am snaking out into the dunes, trudging forward, as the blue and lemon glow of

473

morning dawns. As I leave the shadow of the demolished dome, from out over the plain, I hear a few muffled detonations behind me—fainter and fainter, receding thunder. There has been further catastrophe back there. Further collapses. But I don't turn around to look, the turning back is for later (and not for me). Alterberg, O, Alterberg!

The ties are cut.

"This is where my dream has brought us?" I think, knowing full well.

And I make a kind of

$$\neg\_(ツ)\_/$$

gesture to myself, before continuing on, stumbling forward into the brightening wind. One more *boom*, and I know that the Institute has fallen finally; sunk with all hands.

Don't look back.

There is no time for mourning the Institute, its occupants, or the bubble which housed us. That's behind. My thoughts are for the now.

I squint at the sun, a single lens flare: an anemone in the frame. The sun is high and impassive—or passive; or passive-aggressive, actually. The sun is being an a**hole. Whew, it's hot.

The trip will take some time, obviously. Days and nights. There will be adventures, sights-to-behold (ruined castles, tombs, Great Walls, Lighthouses, Eiffel Towers, wavering trails of wayward robot jockeys . . .). There will be terrible predicaments, jubilant escapes, so on.

The trip through the desert to be indicated by question marks, which,
themselves, indicate other things entirely, like confusion, excitement,
but also exhaustion, thirst, itchiness, gratitude, nausea, anguish,
glimmers of false hope, recognition, discharges, both solid and liquid,
prayer, fist-shaking, delusional merriment, etc.

???????????????????????????????????? ????????????? ???????? ?
???????????????????????????? ??????????????????????? ?????????? ????
?????? ?????? ???????????????????????????????????? ??? ???????????
?????????? ??????????????????????????????????? ????????????? ?
????????????? ???????? ? ????????? ?????????? ?????????????
??????   ?????????   ?????

I have not disappeared from sight yet though; far from
it. I travel across the desert, past the esoteric, sunken mon-
uments, over the bay (yes *over* the bay), and by the time I
reach the outskirts of the city, the trip has taken my humanity along with my clothes, my shoes, several layers of skin,
bodily moisture, and much of what is left of my reason.
Do not shed a tear on my behalf, though, I'm still going.
My feet carry me on still. Out of the flatlands. One step
and another. Into the heart of town, past the outskirts, the
Spar, in and around the Electronics Roundabout, past the
perfume district, past the casinos, past the mosques and
the barbican of business towers, toward downtown, and
deeper. Into the tangle of smaller streets. Into the heart of
the city's ghettos—in and in, retracing the journey into the
obscure center of the metropolis. Then: the alleyway, the
end of the alleyway, the door. I stare at the front of the shop

PETER MENDELSUND

for an elastic moment, a caesura of indefinite, or perhaps
mutating length, and, low-slung and bowlegged under the
fatigue, I take the last few steps and reach for the knob,
give it a stiff, quick pull, and walk in under the familiar yellow fluorescents.

Exit/Entry Visas.
The first thing I see in the Same Same shop is the proprietor. He is amused. No, smirking. He seems proud. Unusually so. Why so arrogant, I want to ask? But before I can say
a word, he turns, ducks back through the counter, opens the
door to that back room of his, and disappears through it.
    Time passes.
    (More time.)
    Sounds from back there.
    Rustling. Conversation?
    I wait, and when the door finally opens again, it isn't
him who emerges from it.
    No, it's something else entirely. A visual disruption pat-
tern, some weird species of cancerous pixel-generation, in
which, it appears that a man is standing, right in front of
me, a man who looks for all the world like . . .
    "Hello, Percy," I say.
    "Hello," say I, in the exact same (tone of) voice.
    There I am, I think, and I've changed.
    I am older. Grayer, obviously. The work of gravity on the
face of a man is the saddest yet most inevitable thing—the
sagging; not that it is that noticeable, though it's noticeable

476

enough to me. Sorry to think that, in moments like this, vanity still rears its (Ugly? Beautiful? Self-recriminating?) head.

God, Percy, you could have at least shaved.

Show some pride, man.

And boy oh boy, you've really let yourself go around the middle. Would a little exercise have killed you? (I recall, now, the trip up the Landau-Schmidt, and the desultory stabs at the gym. Stick-to-itiveness has never been my forte though, has it. But in my defense, who has the time? The time for the project, and one's vanity? Time, time, time. The project takes up one's allowance of time and of vanity, I'm afraid. All of it.)

Eyes are pretty bloodshot, though the good news is that they are also slightly more animated than they used to be. A little less dull, flat, a little less dark. But still sad and wet. The hair? The hairline? Bloody hell if that isn't the worst part of all of it. It will be gone soon, and that. Dying off like a poorly sprinkled parkland. I'll soon have a metastructural dome of my own, Lolz.

Okay. Never mind. Good riddance.

Less maintenance I suppose, less work.

Other than this, other than my reduced appearance, there is little else to recount. He (Percy, I) is (am) standing behind the desk, in front of the curtain which hides the back room. He's me (or us), he is me in every detail (but you know, denatured). He is me in a way which is so powerfully insistent that it threatens the assimilation of us both.

I feel a gravitational pull from our congruities. He must feel the same, for he levers open a gate in the counter, and steps through to the other side, folds the counter back down again, turns, and walks closer.

The unmitigated likeness threatens to pull us and the entire world into a collapsing singularity. It is nauseating. He stands there, eyes open and unblinking, as if they were painted on the placard of his face. (God this is exhausting.) He doesn't speak, and doesn't acknowledge my having spoken in any way. It isn't clear to me whether this dumbness is due to incomprehension or intransigence. Perhaps he is simply unable to respond, as our bodies, our features, our very organs of comprehension and communication are beginning to merge toward an indistinguishable point.

"Shouldn't it end now?" I suggest to him (me), mildly.

And a pilot light goes on inside him (me). He (I) nod(s).

Rooting in his (my—okay enuf of this, let's go with "he" and "his") pocket, he finds something and pulls it out. A single piece of paper. He smooths it, and puts it on the countertop. Hands a pen to me.

He taps on the paper with a finger.

"What's this?" I ask. "Will this . . . Ah, I see. Okay. I'm supposed to . . .

Signature of Holder.
"Sign . . ."

Scribble, scribble.

"And initial . . ."

Scribble, scribble.

"Oops, date, also . . ."

Scribble.

"There," I say. "That should be it."

He pulls a pair of reading glasses out of his pocket (since when did I need . . .) and looks over the paperwork.

Tick tock, tick tock.

"Does everything seem in order?"

He palms his thin, errant hair back along his sweaty head. (I do the same.)

Tick tock.

"All good, Percy? Jesus Chri—"

And then, with a sudden movement his body jerks into motion. He grabs the pen out of my hand before I know what is happening, and now he does what second men do; what they have always done, ever since the very first of the second men. With the pen held like a dagger, he swings it back in a wide arc above his head:

and my face falls,

and the pen falls,

and the stain grows, that moist spot seeping outward,

then the curtain falls,

and that's just about that.

53

THE FINAL FUNDAMENT

Fundament 32. Not a rule, but a toast. A salute. To the chewed-up. To great, and variously nasty cuds. Here's to junk heaps; crap made of other crap. To shit. Junk, cut with other junk. Our admixed stuff. Interwoven; layered, mashed to a paste. Here's to the pulverized and indistinguishable contents of our eating mouths; to the acid baths of our stomachs, to the hot stews we vomit, or otherwise expel. The miscellanies, jumbles, alloys, and dyspeptic brews which are the circulating units of production in each and every cycle of consumption and manufacture, from our Frankenstein-monster-like genomic birthrights, to the planetesimals of the solar nebula from which earths are forged. Cheers to the process of consumption and manufacture itself: mastication, assimilation, ingestion, absorption, consolidation, evacuation, so on. Raise a glass (that is) to the digestive, in its various material forms and in all of its magnificent phases (and in the case of the paper: the amalgamation of natural ingredients, the great "chipping together" of woods, the manufacture of pulps through molecular disintegration, reorganization, and reintegration, the separation of wastes, the supplementation of additives . . .). A moment to acknowledge the peristaltic nature of creativity. To recognize, most of all, the seat of invention, the cloacal; the most trafficked sites of egress, internal to external, private to public. The creative voice? The mouth has little to do with anything; vocal cords even less so. Here's to the true birthing canals. The sewers, not the spires. As if anything in the endeavor of creation were easy, or cute. As if the products of creation were anything but impure and despoiled; violently puréed. Nothing springs forth as if newly struck—God's own first coin, golden and bright. Births: disgusting, Imho. Wet, sticky, malodorous, dangerous, Tmi. So *Prost* to the absolutely repulsive process of creation. *Santé*, and *salud* to birth, retch, mucus, and pus, the foul miracle of discharge, and I'm nearly there, so pipe down, show some manners, a little patience, there's a plan here: I'm aiming for thirty-two of these Fundaments, thirty-two exactly, like those fucking variations (you know the ones) which pretty much could've gone on indefinitely given the fecundity of the ground (and what piece of music, ultimately, is not a set of variations I ask you), but one has to end a composition somewhere, doesn't one, so it might as well be with a quodlibet; a chaos of public domain ditties (Cheers, to the quodlibet), because after that, after that: the theme, the same old theme comes around again, identical, but never really identical, another example of the very same, outrageous ourobouros I've just been praising, the triumphal human centipede of human invention. So there's a final toast for you: to endings. To endings! (And let's get on with it already, shall we? Save some paper; now, as good a time as any?) Everything needs an end, Imho, and guess what, voila, it has already arrived. Yes. You made it. Here's to you. Here's to us. *We* made it. The final Fundament. The Fundament of Fundaments. It's over now. At last. Phew. No more nonsense. No more project. No more *words*. All that's left is for me to hitch up the uniform at the belt, pull it down at the crotch, brush the evidence off myself, square my shoulders, step carefully over my own body, and, before I can change my mind, slip out the front door of the shop. And that's precisely what I intend to do. My prospects out there may be poor, but who knows? Who knows. Not me. That's for sure. Though time will surely tell. Tbd.

Tbd.

The End.

ACKNOWLEDGMENTS

I would like to thank, first off, my good friend Ben Shykind, who introduced me to Same Same shops (specifically, the Same Same shop near the Karwa bus station in Doha, Qatar) and without whom (for better or worse) this book wouldn't exist. I'd also like to thank my editor, Lexy Bloom, my agent, Chris Parris Lamb, Ben Marcus, Caleb Crane, Sonny Mehta, Anne Messitte, Edward Kastenmeier, Gerry Howard, Andrew Ridker, Michael Theodore, Oliver Munday, Maria Goldverg, Jennifer Olsen, Peter Terzian, Ruth Cohen, Dan Wilhelm, Tom Pold, Lisa Silverman, Anna Knighton, Edward Allen, Kate Runde, and, finally, though most important: Violet, Ruby, and Karla.

This book was heavily influenced (rather obviously) by Thomas Mann's *Magic Mountain*. Most of the chapter headings—as well as the short excerpt on pages 250–51—are taken from John E. Wood's translation. There are many other references (less obvious, perhaps) to other books (novels mostly, though not exclusively) scattered throughout this one as well, but I leave it to you to sort those out.